REDEMPTION IN CAJAMARCA

REDEMPTION IN CAJAMARCA

RICHARD WALTER

iUniverse®

REDEMPTION IN CAJAMARCA

iUniverse books may be ordered through booksellers or by contacting:

iUniverse
1663 Liberty Drive
Bloomington, IN 47403
www.iuniverse.com
844-349-9409

Because of the dynamic nature of the Internet, any web addresses or links contained in this book may have changed since publication and may no longer be valid. The views expressed in this work are solely those of the author and do not necessarily reflect the views of the publisher, and the publisher hereby disclaims any responsibility for them.

Any people depicted in stock imagery provided by Getty Images are models, and such images are being used for illustrative purposes only.
Certain stock imagery © Getty Images.

ISBN: 978-1-6632-3205-2 (sc)
ISBN: 978-1-6632-3206-9 (e)

Print information available on the last page.

iUniverse rev. date: 11/24/2021

Dedicated to the memory of my *buen amigo*, Aníbal Zambrano,
a true son of Cajamarca

One

I WOKE UP WITH THE mother of all hangovers.

I had all the classic symptoms: a splitting headache, the whirly beds, a terrible thirst, and an awareness that if I didn't get to the bathroom soon, I'd be spilling the contents of my stomach all over myself. Despite the urgency, I was afraid to move, sure that any sudden motion would make things worse.

Then, sure enough, things got worse. In my left ear I could hear a sound that seemed to reverberate off the walls of my apartment like the steady beat of a bass drum. Turning on my side I saw a stranger in my bed. She was flat on her back, her bare breasts with flower tattoos exposed, the sheet covering her from the waist down. And she was snoring as peacefully as a virgin with a clear conscience, which I knew she was not.

Groping through the fog of my mind I remembered. We had met last night at a local bar. She was already half in the bag, downing shots of tequila like a metronome. I foolishly tried to keep up and by the time we got to my apartment we were both so drunk it was a miracle we were able to walk. Our scattered clothes on the floor attested to the fact that we had retained enough of our motor skills to get into bed and connect our body parts.

I reached under the sheet and confirmed the fact that I was naked. Dried semen in my groin area confirmed my suspicions that we had done the dirty deed. I prayed that through my drunkenness I had used a condom. Turning to my right to check the floor for evidence I experienced a dizziness that threatened to land me head first on the hardwood. Much to my relief, I saw my used condom where I had flung it after it had served its purpose.

Looking again at my bedmate, I struggled to remember her name. What was it? Rhonda? Ruth? Rosie? Roxanne? I was pretty sure that it was something that started with an R.

I wasn't too worried that she would be insulted when she awoke. She probably didn't remember my name either.

As she snored away, I made a closer inventory. The cold light of day coming through my window was not kind to "R." She had dirty blonde hair, and by that I mean really dirty. It had been a while since her last shampoo. And, through my haze, I remembered that she was not a natural blonde. When I picked her up I had guessed she was a little over thirty. Now I added ten years. Her breasts were beginning to sag and a twinge in my back reminded me that it had been an effort to carry her onto the bed. In a moment of panic, I looked for needle marks on her arms but saw none. That didn't mean she wasn't a user. But I wasn't about to do a thorough inspection.

As you might have guessed, this was not the first time I had found myself waking up in bed with someone I had just met. Ordinarily, I enjoyed getting reacquainted and having a go at morning sex. Even with a hangover it had its charms, but not this time. Definitely not. I would let my companion enjoy her snooze – I owed her at least that – and then send her on her way.

I summoned my resolve and swung my feet onto the floor. My head felt like it was about to explode. I staggered to the bathroom and barely got the toilet lid up before I puked my guts out. Sinking to my knees, I hugged the commode like a long-lost friend and spent ten minutes emptying all the contents of my stomach into the bowl.

After flushing the toilet, I closed the lid and pulled myself up to the wash basin. I was following a familiar routine, one that I had polished to perfection. Opening the medicine cabinet, I took out four extra-strength Tylenols and downed them with several glasses of water. Next, I lifted the toilet lid and ignoring the lingering odor of my own vomit, peed freely. As had become my custom lately, I checked to see if there was any blood in my urine. There wasn't. But I didn't know how long my luck would hold. I had been experiencing some sharp back pains recently and suspected my kidneys might be compromised. The smart thing would be to see a doctor. But I was too chicken to face the possibility of the bad news that would alter a lifestyle to which I had become accustomed.

After another flushing, I again closed the lid. The next step on my path to recovery was to brush my teeth. I had to get that taste of vomit out of my mouth if I planned to rejoin the human race. I applied some Crest to my toothbrush and spent a good two minutes giving my pearly whites a thorough going over. After spitting and rinsing, I took a washcloth, ran it under the faucet, applied some soap, and scrubbed my face clean of any debris. I thought about washing my hair to make sure all bases were covered, but didn't see any obvious chunks of matter that needed to be removed. I would take a shower later, after I had gotten something into my now thoroughly empty stomach.

As I wrung out my washcloth, I looked in the mirror. For a second time that morning, I thought I saw a stranger. The basic ingredients were there – the shoulder-length jet black hair, usually pinned back in a ponytail but now hanging free, the de rigueur goatee, the square jaw with a slight Kirk Douglas cleft, the dark eyes. But the eyes gave it away. They used to sparkle, at least on occasion. Now they were blood-shot and dim. My nose, trending slightly to the left after absorbing one too many punches, was shot through with red veins, the legacy of my heavy drinking. My skin was beginning to show the ravages of time and my hair had streaks of gray. *And I thought "R" was ten years older than she had first looked.* I was in my mid-thirties and looked about ready to join the AARP.

I stumbled out of the bathroom and searched for some clothes to cover my naked body. Rummaging through my Goodwill-purchased chest of drawers, I found a pair of shorts and a 49r's tee shirt that looked reasonably clean and put them on. Padding barefoot to my miniscule kitchen, I took a can of coffee from the icebox, filled the filter on my machine to the brim, and pressed the start button.

For several weeks, I had feared that my coffee-maker was on its last legs. It was sending me distress signals on a daily basis. But it still worked. After a couple of minutes of gurgling and gasping, the water began to percolate through the filter and into the carafe below. As soon as there was enough to fill a mug, I poured some and waited for it to cool.

Sitting down on my sole kitchen chair, I glanced at my bed. Sleeping beauty was still at rest, her snores a pleasant background noise now that the Tylenol was beginning to work its magic. I had been afraid that my up-chucking in the bathroom and rustling in the kitchen area would wake her. But she was dead to the world.

Starting to sip my coffee after it had cooled, I glanced around my apartment. It didn't take long. I had a studio about the size of a room you would find in a bargain motel. The bed where "R" was currently sawing wood was actually a fold-out couch, which, along with a small kitchen table, the kitchen chair I now occupied, the aforementioned chest of drawers, and a small television resting on top of a wooden crate were my only pieces of furniture. As you might guess, aside from the occasional one-night stand, I didn't do much entertaining.

My apartment was on the third floor to the rear of a five-story building just south of Market Street in the Mission District of San Francisco. Out my kitchen window I had a lovely view of an inner courtyard, where junkies and the homeless, often one in the same, had taken up semi-permanent occupancy. At least they were quiet and, so far, had not caused problems for any of the tenants. Having spent some time on the streets myself, I could sympathize with their plight.

For the privilege of enjoying such digs, I paid a rent of almost three thousand bucks a month. That was more than half the salary I pulled in as a construction worker. Up till now, I had been able to make it. I didn't have or need a car. I could find everything I required – food, drink, companionship – within easy walking distance. For getting to work, I depended on public transportation or hitching a ride with a co-worker. So I got by and actually managed to save for the occasional trip out of the city, usually down the coast to L.A.

But there were clouds on the horizon. Silicon Valley billionaires were beginning to gentrify what had once been a down at the heels but funky neighborhood and the rent would soon reach beyond my ability to pay. I had heard talk from other tenants that a guy from Palo Alto was planning to do a gut rehab of the entire building and turn the apartments into condos that would go for a million or more.

I would hate to leave. I had been in San Francisco for three years and loved living in the city. The thought of moving into some distant but affordable suburb sent chills up my spine. Maybe I would join the homeless just to stay put.

The vibrating buzz of my cellphone jarred me from my musings. I looked at my watch. It read 8:37. Who could be calling on a Sunday morning? Then I remembered. My construction crew was working on a project in Daly City. We usually didn't work on Sundays. But this project was running behind schedule. The foreman wasn't sure he would need me, but said he would call if he did.

It took me a few moments to locate the phone. I had left it in my pants, which were now lying on the floor next to the bed. I hustled over, picked up my pants, and returned to the kitchen table, extracting the phone along the way. My bed-mate stirred and for a moment her snoring ceased. But then I heard the familiar drone resume. In the meantime, my phone was vibrating in the palm of my hand like a captured sparrow.

I looked at the screen, fully expecting to see my foreman's name and number. Instead I got a shock that threatened to turn my guts inside out for the second time that day. There was no name, only "private caller," on the screen. I didn't recognize the number, but the area code was all too familiar: 636, the suburbs of my hometown of St. Louis.

It could only be one person. And the last thing in the world I wanted to do was to talk to him.

I covered the phone with both hands; partly to muffle the sound, partly in the hope that somehow that would discourage the caller. But I knew better. He would never give up. He knew I was at the other end and would keep calling until kingdom come. A part of me also had to admit that I was being childish.

Finally, I opened my hands, pressed the talk function, and grunted "What?"

"Hi Clint. It's me John. Please don't hang up. It's important."

I hadn't heard his voice in over three years. But it was instantly familiar; deep, resonant, all traces of a native "Missoura" accent erased; a voice brimming with confidence; a voice that demanded respect - the voice of my older brother.

A few seconds of silence ensued as I struggled with a response: Maybe something along the lines of "Sorry, but I'm expecting an important work-related call." Or, "I can't talk now John. Get back to you later." Or, more truthfully, "I don't want to talk to you or anybody else in St Louis. And don't bother calling again."

But instead, I replied, "How did you get my number?"

"It wasn't hard. But that's not the point. I just..."

My brother had lots of friends in high places. I suspected that he had called some contacts in the national security bureaucracy to get my number. I had done my best to stay off the grid, but in these days of government surveillance, that's not easy to do.

I interrupted, "Okay Bro. What's so important?"

"Dad's had a stroke. He's at home, but he's in bad shape. Mom and I want you to come back to St. Louis. We're not sure how much time he has left," he said, a slight tremor in his usually steady voice.

There were a lot of things a good son would have said at this point. But that was not me, as my father had made crystal clear throughout most of my life. For him, John was the good son, I was the bad son. And that was the main reason I was about as far away from St. Louis as I could get.

"Uh, Listen Bro," I said, trying to sound sincere. "I'm really sorry to hear about dad." In fact, I wasn't sure how I felt. I didn't wish death on him. I hadn't gotten to that point. But I also didn't feel I owed him anything either. I had made my break with him and any forced reconciliation would be phony. "But I'm awfully busy right now and..."

Just as I was about to offer my excuse, my brother interrupted. "There's more bad news. Mel has gone missing in Peru. Nobody has seen or heard from her in almost a week. That's what precipitated dad's stroke. And mom is going crazy with all this. We need you to help us find her. *Please* come home," he pleaded.

That bit of news hit me hard. Mel, short for Melanie, was our kid sister, born five years after me. Overcoming some sibling jealously, John and I had become protective big brothers, helping her navigate the shoals of a turbulent home life. Once she went off to college on the east coast, we saw less of her. But until I broke off all ties, we had kept in touch. She seemed to sympathize with and understand my discontent. Once I had headed west, I thought about maintaining contact with her but was afraid she would try to guilt me into some sort of effort of reconciliation. The last I had heard, she was studying anthropology at Cornell, working on her doctorate.

If it had just been a case of going home to see my dad, I might have held off. But what John told me about Mel changed the equation dramatically.

After a few moments of silence, I said, "Okay John. I'll come home." I could hear his sigh of relief. "What can you tell me about Mel? Where…"

He cut me off. "It's complicated Clint; very complicated. Why don't we wait until you get here? It's better if we go over all this in person." Then, after a pause, he added, a catch in his voice, "I'm really glad you're coming. We need you here."

We then discussed the details of my trip. It had been years since I had flown on a plane. I had made my way to San Francisco in stages, mostly by bus with stops along the way to work odd-jobs. John told me he had already booked a flight to St. Louis in my name for that afternoon. Because it was a last-minute booking, the cost was close to two thousand dollars. I had that much and more in cash, but my brother chuckled when I told him I would pay for the fare myself at the counter. "You'd likely end up in jail," he said "suspected of being a terrorist." I didn't tell him that I probably looked the part.

"I've already put it on my credit card," he said. "Don't worry about it. Now I need your e-mail address so I can forward the ticket to your phone."

It was my turn to chuckle. "E-mail account? I don't have no stinking e-mail account."

He laughed. We were beginning to slip into the easy banter that once had made us close. "No problem," he replied. Then he described some sophisticated technical maneuver that would transfer the ticket to my phone. All I had to do was show the app on my phone at the gate and I would be able to board. I expressed my doubts, but he told me not to worry.

After he hung up, I tried to organize my jumbled thoughts. My brother's phone call had come from out of the blue. It had caught me off guard. I still had my reservations about returning to St. Louis. The call had stirred up old memories, most of them bad. But I did love my sister. And if I could help find her, then that was what I would do.

Two

I SHOOK THE BLONDE IN my bed awake. She rubbed her eyes and looked at me with no evidence she recognized who I was or where she was. But it was not her first rodeo. Without a word, I simply pointed to the bathroom. She struggled out of bed, doing nothing to cover her naked body, and stumbled to the bathroom. I gathered her clothes from the floor and stacked them neatly on the bed.

Through the bathroom door, I could hear the shower running. Under other circumstances, I might have joined in. After all, San Franciscans are big on conserving water. But that was the last thing on my mind. Instead, I grabbed my backpack and began to fill it with underwear, a change of clothes, and other necessities. I didn't know how long I would be gone, but assumed that I would find some of my own clothes at home. If not, I could borrow from my brother.

By the time I had finished, the blonde emerged from the bathroom. She used a towel to cover herself, perhaps out of modesty, perhaps not wanting me to see parts of her that looked better in the dark than in the harsh light of day.

"Hi...uh...Chuck," she said.

I didn't correct her. After all, I didn't remember her name. "Hi yourself," I replied. "Listen, I'm sorry to have awakened you. But something's come up and I need to get going."

She didn't seem disappointed. Looking at my crummy apartment, she probably realized that I was not worth a long-term investment. "No prob," she said, dropping the towel and giving me a full view that I could have done without.

"I have stuff to do as well," she said as she began to dress. I doubted that, but simply nodded.

A few minutes later, she was out the door and out of my life. As she was leaving, I finally remembered her name: Marcie. Well, at least it had an "R" in it.

The next order of business was to call my foreman. I got him on the third ring.

"Hey Clint," he said. "What's up? Is it about the job in Daly City? I was just about to call to see if you were available. We need a couple of guys. So if you…"

I interrupted. "Sorry Craig, but not today. In fact, I need to take a couple of weeks off."

The news caught him off guard. Craig Weston was my foreman, one of the best I had ever worked for. And I had worked for quite a few. He was tough but fair. He expected a lot from us and demanded quality work. He took a lot of personal pride in every project we completed. Despite his exacting standards, he also was willing to overlook individual flaws as long as they did not interfere with the job. In my case, that meant ignoring my worst habit. I never, *ever* drank on the job. But that didn't mean Craig didn't notice the times I had to find a place to throw up or fight through a Grade-A headache. Fortunately, I never had the tremors while working. I think that would have sealed my fate.

But Craig let me stay on. It helped, of course, that I was one of the most skilled workers he had. In fact, I think I was probably one of the most skilled in the city. On a construction site, I could do almost anything, from brute manual labor to installing plumbing and electricity. Laying brick, plastering, painting, carpentry – you name it, I could do it. I was like one of those invaluable utility men on a baseball team. I could play any position and pitch with either hand. So when specialists got sick, hurt, or didn't show up for whatever reason, Craig could plug me in, save time and money, and be confident that the job would be done right.

After a pause, I heard the disappointment in his voice. "Gee Clint, I don't know. We've got a lot of deadlines. We really need you buddy. I can maybe give you a week. But two? I just don't know. Do you really have to be gone so long?"

In truth, I had no idea how long I would be gone. Two weeks was just a ballpark guess. It could be that we would locate Mel or find out what had happened to her right away. Maybe she would show up tomorrow. Who knew? But even though I didn't have all the details, the mere fact she had gone missing in Peru indicated that the search for her was going to be a lengthy one.

Although I could probably find work with any construction crew in the city, there were not many who treated their men – and women – better than Craig. I would hate to break with him. He and the guys I worked with were like a surrogate family. In fact, Craig reminded me a lot of my father – without all the bad parts. But I had to be as fair and honest with him as he was with me.

"Listen Craig," I said. "I just got a call from my brother in St. Louis. Something has happened to my little sister. She has disappeared somewhere in South America and I need to get home and help look for her. And I honestly don't know how long it's going to take. Maybe two weeks. It could be less but likely more. But I've got to do it. And I understand if you say no." But, I thought to myself, I hope you say yes.

"Geeze," he said, "I'm sorry, really sorry. I mean I didn't even know you had a sister. It must be awful not to know where she is."

I had not said anything to Craig – or to anybody else – about my family. As far as he knew, I was just a Hippie drifter without roots, one who just happened to have exceptional construction skills.

"Yes it is Craig. I'm pretty shook up."

"Okay Clint. I'll need to inform the boss. But here's the deal. We'll keep your job open for two weeks. After that, we'll have to look for someone else. I can't guarantee anything, but if you do come back after we've hired a replacement, I'll do my best to get you onto the crew. Luckily, you can fit almost anywhere. But again, there are no guarantees. We might be full up when you return. Sorry, but that's the best I can do."

"Thanks Craig. That's more than fair. I really appreciate it, "I said, my voice cracking.

"And good luck on finding your sister. We'll be praying for you. Okay if I tell the guys why you're not with us?"

"Sure Craig. And thanks again."

"No problem Clint. Let's hope we see you soon."

"Yeah. Let's hope so."

As I shut off the phone and put it on the table, my hand shook as though I had some kind of fever. Maybe it was the result of emotion. But I suspected it was due to something less noble and more common. I needed a drink, and I needed one badly. Under the sink, I found a bottle of my old friend Jim Beam. Unscrewing the top, I took two deep swallows. I was tempted to take more, but I had to be sober enough to get from my apartment to the airport. Reluctantly, I put down the bottle, replaced the top, and returned it to its original location. Maybe if I couldn't see it, I wouldn't be tempted. As always, I felt a little ashamed that I had become so dependent on alcohol, dependent enough that on the days I didn't work I was a pretty steady morning drinker, one of the classic signs of serious alcoholism. A friend had suggested I try Alcoholics Anonymous, but I had fended him off with the usual excuses: *I've got it under control. I never drink on the job. I'm not like those street winos. I can quit whenever I want. I've got it under control.* Deep down, I knew this was all bullshit. But I wasn't about to turn my back on my best friend just yet. And as I looked down at my hand, it was now steady as a rock. I knew the best medicine to take for that particular affliction. And it had worked like a charm.

Three

I T WAS A LITTLE after twelve when I left my apartment. I had taken a long shower, washed my hair, and trimmed my goatee so as to look reasonably presentable. It was mid-July and I knew that it would be at least ninety degrees in St. Louis with a suffocating humidity. I dressed accordingly in a blue polo shirt and light-weight tan cargo pants. My once-white New Balance shoes showed considerable wear and tear, but they were still serviceable. I debated wearing my San Francisco Giants cap but remembered how fanatic St. Louisans were about the Cardinals. Instead, I placed a dark blue cap with my construction company logo on top of my head. While it was going to be hot in St. Louis, it was cool in San Francisco and I added a light gray jacket to my ensemble.

I had arranged with the Hispanic couple who lived on the first floor to collect and save my mail. Most of what I got was junk, but there was the occasional important correspondence, including some outstanding bills, that I didn't want to lose track of. Not trusting banks after the crash of 2008, I had kept about five grand in cash in my apartment. That represented my life savings. The money was pretty well hidden, but a determined thief would likely find it given some time. I decided to take three grand with me and leave the two grand to fate. The building had not had a break-in during my three years of residence, but there were no guarantees.

It got to the BART Station on Market in five minutes. Twenty minutes later I was at the airport. My watch read 12:40. The flight to St. Louis departed at 1:45. I got in the nearest and shortest security line, untying my shoes before I did so. Since I didn't own a car, I had yet to get a California driver's license. A few times on the job I had been needed to drive a pick-up truck somewhere to get supplies. One of these days that would cost me. I made a mental note to apply for my license when I returned. On the other hand, a little voice whispered in my ear that not having a license would deter me from driving and getting a citation for DUI – or worse.

Fortunately, I had a passport that I had recently renewed. I had needed it for my occasional trips to Canada and Mexico. When I reached the security check-in point, I showed the TSA agent the ticket on my phone and my passport. I must have been a little nervous. I could feel some sweat on my forehead even though the airport was cool. To my surprise, he paid only slight attention to the screen on my phone. I suppose he was now quite familiar with this latest technological breakthrough. But he gave my passport a thorough going-over, raising it to the light and shifting his eyes back and forth between my photo likeness and the real me. It wasn't a great picture, but I didn't think I had changed that much in the nine months since I had received my new document. For a moment, I thought he was going to ask me to step aside for a more thorough inspection. But he finally handed over my passport, waved me through, and wished me a good flight.

It had taken me more than half an hour to navigate the security line. Re-tying my shoes, my hands began to shake again. I needed the usual remedy. I hoisted my backpack and quick-stepped toward the gate my eyes darting to the left and right to locate the needed oasis.

There it was on the right: The Gold-Rush Bar. I took a stool and ordered a double bourbon straight. I laid a twenty on the bar and told the server to bring me another drink in five minutes. He looked at me with a knowing eye. He had seen my type before, probably many times. "Certainly sir," he said. "But just a reminder, we have a four-drink limit. Airport rules," he said with a shrug, as though he thought them unreasonable.

I looked at my watch. One twenty. My flight would begin boarding soon and I was still a ways away from the gate. I would have liked to have tested the drink limit, but I needed to be on the move soon. I swallowed the first bourbon in several gulps, feeling the fiery liquid hit my empty gut like molten lava. It would have been smarter, of course, to have had some real food rather than a liquid diet. But I immediately felt better as the alcohol took effect. My hands no longer shook.

After draining the second glass, I headed to the gate. I was a bit light-headed and wobbly, but arrived for my flight just as the final boarding call was issued. Somewhere in my foggy memory, I recalled that the airlines could deny you boarding if they suspected you were inebriated. I had had a lot of practice faking sobriety. And after all, I had *only* had two drinks; albeit straight shots in less than ten minutes.

Having been caught in similar situations, I made it a practice always to carry chewing gum. As I got in line to board, I popped a couple of sticks in my mouth and began to chew. In this instance, the gum would serve two purposes: hide the smell of alcohol on my breath and help with the ear-popping of takeoff.

If there was a test, I passed. With only a passing glance, the attendant who checked my ticket took the phone, passed it over a screen, saw and heard the proper response, and handed me my boarding pass. After she had wished me the perfunctory pleasant flight, I sauntered down the gangway to the plane.

Since he had booked my flight at the last minute, John had only been able to find me a seat near the rear in coach on the left side of the plane in the next to the last row. Not much, I thought, for two grand. "It was a totally full flight so stop griping," I said to myself. At least I was on board.

Four

WE TOOK OFF RIGHT on time. I chewed my gum vigorously as we ascended. I had a window seat and a spectacular view of the Bay Area as we circled north and then headed east across the San Joaquin Valley toward the Sierras and beyond to St. Louis. For a few seconds I had a premonition that I might never be back. I pushed it away, attributing it to my addled state. The shocks of the day had taken their toll and had put me in a dark mood. That was all.

Sitting down, I hadn't paid much attention to my seatmates. I took a closer look. On the aisle was a guy about my age but at least a hundred pounds heavier, most of it hanging over his belt. He was already fast asleep and I could hear him breathing heavily and emitting little sounds that seemed almost dainty coming from such a big source. It appeared to be my fate today to share space with a snorer.

In the middle seat was a cute brunette. I guessed she was in her early twenties. She was dressed in tight jeans, a tee-shirt with a likeness of the Golden Gate Bridge, open-toed sandals, and a Fisherman's Wharf cap on her head. She had a loaf of sourdough bread under the seat in front of her. I was no detective, but all the clues suggested a tourist on her way back home.

Usually, I tried to avoid conversations on planes. It was bad enough to be trapped with total strangers in a tin can traveling hundreds of miles an hour five miles up. But to be trapped with a bore turned it into a real nightmare. Better my own thoughts than some annoying fellow-passenger.

But in this case, I decided to make an exception. Turning toward the brunette, I extended my hand: "Hi," I said with a smile. "My name is Clint. What's yours?"

She looked startled. After some hesitation, she ignored my hand but said, "I'm Teresa."

It was clear that I had made her uncomfortable. I could read her mind. On one side was a fat slob who had taken control of her arm rest, his body impinging on her space. On the other was a sketchy looking guy who, I reminded myself, appeared twice her age and seemed intent on striking up a conversation that she desperately wanted to avoid. Her arms were crossed over her chest in a protective gesture and she was doing her best to avoid any physical contact with either of the men to her side.

I didn't push it. We exchanged some basic information. She was indeed returning to St. Louis after a fabulous week in San Francisco with some college friends from the Bay Area. I told her that I lived and worked in San Francisco and how much I loved it. I was making a trip to St. Louis to visit family, but didn't say anything about the reasons. I was tempted to play the old St. Louis game of asking her where she went to high school. But while she had relaxed a bit, she was still eyeing me nervously so I let the conversation peter out.

By this time, we were somewhere over Nevada. Teresa got out her headphones and her I-pad and did her best to create a protective cocoon. I had brought a John Grisham paperback to pass the time and started to read, but found it hard to concentrate.

When the seatbelt sign went off, the flight attendants began their service. I badly needed food and a strong drink, maybe two, but didn't have a credit card. I was pretty sure Teresa had one, most people do. I thought about asking if she would purchase a sandwich and a couple of bourbons for me. I would give her cash in return with a little bit extra. But I decided that while I might be desperate for a real drink, I wasn't *that* desperate. Instead, I took a couple of the complimentary Diet Cokes and made do with the peanuts and assorted snacks.

The sodas helped settle my stomach and I returned to my reading. But I couldn't focus. Usually Grisham's writing held me spellbound. But I had too much on my mind. Sitting next to Teresa, a fellow St. Louisan, combined with my rushed return home unleashed a torrent of memories, most of them unpleasant.

Five

I HAD BEEN BORN AND raised in St. Louis, my mother's hometown. My father came from a small town in the mountains of eastern Tennessee, north of Knoxville. His last name was Jackson, a not uncommon surname in that part of the woods. Somewhere in the family lore was the belief, never proved, that he was related to the famous Civil War General, Stonewall Jackson. Or maybe it was Andrew Jackson. Whatever the truth, he descended from a long line of Tennessee Volunteers who took pride in their military service. Wanting to set him on the right course, his parents had named him Alvin Gary Jackson after the World War I hero Sergeant Alvin York who hailed from nearby Pall Mall, Tennessee and the actor who portrayed him in the movie "Sargent York," Gary Cooper. Almost immediately, he became known as Al and that is the name that stuck.

Growing up in a rural area my father spent a good part of his youth in the outdoors, hiking, camping, hunting, and fishing. He didn't have much in the way of formal schooling, but his father taught him all the useful skills associated with building and maintaining a house, skills that I ultimately inherited. As soon as he turned eighteen, Al enrolled in the Marine Corps. That was in the 1960s, during the height of the Vietnam War. Where Al grew up there was no anti-war movement. Instead, young men from his part of Tennessee were happy to enlist.

Al served two tours, earning a purple heart and a bronze star. His plan had been to return home after his service. But during his first tour he had been shipped state-side to a hospital in San Diego to recover from a chest wound. That's where he met my mother, a nurse in his ward. They fell in love and after my father returned from his second tour, they got married.

Over the course of their married years, my father ruled the roost. But on one thing my mother put her foot down and refused to budge. She would *not* live in Al's hometown, no matter how much he pleaded. Instead, she demanded – and he reluctantly agreed – to return to her hometown of St. Louis to settle down and raise a family.

My mother, Mae Demhoff, of German descent, had been born and raised in south St. Louis. She had an extended family there and could not imagine living apart from them. Al acquiesced. And, as it turned out, for him it was a great move. Mae's family took him in as one of their own, immensely proud that she had married a war hero. My grandfather, Hugo Demhoff, owned a small neighborhood hardware store and immediately hired Al on as an assistant. Mae went to work as a nurse at the local VA hospital. Soon, they were earning enough to rent a small house and to start a family. My brother John was born two years after Al had returned from Vietnam and I followed four years later. My sister Mel was something of an afterthought, coming five years after me and when my mother was in her late thirties.

Now as to our names. My father never really left the Marine Corps. To him, it was a second family. He generally disapproved of tattoos and strictly forbid us from inking our bodies. But when he rolled up the sleeve on his muscular right arm you could clearly see "Semper Fi" and the Marine insignia proudly displayed. And he wanted his sons to follow the tradition. My brother was named for one of dad's favorite actors, John Wayne, who portrayed a Marine in the movies, most notably in *The Sands of Iwo Jima*. In fact, my brother's full name was John Wayne Jackson. In the year I was born, 1986, another Marine movie my father liked, *Heartbreak Ridge* appeared. Accordingly, I was named for its star, Clint Eastwood. My mother prevailed when a daughter was born. She was christened Melanie, inspired by the Olivia de Haviland character in *Gone With the Wind*. My father, who wanted a third son, hid his disappointment by having everyone call her Mel, like Mel Gibson.

As we grew older, my brother and I found this naming business weird, particularly as neither John Wayne nor Clint Eastwood had actually served in uniform. But there were a lot of strange new names out there. And, after all, John and Clint were perfectly good male names, regardless of what inspired my father to select them for us.

Our names were the least of our worries. Once Al had saved enough money, he started his own small construction business. My mother's family helped, recommending him to their wide network of friends, neighbors, and relatives. When my mother quit her job to stay home and raise us, my dad worked like a man possessed. Soon, his reputation for craftsmanship, reliability, and fair pricing began to spread and his company began to grow. By the time I was ready to enter high school, the Jackson Construction Company was one of the biggest in the metropolitan area and my father was becoming rich beyond his and May's wildest dreams.

Al's success allowed us to move from our cozy south city split level to a four bedroom, three-story house in the western suburb of Webster Groves. The public schools there were excellent, but Al insisted that Clint and I attend the Country Day School in Ladue where we would mingle with the sons of the St. Louis elite. "I never had the advantages of a good education," he told us incessantly, "and I want you boys to have what I never did." Unspoken was the fact that while Al had acquired a lot of money, he had yet to crack the local establishment. He desperately wanted membership in one of the snooty country clubs in St. Louis County, but had yet to gain an invitation. "It's alright for me to build their fancy new houses," we once heard him tell our mother, "but they don't want me sitting down for drinks with them."

John didn't seem to mind that he and I were like a small invasion force designed to establish a beachhead so that dad could storm the ramparts of local privilege. My brother adapted well to Country Day, mixing easily with the preppies. It wasn't long before he was a Big Man on Campus. He got straight "A's" back before grade inflation and was a three-star athlete in football, basketball, and baseball, earning all-state honors. Class valedictorian, he made it into Princeton on a full athletic-academic scholarship.

I was the opposite. I hung out with a crowd that constantly got in trouble, earning numerous suspensions. My class-room performance was dismal, largely through lack of effort. I did manage to graduate, but just barely. It was also during these years that I began to get into heavy drinking, racking up several citations for DUI and narrowly avoiding some serious accidents. I did enjoy sports, and actually did pretty well. But I chose not to compete with my brother. Instead of team sports, I stuck to swimming and long-distance running. Even though I won some medals, my father sniffed that these were "sissy" sports and my accomplishments were nothing to be proud of.

My relationship with my father, never great to begin with, deteriorated over time. From the time I was a teenager, he never tired of telling me what a disappointment I was to him. "Just look at John," he would demand. "Why can't you be like him? You are just wasting your life. What's the sense of paying thousands to send you to a great school if all you do is goof off?"

The more he rode me, the worse it got. We would have screaming matches and nearly came to blows on more than one occasion. My mother tried to intercede, but Al would have none of it. "Stop coddling him Mae," he would shout at her, his face red with anger. "He needs to grow up and become a man."

Maybe he was right. I did need to grow up. But somehow I could never get over the hump. One disappointment and foul-up followed another. Despite my mediocre grades, I did gain acceptance at the University of Missouri, largely due to my Country Day diploma and my father's influence. It wasn't Princeton, but at least it offered the promise of a university degree. I started off with the best of intentions, but early in the first semester spent more time in local bars than in the classroom. By mid-year I was on academic probation. I returned for the spring semester, but gave up after a month. I was going nowhere.

By the time I had dropped out of Missouri, John had graduated from Princeton with highest honors. The next stop was Yale law school. But our dad wanted us to do our military service as soon as we graduated from college. John dutifully enlisted in the Marines and was promptly sent to the Persian Gulf as part of the force that would invade Iraq following the terrorist attacks of 9/11. My father demanded that I do the same. He didn't put it into words, but I could read his mind. "You might as well do something with your worthless life. Do something useful for your country."

I actually entered the Corps with a bit of gung-ho spirit. I did

20

want to do my part, although I had my doubts about the wisdom of invading Iraq, which seemed to have little to do with 9/11. That lasted about three weeks. I ended up punching my drill sergeant in the face, knocking him cold. "Well," I thought, "My dad would be proud. I was no sissy." I was lucky. The CO at Parris Island understood that the sergeant had crossed the line in his attempts to make me a Marine. But I had crossed the line as well. No punching of superior officers, no matter the treatment. I was washed out, but without any added penalties.

When I slunk home, my father and I had another confrontation. "Yet another disappointment," he screamed his face as red as a beet and his fists clenched. I tried to explain my side of things, but he wouldn't listen. With my mother watching on in tears, he told me not to bother unpacking. "Get out of this house you good-for-nothing," he shouted at the top of his lungs. "See if you can make something of yourself on your own." I didn't know it at the time, but we would repeat this scene numerous times until I finally took off for good.

Six

I WAS ABLE TO BUNK with a buddy of mine who lived in Maplewood, a mostly working-class St. Louis suburb. After passing most of my days spending what little money I had left in booze and babes, I began to drift from one menial job to another. They didn't last long as I continued to drink heavily, failed to get to work on time, and often got into heated confrontations with customers and employers. It didn't take a genius to figure out that I had, as they say, "anger issues."

I spent a couple of years this way. Then, one day I got into a bloody fight with my Maplewood buddy. I can't even remember what it was about. Maybe it was over the fact that I never contributed much in the way of rent to cover basic household expenses. Or maybe it was over a girl. Whatever the reason, he kicked me out and I spent a couple of weeks on the street. Just when I thought things couldn't get worse, they did.

I was hanging out with other homeless people in downtown St. Louis, begging for change during the day and sleeping in abandoned buildings or under viaducts during the night. One night in early fall, I had found a spot to crash in a vacant lot near Laclede's Landing, an entertainment district on the Mississippi River in the shadow of the Gateway Arch. Wrapped in a ratty blanket I had found in a dump and sound asleep, I was suddenly awakened by an attack from out of the blue by two guys.

I was momentarily stunned. I had heard stories about similar beat-downs of the homeless, but figured they were probably exaggerated. "That would never happen to me," I thought. Now I was getting a painful lesson of how wrong I was.

As the two guys started kicking me, I heard them laughing and cursing. "Way to go Spencer," one of them yelled as his buddy aimed a boot at my head, a kick that would have knocked me silly – or worse – if I had not been able to dodge it at the last second. Spencer's friend then connected with a solid kick to my stomach.

I had several options. I could beg them to stop. I could curl up into a protective ball and take the punishment, hoping that the damage would not be too severe. Or I could try to get to my feet and defend myself. I chose option three.

Luckily for me, my attackers were in a condition I knew very well. I could tell from their voices, their breath, and their demeanor that they were pretty well plastered. I guessed their decision to pick on the poor homeless guy was part of a night of heavy drinking. They hadn't been able to pick up chicks in a bar, I speculated, so why not get your jollies by letting out your frustrations on some loser who won't put up much of a fight.

They were in for a surprise. I managed to avoid enough errant kicks to stagger to my feet. I could see some panic in their eyes when they saw I wasn't some wizened wino. Instead they were confronted by someone who was about their age and size and despite all the dissipation still in pretty good shape.

Long story short, I made them very, very sorry they had chosen me to hassle. By the time the police arrived on the scene, both my attackers were out cold with broken jaws and other serious injuries. In fact, if the cops hadn't pulled me off them, I might have killed them.

An ambulance arrived and the two were carted off to Barnes Hospital. I ended up in the city jail while the cops sorted things out. After I told them my name and showed them some identification (I still had a valid driver's license), I explained what had happened and displayed the assorted bruises I had collected before I had managed to get to my feet. But they looked skeptical. The two guys I had laid out were well-dressed and had been driving a brand-new Audi. I had a week's growth of beard, was dressed in clothes from the Salvation Army, hadn't had a shower in a month, and had been sleeping in a vacant lot.

I had hoped that after I had told my side of things, the cops would let me go. But they decided to hold me overnight until they could check out my story. They put me in a holding cell, where fortunately I was the only occupant. In my storied past, I had spent more than a few nights in the drunk tanks of various jails. Usually, I shared accommodations with other miscreants, many of whom were still inebriated and who made it impossible to get any sleep. The lone cot in the cell smelled of flop sweat and urine, but I didn't care. Compared with where I had spent the last few weeks, it was like being in a luxury hotel.

Seven

A GUARD WOKE ME OUT of deep slumber at eight in the morning. "Time to rise and shine Jackson," he said in a loud voice. "There are some people who want to speak with you."

I opened my eyes, sat up, and looked around. For a moment, I had trouble figuring out where I was and how I had gotten there. But then it all came rushing back.

The guard opened the cell door and handed me a tray with what passed for breakfast. I used the plastic fork and spoon to shovel down some lousy powdered eggs, something that may have been a sausage patty, and bit into a couple of pieces of stale dry toast. A washed it all down with what the plastic container said was orange juice but tasted more like months'-old Kool Aid.

From the other side of the cell door, the guard kept a steady watch on me. I don't know what he expected me to do. Stab myself with a plastic fork?

After I had used the toilet in the corner, the guard opened the cell door and beckoned me out. As he walked me down the corridor to an interview room, he kept one hand on my arm and his other hand on his baton. I adopted the least threatening posture I could and was nothing but polite. He probably had heard about the damage I had inflicted on my two attackers the night before and was taking no chances.

At the interview room, I found two detectives waiting for me behind the kind of plain table you saw in every cop show on TV. Directly above the table was a single overhead light. The room itself was painted institutional gray, with the standard mirror on one side, presumably allowing others to watch and record the interview.

One of the detectives was tall and lanky, with thinning sandy hair and pale skin, dressed in a well-worn off-the-rack dark suit. I guessed he was in his forties. The other was short and stocky, with curly red hair, a florid complexion, and about the same age as his partner. He wore a checked sport coat and brown trousers. For some reason, they reminded me of Bud Abbot and Lou Costello. But as I soon found out, they were as far from comedians as one could get.

"Have a seat Jackson," the tall one said without standing, pointing a bony finger at a chair opposite them.

As I sat, he introduced himself. "I'm Detective Swanson," he said. "And this is Detective O'Malley." O'Malley didn't say anything, just nodded. I began to wonder just how much trouble I was in.

"Listen," I said, "I don't know what you guys want with me, but..."

Swanson cut me off. "We just want to talk Jackson. Get your side of the story again. Go over a few of the details you provided to the officers last night." Then he paused, "You want some coffee before we begin?"

"Sure. Thanks. That would be great."

"Back in a minute," he said, "Cream and sugar?"

"Just black will be fine, thanks."

While Swanson fetched the coffee, O'Malley stayed seated. He simply stared at me with a hostile expression on his face. It was pretty clear who was going to be the "good cop" and who the "bad cop" in this scenario.

Less than a minute passed and Swanson returned with my coffee. I let it cool for minute and then took a few sips. It tasted as though it had spent a rough night, but I needed the caffeine jolt. My hands were trembling as I put the cup down on the table. The detectives probably read this as nervousness, maybe a sign of guilt. But what I saw was the familiar sign that I needed something stronger than coffee to drink.

As I went over my story again, Swanson and O'Malley stared at me without expression. From time to time, Swanson would look down at a notepad, presumably checking my morning version with the one I had given last night.

When I had finished, Swanson let me sweat for a couple of minutes before he responded. "Look Jackson, we're checking into your story. But so far, we have no witnesses. So we just have your word to go on."

"What about the two guys who attacked me? I'm pretty sure they were drinking heavily when they decided to get their kicks by hassling me. They probably got lubricated at the Landing and stumbled upon me on their way home. I don't mean to tell you your job, but..."

I was about to suggest they check some of the bars at Laclede's Landing when O'Malley interrupted, speaking for the first time. "Then don't try Jackson," he said in a threatening tone, definitely playing the "bad cop."

Swanson, playing the "good cop," took it down a notch. "We've been looking into the two victims as well..."

Now it was my turn to interrupt. "What do you mean 'victims'?" I said with some heat. "I was the victim here, not them."

"Okay Jackson, okay," Swanson said, raising his hands in a placating gesture. "We've been looking into the two guys you sent to the hospital, okay? And you're right. It seems they were out bar-hopping last night."

"So you see...," I started to say, when O'Malley took his turn.

"Right now, we don't *see* much of anything Jackson. You tell us that the two 'victims' decided to beat you up for no reason. But why would they do that? You, on the other hand, might have lured them into a fight, maybe said something to provoke them. Maybe you had an eye on their fancy car. Maybe you thought they would be easy marks and you could mug them. You probably thought they must have some money on them and they were vulnerable, having been drinking and all. Maybe..."

I could feel my blood boiling. I was about to say how ludicrous all that speculation was when I realized that O'Malley wanted to goad me into saying something stupid. So I just kept my mouth shut and shook my head as he went on spinning fairy stories.

Once O'Malley ran out of theories, Swanson took the baton. "Look Jackson," he said somberly, "we need to hold onto you until we can straighten things out."

"How long is that going to be?" I asked, a sense of panic beginning to build.

Swanson shrugged. "We really don't know. Both of the vic...both of the guys you say attacked you are still unconscious. In fact, one of them is in a coma. We just have to wait until we can get their side of the story. Sorry. But that's the way it is."

I didn't know how genuinely sorry Swanson was. But I was desperate to get out of jail.

"Have I been charged with anything?" I asked.

Swanson and O'Malley exchanged looks. "No," Swanson said. "We are just holding you for questioning. We can keep you for forty-eight hours without charging you."

"Do I at least get a phone call?"

Again they looked at one another. Both shrugged. "Sure Jackson," Swanson finally said after letting me sweat a little. "One call," he said, pointing to a phone in the corner. "You can make it now if you like. But we need to be present to make sure that you only make the one."

"Thanks. That's all I'll need," I said with feigned nonchalance. In fact, I wasn't at all sure that was going to be the case.

Eight

I FELT LIKE ONE OF those contestants on a game show. I had a lifeline to help me out of a jam. The big question now was: Who to call? And the answer to that was not an easy one.

Under ordinary circumstances, the logical choice would have been my brother. John was a lawyer and had begun to have some clout in local legal circles. But we had not been on good terms for some time, and it was all my fault. Five years ago, after he had graduated from Yale Law, he had married his high-school sweetheart, Tiffany. They had met when Tiffany was a student at Country Day's sister school, Mary Institute. Blonde, blue-eyed, and I had to admit, knock-out gorgeous, she came from one of St. Louis's best families and was a perfect match for my driven, straight-arrow, good-looking brother. Their wedding took place at the Old Cathedral near the river and was attended by a representative cross-section of the local elite.

My parents couldn't have been happier. It was like a coming-out party for Al and Mae Jackson, children of humble working-class parents, who had achieved the American Dream. There was only one fly in the ointment: Me.

John had chosen me as his best man. Back then we were still close despite my wayward existence. I had managed to stay upright during the ceremony and perform my expected duties while nursing one of my monumental hangovers. The bachelor party I had thrown the night before, I was later told, was one to remember. However, I had drunk so much I had only a hazy recollection of the details. I did recall my brother driving me home from a strip club in Sauget, Illinois across the river in East St. Louis. He was not happy. The kind of debauchery I specialized in was not his cup of tea. He had only gone along with my plans out of filial duty; as something that was expected of him, not out of enjoyment. He barely touched the drinks I tried to force on him and, fortunately for me, remained sober enough to make sure we got home safely.

At the wedding reception, held in a Ladue country club where Tiffany's parents were card-carrying members of long standing, I made a total fool of myself. Six sheets to the wind, I gave a rambling, incoherent toast that seemed to go on forever. In the course of my remarks, I managed to insult just about everybody in the room. Before I could finish, one of the groomsmen pulled me from the microphone and mercifully shut me up. I had made it an occasion to remember alright, but not in a good way. My parents were embarrassed beyond measure and John was livid. If I hadn't been so drunk, my brother probably would have beaten the crap out of me. Instead, he told me in disgust, "Thanks a lot Clint. You managed to turn what should have been a magical day into a nightmare. Maybe God will forgive you (he had always been the religious one), but I sure won't."

After John and Tiffany returned from their honeymoon, I tried to patch things up. I practically groveled at his feet. But he would have none of it. The wound was too deep. When forced together at family gatherings, he kept a cool distance. There was a slight warming when his and Tiffany's daughters were born. Heather came first, almost nine months to the day after the honeymoon. I was genuinely happy for them and felt more affection for their little bundle of joy than I had expected. When Tiffany let me hold Heather in my arms for the first time, albeit eyeing me anxiously, I couldn't constrain my tears. *Where had that come from?* A year and half later equally adorable Willow arrived.

With my two nieces, I became the slightly goofy adoring uncle. Whenever I had a little extra money, I bought them presents and never failed to remember their birthdays.

My being "Good Old Uncle Clint" went only so far with my brother. One fine spring day, I volunteered to take the girls to the zoo. Both John and Tiffany were swamped with work and obligations and I thought my offer to take the girls off their hands for a day would be welcome. I also hoped that the memory of my wedding-reception debacle might have dimmed. Boy was I wrong. "Absolutely not," John said in no uncertain terms. "We're not putting our daughters' safety and wellbeing in *your* shaky hands. What are you going to do? Stop off for a few beers to steady yourself before you pick them up?"

The words hurt. I was going through one of my ritualistic sobering-up periods and hadn't had a drink in almost two months. Actually, forty-five days, but who's counting? But my brother was right. How could he trust me not to fall off the wagon? I could swear on as many bibles as he could pile up that I would do nothing to put the little girls I adored at risk and he still wouldn't believe me. Just to prove the point, that night I put a spectacular end to my forty-five days of sobriety and started yet another downward spiral.

To return to the matter at hand, I thought John, despite the lingering resentment, still might have enough residual brotherly love to come to my rescue and get me out of jail. But there was a more practical matter. I had heard from my mother, with whom I remained in touch, that he was out of the country on some legal business. I couldn't very well expect him to rush home on my behalf, even if I had known how to reach him.

My sister Mel was another possibility. But she was in graduate school on the East Coast. As with John, I had no way of reaching her even if I had been so inclined.

I went through a list of friends, but by now it was a short one. I had burned most of my bridges.

Finally, I reluctantly came to the conclusion I had been avoiding. I had to call my mother. She was the only one I could count on. I imagined my father reacting to the news that I was being held in jail with disgust: "Let him stew in his own juice, lie in the bed he has made for himself. Learn some lessons the hard way."

As I picked up the phone to enter my home number, I felt a sense of shame. *Thirty years old and still depending on your mother,* I thought. But what choice did I have? I didn't want to spend another night in jail. And while I knew the detectives were playing some games with me, I could be in real trouble if they believed any of the scenarios O'Malley had been spinning. And if I didn't call, I would end up with a court-appointed public defender. The stakes were too high. I needed solid legal representation, the kind my mother could arrange for me; that is, if my father would allow her to do so.

I punched in the numbers. Swanson and O'Malley were watching, their faces masks of indifference. My hand held the receiver in a death grip as I heard the rings on the other end. I guessed that it was around nine o'clock. I prayed that Al had stuck to his usual schedule and had left two hours earlier, leaving my mother and our maid alone in the house.

When there was no answer after ten rings, I began to panic. But on the eleventh, someone picked up the phone. When I heard my mother's voice say "Hello" I felt a wave of relief. My lifeline had been connected.

"Hi Mom," I said, my voice hoarse and cracking.

"Clint," she said a catch in her voice. Then her maternal instincts kicked in. I did call her from time to time but never this early in the day. "What's wrong? Are you in some kind of trouble?" she asked.

"I'm afraid so Mom," I said. Then I explained the situation. As I presented my side of the story, I could see Swanson and O'Malley exchange smirks.

After I had finished, my mother said, "Listen Clint, I'm going to call Ted Stevenson right away. I'll tell him what's happened and I'm sure he or one of his associates will be there soon to get you out of jail."

I breathed a sigh of relief. Ted Stevenson was the family attorney, a member of one of the most prestigious law firms in St. Louis. As far as I knew, he didn't do criminal law, but there were plenty of members of his firm who did. And I was sure he would act promptly. He not only was a close family friend, but also received a healthy yearly retainer to handle the many legal issues involving my father's business. Whether he or somebody from his firm came to my rescue, I was a lot better off than being represented by some wet-behind-the ears and poorly-paid public defender.

"Thanks a million Mom," I said. "But what about Dad?"

I could hear her take a deep breath. "Don't worry about your father. I'll think of something." She might have added what she was probably thinking: "I have had a lot of practice trying to protect you from your father."

After thanking her again, I hung up. Turning to my inquisitors, I said with a little smirk of my own, "I think we are through talking detectives. I'm going to wait for my lawyer before saying another word."

Actually, I was a little hazy on the law, depending mainly on what I had learned from watching television. Maybe they didn't have to stop interrogating me. I wasn't officially under arrest. I hadn't been read my Miranda rights. But they didn't press the matter. They just shrugged as if to say, "Your choice buddy."

They called in the guard and he took me back to my cell, where I would cool my heels until my lawyer arrived. Before I left the interview room, O'Malley provided a not too-gentle reminder of the serious trouble I was in. "Don't get too comfortable Jackson," he said with snarl. "If your story doesn't hold up, we'll have plenty of opportunities to continue our little chat. And you'd better hope that the two guys you beat senseless recover. Otherwise, you're going to be in a world of hurt."

I struggled to muster a look of indifference. He was just trying to throw a scare into me, I said to myself. But as his words hit home I felt a jolt run up my spine and my heart beat like a drum inside my chest. As I was led to my cell, I uttered a silent prayer that Ted Stevenson or one of his minions was at that moment riding to my rescue.

Nine

I STEWED IN MY CELL for about an hour until my rescuer arrived. "Okay Jackson," the guard said, opening the cell door. "Your lawyer is here. You're free to go."

I just nodded and got up from the cot, hoping never to see it again. The guard led me to the booking area, where Ted Stevenson himself was waiting for me.

When he saw me, a look of surprise appeared on his face, mixed with what I interpreted as disapproval. I couldn't blame him. I hadn't showered in days and a night on a smelly mattress had not enhanced the body odor that even I found repulsive. I had a straggly beard and dirty long hair. I was wearing the same castoff clothing, now with splotches of dried mud and a few blood stains, some of which were mine, some of which came from the guys I had beaten. I looked exactly like what I was – a homeless bum.

Ted recovered quickly. Extending his hand, he said "Hi Clint. Good to see you. Let's get you out of here."

I took his hand in a firm grip. "Thanks Ted. It's good to see you too, believe me."

Taking me by the elbow, he led me out the door to the street, where a late-model black town car was waiting. It was in a no-parking zone, but Ted's influence had kept it free of a citation.

Ted's driver, a big, burly guy named Mike was holding the rear door open as we descended the steps and onto the sidewalk. Ted still had me by the elbow. I jerked it away. "Wait a minute Ted," I said with a note of panic in my voice, "Where are we going?"

I had a pretty good idea of his answer. "You're going home Clint. Please get in the car."

It was the last place I wanted to be. Well maybe the second last. I thought about bolting. Mike must have read my thoughts. He left the car door open and headed toward me, ready to stop me if I tried to run.

I stood frozen. What was I going to do? I had no place to stay. I would have preferred to keep on living on the streets rather than share space with my father. But reality set in. I was still under suspicion. Before I had left the station, Swanson had told me not to leave St. Louis until my situation had been resolved one way or the other. He or Ted had to be able to contact me. My mother had gone out on a limb to spring me. I really had no choice.

Ted clarified things. "Okay Clint. You have two alternatives. You can go home to your mother and father. Or..." He gestured over his shoulder to the jail entrance.

I gave in. Without a word, I brushed by Mike and got in the backseat of the car. Ted slid in next to me, careful not to get too close. I saw him reach for a handkerchief, presumably to cover his nose, but then he apparently thought better of it. Instead, he cracked his window to let in a little of the fresh air on what was a crisp and cool autumn day.

On the thirty-minute ride to Webster Groves, Ted asked for my side of the story. He listened intently as I described in as much detail as I could the events of the previous night and my grilling at the hands of Swanson and O'Malley. He interrupted occasionally but for the most part simply let me do the talking. When I had finished, he said, "Well, from what you tell me it seems a pretty clear-cut case of self-defense. But, "he added, "The police only have your side of the story. So far as we know there were no witnesses. Maybe one will show up to corroborate your side of things. But if not..."

"Yeah. If not, I could be in deep trouble. The cops made it pretty evident they had doubts about my account."

He tried to reassure me. "Look Clint. We have a long way to go here. We have to wait for the two men you attacked to recover and tell their side of things. In the meantime, we can do a little digging of our own, maybe scare up a witness or two. Somebody who might have seen them drinking and heard them planning to beat up a homeless person.

Maybe something along those lines. Just hold tight, okay? Don't panic. We're going to look out for you."

"Thanks Ted," I said, my voice cracking. "I appreciate it. And I'm sorry I've caused so much trouble."

He waved it off. "Just doing my job. Just doing my job. And helping people in trouble is what I do."

I was tempted to say that some people were worth the trouble. And maybe I didn't fall into that category, at least not at the moment. But enough with the self-pity, I said to myself. It was time to man-up to the next challenge – confronting my parents.

Mike pulled up in front of my family home. He stepped out and opened the back door. Ted stayed seated as I got out. "Thanks again Ted," I said.

"Your welcome," he replied. "We'll be in touch. And try to relax, okay?"

I gave him a wry grin. "Yeah. Sure. Relax. Got it."

I closed the door and stepped onto the sidewalk. Mike gave me a nod and a wink and returned to his place behind the wheel. He then drove off, the purr of the sixty-thousand dollar car barely discernible in the quiet suburban street.

I kept an eye on the car until it rounded the corner and disappeared from view, delaying the inevitable for as long as possible. For a moment, I thought about turning around and hightailing it out of there. But the moment passed. I took a deep breath and turned toward my house.

Our home had been constructed to Al's specifications. It was a stately three-story brick house, fitting nicely into some of the older residences in the neighborhood. Two oak trees bordered the walk up to the front porch. Their leaves were beginning to turn gold and red in the early fall. As kids, John and I enjoyed climbing the trees. As I gazed at them, I tried to recapture memories of happier times. But then I recalled that when I was nine, I fell from one of the oaks and broke my arm. It was a typical young kid accident. But the way my father screamed at me, you would have thought I had robbed a bank or something worse. My mother tried to reassure me that he had reacted that way because he loved me and I had scared him by my reckless behavior. Maybe that was true. But he had a long history of abusing me, verbally and physically and it would take a lot to convince me that his reaction was out of love and not some other twisted motivation that perhaps he himself did not understand.

As I headed to the front door, I saw Al's red pick-up truck with the "Jackson Construction Company" white lettering. I felt my heart sink. I had hoped he would not be home. But obviously my mother had called him and he was there to greet me. I didn't expect it to be with open arms.

I was not disappointed. I was about to ring the bell, when the door opened and my mother rushed onto the front porch to throw her arms around me. It was a test of motherly love that she did not immediately recoil from the sights and smells I presented. Instead, she hugged me so tightly I had trouble breathing for a few seconds.

"Oh Clint," she moaned. "I was so worried. I've missed you so much. It's so good to have you home, safe and sound." Still holding me tight, she began to sob.

I gently grabbed her by her upper arms and pulled her away. When I saw her haggard face, her eyes red from crying, I was overcome with guilt and shame. While I had called her from time to time, I hadn't seen her in months. I was as shocked by her appearance as she probably was by mine. She seemed to have aged ten years since I had last seen her. And it didn't take an Einstein to figure out that I was to blame.

At first, I didn't know what to say. I could feel tears begin to form. "I'm sorry mom," I finally said. "Sorry to have caused you so much grief."

She gathered herself. "That's okay. You're home now. That's all that matters."

My mom was about a foot shorter than I was. Looking over her head, I saw Al standing about three feet away in the hallway beyond the open front door, his arms crossed over his chest. He didn't say anything, just stared at me with the typical mixture of disappointment and disgust. His expression seemed to say it all: "See what you have done to your mother you ungrateful bum! You should say *sorry*. You have a lot to be sorry about."

"Come on in Clint," my mother said, tugging at my arm. Then, turning to my father, "Say hello to Clint Al. He's home."

"Yeah, he's home," my father said, his voice dripping with disdain. "How lucky for us."

For a second, I thought he might grab me and kick me out the door. Not that I would have blamed him. And maybe it would have been best for all concerned. But he just stood aside and let my mother guide me into the hallway.

Ignoring my father's sarcasm, she said "Your room is just as you left it. Why don't you freshen up? And then we'll have a nice lunch. Wouldn't you like that?"

"Yeah Clint," Al said, his voice dripping with sarcasm. "Why don't you do that? Then we can have a nice lunch – and a nice long chat."

As I made my way up the stairs, all the old ghosts came back to haunt me. I was home alright, but for how long? I knew the "chat" Al wanted to have would indeed be long. I doubted it would be nice.

Ten

A S IT TURNED OUT, I was half right. We indeed had a long chat. But it was marginally "nicer" than I had expected.

After I had showered, shampooed, shaved, and changed into clean clothes, I went downstairs to face the music. My mother had sandwiches, soup, salad, and dessert waiting for me. While I hungrily downed everything in sight, my first decent meal in weeks, she kept up a steady stream of chatter, filling me in on what the rest of the family had been up to during my absence. My father kept silent, staring at me over the rim of his coffee cup as he watched me eat.

When I had finished, we got down to brass tacks. I told both of them my side of the story, my mother nodding sympathetically and gasping when I described how I had been kicked awake while sleeping in a vacant lot. As I had expected, my father looked on impassively and said little, uttering the occasional non-committal grunt. When I had finished, he started in on me in familiar fashion.

"Well Clint, I could have predicted something like this. You have been on a self-destructive path for years. You were lucky those two guys didn't do more serious harm." He sounded almost sorry that they hadn't.

I was about to say, "Hey, how about a few points in my favor for taking on two guys who thought I would be easy pickings and turning the tables on them?" Maybe that would appeal to his tough-guy instincts.

But before I could speak, he surprised me. "Your mother and I think that maybe this time you have learned your lesson. That maybe, just *maybe*, you realize that you have reached rock-bottom and are ready to get your life together. So, we're willing to give you one last chance to set things straight." He paused, giving me his familiar no-nonsense glare and adding a steely tone to his voice. "Here's the deal. You stay here with us, where we can keep an eye on you. You agree to stop the drinking. No more fights, no more trouble. And you work for me on one of my crews to pay for your room and board. In return, we'll try to get you out of the current mess you've made."

I could feel my blood begin to boil. I was no longer a kid, forced to accept a punishment that sounded like "go to your room" or "you're grounded." I was a grown man, capable of making my own decisions, of going my own way.

"And if I don't go along with your plan?" I said, mentally preparing to get up from the table and head out the door.

"Then you can forget having us pay to have Ted Stevenson – or anybody else – represent you."

"Please Clint," my mother said. "Listen to your father."

I stared at both of them for a few seconds, my fists clenched. I felt trapped. I took a deep breath and collected my thoughts. In the cold light of day, I began to reassess my situation. As much as I hated to admit it, my father's words struck home. I *had* been on a self-destructive path. Maybe he was right. Maybe I had hit rock bottom and needed help to get out of the pit I had dug for myself. I had serious doubts that staying at home and being under Al's thumb was the best way to get on track. I blamed him for the course my life had taken. But there was no realistic alternative. I desperately needed the first-class legal representation Ted Stevenson could offer. Otherwise, if things went bad, I could end up in prison. I didn't know the exact condition of the guys I had sent to the hospital, but a charge of assault and battery with deadly intent was not out of the question.

"Okay Dad," I said with some reluctance. "You've got a deal."

I reached across the table and offered my hand. I couldn't read the look on his face. It seemed to be a mixture of satisfaction and sadness. He took my hand in his and squeezed it in his powerful grip. "Deal," he said.

My mother was beaming. "Oh Clint," she exclaimed. "It will be wonderful to have you home again. Just wonderful."

She got up from her chair and gave me a hug. I didn't expect my father to join in. He never had and he wasn't about to do so now. A manly handshake was as far as he would go in terms of affectionate physical contact with his sons. Slaps, spanks, and punches, that was another matter. Under his breath I could hear him mutter, "Yeah. Just wonderful."

For the next few months, the bargain I had struck with my parents held. I stopped drinking, going cold turkey. The day following my return, I woke at six and, after a big breakfast, was out of the house by seven to begin work on one of Al's projects. It was the start of long days of doing whatever needed to be done – pouring cement, laying brick, installing plumbing and wiring, painting, plastering; you name it, I did it. I blamed my father for a lot of things that had gone wrong in my life. But one gift he did provide were the construction skills I inherited from him. So long as I kept reasonably sober, I could always find a job.

One night about two weeks after I had returned, we were sitting around the dinner table when my father gave me the first compliment from him I could remember. "You know Clint," he said over dessert, "I have to admit that while you may be a jack of all trades in the construction business you are the master of most of them. I don't have many men who can do all the things you can on a site and do them well."

I was so shocked I didn't know how to respond. But then good old Al stuck the knife in: "So if you ever find yourself on the street again, you don't need to be homeless. You can build your own place."

He might have meant it as a joke and I laughed half-heartedly. But behind the joke was a meaning hard to miss: "You're doing okay so far. But you're going to foul up again. It's inevitable."

The next day, I got good news on the legal front. Ted Stevenson told me that the two guys who had attacked me were, as I had suspected, a couple of spoiled brats from the suburbs. They had spent a few days in the hospital, but had been released. Their injuries were not considered life-threatening, although it would take them awhile to recover fully. They wouldn't be chewing steaks anytime soon. Their families were well-known in St. Louis social circles and planned to press charges against me, claiming, as O'Malley had suggested, that I had lured them into that vacant lot so I could mug them and take their car. So, it would be attempted robbery and assault.

When my father got this bit of news, I thought he would hit the roof. These families had clout and my run-in with the two kids might harm his business. They also sat on the boards of the elite country clubs he so desperately wanted to join.

For a while, I feared Al might throw me to the wolves. I imagined him saying something along the lines of, "Hey. I can't control my son. What can I do but apologize for his behavior. His mother and I have tried our best; he's beyond our influence."

But Ted Stevenson proved to be worth his retainer. While the police seemed inclined to go along with the story spun by powerful St. Louisans, Ted had a private investigator do some digging. He found that the two guys who had attacked me had indeed been drinking heavily at a bar on the Landing. They had tried to pick up some girls, but with no success. A bartender had overheard them talking about "cleaning up the area" by rousting some of the nearby homeless. He was willing to testify if called. He wasn't happy that the two jerks had failed to tip him.

While it wasn't conclusive evidence, it was enough. Ted had been able to convince the attorney representing the two families that the case against me would be difficult to prove without eyewitness testimony and the subsequent trial would expose the less than gentlemanly behavior of their two sons. We would offer to pay their hospital expenses if they dropped the charges, which they did, leaving me in the clear and lifting the dark cloud over my head.

While my mother and I received the news with relief, Al remained Al. I don't think he really wanted me to end up in prison, if only because it would be so embarrassing for him. But he also clearly still had doubts about my side of the story. And, to be fair, I had lied to him on too many occasions to recall. In this case, I was telling the honest truth. But I could understand his skepticism, the bartender's account notwithstanding. He was judging me by my overall track record, not by just one race. Also, he probably thought the dismissal of charges was more the result of Stevenson's legal maneuvering than the veracity of my side of things.

The next few months were pretty good. I stayed sober and continued to work hard. The combination of long hours at a construction site and my mother's cooking helped me restore some of the weight and muscle I had lost on the streets. No booze helped me feel better as well. I had no trouble sleeping after a long day's labor and woke up refreshed and with my head clear for the first time in years.

I was feeling better emotionally as well. One of the few things I admired about my father was his commitment to doing quality work on every project he undertook. Unlike many of his competitors, he never cut corners, never tolerated shoddy work, never ran up phony charges, and demanded the highest standards from everyone who worked for him. Before beginning any project, he gathered all the workers together at the site and gave them a pep talk. "I want you all to think of this project not as something you are building for a client. Instead, think of it as a home you are building for yourself or your family." If it was an office building or a store, he would amend the speech: "Think of it as a place where you would want to work or where you and your family would want to shop."

And he meant what he said. Even if he had a dozen projects going on simultaneously, and had foremen he could trust, he made it a point to visit every site three or four times a week to make sure everything was going as planned. And if someone couldn't cut the mustard, they were gone in the blink of an eye. There were plenty of replacements eager to fill the vacancy. Al had the well-deserved reputation of being tough but fair. If you did your work well, you got rewarded with generous wages, incentive bonuses, and other benefits. Al also was a fanatic about safety on the job, something that could not be said of many of his competitors. The accident rate at his sites was the lowest in the city. My co-workers told me that every construction laborer in St. Louis wanted to work for Al. Any vacancies were usually filled the day after they occurred.

And as I got into the work, I began to feel some of the same commitment to high standards and high quality that my father preached. When we finished a job, I took pride in the result – and in being part of the team that had produced something that would stand the test of time. Be it a fancy home in the suburbs, an office complex in the city, or a new store in downtown Webster Groves, I knew it was a structure that was solidly built, would provide satisfaction to its inhabitants, and included my contribution of sweat and skill.

I also found that I enjoyed working with a team. I had always been a loner and it took a while for me to fit in. When I showed up for work the day after I had cut my deal with Al, I could see the questioning looks as the foreman introduced me: "What have we got here?" their faces seemed to say. "The boss's son dropped on us out of the blue. What's he going to do, report back to his daddy if we fail to drive a nail to his specifications? Fill a spot that a family man needs? Replace one of us? Think that he can sit on his butt all day while we do the work?" And I couldn't blame them if that was what they thought. But by the end of the day I had shown them that I was no slouch on the job, that I could more than pull my weight, and that being the boss's son in no way meant that I was there to spy on them. By the end of the week we were swapping jokes and stories and I was invited to join most of the crew at a local bar after work. I went along, but stuck to Diet Coke, a fact that raised some eyebrows but no overt questions. Most of them probably knew of my sordid past and were discreet enough not to embarrass me.

A month into my stay at home, I started to see a girl I had known from high school. She was going through a tough divorce and wasn't looking for any long-term commitment. Neither was I. Our relationship was more one of convenience and mutual support rather than any great passion. We enjoyed being with each other and I found I could actually get through a pleasant evening and have a nice conversation without the lubrication of alcohol. My parents knew her and her parents and gave their blessing to our dating, although I would have seen her regardless.

It was all too good to last. Every time I heard one of my co-workers praise my father, I thought to myself, "Yeah. But you don't have to live with him." Relations at home were civil, but there was a constant tension. I was on trial and I knew it. Over the dinner table, my father peppered me with questions about how things had gone on the job that day. I could see him constantly check for signs that I might be hitting the bottle, staring at my hands to see if they shook and at my eyes and nose for tell-tale signs of alcohol abuse. I thought he looked disappointed when he didn't find that I was back to my old bad habits. And he constantly reminded me that I would have to work for him for a long time if I meant to pay back the substantial fee that Ted Stevenson had charged to assure I didn't end up in prison.

The way he figured it, I was doing the job of someone he would have to hire. He kept a weekly account of the savings, minus the one hundred dollar "allowance" he gave me. "At this rate, just three and a half more years to go," he informed me with a glint in his eyes that reflected his glee in my predicament. It was practically a weekly ritual for him to state where my balance stood.

My mother tried to intercede on my behalf. "Oh please Al," she said about a month into this performance. "Let Clint be. He's working as hard as he can. Let's not keep Ted's fee as a cloud over his head. Besides…"

He cut her off. "No coddling Mae," he said. "He's got to learn to pay his debts and that's all there is to it."

My mother didn't argue. She knew it was no use. And, so did I. She rarely won arguments with my father. Furthermore, I had to admit, Al was right. I owed him for bailing me out. I couldn't deny it. But it stuck in my craw that he felt it necessary to bring it up on a regular basis. And I chafed at being treated like a wayward teenager, with little if anything in the way of positive reinforcement. How about a few "atta boys" on those occasions when I had handled a problem on-site that no one else could. But not a peep from Jarhead Al.

Finally, after six months at home, we had one of our familiar confrontations. I can't even remember what it was about. Something trivial no doubt that spun out of control. We ended up in a shouting match that threatened to turn physical until I packed my bag and fled the house, slamming the door behind me with my father's taunts – "you ungrateful good-for-nothing, you loser" – ringing in my ears. That night I broke my vow of sobriety and got roaring drunk.

Over the next two years, the cycle continued. I would spend a few months either bunking with a buddy or again on the streets. I would get into some kind of trouble with the law and my parents would bail me out. I promised to reform, returned to my room at home, and got back to work. My mother protected me, my father abused me. Then Al and I would have an argument and I would storm out.

This cycle played out several times until I finally broke it. This time, I had only been home for a week when Al and I really got into it. We were both frustrated with each other and reaching a breaking point. One night, I got plastered and came home well after midnight. Al was waiting up for me in the hallway. As I stumbled in, he read me the riot act. "Get out of here you bum," he shouted, his face red, his eyes bulging, and his fists clenched. "This is it. No more chances. You're on your own."

Up to this point, our arguments had remained verbal. But this time was different. I just exploded. With an anguished cry, I lunged at him, my hands headed for his throat. I caught him by surprise and he fell backward onto the floor with me on top of him. He managed to recover and hit me on the side of the head with a round-house right. Ordinarily, it would have stopped me in my tracks. It hurt like hell and for a second I saw stars. But my alcohol-fueled rage allowed me to shake it off. I remained on top of him and managed to get both my hands around his throat, prepared to choke the life out of him. When I applied my grip, his eyes bulged and I saw fear in them. And, while it might have been my imagination, I thought I also saw a grudging respect as if he was saying, "Well it took you long enough."

Before I could do further damage, I heard my mother at my side screaming at the top of her lungs, "Clint! Clint! Please stop it. Please." Tugging at my right arm, she said "You're going to kill him."

"Damn right I am," I said, my voice slurred.

As my mother tugged at my arm, I began to loosen my grip. For a second, I had the thought of knocking her aside so I could finish the job. But that image sobered me up. Instead, I loosened my death grip and fell off my father. My mother went to him as he struggled to regain his breath. I just lay on my back at his side, breathing heavily and fearing I was about to vomit.

"Get out," my father said in a hoarse voice, sitting up with Mae's help. "Get out and never come back. From now on you're dead to me. Get it. You are no longer my son."

"Fine with me," I said, my voice cracking. "And you were never really much of a father."

My mother just stared at me, her eyes filled with tears. I struggled to my feet, went up the stairs to my room, packed my bag, and left the house, this time for good. Through the haze of my jumbled thoughts, I knew I had to get as far away from Al and St. Louis as I could. If I didn't, I was afraid that any more contact with my father would find me finishing the job I had started that night.

Eleven

AS MY FLIGHT BEGAN its descent into St. Louis, those painful memories refused to fade. Down below I could see the lush farmland of my native state in all its glory and began to pick out familiar landmarks. Coming in from the west, we crossed the Missouri River, its muddy waters reflecting the rays of the setting sun. As we got closer to the ground, I could make out some office buildings that I had helped construct in what seemed a lifetime ago. Finally, we touched down light as a feather on the runway of Lambert International Airport. The flight attendant welcomed us to St. Louis where the local time was 7:30 pm and the temperature 95 degrees. I was home.

Sitting in the back, it took me time to disembark. I was in no hurry. I knew what awaited me was not going to be pleasant.

Our plane had docked at the end of Terminal C and it was a long walk to the exit. Even though I knew my brother was waiting for me, probably anxious to pick me up and get going, I strolled leisurely along the corridor. About halfway down, I spied what I was looking for – an airport lounge. I sat at the bar and ordered two double scotches straight up and downed them in thirsty swallows. I felt like a wanderer in the desert who had stumbled across an oasis.

Thus fortified, I made my way to the exit. My stomach was burning from quaffing two heavy drinks so quickly and I felt light-headed with the booze going directly to my brain. But as always, my faithful friend helped me to blur the past and strengthened me to face the future.

Passing through the exit, I spied my brother John amidst a cluster of people in the waiting area. Some of them had balloons and signs with special welcomes for loved ones. I didn't expect the same treatment.

John came forward to greet me, a look of annoyance on his face. He undoubtedly had checked the arrival board, had seen when my flight touched down, and knew instinctively what had caused my delay.

Anyone seeing us might not have guessed we were brothers. We were about the same height, a little over six feet tall, and the same weight, around 180. But John had inherited my mother's blond hair and cornflower blue eyes while I had picked up the dark hair and eyes of my father. John looked like the All-American boy that he was while I looked like someone you might want to avoid if you passed him on the street. His hair looked as though it had been cut by a barber who charged three figures. Although it was not a Marine crew-cut, it still was neat and trim. He wore a gleaming white dress shirt and dark pants, the only concession to the heat and the circumstances was the suit coat slung over his shoulder and the loosened tie at his throat. I guessed that the suit cost at least half my monthly rent. And I was dressed... well you know.

But if you looked closer you could detect the family resemblance. We both had the same prominent cheekbones, the same nose slightly altered, in my case by fights, in John's case playing football. We both had square jaws, broad shoulders, and reasonably narrow waists. We both were muscular, me from my construction work John from his obsessive workout regime. If you looked at the eyes, however, you could see that John's were clear and bright while mine had those telltale traces of red. But although John's eyes were clear, I could see that he was troubled. There were also new worry lines that were beginning to wrinkle his brow and bracket his mouth. He was usually as cool as the proverbial cucumber, but I could sense the tension and strain he was trying to control.

"Hey Clint," he said, grabbing me in a hug that surprised me. "It's great to see you. Thanks for coming."

I mumbled something in response, feeling a little disoriented. My brother could probably smell the liquor on my breath, but refrained from saying anything.

"Any baggage aside from your backpack?" he asked.

"No. This is it."

"Then let's get going."

We walked down the corridor by the baggage carousels and then out the exit into the parking garage. When we left the air-conditioned terminal, the heat and humidity felt as oppressive as I had remembered. Living in San Francisco had spoiled me and I had almost forgotten how brutal St. Louis summers could be. Just walking to John's car, not that far away, found me sweating profusely. All I could think of was how good a cold beer would taste.

Once in the car, a brand-new BMW in classic black, John turned on the AC full blast. Leaving the airport, we headed west on I-70. For a minute I thought about suggesting to my brother that we just keep on going until we hit the Pacific Ocean. I really was not looking forward to my homecoming and was having serious reservations about agreeing to return no matter how dire the situation.

We motored along in blissful air-conditioned comfort at seventy miles per hour, all traffic noise blocked out by the marvels of German engineering. I was tempted to tell John to slow down, that I was in no hurry. But there was no sense delaying the inevitable. Might as well sit back and enjoy the ride as the familiar sights and landmarks flashed by.

"So, Clint," John said, shooting me a sideways glance, "How are you? It's been a while."

"Not too bad. I love San Francisco and like my job."

"Hmm," he said. "And what job is that?"

"Construction, actually. I found a good company and crew and things are going well. Real well."

He cocked an eyebrow in my direction. "Glad to hear that. I guess the apple..."

"Doesn't fall far from the tree?" I finished. "Yeah. Of course, there are the good apples and then the other kind."

I immediately regretted the self-pitying tone and switched the conversation.

"So, what's the deal? What's happened to Mel? You said you'd fill me in when I got here. What's up?"

"Let's wait till we get to mom and dads. As I said on the phone, it's pretty complicated and we need to have a family discussion."

"I thought you said Al had had a stroke. How's he going to participate?" I asked.

49

"Yeah. Well, Dad had been in bad health for some time, losing a lot of weight. Of course, being Big Al, he wouldn't admit anything was wrong. We finally got him to a doctor and he diagnosed diabetes along with other ailments, including damage to the liver and kidneys. The prognosis was pretty grim, maybe six months and everything would shut down. Then, when we got the word about Mel, he had a stroke that left him unable to talk or move. He's now confined to a wheelchair and on a steady supply of oxygen. But the doctors say he can hear and understand. And Mom wants him to be there when we go over what we aim to do. She thinks it will bolster his spirits to know that the family is planning a response, although how she can tell anything might be sinking in is beyond me. But she says she can, so…"

"So we go along with the charade to please Al," I said with some bitterness. "Well we've all had practice doing that."

He just nodded, not arguing the point. Even though he was the "good son," he had had his share of problems with our father and was under no illusions about his abusive and overbearing nature.

"Hey Bro," I said. "Aren't we going in the wrong direction?"

We had turned south onto the I-270 outer belt and when we got to I-64 running east and west I had expected we would turn left and head toward Webster Groves. Instead we took a right and headed west toward the Missouri River.

"I forgot that you have been out of the loop. Mom and Dad moved from our old house about three years ago, not long after you left."

Probably too many bad memories, I thought to myself. *Most, if not all of them, associated with me.*

"They live in a gated community in St. Albans near the Missouri. They found a house with a great view of the river and enough room to accommodate several families. And most importantly for Al, complete with its own country club and golf course where he automatically became a member just by being a resident."

I couldn't hold back a laugh. "So he finally realized his dream, even if he had to buy it. And I assume it cost a pretty penny."

"That it did. That it did."

Although I laughed, the news shook me. For some unexplained reason, I thought my mother and father would end their days in their Webster Grove home. It had been built to Al's specifications and he even had taken part in its construction. It's where their three children had been raised and where they had a lot of close friends in the neighborhood. I had an image of them growing old together in familiar and comfortable surroundings. And even though it had often been hell for me to live there and I had sworn never to return, it was still what I thought of when I heard the word "home." And now Al and May had abandoned the security and comfort of the home they had built for themselves, along with the web of congenial and supportive friends, to live in virtual isolation in a community that whatever the amenities could not replace what they had. To add to the irony, Al's stroke meant that he could not even savor the benefits of the country-club membership he had sought for so long. I had to ask myself: *Would they have made this move if it hadn't been for me, the trouble I had caused, and the painful memories of that last awful night when I almost chocked the life out of my father? Well what if they had?* I said to myself. *Al was just as much to blame for what happened as I was, maybe more so.*

I considered asking John if my suspicions about what lay behind the move to St. Albans were on target. But instead I kept mum. He and I had more immediate concerns. To find out what had happened to our baby sister and how we could get her back safe and sound. Compared to that, my personal angst counted for little.

Twelve

PASSING THE CHESTERFIELD MALL on our left, we took the exit to Wild Horse Creek Road, which would carry us to St. Albans. It was a narrow two lane for most of the way, twisting and turning over small hills. There were trees close by on either side and with dark approaching, Clint slowed his speed and focused on his driving. As teenagers, we had come out this way for bike rides, stopping at a local grocery store for its famous sandwiches. I could still make out some of the rural charm, but could also see that new subdivisions had sprung up at regular intervals on our route, signs that urban sprawl was continuing its relentless spread westward.

While Clint drove in silence, my thoughts turned to Mel.

I could still recall the day when Al and Mae brought home my baby sister from St. Johns Hospital. I was five and John was seven at the time and despite my mother's initial fears that we would resent this intrusion, we instead could not conceal our delight with the new addition. Another recruit to help stave off our father's wrath we thought. Maybe the presence of a little baby girl would soften his rough edges.

For a while, it seemed to work. Mel was a beautiful baby with her mother's hair and eyes and an easy disposition, even as an infant. Al had wanted a third son and initially did little to hide his disappointment. But Mel won him over and he was soon increasingly besotted with his new daughter. That did little, however, to change his attitude and behavior toward his sons. He stuck to his hectoring ways, riding us and pushing us at every opportunity. And as Mel grew older she began to get some of the same treatment, although never with the physical abuse we suffered. Nonetheless, his verbal pummeling began to take its toll on

Mel. We tried to protect her as best we could, but it was a tough slog. Fortunately, as Mel grew into a beautiful young woman, she began to show a dogged determination not to let Al get to her. While she didn't engage in the kind of teenage rebellion that I did, she quietly charted her own independent course. She developed her own tight circle of friends, concentrated on her school work, and lost herself in books and music.

Like my brother, she excelled at everything she did – academics, athletics, music, you name it. As was the case with John at Country Day, she was valedictorian of her class at the sister school, Mary Institute. She followed in John's footsteps into the Ivy League, in her case choosing Penn over Princeton. The main reason was her budding interest in Archaeology and Anthropology, areas in which Penn enjoyed a sterling reputation. As a teenager, she had become fascinated with the remains of the pre-Colombian civilizations that had inhabited the nearby Mississippi River Valley. When her class took a field trip to the Cahokia Mounds across the Mississippi in Illinois, she became hooked on finding out all she could about what had been one of the largest cities in the Americas thousands of years ago. She volunteered for digs around the area. Already a superb athlete, winning awards for volleyball, basketball, and softball, she had the necessary physical skills and stamina to equal and often outperform her male colleagues at the excavation site.

Al seemed ambivalent about Mel's interests and ambitions. He remained stubbornly old-fashioned in his attitudes toward women. In his eyes, if a woman was not planning to marry, have children, and stay at home to raise them, then she should embark on a career that had a practical application – law, medicine, business – not one that looked for ancient relics. I suspected, too, that when it became apparent my brother was going to be a lawyer and I had proved unreliable and unworthy, in the back of his mind he harbored the idea that Mel one day might inherit and run Jackson Construction.

By the time Mel was making decisions about where to go to college and what to do with her life, John was not around much. I was and witnessed first-hand the numerous arguments around the family dinner table between Mel and Al, each stubbornly sticking to their respective guns. While Mel had inherited our mother's looks, and to some extent her gentle nature, she also had many of the same traits as our father, which made their clashes long and drawn-out affairs with neither side willing to budge.

Ultimately, Mel won out. In practical terms, there was little that Al could do to stop her from attending Penn short of locking her in the basement. Knowing my father, I imagined that was a thought that crossed his mind. Mel had won a full four-year scholarship and had saved enough of her own money to forestall any thoughts Al might have of using his financial power to thwart her ambitions. Finally, he gave in and grudgingly gave his blessing. Secretly, I thought he felt a sense of pride in his accomplished daughter who had stood up to him to get her way. Not that he would ever admit it. When my parents returned from settling Mel into her first year at Penn, my mother told me that as they left my sister with her roommate in her dorm Al had to fight to keep back the tears.

While I had been witness to many of the heated discussions between Mel and my father, my sister, unfortunately, was also frequently present when Al and I had at it. Their arguments were fierce but relatively civil; no unduly harsh words, no irreparable damage done. My set-tos with my father were just the opposite: loud, profane, bitter, and skirting the edge of violence. On one occasion, when one of our periodic disputes erupted while John was gone and the four of us were around the dinner table, Al became so infuriated with me that he lurched from his chair and came at me with his right fist balled, ready to land a punch to the side of my head. As I got up to defend myself, I could hear my mother scream: "Al. Clint. Please don't! For the love of God, stop it!" At the same time, Mel got up from her chair and grabbed my father from behind, trying to pull his right arm down so he wouldn't hit me. In a rage, Al used his left arm to ward her off, sending her tumbling to the floor. Mel screamed, more out of shock and surprise than from pain.

Realizing what he had done, Al lowered his right hand. I had risen, ready to defend myself and we stood inches apart starring daggers at one another. After about ten seconds, he shrugged his shoulders and turned to help Mel back on her feet. "I'm sorry sweetheart," he said. "I'm sorry. I just lost control. I won't let it happen again."

Mel just looked at both of us, sadness mixed with anger on her face. Without a word, she turned and left the scene of the crime. The sound of her slamming the door of her room reverberated throughout the house. Al turned to me: "See what you have done Clint. This is your fault. You should be ashamed of yourself!"

I thought about responding: "How was it my fault? You were the one who got up ready to punch me. You were the one who threw Mel to the floor." But I knew that whatever counter-arguments I might present would simply be batted down and exacerbate a still tense situation. Instead, I followed Mel's lead and left the dining room without a word. But instead of going to my room, I went out the front door, giving it a good slam as I did so, and headed for the nearest bar.

The next day, I apologized to Mel for what had happened. "I'm sorry sis," I said, "Sorry that you got caught up in the middle of the fracas last night. No damage I hope."

She gave a sigh of exasperation. "Not really." Then with a grin, "But my butt is a little sore."

We laughed. But then she turned serious. "But you and Dad need to stop this constant fighting. It's killing Mom and not doing anybody any good. Maybe you and Dad should get some counseling. See if you can't get to the bottom of this mutual antagonism. If you don't, I'm afraid you are really going to hurt each other."

I didn't blow her off. But I knew that it was a vain hope. Al would never agree to counseling. That's not the way ex-Marines handled problems. And while I might have given it a shot to avoid putting Mel and my mother through more agony, I had my doubts it would do the trick for me either.

Once Mel went off to college, we saw less and less of her. She spent her summers doing anthropological field work on archaeological digs in various exotic locales. We only saw her during the Christmas holidays, and sometimes not even then. On one of her rare trips home, I asked her why she saw us so rarely. She gave some half-baked answer about how demanding school was and how she couldn't take the time off, even for the holidays. Her excuses were far from convincing. I finally got her to admit that she dreaded entering the poisoned atmosphere that existed between me and Al. Until we had resolved our "issues," she said, "Don't expect to see much of me."

After she told me that, I felt crappy for about an hour. But it passed. I didn't say it to Mel, but I thought to myself, "Well sis, it takes two to tango. Why don't you ask Dad if he is ready to bury the hatchet? Why does all the compromise have to come from me?"

Well, as you know, there was no compromise. Things just got worse.

True to her word, Mel stayed away. She kept in touch through emails and phone calls, but even those became less frequent. My parents went to see her once or twice a year, but she was usually too busy with her work to spend much time with them. Their last visit was to Cornell, where Mel was pursuing her doctorate in anthropology. This was just before Al and I had our final blow-up and I set out for California. That was the last I had heard about Mel until John's phone call this morning. Now, it appeared, she had gone missing and I was expected to help find her. Whether I would be of much use in that effort only time would tell, but I had my doubts.

Thirteen

ABOUT TWENTY MINUTES AFTER leaving the Interstate, we descended into a broad valley. To our right I could make out the fairways and greens of a golf course. John slowed and made a right turn off Wild Horse Creek Road, stopping at a gatehouse with a lowered bar that blocked our way.

A guard dressed in brown with a revolver strapped to his waist, stepped out to greet us, a clipboard in his left hand. John lowered his window and turned on the interior light.

The guard recognized him immediately. "Good evening Mr. Jackson," he said. "And you have a guest."

"Yes Ralph," said. "This is my brother Clint."

Ralph leaned down to get a closer look and did little to hide his surprise. Maybe it was the scruffy face, the long hair, and the casual clothes. Or maybe this place was like a small town where everybody knew everybody else's business. I pictured him picking up the phone later and telling all and sundry, *the prodigal son has returned.*

Straightening up, he jotted something on his clipboard, presumably our names and the time.

"Nice to meet you Clint," he said.

"Same here Ralph," I replied.

With that, he returned to the gatehouse, put down the clipboard, and raised the bar blocking our way, waving us through.

This was not my first experience with a gated community. I had worked construction jobs in my share of this new form of suburban living. But I found it jarring to be a visitor to a place like this, a place that made me feel strangely unwanted and uncomfortable. Give me the seedy Mission District anytime.

"So, John," I said, "Is an armed guard really necessary?"

He shrugged. "Probably not. But it's what the owners here want. An extra layer of security. And, to be fair, even though these homes are about as far from high-crime areas as you can get, they are in an isolated place and provide a tempting target for burglars. What is that Willie Sutton said when asked why he robbed banks? 'Because that's where the money is.' Well, to a burglar these homes are like banks."

"Have there actually been any break-ins?" I asked.

"Not that I know of. And in addition to Ralph and the other guards, all the houses have the latest in home security – motion detectors, cameras, alarms. Some even have electrified fences."

I wondered how much good any of that would do if a sole burglar or a gang was determined enough to rob any of the palatial mansions I saw on my right and left as we wound our way up a bluff that ran parallel to the Missouri River, the moon reflecting off its surface.

We followed the ridgeline for about a quarter of a mile. "Here it is," Clint said, turning left into a circular driveway. Looming in front of us was a massive three-story mansion with stone walls, a slate roof, and an attached garage with room for three vehicles. Floodlights illuminated the entrance to the front door and the driveway, turning night into day. I was amused to see Al's trusty red pick-up parked prominently in front of one of the garage doors for all to see. If anyone had any doubts as to who lived in the mansion, the "Jackson Construction Company" painted in white on the driver-side door removed them.

John parked and turned off the engine. "Let me warn you," he said, gripping my arm. "You're going to be in for a shock. You better prepare yourself for when you see Al and Mae. They're not the same."

I nodded. "I understand."

He patted me on the shoulder. "Let's go. Mom is anxious to see you." Left unsaid was whether Al felt the same.

By this time, the effect of the drinks I had gulped down at the airport had worn off. I could feel a dull pain in my gut and acid rising in my throat. I had a slight tremor in my hands which I knew would get worse unless I had another drink - and soon. But that would have to wait.

As I unlatched my seat belt and reached for the door handle, I had the wild impulse to shove John out of the car, somehow snatch the keys from his hand, and head west for California. But I repressed the impulse. I took a deep breath, grabbed my backpack, and followed John to the entrance of my parents' pretentious new home. The front door was an imposing combination of solid burnished oak with black iron hinges, handle, and knocker. It reminded me of the entrance to a medieval castle. I steeled myself for what I would find on the other side.

I half expected the door to be flung open, my mother, as she had so many times in the past, welcoming me back with tears in her eyes and her arms enveloping me. But instead, John took out a set of keys and went through an elaborate ritual of unlocking at least three separate locks, including what appeared to be an electronic dead bolt that made a faint buzzing noise through the solid oak. "I told you," he said with a wink, "Lots of security. Look up there," pointing to the left and right above my head. When I did, I saw two surveillance cameras about twenty feet apart staring back at me. Having helped in the construction of similar homes, I was aware of all the newfangled elaborate security measures now available. Nonetheless, it jarred me to find the same kind of set-up in my parents' new home. On one level, it should have provided some comfort. After all, they were old, infirm, and vulnerable and anything that would make them safer should be welcome. On another, however, I found it sad that they had abandoned a comfortable, friendly neighborhood to live in splendid isolation behind various layers of security. And I could not avoid the guilt that came with knowing that I was largely responsible.

After John had finished the unlocking, he pushed the doorbell. I could hear the chime echoing on the other side.

"Can't we just go in?" I asked.

"Yeah. We can. But I wanted to warn the staff before we did so. Even though they are expecting us, I didn't want to surprise them. They might get nervous and…well, overreact."

"The staff?"

"Three full-time live-ins. There's Dad's caretaker, Rosa. She's a registered nurse. Then there's Evelyn who helps Mom with the cooking and cleaning. And you remember Gus Freidrich?"

I searched my memory. "Sure. One of Dad's foremen. Big strong guy who didn't mind pitching in wherever or whenever he was needed."

"That's him. Well when Dad had his stroke, Gus, who had just retired, volunteered to help out. He's a combination butler, chauffeur, and bodyguard. Then we have half a dozen others who come by to do the gardening, pool maintenance, and whatever else needs to be done."

I shook my head in wonder. Quite a change from what I had been used to. My father taking care of house repairs, the lawn, and the vehicles on his own and my mother doing all the usual domestic chores with an occasional assist from her children.

"Must cost a lot," I observed.

John shrugged. "It does. But Al has a lot. On that front they have no worries." Then he turned somber, "But on the other…"

"There's Mel."

"Yes. There's Mel."

As we waited for one of the staff to open the door, I again felt a growing sense of remorse and regret. Things had gone terribly wrong for my parents while I had walled myself off in my own kind of splendid isolation, letting my antagonism toward my father distance myself from my mother, my brother, and my sister, who loved me unconditionally and who were now in desperate straits. I had broken my mother's heart more than once, let my brother assume the burden of looking after the family's wellbeing instead of sharing the load with him, and lost touch with my sister whose life might well be in danger. *And to think that just minutes ago I was tempted to turn tail and run!* I pushed down the self-loathing, tried to square my shoulders, control the tremor in my hands, and prepare to do my part in helping John and my parents deal with the current crisis. But at the same time a little voice sniggered, *Yeah, we've heard that one before.* I tried to ignore it, but it lingered.

As I pondered these thoughts, the door opened. It was so thick I hadn't heard the approaching footsteps on the other side. Mentally, I had been preparing myself to have my mother throw herself into my arms. Instead, it was Gus Freidrich. Even though it had been a few years, I recognized him immediately. There were few signs of age. He was still tall, muscular, and in incredibly good shape for a guy in his sixties. In fact, he probably looked better than I did. His brown hair showed few signs of gray. He had a hawk nose, clear brown eyes, and a square jaw. I had only seen him in work clothes but tonight he wore a light-blue blazer, an open-collar white dress shirt, and tan slacks. The blazer was unbuttoned and I could see that he had revolver attached to his belt.

"Good evening John," he said as we passed through the door. Then, his eyebrows raised and with a look of disgust he did little to hide, he greeted me with a dismissive nod and a curt, "Clint."

"Hello Gus," I said, extending my hand which he took reluctantly. "Good to see you again." And I meant it. I had enjoyed working with Gus, who at the time seemed to forgive my faults and to appreciate the effort I put into any job. But my abandonment of the family had soured him. And he probably was not alone. He didn't say anything in response to my "Good to see you." No "same here" or "me too." Instead, he made sure the door was securely locked before he turned to John and said, "Al and Mae will meet you in the family room."

"Come on," my brother said, grabbing me by the arm as though he feared I might bolt.

The three of us walked through a high-ceilinged living room over polished hard-wood floors interspersed with oriental rugs. A large chandelier lit the room and off to the side I could see a massive fireplace. I didn't recognize any of the furniture, which looked new and very expensive, so new that it hardly looked used. John read my thoughts.

"Mom and dad decided to start fresh out here, junking most of the furniture from the old house except for Al's work desk and Mae's sewing table. They didn't do much entertaining, even before the stroke. So this room looks pretty much as it was when they moved in. They spend most of their time in the kitchen or the family room."

I just nodded, taking it all in. We passed the kitchen and with a quick glance I saw that it was about three-times the size of my San Francisco apartment and with the latest in restaurant-grade appliances. Further on was the family room, which unlike the cold and antiseptic living room, was warm and welcoming. It had the same hardwood floors and plush oriental rugs. The lighting came from table lamps, which provided a soft glow. In the center of the room was a beautiful cherry-wood coffee table situated between three small sofas forming a U. To the right was another fireplace, but this one was smaller than the one in the living room and I could tell had received some heavy use. My mother loved a crackling fire in the winter. Straight ahead was a picture window that ran from wall to wall and floor to ceiling and provided a spectacular view of the woods leading down to the Missouri River.

As I was absorbing all this, I heard a slight thumping sound behind me. Turning, I saw a woman approaching me, supported by one of those aluminum canes with a tripod at the end. For a split second I failed to recognize my own mother. She was frail, thin to the border of emaciation, and clearly found it painful to walk even with the cane. She seemed to have aged twenty years since I last saw her. My guilt-o-meter began to skyrocket. I knew that I was not totally responsible for this drastic deterioration, but I had to share a good bit of the blame.

After several seconds of stunned silence, I went to her. "Hello Mom," I sputtered, fighting back tears.

She lifted her hand from her cane and threw her arms around my neck, holding on for dear life. I could feel her body shake with sobs. "Oh Clint. Oh Clint," she said. "It is so good to see you. So good to have you back. I've missed you so."

I didn't know what to say. Anything I could come up with would sound insincere. So I just held her. Finally, I said, "I'm back now Mom. I'm here to help."

Out of the corner of my eye I could see John looking at us, shaking his head slightly. I couldn't read the expression but I was pretty sure he was thinking that I had a lot of making-up to do.

While I continued to hold on to my sobbing mother, over her shoulder I saw my father being wheeled into the room. He was being pushed by a Hispanic woman in her forties dressed in a white uniform. This I took to be Rosa the caretaker.

Mae finally let her arms fall from my neck and to her sides, almost losing her balance in the process. I held on to her and helped her regain control of her cane. As I put my hand on her back I felt nothing but skin and bones. When I had left, she was still a hale and hearty woman who had kept her figure. She took pride in the fact that she had maintained a weight commensurate to her height, roughly one hundred thirty pounds for five foot eight. Now she was stooped over and appeared to have shriveled to less than a hundred pounds.

"Look Al," she said, raising her voice. "Clint is back. Isn't that wonderful." Then, turning to me, she implored, "Say hello to your father Clint. Please say hello."

John had told me to prepare myself for a shock. But I hadn't been ready for the one-two punch. Still reeling from my mother's appearance, I was knocked further off balance when I saw Al. I had only a vague general idea of what disease and a stroke could do to a person. Seeing it in the flesh and in my own father was almost more than I could take.

It was though I was facing a stranger. The shrunken figure in front of me must have been an imposter. *It couldn't be Al.* If my mother had lost forty pounds, Al must have lost a hundred. He was gaunt to the point of being skeletal. His cheeks were hollow and there was stubble on his face, something he never would have allowed in his previous incarnation. The old Jarhead was always clean-shaven. His thick black hair, which he had always kept in a trim crewcut and which I had inherited, was now almost totally white His once muscular arms lay flaccid at his side, his hands curled helplessly in his lap. He was dressed in pajamas and robe. I couldn't see his legs, but his shins were exposed and the flesh was pale and blue-veined. Drool ran over his lips and down his chin. Rosa leaned over and patted it away with a white cloth. I couldn't believe that a man so strong and vital had been reduced to this shambling wreck. But the evidence was right there in front of me.

I was caught in an emotional turmoil. For a moment, I felt as though I might break down in sobs like my mother. Anybody would, I thought to myself, confronting such a pitiable sight, not to mention one's own father. But all that old resentment and anger still remained. I certainly wouldn't have wished this fate on Al – or on anybody. But I just couldn't let go of the bitter feelings I still harbored.

John read the look of shock on my face. "As I told you Clint, the doctors say that while the stroke has prevented Al from moving or speaking, his hearing is still intact and his mind is still working. So if you talk to him, he can take it in even though he cannot communicate. And it is important that we keep trying to break through."

I moved closer to Al and bent down, placing my hand gently on his shoulder. I could feel the frail bone underneath. I leaned over until my face was only inches from his. I cleared my throat before speaking, afraid of revealing my emotions. "Hello Dad. It's me, Clint. I'm back."

Straightening up, I stared into those dark eyes that had so often been full of rage directed at me. All I saw was a blank stare, as though I wasn't there right in front of him. I wondered if that look was because he could not respond - or maybe he could but could care less whether I was back or not.

Fourteen

I KEPT LOOKING AT MY father, hoping for some response. But there was none. For a few seconds there was nothing but silence aside from Al's labored breathing. The oxygen mask hanging around his neck had been removed when I had spoken to him. Rosa reached around and replaced it over his nose and mouth. Al didn't move or change expression as the oxygen began to flow, but his breathing became easier.

My brother took charge. "Clint, why don't you and I and Mom have a seat? We have a lot to discuss." He then assisted my mother to a place on one of the couches, helping her down until she was comfortable, placing a cushion behind her back for support.

Once Mae was settled, she patted the couch. "Please sit next to me Clint. I want you close. You've been gone too long."

"Sure thing Mom," I said with a catch in my voice. I settled in next to her. She grabbed my arm and held on tight.

"I bet you're hungry," she said.

Good old Mom, going to her default mode upon seeing me for the first time after one of my many absences. "That I am Mom. I'm starving," I said with a smile.

She smiled back. "Rosa," she said, "Could you please bring the food Evelyn prepared from the kitchen and set it out on the table?"

"Yes Mrs. Jackson," Rosa replied in a thick Spanish accent. "What about Mr. Jackson?"

John again took charge. "Move him over here," he said, pointing to a spot near where Mae and I were sitting at the end of the couch. Rosa wheeled Dad over so he was only a foot or so away from where I was seated. I could hear the steady hum of the oxygen pump in my left ear while Mom clung to my right arm for dear life. Al's eyes still remained fixed in a blank stare, no sign at all that he was aware of where he was or what was happening. I felt a momentary sense of claustrophobia, what with my father's wheelchair blocking my way off the couch to the left and my mother's weight on my arm to my right. But I fought the rising panic with deep breaths and did my best to relax my tense muscles. John, who had pulled up a chair next to Al, seemed to notice my predicament and sent me a hand signal to calm down. Easier said – or signaled – than done, but somehow I managed to get myself under control.

Leaning back in the couch, I tried to gather my thoughts. I was feeling disoriented, partly due to beginning the day with a massive hangover in San Francisco and now transported to a place that was both familiar and strange. I longed for a drink, the effects of the two scotches I had downed at the airport having long worn off. But I didn't dare ask for one in the present circumstances.

I looked at my brother. "So, John, what's this all about? Why, exactly, am I here?"

He sensed my anxiety. "Let's get something to eat first; then we can talk about Mel."

I heard my mother whimper at the mention of my sister's name and her grip on my arm tightened. "Yes Clint. You need some nourishment. You don't look well. A little pale and you've lost weight."

I was tempted to tell her that a few cold beers would make me as right as rain, but kept my mouth shut and simply nodded.

As if on cue, Rosa appeared with a heaping plate of sandwiches, some assorted fruits, and a pitcher of iced tea. Placing them in front of us on the coffee table, she retired to the kitchen, leaving us alone with our food and our thoughts.

While we ate, Mom filled me in on what had been going on since I had made my dramatic departure. The way she put it, moving to St. Albans was a way to fulfill Al's long-time dream to be accepted as a full-fledged member of the local elite with no mention of what I suspected really lay behind the move – to get away from too many bad memories, mostly generated by me, in Webster Groves.

The sandwiches were delicious. If this Evelyn had prepared them, she really knew what she was doing. Of course, everything tastes better when you're hungry, but the bread was fresh and the various cold meats between the layers were superb. I greedily drank several glasses of iced tea, slaking my thirst and wishing for something stronger.

As we ate, I stole glances at Al. Still nothing but that vacant stare, no sign that he was aware of what we were saying.

After we had finished, John signaled that it was now time to get down to business. "Okay Clint," he began, "let me explain what's happened to Mel and why we need you to help find her."

I leaned forward. "Okay. I'm all ears."

"Let me fill you in," John began. "Mel was doing field research for her doctorate at a site near Cajamarca, Peru in the Andes, working with a team of fellow students under the direction of her dissertation advisor. She and the team have been at the site since January. A week ago, Mom and Dad got a call from the State Department that the Cornell team had reported to the embassy she had gone missing. The embassy then contacted the local police to look into the matter. The police reported back that a week ago, when the team gathered for breakfast, Mel wasn't there. At first, they didn't think much of it, even though it was unusual for Mel not to be on time for anything. But they figured she had just slept in. They had all worked hard the day before and needed the rest. After breakfast, one of the team went to Mel's tent and found it empty. That's when they began to get worried. They searched the site and its surroundings, shouting out her name. But no Mel."

Next to me, my mother let out another little sob. I could feel my own stomach clench.

John looked at us both, his expression somber and his blue eyes showing pain.

"So," he continued, "the team leader decided to wait a few hours before reporting Mel missing to the local authorities. He speculated that maybe for reasons of her own, she wanted a break from the group and had decided to take some time off."

"Without telling anyone? That's not the Mel I know," I said with some heat.

John nodded. "I agree. But we weren't there. We don't know what had been going on within the group. Maybe the team wasn't as friendly and cooperative with one another as the State guy implied. Maybe there were the usual tensions and inter-personal conflicts that crop up when any group of persons are in isolated conditions and engaging in what was probably a competitive atmosphere." He gave a "who knows?" gesture with his hands. "At any rate, they didn't report to the local authorities that Mel was missing until later in the day. By then, it was getting dark and too late to organize a search party."

I could feel a familiar feeling of anger rise in my chest and turn my cheeks red. If the team leader had been in front of me, he would have gotten a severe tongue lashing at best, a severe beating at worst.

John read my thoughts. "To tell you the truth, I don't think it would have made much difference if the local authorities had been advised earlier. From what the State Department guy told me the locals wouldn't have been of much use regardless of the timing. The regional boss is an anti-American radical who was not happy that the national government had given the team permissions to work at the site in the first place. So, the people operating under his direction are not going to make much of an effort to find Mel. And they threw up some wild theories to cover their lack of action. One policeman suggested Mel had run off with a local boy she was seeing. He also threw out the unlikely theory that she and he might have joined a revolutionary group."

"Sounds pretty far-fetched," I said. "What about an old-fashioned kidnapping? Some of the Mexican guys I work with in San Francisco say that happens a lot south of the border."

"Actually, that would be good news. At least we would have some indication she is still alive and would have a chance to get her back."

Hearing this, my mother broke down into uncontrollable weeping. I can't say I could blame her. I was feeling angry, frustrated, and saddened, close to tears myself.

We both consoled May with meaningless reassuring words and after a few minutes of sobbing she finally calmed down. John shot me a look that said "I could have phrased that more delicately." Al still showed no reaction, simply staring into space.

"I asked the State Department guy the same question. He said a kidnapping for ransom was not out of the question. There have been several in Peru in recent years. But there have been no ransom demands, at least until now. He didn't rule out that possibility completely, but thought that it was unlikely. Usually, the demands come right after the capture."

I slumped back against the couch, feeling like I had been punched senseless. Guilt swelled up inside me like a tidal wave. While my parents and my brother had been going through hell, I had been lost in a cloud of self-pity and self-destructive behavior.

I straightened up. "So what do we do now?" I asked.

John looked me square in the eye. "That's where you come in Clint. We want you to go to Peru and see what you can do to find out what happened to Mel."

I expected the answer, but I immediately began to protest: "Why me? Why not send a professional? You know, hire a private investigator."

"We looked into that," John said. "But we couldn't find anybody who fit the bill. There were a few who seemed eager to take the case, but when we checked their references it was clear they were only in it for the money. They had no experience working abroad and more than likely would only go through the motions and report back they couldn't find anything."

I wondered if that was really the case. There must be ex-spooks around who could have filled the bill. But I didn't want to argue the point. I trusted my brother's judgement in such matters and was in no position to question it.

After a few seconds, I asked, "Then why me and not you John? You are the one with the connections and the experience."

What I said was true. But behind it were my own self-doubts that I could be of any use whatsoever in trying to find my sister. The only thing I had going for me was a pretty good grasp of Spanish picked up during my construction work and a few trips to Mexico. Otherwise, my sister's fate, presuming she was still alive, would hinge on her irresponsible – and let's be honest – alcoholic brother.

John hesitated for a moment, looking uncomfortable and seemingly caught off guard. I couldn't figure out why. Surely, he must have anticipated my question, which any objective observer would see as perfectly natural. For a few seconds I thought he was about to unload on me. I could imagine the thoughts whirling through his head: *Typical Clint, trying to avoid responsibility and putting the whole burden on his big brother's shoulders. And, given his track record, why entrust him with anything?*

But instead, he took a deep breath and told me calmly, "I wish I could Clint, but I can't. Somebody has to look after Al and Mae. Plus, I've got work up to my eyeballs, including some important cases that are coming to trial. In fact, one of them," he said, looking at his watch, "begins at eight-thirty in the morning tomorrow."

I wasn't convinced. It seemed to me that with Rosa and other staff on hand my parents would be all right for however long it would take John to try to find Mel. Moreover, he worked for a pretty big firm and they could probably find someone to assume his load given the emergency situation he confronted.

"But," I began, "can't you...?"

He interrupted me, reading my mind. "Yes. If necessary, I would put all that aside and go to Peru myself. If you don't want to...."

He let it trail off, letting me stew.

"Please Clint," my mother said, "John has so many responsibilities here. We need you now. We need you desperately. Please help us. Please go and find Mel. Please." She then again dissolved into tears. I took her into my arms and let her cry herself out against my chest, awkwardly stroking her back to comfort her while my brother looked on with a face that seemed to mix sorrow with frustration.

As I held my mother, I tried to sort out my thoughts and my emotions. On the one hand, I could feel familiar resentments bubbling up to the surface. My mother and my brother were double-teaming, trying to force me to do something I was resistant to doing, producing my usual rebellion against parental – and in this case – fraternal pressures. On the other hand, I had to accept the fact that what they said made sense. John *did* have many more responsibilities at home than I did. I had little to tie me down. Even if I lost my current job in San Francisco, I could easily find another. At the bottom, of course, was my realistic appraisal that I was not really up for the task they wanted me to carry out. I was a pretty slim reed to rely on, deeply flawed in so many ways. Stacked against this was the fact that I loved my sister and was devastated by the news of her disappearance I finally determined that whatever my flaws I would do my best to try to find out what had happened to her.

"It's all right Mom," I said, choking back some tears of my own. "I'll go. I'll find Mel and bring her back safe and sound. I promise." That was probably a promise I shouldn't have made. But at the time, it was one I had every intention of trying to keep.

John joined us on the couch. "Thanks Clint," he said, clearly relieved.

My mother, now nestled comfortably between her two sons, shared his relief. "Yes. Thank you, Clint. I know you can find Mel. I just know it," she said, her eyes shining.

Again, I looked at my father. The stare was still there, but I thought I saw something in his eyes as well, something I hadn't seen before. Maybe it was just the angle of the lights. But perhaps he had absorbed more than we knew. I could only speculate as to what he might be thinking. But if I had to guess it would have been something along the lines of *Just how will he screw up this time?* I swore to do my best to prove him wrong but had to admit that history and the odds were on his side.

Fifteen

THE NEXT DAY FOUND me back at Lambert Field ready to board the 11:30 am American Airlines flight to Miami. From there I would take the overnight flight to Lima, the capital of Peru. It was from Lima that my search for Mel would begin.

After I had made my decision and our parents had left, John and I had hammered out some details for my upcoming trip. Even without knowing for sure that I would agree to go, my brother had made preparations on the assumption that I would. He had booked the next day's flight to Peru in my name, had withdrawn two thousand dollars in cash for my immediate expenses, and provided me with a credit and debit card as well as the code to an account number that I could use to withdraw more cash beyond the standard limit. If it turned out that Mel was indeed being held for ransom, I would have access to whatever it might take to get her back. He also had booked a room for me at the Sheraton Hotel in downtown Lima.

John was nothing if not thorough. "What if I had said no?" I asked him.

"I don't really know. I guess I would have gone down there myself. But I had a strong hunch that you would agree. I know how you feel about Mel. I couldn't imagine that you wouldn't want to do everything possible to find her and bring her back."

I was about to say, "You mean dead or alive?" but figured there was no need at this point to be unduly pessimistic. However, we both knew it was a real possibility we might never see our sister again.

Instead I said, "I guess your hunch was right" and left it at that. "And by the way," I added, "I have about three grand of my own to add to the kitty, if needed." I wanted him to know that I had not been totally shiftless and could at least carry some of the financial burden in trying to find Mel.

I could see the barely concealed look of surprise on his face when he said, "Well great Clint. That's a big help."

In addition to the plane ticket, the money, and the credit cards, John gave me the name of the guy at the embassy in Lima with whom he had been in contact – Charles Macalister. He also gave me another name – Lamar Jenkins, a close friend from his days in Princeton who was currently working for a U.S. mining company in Peru. "I contacted Lamar as soon as I got the word Mel was missing. He told me he would do what he could. But the day I called, he was off for a ten-day tour of mining sites in the jungle. He should be back in Lima by now. Look him up as soon as you can. I trust him more than I do some suit at the embassy." Then he added, "It seems to me that the embassy guys could be doing more to help us find Mel than they have been so far. You need to push them when you get there. I'll try to put on a little pressure from my end, but you might have more luck being there in person."

I just nodded. I planned to do my best, but wondered if that would be enough. John would have been a much more commanding presence in the face of officialdom than his bedraggled and scruffy brother.

By the time we had wrapped up the details of my trip, it was past midnight. We were both exhausted. I assumed that I would be crashing in a guest bedroom somewhere in this McMansion. But instead, John escorted me upstairs to the second floor, past the master bedroom and then down the hallway to where there were two doors facing one another on each side. Pointing to the door on his left, he said, "This one is mine." Then, pointing to the opposite door "And that one is yours."

I was about to enter my room, when John grabbed my arm. Keeping his voice low, he said, "Before you go in, there are a couple of things I need to tell you." Suddenly, a look of anguish crossed his face. "I should have told you earlier, but I've been under a lot of pressure recently. I didn't want to mention it in front of Al and Mae but it looks as though Tiffany and I are splitting up."

In a day full of surprises, that one really knocked me for a loop. "But…"

Before I could get the usual questions of out my mouth, he held up his hand. "It's not final. We are going through couples counseling and we are cooperating in parenting the girls. But they are probably picking up on some of the tension and have begun to act out in ways that go beyond the usual adolescent rebellion."

I could see the strain and sadness in his face as he ran his hands through his hair, where I noticed some streaks of grey I had missed before.

"But...?

Again, he held up his hand. "One of our main "issues" has been Tiffany's feeling that I spend too much time at my job, travel too much, and not do enough to help with the girls." He looked exasperated. "And I have to admit, she probably has a point there. So, while I didn't want to mention it when we were discussing why you should go to Peru and not me, that's one of the reasons. Given the precarious state of our marriage, I'm terrified that even though Tiffany loves Mel and understands the emergency, another long absence would be the final straw. So..."

"So why not me?" I said, "Unencumbered with family responsibilities."

"Yes Clint," he said, "I'm afraid so. Why not you?"

I didn't know how to respond. I had never seen my brother appear so desperate and in such despair. Everything had seemed so effortless for him – school, career, marriage – and now what was most important to him was on the verge of falling apart.

"I'm really sorry to hear that Bro." I was about to add, "If there is anything I can do..." when I realized that what I had committed to do – try to find Mel – was the best thing I could do for him.

John gathered himself, wiping away a tear. "Thanks Clint."

"One more thing. Before you go to your room, prepare yourself," he said, with a wry look.

"That sounds ominous," I said.

He chuckled. "Not really. Remember when I said Al and Mae had left most of their furniture behind in Webster Groves."

I nodded. "Well, there were more exceptions than those I mentioned."

I grinned at him. "I think I know what you mean John."

He grinned back his equanimity momentarily restored. After an awkward moment of silence, he pulled me towards him and gave me a hug. "It's good to see you again little brother." Pulling away, he turned toward the door to his room. "We better get to sleep. I don't know about you, but I am bushed. See you in the morning."

"Yeah," I mumbled. "Me too." Then to lighten the mood, I added *"Hasta Mañana."*

He grinned. "See. Your Spanish is just fine." With that, he opened the door to his bedroom, stepped over the threshold and gently closed the door behind him.

I stared silently at the door to "my" bedroom. I had a premonition of what I would find on the other side. And I was right. Turning the knob, I opened the door and switched on the light. When I saw the room, I let out a sound between a chuckle and a moan. The house was different, the dimensions and the windows were not the same, but in every other particular it was exactly like my old room in Webster Groves. The bed and the furniture were the same. The pictures on the wall were the originals. My trophies and awards, such as they were, were arranged neatly on the same table. I opened the door to the closet and hanging there were the clothes I had left behind, hanging neatly in an orderly row. I was sure the bureau would be the same. An old pair of pajamas lay on the bed and my seldom-used bathrobe was draped over a nearby chair. I half-expected a rose and a chocolate on my pillow, but thankfully it was bare.

I felt tears form and brushed them away. Once again, a deep sense of guilt washed over me. My father might have given up on me but my mother had not. She had fitted out the room in her new home as a kind of talisman to lure me back. The message was clear: so far as she was concerned, I was always welcome. My father must have gone along with the scheme, if only to keep Mae happy, but I am certain he did not share the sentiment and probably never expected that I would actually spend a night in the shrine my mother had constructed.

The whole thing felt both weird and comforting at the same time. I was exhausted, too tired to mull over all of the ramifications of my mother's actions and strangely pleased to find myself in familiar surroundings. I stripped quickly, leaving my clothes in a messy pile, pulled on my pajamas and slid between the sheets.

I expected sleep to come immediately. But doubts kept me awake.

Was I up to what my parents and my brother expected of me? Could I stay off the booze long enough to be of any use or would I just add to their burdens? How would I manage in a country I did not know and in a language I only understood at the rudimentary level? Finally, fatigue overcame me and I drifted off to sleep.

I was in the middle of a crazy dream when John shook me awake. "Time to rise and shine Bro." Then, giving me a second look and a grin. "Well at least to rise."

I stumbled out of bed, momentarily disoriented. I was back in my old room but in a different house. *What was going on? Was I losing my mind? Had alcohol finally eaten away at vital parts of my brain?* But then it all came rushing back: my brother's phone call - *Had it only been twenty-four hours ago?*- the news that Mel was missing; the flight to St. Louis; seeing my parents, Al now practically comatose; spending the night in a room that had been preserved for me; my promise to do all I could to find out what had happened to my sister.

John was already dressed in shirt and tie. "Breakfast is ready. And we have to go over some things before I head out. I need to leave in about thirty minutes," he said with a sense of urgency.

I looked at my watch. It read six-thirty. Only five or six hours of sleep, but it would have to do.

After using the bathroom, I joined John in the breakfast room, which was just off of the kitchen. There I was introduced to Evelyn, the cook. She was a fortyish, pleasant woman, who, she informed me, like Mae had been born and raised in South St. Louis, and who had prepared enough food for a small army. She fussed over us, pouring juice and coffee and asking if we needed anything more besides the eggs, bacon, toast, hash-browns, and pancakes set before us. We both shook our heads as we dug in.

As we ate, John informed me of the preparations he had made. He handed over the plane ticket, the cash, the credit cards, the hotel confirmation, and the names and contact information of the embassy official and his Princeton friend. He also supplied me with a map of Lima and another one of Peru.

As I assembled these materials, he reached into his pocket, took out a cell phone and passed it to me. "You'll need this Clint. It has unlimited minutes and I have set it up for international calls." He hesitated for a few seconds, then said "I want you to call me every day, okay? If I don't hear from you on a daily basis, I am going to assume the worst and head down to Peru at once."

I couldn't read the look on his face or the tone of his voice. Assuming "the worst" might mean something bad had happened to me. After all, I was heading into a situation that clearly posed some serious risks and dangers. If that was what he meant, I could only be touched by his fraternal concern. But if "the worst" meant that I had gone off the rails, descended into one of my bouts of drunken oblivion then there was an entirely different message behind his warning. Perhaps it was a combination of both.

I chose not to guess. Accepting the phone, I assured him, "You got it. Every day like clockwork. You can count on me."

For a split second I saw a look in his eyes that said, *Yeah. Sure. Just like always.* But it faded. He simply nodded without comment.

When we had finished our breakfasts, John headed for the front door, grabbing his briefcase and his suit coat along the way. I followed him. Before he opened the door to leave, he gave me another hug, pounded me on the back, and said, "Best of luck Bro. We're all counting on you." He finished the pep talk with something that still rang in my ears, "If anyone can bring Mel back safe and sound, you're the one."

"I'll do my best," I promised, not at all sure that he was right in his assumption.

After he left, I headed back to my room and began to pack for the trip. The backpack I had traveled with from San Francisco would not be enough for what I would need. I thought about asking Rosa or Evelyn to find me something larger when I remembered that I had a good-sized duffle bag left over from my brief Marine stint, about the only thing I had to show for my service. Maybe Al had thrown it out in disgust but maybe Mae had held on to it. When I looked in a shelf above the closet there it was.

I hauled the canvass bag down and proceeded to fill it with the basics from my bureau. It was winter in Peru so I included some sweaters and long-sleeved shirts. I packed enough underwear and socks to last two weeks and included an old pair of hiking boots, which I figured I might need if I were to spend any time in the mountains where Mel had gone missing. I added a worn leather jacket that had seen better days but was still serviceable. I put a light-weight jacket into my backpack for easy access just in case. I carried the bag along with my backpack down to the entrance hallway, where I found my mother waiting for me.

She was dressed in a shirt and slacks and had put on some light makeup. She looked relaxed and rested a marked improvement over last night. Evelyn was at her side and helped her maneuver with her cane to draw near and give me a hug and a peck on the cheek. "Good morning son," she said cheerfully, "I see that you are all packed and ready to go."

I nodded. "Did you sleep well?" she asked with a sly smile on her face.

"Yes I did Mother. Good to be back in familiar surroundings." I wasn't sure that was true, still feeling that it was all a little weird to have spent the night in a kind of shrine. But I had slept like a log and, for the first time in longer than I could remember had awaken without a hangover.

"I slept well too," she said with a smile. Then it faded. "It's been a long time since I had a decent night's sleep. First Al's stroke and then this...,"she struggled to find the right words, "...this *business* with Mel." Her voice wavered and for a moment I thought she was going to break down as she had last night. But she recovered and the smile returned. "And you know why I got my first restful night in months, don't you?"

I suspected I did know but didn't' want to say it. When I didn't answer, she replied for me. "It's because you are back with us. And I know you are going to find Mel for us. I just know it. I feel it in my bones."

Her eyes were shining and she looked so happy I didn't want to spoil the moment. Instead, I gave her the same answer I had given my brother. "I am going to do my best Mother. I promise you that."

"I know you will son. I know you will."

Just then I heard a car horn sound. "That must be your taxi." Since my brother was going off to work and was not going to be able to drive me to the airport, we had decided the night before to reserve a taxi. It was now waiting outside.

As I turned to gather my bags, my mother grabbed my arm. "Before you leave Clint, would you please go say goodbye to your father? He's in the kitchen. Rosa is feeding him breakfast."

I didn't really want to see him again and to absorb that look of what I assumed was doubt and disapproval in his eyes. I was feeling enough pressure as it was. But I also knew it would be childish of me to refuse.

"Sure thing Mother," I said. "Just let me tell the taxi driver to wait a few minutes." I opened the door and picked up my bags. Outside, a County Cab in red and white was idling. When the driver got out, I gave him my bags to store in the trunk and asked him to hold on while I said goodbye to my father. Then, with my mother clinging to my arm, we went to the kitchen.

Al was in his wheelchair and Rosa was spooning what looked to be oatmeal into his mouth, wiping away the parts that drifted down his chin. Seeing him so helpless, being fed like a child brought a lump to my throat. I still hadn't quite adjusted to the reality that this once vital, strong man who I both respected and feared, had been reduced to this helpless state. I imagined that in his mind he was thinking that his current situation was indeed a fate worse than death.

As I approached, Rosa stopped the feeding and stepped aside. "Hello Dad," I said, fighting to keep my voice steady. "I just wanted to say goodbye. The taxi is outside to take me to the airport. I'll be in Peru this time tomorrow, doing my best to find Mel."

He just gave me his vacant stare, his eyes dull and lifeless. There was nothing to be read in his expression. I gently grabbed his upper arm in a gesture of reassurance, again shocked to feel the once solid muscle now flaccid and soft, the bone underneath brittle and vulnerable. I let go of his arm and tried to hide my feelings with what I hoped was a confident smile. Then, before the tears began to flow, I turned away and walked with my mother to the door and the waiting taxi. She gave me a final hug and kiss on the cheek as we parted. As the taxi made its way down the driveway, I turned my head and saw her waving bravely until the turn down the entrance road hid her from view.

Sixteen

WHEN MY FLIGHT FROM St. Louis arrived in Miami at three in the afternoon, I learned that the connecting flight to Lima had been delayed and would not be departing until around midnight. That meant I had a long nine hours to kill. I considered my options. I could try to find a quiet corner and get some sleep. I still had some catching up to do. Or, I could just wander around, getting some exercise by pacing through the terminals, maybe get in a good five or six miles while taking in the sights. Then I would grab some dinner, which would help pass the time. After that, I could head to the departure lounge and strike up a conversation or two with a fellow passenger. And, if all else failed, I could resume the Grisham thriller that I still had in my backpack with more than half left to be read.

These were good options, all of which would keep me on the straight and narrow. But who was I kidding? I *did* start out with good intentions. I walked around the terminal for about an hour, observing the masses of moving humanity – the sun-burned passengers returning from a Caribbean Cruise, the exhausted couples with their kids lugging their trophies from a recent trip to Disneyworld, the business types glued to their cell-phones with the weight of the world written on their unsmiling faces. Around me I heard a buzz a languages and accents – the lilt of the British Caribbean, snatches of French and German, and lots of Spanish. I didn't hear much of the Mexican accent so common in San Francisco but a lot of what I assumed had to be the Cuban variety given the large exile community in Miami, along with a mixture of South American variations and a smattering of what I guessed was Portuguese from Brazilians.

Figuring I had gotten enough exercise, I found a quiet spot and dug out my Grisham novel. I had finished about thirty pages when I felt my head nod and began to doze off. I woke up about an hour later, feeling a chill. I only had on a light polo shirt and the temperature in the airport must have been in the sixties. I grabbed the light jacket from my backpack and put it on, then looked at my watch. It was five o'clock, still a little too early for dinner. But I was thirsty. The wise course would have been to get some water, either the bottled kind or directly from a fountain. But I knew deep-down what kind of thirst-quencher I craved.

I went through the usual internal argument, almost like a catechism, but knew how the debate would end. Gathering my things, I looked for the nearest watering hole. I didn't have far to go. There was one just fifty feet away. I went in, found a seat at the bar, and ordered a draft beer. Like so many alcoholics, I rationalized that beer and wine were not really all that damaging, not like the hard stuff. Just keep it under control. When the barmaid brought me a sixteen-ounce glass of dark amber beer, the foam edging down the outside of the glass, I grabbed it like a prospector lost in the desert and took a grateful swallow. Nectar from the gods.

I drained the glass dry and signaled for another. The usual feeling of temporary well-being gradually took hold. The recent trauma of coming home and even what had happened to Mel began to recede as I became more and more relaxed. As was my custom, I looked around to see if there were any attractive – or available – females with whom I might strike up a conversation. But the pickings were slim. Instead, I turned my attention to the large flat-screen behind the bar and tried to interest myself in a baseball game between the Marlins and the Mets. It was a way to pass the time but I found the game less than absorbing. Despite moving to the Bay Area, I remained a die-hard St. Louis Cardinals fan and had little interest in any other teams.

By the time I had drained my fourth beer, feeling none the worse for wear, I decided I needed some food in my belly. I had had nothing since breakfast aside from some snacks on the flight from St. Louis and was sober enough to know that more alcohol on top of an empty stomach was a recipe for disaster.

As I paid my bill, I asked the barmaid if she could recommend a good place to eat. In my limited experience, restaurants in airports left much to be desired.

"Try *La Carreta*," she said. "They serve good Cuban food at reasonable prices. You'll see a lot of airport personnel and flight crews there. Kind of like truck drivers who know the best diners along the interstate. Just head down the terminal to Gate 34, you can't miss it."

I thanked her and left a generous tip. So far, I was using my own money, leaving the wad that my brother had given me for when I really needed it.

After stopping at a bathroom, I found *La Carreta* without any trouble. It was about six o'clock and there was a substantial line waiting to enter. But it was cafeteria style and the line moved quickly. I took a tray, picked up a key-lime pie, and asked for lechón, or roasted pig, that I had tried in Mexican restaurants in San Francisco. I hoped the Miami version met the same standard. I added yellow rice and fried plantains and headed to the check-out counter, where I had a choice of beverages. The sensible selection would have been water or a soda. But I was still feeling a slight buzz from the four beers I had consumed and decided to continue feeding my addiction. I got a bottle of Heineken, found an empty table, set my tray down, and begin to attack my food.

It was as good as advertised. Half-way through, I got another beer. By the time I had finished, I could sense that my buzz had become more pronounced. In a moment of clarity, I determined that I had to cut out the alcohol and sober up. Fortunately, there was a Cuban coffee stand at the side of the restaurant. It was as popular as *La Carreta* and I had to wait in line for about ten minutes before being served. I ordered a double expresso, added a lot of sugar, and sipped it slowly.

I immediately felt the jolt and my head began to clear. But just as I began to congratulate myself on my self-restraint, I looked across the terminal and saw a huge sign for Johnnie Walker Blue. At a stand, employees were pouring free samples and offering vouchers for duty-free bottles at half price.

My good intentions melted like an ice-cream cone in Death Valley. I rounded up the usual rationalizations. I would only take one small sample. I had never had the "Blue" version, which was the top of the line for the brand. Why not give it a try? I'd never graduated beyond the cheapest "Red" label. Why should I pass up this golden opportunity staring me in the face? Besides, I still had five or six hours to kill before my departure. What else was I going to do? I could handle it. No problem.

You can guess the rest. After the first free sample, which went down as smooth as silk and soon began to erode the barrier of sobriety provided by the strong Cuban coffee, I cadged another from the cute young female rep who was sensing an easy sale. She wasn't wrong. I asked for a voucher, which she handed over with a smile and a wink, and made right for the nearest duty-free shop. There, I decided to buy two bottles, which were on sale for the price of one. My plan was to keep one for immediate use and take the other with me on the plane. But when I carried them to the check-out counter, I discovered belatedly that I could only pick them up as I boarded the plane. No instant gratification allowed. I suppose that if I had been a more sophisticated international traveler I would have known this.

I pondered my options as the sales clerk waited for me to proceed. I thought about the future. If I had the bottles with me on the plane, it seemed unlikely that I would be allowed to open them and begin to guzzle. I did know enough to realize that airlines were cracking down on such practices, both for safety and economic reasons. I might even be subject to arrest when we landed, hardly an auspicious start. On the other hand, I could carry the two bottles unopened to Peru, where they would be available for consumption later. But how would that square with my vow to straighten out, sober up, and find Mel? Ultimately, my better angels prevailed and I told the sales-clerk to cancel the sale.

Leaving the shop, again congratulating myself for conquering my demons, I still faced the familiar dilemma: How to kill the time remaining until my plane took off for Lima?

I decided to try Grisham again. Locating an empty seating area, I plopped down, opened the paperback, and began to read. But I couldn't concentrate. After twenty minutes of scanning the pages without retaining much, I gave up. Hoisting my backpack, I began to wander the terminal once again. Along the way, I dropped into several stores, just to browse the merchandise. But it wasn't my thing.

My thing was to go to a bar, enjoy the atmosphere, and down some drinks. So that's what I did. I knew I shouldn't. I knew that it was exactly the wrong thing to do. But old habits die hard.

I went back to the bar I had frequented before. The same barmaid, a good looking brunette with an engaging smile, came right over as I slid into the same stool I had occupied before.

"How was *La Carreta?*" she asked.

"As good as advertised. Thanks for the recommendation."

"Glad you liked it," she said. "What can I get you? The usual?"

I hesitated. The smart choice, I knew, was to stick to beer. While it was still alcohol, I knew that I could tolerate it better than the hard stuff. But I could still taste that premium Scotch on my tongue, a taste I wanted to savor again.

"No. I think I'll switch. Do you have Johnnie Walker Blue?"

She seemed surprised for a second. Then she shook her head. "No. But we do have Johnnie Walker Black. Will that do?"

"I guess it will have to," I replied, disappointed.

"Straight up or on the rocks?"

I was tempted to take it straight. But that way, hard experience told me, led to a full-out drunken state, a state I could not afford if I were to get on the plane.

"On the rocks, please. And with a glass of water."

"Sure thing," she said. "I'll be right back."

Wow, I thought to myself, the familiar self-loathing reasserting itself, *What maturity! On the rocks instead of straight. Way to go.* I imagined my brother sitting at my side, uttering the same sarcasms. The thought of John beside me triggered a sense of resentment. *Why wasn't he beside me? Wasn't he my brother? Didn't he want to find Mel as badly as I and Mom and Dad? Why couldn't he be here? Was his work so damn important that he couldn't take time off for a family emergency? And why put me in this position? Didn't he know better? Didn't he know that I was seriously damaged goods? Why put all the burden on me? If he had been with me, if we were doing this together, then I wouldn't be sitting on this bar stool getting ready to drown my sorrows?*

Then, from somewhere in the depths of my psyche, another voice entered the conversation. *So, you sitting on this bar stool is all your brother's fault? The brother who is trying desperately to save his marriage and keep his two girls, who you supposedly adore, from the trauma of divorce? And I suppose it's Al's fault too? When are you going to grow up and admit responsibility for your own actions? What happened to all those promises you made – what? – twelve hours ago? It's time to get with the program and stop your whining.*

I did my best to shut off both voices, the argument to be continued later. At least I was where I was most comfortable, in my natural surroundings you might say. Time for more sober reflection later.

The barmaid, whose name was Natalie, brought me a glass half-filled with ice and the bottle of Scotch. She covered the ice up to the rim of the glass, undoubtedly remembering the generous tip I had left her before. She followed up with a glass of water.

I took a tentative sip of the Johnnie Walker Black. It wasn't quite up to the Blue, but it was more than acceptable.

The flat screen was still showing baseball. But by chance, now it was the Cardinals versus the arch-rival Cubs. It held my attention and helped keep my drinking under control. I had several glasses, but sipped them slowly. From time to time, I chatted with Natalie and felt some sparks. When I said I was leaving on the midnight flight to Peru, she suggested that if I came back through Miami, I should look her up and passed me a napkin with her phone number. As I slid unsteadily off my bar stool, I pocketed the napkin and promised Natalie I would call if I returned through Miami. She gave me a smile and a wave goodbye as I weaved my way onto the concourse and headed for my gate, hoping I wasn't so drunk I would be denied boarding. But I had fooled airport personnel before and was sure I could do it again. Practice makes perfect.

Seventeen

I GOT TO THE GATE just as my group for boarding was being called. Along the way, I had managed to gulp down a bottle of water, which helped me sober-up enough so that I wasn't staggering. I also chewed some gum vigorously to hide my breath. Tricks of the trade.

As I waited my turn to show my ticket and passport to the boarding agent, I had a sudden panic attack. *What if I was judged inebriated enough to deny me boarding. One more delay and one more embarrassment.* But I was used to putting on a good act and the boarding agent let me pass without comment.

The flight was full with what seemed to be an even mixture of foreign tourists and native Peruvians. My seat was half-way down the aisle by the window. The aisle and middle seats were already occupied when I arrived. Fortunately, there was still room in the overhead bins for my backpack, which I placed carefully over a neatly-folded dark suit coat. I had checked my duffel bag in St. Louis all the way to Lima. After stowing my gear, my two seat mates, a woman who I took to be a Latina on the aisle and a guy who looked to be from the U.S. in the middle, got up to let me pass to the window. I nodded my thanks and settled in. Before buckling up, I put a black leather case containing my passport and airline ticket in the seat pocket in front of me where I could reach it easily if needed as well as keep an eye on it.

By this time, I had more or less achieved something close to sobriety. As we waited for takeoff, I figured I could engage in conversation without slurring my words.

I turned to the guy in the middle seat and said in English, "Hi. I'm Clint."

I'm not sure he was interested in conversation. But after a slight pause, he extended his hand. "Blake Anderson. Pleased to meet you."

Definitely a fellow gringo, with a slight Texas drawl. He had, I guessed, about ten years on me. He looked trim and fit with blue eyes, well-trimmed dirty-blond air that was showing touches of gray, and had on a white shirt and a blue tie loosened from an unbuttoned collar. His suit jacket, I assumed was in the overhead bin and I silently hoped I hadn't put my bag right on top of it.

I asked the standard question: "So Blake. What takes you to Lima? Business or pleasure?"

Once more the slight pause, as though considering carefully what to say next. "Business I'm afraid."

Then the natural follow-up: "Oh. What do you do that takes you abroad?"

I figured him working for some kind of multi-national that had its fingers in pies across the world. Of course, if that were the case, he most likely wouldn't be flying coach but instead be up front in business class.

He looked at me in a calculating way, sizing me up, before responding: "I work for the U.S. government. Treasury. I'm headed to Lima to consult with our Drug Enforcement Administration representatives, helping them trace the money trail as best we can."

"Wow," I said. "That sounds interesting. Any danger involved?"

I couldn't read his look, but it seemed to say: "*What an idiotic question! We're dealing with one of the most violent activities on the planet. Of course, there is danger.*"

If that was what he was thinking, he hid it well. "There's always some element of risk. But I'm not on the front lines like our DEA guys. Just a bookkeeper with a low profile."

I didn't know much about the details. I had a vague impression that Peru was like several South American countries, involved in the growing of coca, the processing into cocaine, and the distribution north. I did know about the violence. The stories were pretty gruesome. I could also imagine, whatever Blake's attempt to downplay his position in the chain of U.S. efforts, money was the bottom line and anyone involved in trying to trace it would not be a welcome presence for the cartels. I refrained from saying this. I also stifled the temptation to tell him that

87

I thought the whole "war on drugs" was futile. We had been at it for decades and things seemed only to get worse. But I supposed that from his point of view the only recourse was to keep at it.

"So," Blake asked, turning the tables, "What takes you to Lima?" Glancing at my casual dress, "Off to see the sights?"

"I wish," I said with a grimace. Then I explained what had happened to Mel and what I planned to do to try to find her.

My story took him by surprise. He listened attentively and when I finished said, "That's terrible Clint. I'm really sorry," a look of genuine concern on his face.

Reaching into his shirt pocket, he pulled out a business card and handed it over. "I'm going to be in Lima for at least a week. If there is anything I can do, give me a call on my cell phone."

"Thanks," I said. "I appreciate the offer. Also, thanks for listening. It did me good to share with someone else."

"No problem." Then his brow wrinkled. "You say your sister disappeared somewhere near Cajamarca?"

I nodded yes.

"Well, that's not known as a major center of drug activity. Most of the activity is in the jungle or the eastern slopes of the Andes. But no place is immune." Another pause. "I don't want to alarm you unnecessarily, but kidnapping and drug trafficking often go hand in hand. It may be that your sister fell into something that touched on a gang's activity and they took her captive to cover their tracks and use as a hostage for future leverage. There are cases in Colombia where female hostages have been held for years. You may have read about one involving Ingrid Betancourt, who fortunately was released after going through several years of hell."

The name and the incident rang a distant bell. I must have read about it when she was released. The image of Mel held captive by a similar group and going through the same experience chilled me to the bone.

Blake saw the anguish on my face. "Sorry Clint. Just speculating, that's all."

"It's OK. No sense in ignoring the possibilities. I need to face reality." *And about time, too!*

Then and there, for the umpteenth time, I made a vow to myself to stay sober, at least until I found Mel – or more somberly – found out what had happened to her. After all, I rationalized, I had never drunk while on the job, and this was another job. In this case, however, it was a round-the-clock job. Could I really keep off the wagon twenty-four seven? I swore to do my best, knowing how high the stakes were. In the back of my mind, however, the familiar self-doubts and self-loathing lingered, whispering in my ear, *Yeah, right. Where have I heard that one before?*

By this time, we had taken off and were headed over the Caribbean toward the South American continent. Even though it was almost one in the morning, the crew determined to serve us dinner. Before that, the drink tray circulated and we were offered our choice of beverages, including complimentary wine. Blake and I asked for water, knowing that on a long flight it was important to keep hydrated. I silently congratulated myself for foregoing the wine. *Way to go!* the cynical voice in my head said, *passing up some wine that came in a box!* When the dinner cart came by, with the choice of chicken or pasta, we declined. Soon thereafter, we turned off the overhead lights and shut our eyes. I don't know about Blake, but within seconds the aftereffects of the alcohol I had consumed during the past hours kicked in and I was dead to the world.

Eighteen

I WOKE WHEN THE OVERHEAD lights went on. As I blinked my eyes open, I checked my vital signs. While I had a slight headache, overall I felt reasonably good with the level of my hangover symptoms somewhere between ten and fifteen on a scale of one hundred. Nonetheless, when the breakfast cart arrived at our row, I welcomed the warm rolls, coffee, and water and consumed them quickly and gratefully.

Blake had been awake when I had cracked open my eyes. "How'd you sleep Blake?"

"Not as well as you," he said wryly. "Boy, you were out like a light. I'm envious. I have real trouble sleeping on airplanes. I probably got one or two hours shuteye, tops."

I thought about suggesting substantial quantities of alcohol pre-boarding as a remedy, but refrained. Despite the lack of sleep, he still looked fresher than I felt.

After we had finished breakfast, it was announced that we were beginning our descent into Jorge Chávez Airport in Lima. I lifted the window shade and looked out onto nothing but low-lying clouds. If my geography was correct, the Pacific Ocean was somewhere close by on my right with the Andes Mountains to my left. The announcement said the local temperature on the ground was about sixty degrees Fahrenheit, about thirty degrees cooler than St. Louis or Miami, making me thankful that I had my trusty light jacket in my backpack to accommodate the shift from the North American summer to the South American winter.

We touched down at six-thirty a.m. on the dot. As we taxied to the terminal, numerous passengers ignored the crew's admonition and unbuckled their seatbelts, stood in the aisles, and downloaded their carry-ons. I was tempted to follow suit, but Blake put a restraining hand on my arm.

"Take it easy Clint. I've been through this before." Lowering his voice, he said, "Peruvians are not great at following the rules and tend to get a bit excitable in situations like these. In fact, they are not going to get through the airport hurdles any faster this way than if they waited. All they are doing is clogging up the aisles. Don't worry. I've been through this more than once and I can get us through the landing hassles without the waits in long lines. Just follow my lead. I assume you have some luggage to pick up."

"Yeah. Just a duffle bag."

"If you don't mind, can I see your baggage claim receipt?"

"Sure." Retrieving my ticket from the leather case in my seat pocket, I pulled out the claim receipt. Blake took it, placed it on the tray table along with a receipt of his own and took out his phone. He snapped a picture of the receipts, touched some buttons on the keypad, and sent the message off.

Turning to me, he said "The miracles of modern technology. Our luggage should be waiting for us once we clear immigration. It will save us a lot of time. When we arrive at this hour so do numerous other international flights. Be warned. It will be a madhouse in the terminal. The wait for your bag to arrive on the carousel can seem an eternity."

"Thanks a lot Blake. I really appreciate your help."

I was pretty sure not everybody could get this kind of service. Blake, I assumed, had some serious clout despite the low profile of flying with the plebes in coach.

I relaxed and sat back in my seat until the crowd cleared. Once it did, we got up and collected our belongings from the overheads. Blake handed me my backpack and retrieved his suit jacket, which thankfully in my semi-sober condition I had taken care not to mess up, along with a bag containing what I took to be a laptop. He shrugged on his coat, straightened his tie, and we made our way out of the plane and into the terminal. Once there, we followed the signs in the corridor toward immigration along with what seemed thousands of others. The crowd, as on our plane, was a mixture of Peruvians and foreign tourists speaking a variety of languages.

"Lots of tourists," I said to Blake, belaboring the obvious.

"Yep. Peru has become a very popular international tourist destination, especially for those who want to visit Machu Picchu." I could see that most of all ages were decked out in hiking gear. "Probably half of the foreigners you see here will soon be boarding local flights to Cuzco. If you have the chance while you are here you should try to go. It's something to see." Then, remembering the reason for my visit, added, "Sorry. I know you have more important things to do."

"Yeah. I do. But maybe some time."

When we go to the hall where we had to pass through immigration controls, it was a madhouse. Lines snaked through roped off lanes, bedraggled and sleep-deprived passengers waiting impatiently their turn to be processed. Many, I assumed, were afraid they would miss their connecting flights.

I got ready to enter the queue when Blake took me by the elbow. "This way Clint," he said, heading to our far right where people were moving through briskly. The sign above the desk read that this lane was designated for airline crews, diplomatic personnel, and the handicapped. We passed by a line of mostly elderly passengers waiting in wheel-chairs.

I felt a tinge of guilt, but Blake pulled me along. "Give me your passport Clint and I'll get you processed." I dug it out and turned it over to him.

At the counter, Blake showed the stoic and slightly bored agent his credentials. After a brief exchange, with some quizzical looks in my direction, the agent stamped both our documents and waved us through. It reaffirmed the fact that my new-found friend had more than a little influence.

As we headed toward the baggage claim area, a guy in some kind of uniform approached us and I felt a tinge of apprehension. But he greeted us with a pleasant smile. "Right this way gentlemen. Your luggage is this way."

We threaded our way through a duty-free shop, where I studiously ignored the various liquor offerings, and entered the cavernous baggage-claim area. Our uniformed guide led us past the chaos to the customs area, where, miraculously our luggage awaited us. There was my battered duffel in all its glory, the Marine Corps logo now faded. Blake's suitcase was a shiny gun-metal gray model on wheels that looked sturdy enough to withstand a bomb blast. And maybe, I thought to myself, given Blake's job, that was the point. I tried not to dwell on it. I had my own problems to worry about.

Blake thanked the guy in uniform and slipped him a twenty, which the guy pocketed without expression. We were then waved through customs with barely a glance.

Before we passed through, Blake asked "Where are you staying?"

"My brother booked me at the Sheraton, which I guess is downtown."

"Yes, it is. Let me get you there. I have a ride waiting and we can drop you off."

"That's very kind of you Blake. But I can make it on my own. I don't want to put you out of your way."

"Don't worry Clint. I'm glad to help." Then, lowering his voice he said, "I know you have a lot on your plate and are under a lot of stress. I'm happy to help any way I can. I mean it. Giving you a ride in a government car is the least I can do."

I was beginning to reassess my generally dim view of government bureaucrats. Blake seemed to be the genuine article. I wondered whether the others I might meet along the way would prove him the exception to the rule.

As we exited the baggage area, we entered an area where a minor riot seemed to be in unfolding. We were bombarded with men approaching us to offer their ride services, which Blake deftly turned away. On the other side of a rope line, people were six deep carrying signs, jumping up and down, and shouting out names. Blake ignored them all, scanning the crowd until he saw a sign with his name on it. Grabbing me once more by the elbow, he dragged me through the jostling crowd.

After shoving our way through what seemed the Peruvian airport version of a rugby scrum, we met up with Blake's driver. He put down the sign and shook Blake's hand. "Hello Mr. Anderson," he said in English. "Welcome back to Lima. Good to see you again."

"Hello Jorge. Good to see you as well."

Jorge was in his mid-thirties with bronze skin, glossy black hair, and pronounced indigenous features. He wore a non-descript spotless and neatly-pressed gray suit along with a white shirt and tie. Standing next to him was another man who could have been his twin from looks to clothes, although with a more intimidating look on his face. He stared at me with some suspicion until Blake reassured him. "Don't worry Eduardo. This is Mister Jackson. He's a friend of mine and we are going to take him to his hotel. And by the way, good to see you as well."

"Good to see you too Mister Anderson. Welcome back to Lima." Then he added, without smiling, "You too Mister Jackson. Welcome to Lima."

Eduardo's English, like Jorge's, was heavily accented but clearly understandable. I wasn't so sure about my Spanish but figured I'd give it a try. "Muchas Gracías Eduardo. Es un placer de estar aquí en su país."

All three chuckled. "Not bad Clint," said Blake with a grin. "Keep practicing."

"Don't worry Blake. I need to."

With the ice seemingly broken, Jorge insisted on hefting my duffel while Eduardo guided Blake's wheeled suitcase to our waiting vehicle. It was not far away but I noticed Eduardo keeping his head on a swivel as if expecting trouble at any moment. Next to me Blake whispered, "Jorge is our driver. Eduardo is the bodyguard. They are both top-notch."

"I see them on high alert. Is there really that level of danger here in the open?"

Again, the look that said *How naïve can you be? Don't you follow the news?* "I'll explain once we get into our ride."

Our ride was a humongous black SUV with tinted windows. What's next, I thought, a police escort?

Jorge used a remote to open the trunk where he deposited my duffel. He then assumed the lookout pose while Eduardo wrestled with Blake's much heavier luggage. Once finished, he closed the trunk and opened the rear door and gestured for me to get in. I slid onto the soft leather seats while Jorge shut the door firmly. Eduardo followed the same procedure for Blake on the other side. Once seated, we buckled up as Jorge got behind the wheel and Eduardo took the shotgun seat, which, under these circumstances might literally have been true.

"Jorge," Blake said, "We are dropping Mister Jackson off at the Sheraton."

"Very well Mister Anderson." With that, he started the engine and we began to inch our way out of the parking lot, through the airport exit, and then onto a highway that seemed to contain every vehicle in the country inching along at a snail's pace. Jorge kept a steady eye on the road, looking for opportunities to switch lanes so we could advance. Eduardo kept his head on such a swivel he began to remind me of Charlie McCarthy and I wondered how he avoided getting a stiff neck at the end of the day.

"Now this is the *real* welcome to Lima Clint. A metropolis of about ten million souls with what seems like twice as many cars, buses and trucks, all on the highway at the same time. And despite the red lights you see along the way, rules are followed only in the abstract. There *are* some unspoken rules that are usually followed, otherwise the accident toll would be astronomical. But it takes a long time to figure out what they really are. In the meantime, just relax and let Jorge handle the traffic."

As if I had a choice. "Makes L.A. look like a breeze," I observed. "Now," nodding in Eduardo's direction and adding a note of concern in my voice, "Are you in *that* much danger here? Would you really be attacked at the airport in broad daylight?"

Whatever he might of thought of my cluelessness, he took the question seriously. "Probably not. But we can't take any chances. Not to be overly dramatic, once I step on the plane – and maybe even on it – I could be a target. It has happened to others and I've had a few close calls over the years. In this business, you cannot assume anything. In lots of these countries, with Mexico a good example, corruption goes all the way to the top. The cartels have enormous influence. You've heard the phrase 'narco-state?'" I nodded. "Well Peru isn't there yet. But it could be. That guy who got our luggage at the airport, for example. Next month or maybe even tomorrow, he could have been bribed – or coerced with threats to his family – to put a bomb in my suitcase. You probably didn't notice, but before we were passed through customs, I checked to make sure there had been no tampering with my suitcase. I'd laid a few traps and none had been sprung. If I had seen any telltale signs, I would have taken it off the area for a special screening."

Once more, a reality check for me. This was the real world and I was in it, like it or not. "Not to sound like a wimp, but how safe are we now?"

He didn't brush me off. "About as safe as you can hope to be. This SUV is made of reinforced steel. The windows," he said, tapping one with a knuckle, "are bullet-proof. We could probably withstand a round from an RPG. It's also pretty bomb proof, fortified all around. Nonetheless," he added with a wry look, "I wouldn't look forward to an actual test."

My admiration for Blake went up yet another notch. He described all of these terrors in a calm, cool, and collected manner. All routine for him, I supposed. I also presumed that he was some kind of high-powered accountant who could make a fortune in the private sector but instead determined to serve the public interest as best he could. I couldn't help but feel embarrassed by my own failings.

"So, Clint," he asked, as we remained stalled in traffic, "What's up for you once you settle in at the Sheraton?"

"My brother has set up an appointment at the U.S. embassy with the guy who's handling Mel's disappearance." Glancing at my watch, "I'm supposed to meet him at two this afternoon."

"What's the guy's name?"

"Charles Macalister."

Blake nodded. "Yeah. I know him. Pretty good guy. A professional diplomat, quite ambitious. He's been posted here for a while, so he knows the terrain. He's also number two to the ambassador, who is a recent political appointee out of his depth. For now, Macalister is more or less running the show. Well-intentioned and generally a straight shooter, but swamped with work. Don't expect too much from him or from the embassy in general. I'm afraid you're going to have to do most of the digging on your own."

He saw my face fall. "Just being realistic Clint. You're in a tough spot." He paused. "If I weren't so busy, I'd go with you to Cajamarca. But I can't. Too much on my plate, and my bosses would never allow it."

"I understand Blake. And I appreciate the offer – and the frankness. I kind of figured that it would mainly be up to me to find my sister."

By this time, we had begun to make slow progress along the highway. "Listen Clint. A few friendly tips for dealing with Lima. First, keep a close watch on your personal belongings. There is a lot of petty crime in this city. Lots of muggings, especially at night and in the downtown area. I'd stay as close to your hotel as you can. Second, as you can see, traffic here is horrific. If you have a two o'clock appointment at the embassy, you probably should leave your hotel by one at the latest. Even though it isn't that far away, when you get into a traffic jam you can be stuck without moving for a long time. Third, avoid taking taxis from the street. Do you have Uber on your phone?"

I shook my head. "If you have time, try to install it. Otherwise, have the hotel arrange for your ride to the embassy and the pick-up as well. It's not unheard of for unsuspecting tourists to hail a street taxi and end up in the suburbs without their belongings or their clothes. Better safe than sorry, even if it's going to cost you a bit more."

"Thanks for the tips Blake. I've spent some time in Mexico, but not in the big cities. The advice is welcome." I didn't add that most of my time south of the border had been passed in a semi-alcoholic daze, where I had been fortunate not to have been picked clean – or worse – at some point.

As I looked out the window, what I saw of Lima didn't leave the best impression. We had finally turned off the airport highway and were beginning to make decent time as we headed for the downtown area. The avenue we were on was bordered with a mixture of cheap hotels, cut-rate restaurants, large shopping malls, and casinos. The sky was overcast with a slight drizzle, forcing Jorge to put the wipers on intermittent. Everything seemed gray. We passed a large hospital that from what I could read was dedicated to the military, maybe a kind of Peruvian Walter Reed. As we entered the downtown area, the hotels became more up-scale and there were some impressive homes that seemed to take up entire blocks.

Once again, the traffic snarled and slowed. We got onto a main drag that took us to a large plaza with a column in the center. Traffic was controlled, if that was the right word, by policewomen in circular stands at the crossroads, wearing large white gloves whereby they signaled stop and go. It seemed to be a terrible job, caught in the midst of a maelstrom of blaring noise, noxious exhaust, and unseen but felt anger as drivers and pedestrians jostled for advantage. They wore face masks but I doubted they did much good in an air thick with fumes.

While we waited to be waved ahead, Blake pointed out across the circle to the Sheraton Hotel. It was a multi-story hotel in the modernist style of the 1960s with all the charm of a soulless office building. Jorge navigated the circle and as we approached the entrance, I asked Blake, "Any chance I'll see you at the embassy."

He gave me a tight smile. "Who says I'll be at the embassy? Sorry Clint. My whereabouts are classified. But you have my cell phone number. Keep in touch and let me know what develops. Let's hope for the best."

As the SUV came to a halt, a bellman rushed out to open the door. Eduardo beat him to it. Putting his hand up, he kept the bellman at a distance while he did the honors. Lifting the trunk lid, he effortlessly pulled out my duffel and then opened my door. With everything under control, and with both hands free and his head on its perpetual swivel, he motioned the bellman over to collect my luggage. After shaking Blake's hand and thanking him once again, I stepped out of the SUV and headed for the hotel entrance. I turned to thank Jorge and Eduardo as well, but by the time I did, it was too late. The doors were closed and Blake and his team were on their way to whatever destination awaited them.

I saw them depart with some wistfulness. Now I was truly on my own and for a moment felt lonely and a bit overwhelmed. I had appreciated Blake's frankness, but as the challenges that lay ahead of me became clearer, the old doubts resurfaced. And would I be able to meet them without the comfort of my old friend – a good stiff drink. Shaking these thoughts from my head, I entered the Sheraton determined to do the best I could to fulfill the promises I had made to find my baby sister and bring her home.

Nineteen

WHEN I CHECKED IN at the Sheraton it was a little after nine. At the desk, I asked the clerk to order a car for me at one. He said he would and gave me a map of the city's downtown. Once I had finished the check-in procedure, he wished me a pleasant stay.

I wasn't used to such fancy accommodations and was not sure of the proper protocol. Usually, I would have lugged my duffel up to my room without assistance. But the bellman, whose nametag read "Mario," seemed pretty insistent on doing it for me. He probably lived on tips so I let him put my duffel on a cart and lead me to the bank of elevators that would carry me to my twelfth-floor room. We chatted a bit as we rode up to my floor, mostly about the weather and my first impressions of Lima. We spoke in English until I insisted that we switch to Spanish. I needed the practice.

When the elevator door opened on twelve, Mario led me down the lushly-carpeted hallway to my room. He opened the door with a key-card and gestured for me to enter while he followed with my duffel, which he placed on a suitcase rack. He showed me the features of the room, which was more luxurious than any I had stayed in before.

"Anything else Señor Jackson?" he asked as he prepared to leave, looking at me expectantly.

He didn't have his hand out, but I knew he was waiting for his tip. I fumbled for my wallet and after some hesitation drew out a ten. It probably was too much, but again, this was all kind of new to me.

When I handed it over, he remained expressionless but I thought I saw his eyes widen a bit. Maybe I had been too generous. Or maybe not generous enough. At any rate, I had bigger things to worry about.

Then I realized that he might have expected his tip to be in the local currency, of which I had absolutely zero, having failed to change my dollars to the Peruvian *sol* at the airport.

"Sorry Mario. I only have dollars at the moment."

"That's fine Señor Jackson. No problem. You can use dollars almost anywhere in Peru. Credit cards too. But you might want to get some *soles* if you plan to stay for more than a few days. There is a *casa de cambio* close by where you can get a good rate. When you leave the hotel, it's two blocks to your left on the corner. It has a blue sign that says *Cambio.* You can't miss it. Just tell them that Mario at the Sheraton sent you," he said with a grin. I guessed that he would get some cut of whatever transactions he sent their way. I was happy to accommodate.

"Thanks Mario. I'll do that."

He turned to leave "Have a nice stay Señor Jackson. I hope you enjoy Lima."

With that, he closed the door, leaving me to get settled in. I looked at my watch. It read nine twenty. I had plenty of time to kill before my two o'clock with Macalister at the embassy.

The issue of changing dollars to *soles* brought to mind Blake's warning about protecting my valuables. So far, I had been pretty cavalier, toting John's two thou in cash in my backpack, keeping my wallet with its precious horde of credit cards in my back pocket, and my new phone in my front pocket. This made me easy prey for any muggers or pick-pockets, who, Blake suggested, were thick on the ground in Lima.

Fortunately, my room had a safe. Mario had showed me how it worked and I stored all my valuables, including my passport and return airline ticket there, keeping a couple of hundred dollar bills to be exchanged for *soles*. I made a mental note to buy a money belt, something I should have remembered before I left.

My next order of business was to clean up. I badly needed a shave and a shower. Looking into the bathroom mirror as I shaved around my goatee I didn't much like what I saw. It wasn't as bad as my hungover state in San Francisco, what, two days ago? But it wasn't pretty either. My eyes were marginally less bloodshot, but still were far from clear. My hair was a mess, dirty, matted, and in general disarray. I wonder what Blake must have thought when he saw me sit next to him. My body odor alone would have been enough for him to recoil in disgust.

Enough with the wallowing. Time to get squared away. After shaving, I got into the shower and soaked and soaped myself in steamy hot water for about ten minutes, shampooing my hair in the process. Drying off, I determined to find a barber shop and get my hair trimmed to an acceptable length and get rid of the goatee, changing from hippie to square. Or maybe just normal. Now could I do the same cleansing and cleaning for the interior as the exterior? Maybe not, but at least I felt I was taking steps in the right direction.

I pulled some fresh under and outerwear from my duffel and got dressed to go out. A blue button-down shirt, tan Dockers, a light dark sweater, my light jacket, New Balance running shoes, and a baseball cap made me feel like a new man.

Before descending to the lobby, I drained two bottles of water and brewed some in-room coffee. I downed a couple of cups with plenty of sugar. So far, there were no serious signs of my usual post-binge condition, but past experience showed that to ward them off there was nothing better than plenty of coffee along with multiple glasses of water.

It was about ten o'clock when I crossed the lobby and headed for the main entrance. I nodded at Mario as he held the door for me.

"Two blocks to the left?" I asked, just to confirm.

"Yes, Señor Jackson. Two blocks to the left."

I followed his directions, walking briskly. The weather hadn't changed much; still cloudy, chilly, and damp. I zipped up my jacket and was glad I had added a sweater. Nor were the surroundings any more pleasant. The traffic noise, the smells, and the pollution surrounded me and assaulted my senses. I had been spared most of the effects in the floating fortress of the SUV, but now I was in the middle of it all full force.

At the end of the first block, a crowd of pedestrians waited to cross the street. Busses, taxis, and private vehicles streamed by. There was no stoplight so it wasn't until the traffic came to a stop on its own that we were able to cross to the other side.

The next block was no better, just more of the same. I kept walking at a brisk pace until I arrived at the next corner where, as promised, I saw the blue sign reading *Cambio* above the doorway. Fortunately, there were only a few customers standing in front of the window where money was exchanged. In the corner was a counter for sending Western Union wire transfers.

I waited patiently for about five minutes until it was my turn. I encountered a female clerk who looked to be in her twenties sitting behind a protective plastic shield reinforced with vertical bars. I smiled and said in Spanish "I would like to change dollars for *soles*." My charm failed. Without a word, she somewhat disdainfully pointed to a chalkboard that listed the current exchange rate, approximately 3.3 *soles* to the dollar.

Then I remembered. I had forgotten the magic words: "Mario from the Sheraton sent me here."

It did the trick. She gave me a dazzling smile. "Certainly Señor. Pleased to be of service."

I passed the two c-notes through the window at the bottom of the shield and she scooped them up. She then lifted them to the light, presumably to check the watermark. "Sorry Señor..."

"Jackson."

"Señor Jackson. But we need to be careful. There are a lot of counterfeit dollars in circulation. But these," she assured me, "are legitimate."

She picked up a calculator, ran her fingers over the numbers and entered them into a machine that spat out a white ticket with the totals. She handed the ticket over to me and I glanced at it quickly. Doing the easy math in my head, I saw I had gotten a small break on the commission, undoubtedly thanks to Mario, who probably got something in return for the recommendation. I was happy to help him out.

I nodded to the girl that everything was okay and she began to count out the *soles*, six hundred and twenty in total. Looking at the notes, it seemed I had exchanged two Ben Franklins for famous people in Peruvian history about whom I had not a clue. Nonetheless, I had accomplished one mission. Now it was time to move on to the next – find a barbershop and do something about the unruly mop on top of my head and the hair on my face.

I was in luck. Halfway down the next block there was a sign on the sidewalk saying *Barbero* with a red arrow pointing to the right. I entered a gallery with little shops on each side and found the barbershop near the end of the row. It had three chairs, two of which were occupied. The third barber, who had been sitting in his chair reading what looked to be a tabloid, quickly got up and gestured for me to take a seat.

We exchanged greetings. As he tied the sheet around my neck, I tried my best to explain what I wanted, hoping he got the gist: cut off the dangling locks but don't do a complete shearing. I didn't want to be a skinhead. Just leave me with a normal, trim haircut. Also, shave off the goatee. He said that he understood and went to work with his scissors. I began to feel like Samson as big clumps of hair hit the floor.

While he cut, the barber asked, "Is this your first time in Lima señor?" A typical opening gambit.

"Yes. It is. First time in Peru."

"Your Spanish is very good," he lied.

"Thanks. I've spent quite a bit of time in Mexico."

"I don't know Mexico. What brings you to Peru?"

"Just tourism," I lied. "I've heard a lot about the country and wanted to visit."

By this time, the other customers and their barbers had grown silent, listening in on our conversation. I was probably something of an oddity, a wandering tourist who had stumbled into their midst.

"Well señor…" my barber began.

"Just call me Clint," I said.

"Clint," he said, making it sound like "Cleent." "Like the actor. One of my favorites."

I suppressed a grin. "Yes. Exactly."

"Well señor Clint. While you are in Lima you must try some of our delicious food. It's unlike anything you've ever had anywhere. In fact," he said with obvious pride, "we are now world-famous for our food. Foreigners come from all over the world to try out our restaurants."

"That sounds great. What would you recommend?"

My question produced a chorus of suggestions from the other barbers and their customers. They all seemed to agree that I must try *ceviche, anticuchos, and cuy.* The Chinese food found in places called *chifas* was also excellent with unique dishes that combined Andean, Spanish, and Asian foods. They also urged me to try a *pisco sour*, made from a liquor native to Peru mixed with lime juice and sugar and topped with the foam of a beaten egg white. In fact, there was a festival dedicated to different brands of pisco currently in progress if I were interested in sampling a drink that had been invented back in the twenties at a hotel near the main plaza. They also warned me that a *pisco sour* was *muy fuerte*, very strong, and I should be careful not to overindulge. I wondered if there was something about me that gave off the vibe that I might have problems with alcohol, but dismissed it as excessive paranoia.

No matter how enticing, I determined that a *pisco sour* was definitely off limits. Although I didn't say anything so as not to offend, I wasn't too wild about eating raw fish *(ceviche)*, barbecued beef hearts *(anticuchos)*, or guinea pig *(cuy)* in any form. As a San Franciscan, the idea of trying some Asian cuisine seemed more appealing.

As my barber continued to work away at the major reconstruction project that was my shave and a haircut, I got caught up in the general conversation. I fielded the usual questions about the United States – cost of living, job possibilities, politics – and lobbed back some of my own on the same subjects. The current government, my informants told me, was trying its best to clean up the corruption of its predecessors and seemed to be making some headway. But they were uniformly skeptical that much would change. I asked about street crime and they repeated Blake's warnings that I should be extremely careful as lots of tourists like me were seen as easy targets. On the subject of drug-related crime, there were some slight differences of opinion but a consensus that it had become more serious over time, particularly in the port area of Callao. They advised me to keep well clear, which I assured them I would.

It took my barber almost half an hour to finish the job. In between clipping, buzzing, and using a razor to get the hair on the back of my neck, he would halt the operation to pitch in his two cents worth of opinion. When he finally finished, he held up a mirror to show me the results of his handiwork. He had done an excellent job, returning my hair to a level of normality that I had not seen in many a year. I'm not sure my buddies back in San Francisco would have recognized the new trimmed and clean-shaven me.

The whole experience in the barber shop had been a lot of fun. I had thoroughly enjoyed the friendliness of the others and had picked up some useful insights about local life along the way. The experience also gave me confidence that my Spanish was good enough for me to communicate and understand what I heard without too much difficulty. The cost of the haircut was fifteen *soles* or about five dollars. I gave the barber twice that, explaining that in the U.S. I would have had to pay at least twenty bucks for the kind of service he had provided me.

"*Muchisimas gracías señor* Clint. You are most kind."

"Think nothing of it," I said, putting on my jacket and my ball cap, which now rested a bit loose on my head. Leaving the shop, I accepted the good wishes from the entire group and thanked them in turn for the pleasant conversation and helpful advice.

Out on the street, I looked at my watch. It said ten thirty-seven. I still had time to kill and decided I might as well explore the downtown. Looking at the city map from the hotel, I determined my location and decided to keep on walking east until I hit the main square, the *Plaza de Armas*.

It was still overcast and cool but the drizzle had disappeared. I went at a leisurely pace, glancing at the various stores, cafes, small restaurants, and office buildings along the way. The sidewalks were crowded with pedestrians, many of whom I took to be of indigenous descent, others who were more European in appearance, and still others who seemed to be a mixture of both. For the most part, I was a good head taller than the majority. But my gringo looks drew few stares, presumably because tourists were a common sight.

After about twenty minutes, I ran into a broad avenue called the *Colmena*, or the beehive.

Fortunately, there was an actual red light that drivers actually obeyed and allowed me to get to the other side without incident. There, I followed a pedestrian-only street, where hawkers of various kinds had set-up makeshift sidewalk enterprises that sold a wide variety of household items at what I assumed were bargain prices. A few tried to grab my attention, but I ignored them and kept on walking.

When I reached the *Plaza de Armas*, it was swarming with tour groups. As I walked around, I could hear a babel of languages – Spanish, Italian, French, Japanese and English. I was tempted to attach myself to the English-language group but decided to hover around the Spanish-language tour. I still needed a lot of practice. We wandered into the main cathedral where the remains of the Spaniard who had conquered Peru by defeating the Inca Empire, Francisco Pizarro, were interred. We went to another church a few blocks away, San Francisco, which held the skulls of twenty-five thousand dead from the Spanish colonial era; creepy but interesting. We returned to the plaza in time to see the changing of the guard at the presidential palace. I overheard a fellow gringo tourist observe that the change was incongruously accompanied by the march from the opera Aida. I didn't know beans about opera, but the music seemed okay to me. I also noticed a significant police-military presence at the corners and sides of the plaza with olive-drabbed helmeted men carrying protective shields, like knights in armor, ready to confront any protest that might emerge.

There was more to see but I had had enough. Maybe some other time. It was almost noon and I was hungry. I decided to forego some of the exotic food choices that my friends at the barbershop had suggested. Instead I went into a place called *Bembos*, part of a local fast-food chain located on the southwest corner of the plaza and scarfed down a burger, fries, and a coke. Not great, but not bad either.

It was a quarter to one by the time I got back to the Sheraton. I went up to my room to freshen up and to get my passport from the safe. I knew I would need to show it at the embassy. Just as I finished brushing my teeth, the phone rang informing me that my ride was waiting for me at the front desk. When I got off the elevator, I saw a guy in a gray suit that looked as though it came from the same rack as Blake's driver Jorge standing near the front desk. I headed toward him.

"Señor Jackson?"

"That's me."

He extended his hand, which I took. "My name is Manuel Rodríguez. I'm your driver," he said in English.

"Pleased to meet you Manuel. But let's converse in Spanish," I said in Spanish.

"No probl... I mean, *no hay problema*," he said with a smile. And then led me out the door to where his vehicle, a late-model black sedan, was parked. I thought about sliding into the back seat but decided to sit up front in the passenger seat. That made for easier conversation.

In the car, Manuel waited for me to attach my seat belt. When it was securely fastened, he said "The police here rarely give you a ticket for speeding or changing lanes or running stop signs. But they *will* fine you if you don't wear your seatbelt. Strange, no. But that's Peru," he said with a shrug.

Once more we entered the madness that was Lima's traffic. I thanked my lucky stars that I was not behind the wheel.

After being stalled for about ten minutes, Manuel managed to get us onto a broad multi-lane highway bisected by tracks for an electric commuter train. It was like the Indy Five Hundred with thousands of vehicles going at break-neck speed, many drivers abruptly changing lanes without warning, forcing Manuel to do a quick dance between the accelerator and the brakes. We had enough near misses to get my heart rate up and make my stomach churn.

While I was clutching the arm rest like a drowning man, Manuel remained cool as a cucumber. That helped calm me down some.

"The highway we are on now is officially called the *Paseo de la República*, but everybody calls it *El Zanjón*."

"I'm sorry Manuel. That word is not in my vocabulary."

He smiled. "Of course, Señor Jackson. It means the "Big Ditch" because as you can see it runs through a kind of sunken valley. Pretty soon we'll be exiting onto another main highway that will lead us south to the embassy, which is located in a suburb called Santiago del Surco."

Sure enough, a couple of minutes later we exited onto another highway called *Javier Prado*. Suddenly, we were back to crawling along.

We took advantage of the slowed pace to converse. Manuel started out by asking me my impressions of Peru so far. I gave him a generally favorable picture, the highlight being the friendly exchange I had had in the barbershop, which elicited a chuckle. Then the inevitable, "And what brings you to Peru Señor Jackson?"

I had hedged my answer before. For some reason, I decided to tell Manuel the whole story. As it turned out, that proved to be the right decision. When he heard that Mel had been in Cajamarca when she disappeared, he almost swerved into another vehicle. "No Señor Jackson. Cajamarca? I am from Cajamarca. My whole family still lives there. Maybe they can help you. I have a brother, Enrique, who is an important official in the mayor's office. I'll let him know that you will be visiting Cajamarca soon and I'm sure he can assist you. In fact, I'll call him while I wait for you at the embassy."

"Thank you, Manuel," I said, touched by his earnestness and eagerness to help. "That is very kind of you. I need all the help I can get," which was certainly the truth.

For the rest of the trip, we drifted into general conversations about politics and sports. About the only sport Peruvians seemed interested in was soccer, a sport that was pretty popular in St. Louis but which I had never played. I didn't have much to say along those lines except to nod my head as Manuel rattled on about games and players I had never heard of. By the time he had wrapped up his discussion of how the Peruvian national team might do in the next international tournament, we had arrived at the embassy.

"Here we are Señor Jackson. Right on time. I'll drop you here and pick you up when you are finished. They do not allow me to park close by," he informed me. "Car bombs, you know. I'll be a few blocks away. Just call me on my cell phone," he said, handing me his card with the number on it."

I took his card. As I got out of the car, he wished me good luck. I thanked him and closed the door, watching as he drove off.

Car Bombs! I wasn't in Kansas anymore.

Twenty

I APPROACHED THE EMBASSY ENTRANCE. There was a lengthy line waiting patiently to gain access. If I had to wait in that line, there was no way I would make my two o'clock appointment. I spoke to a uniformed security guard and explained my dilemma. He pointed me to another entry point that had no line. The long line, he explained, was for Peruvians seeking visas to travel to the U.S.

At the empty entry point, a bored-looking official slid open a window and asked what business I had at the embassy. I gave him my name and told him I had a two o'clock appointment with Charles Macalister. He checked a clip-board, nodded, and then asked for my passport, which I handed over. He looked at it carefully and then scanned the face page onto a screen. I inwardly bristled at the Big Brother aspect of the procedure but also realized that if anything were to happen to me at least there was some record of my presence in Peru.

He returned my passport with a slight smile. "Here you go Mister Clint *Eastwood* Jackson."

I smiled back. "It's a long story."

"I bet," he said. Then he touched a button somewhere and a gate to the embassy opened. "Mr. Macalister is expecting you Mister Jackson. Just step inside and someone will be out soon to escort you to his office. Have a nice day."

I followed his instructions and stepped inside as the gate closed behind me. On the other side were two security guards with side arms and steely glares. They looked alert and serious and gave me a careful eyeball.

"Please step over here sir," one of them said.

I did as I was told. I knew what was coming. He took out an electronic wand and asked me to stand with my arms extended.

"Please remove any metal items and place them in this bucket."

I followed orders. My watch, belt, cell phone, and loose coins went into the gray plastic container. Then the guard ran the wand carefully over me, no telltale beeps sounding.

By the time I had recovered my items and returned them to their proper place, my escort had arrived. She was a pleasant surprise. A cute blonde somewhere in her mid to late twenties, who extended her hand in greeting.

"Hello Mister Jackson," she said with a welcoming smile. "I'm Jennifer. I'm here to take you to your meeting with Mister Macalister. Just follow me."

While we walked toward the embassy building, we chatted a bit. Jennifer was a junior foreign service officer from Atlanta, Georgia. Lima was her first assignment and she had been on duty for about a year. So far, so good she told me. She was enjoying it and learning a lot.

As we chatted, I took in my surroundings. The embassy was a multi-story modern building with a colorful façade located some forty yards from the main gate and the street. *Car bombs, remember.* It was set into what looked like a mini-park of several acres encircled by what I judged to be a twelve-foot thick metal fence. There were surveillance cameras everywhere and numerous satellite dishes on the roof. It had a far from-welcoming vibe. Instead, it brought to mind a medieval castle surrounded by a moat.

As we entered the building, we encountered yet another layer of security. This time I had to pass through a body scanner after surrendering my metallic items. Once again, no beeps.

Jennifer had been waved through and was waiting for me as I exited the scanner.

"Lot of security here," I observed, belaboring the obvious.

She nodded. "We've learned from hard experience that you cannot be too careful. Follow me," she instructed, leading me up a flight of stairs to the second floor and then down a long corridor toward Macalister's office. I thought about asking Jennifer, who had no ring on her finger, if she were free tonight but thought better of it. Now was not the time. I had to focus on the task at hand – finding Mel.

About halfway down the corridor, we stopped at a door with Macalister's name on a plaque to the side. "Here we are," Jennifer said. She knocked lightly and, since we were expected, opened the door and ushered me inside to an outer office where Macalister's secretary sat behind a desk.

"This is Florencia, Mister Jackson," Jennifer said. "She'll take over from here."

I thanked Jennifer as she closed the door, giving me an encouraging smile and wishing me good luck. In the meantime, Florencia rose from her desk and knocked on the inner office door to announce my arrival. Opening the door, she gestured for me to pass on through. "Mister Jackson to see you Mister Macalister," she announced as I walked into the office. I looked at my watch. It showed me a few minutes late, delayed a bit by the elaborate security procedures.

Macalister rose from his desk and came around to greet me. "Clint," he said, "taking my hand in a firm grip. When he spoke, I thought I detected a Boston accent. "Good to see you, although I wish it were under more pleasant circumstances."

"Same here," I replied. He gestured for me to take a seat and settled back behind his desk.

Macalister was in his mid-thirties with dark curly hair beginning to recede and dark eyes behind designer glasses. He looked to be about my height and weight, but his complexion was sallow as though he spent most of his time indoors. His suit jacket was hung on the back of his chair, his white dress shirt unbuttoned and tie unloosened. There was an imposing pile of paper on the top of his desk.

While I sized him up, he did the same. He eyed me as I followed his suggestion to get comfortable and take off my jacket and cap. As I did so, I was thankful for the morning clean-up.

Before I could open my mouth to ask him about how things were proceeding on the search for Mel, he held up his hand palm out. "I've asked one of our local FBI agents to join us. He'll be here in a few minutes. In the meantime, would you like something to drink? Coffee? Water?"

"Water would be great, thanks."

"No problem." He touched something on his desk and seconds later Florencia appeared.

"Two bottles of water please Flo."

Flo returned within seconds, handing me a plastic bottle of chilled water and then passing the other over to Macalister. After she left, we opened the bottles and I downed half of mine in two gulps while Macalister took careful sips of his. I was thirstier than I realized.

"The only place south of the border I know," I said, "is Mexico. I presume that like there, I should avoid drinking tap water."

"Right. Better safe than sorry."

Just then, the door behind me opened and I turned my head to see a stocky guy in his forties, dressed in a dark suit, enter the office.

"Hi Mike," Macalister said. "This is Clint Jackson. Clint, meet Mike Hogan, one of the FBI agents assigned to the embassy."

I rose from my seat and shook Hogan's extended hand. He had a firm grip and a no-nonsense look on his face. He had thick brown hair, cut to FBI regulations, and was broad through the neck and shoulders. He waved for me to sit back down and took the chair next to me and opposite Macalister, turning it so he could face both of us at the same time.

"Mike here has been leading the investigation into your sister's disappearance and I thought you should hear from him directly. Mike..."

I shifted in my chair so I could lock eyes with Hogan as he spoke to me. He cleared his throat and spoke with a raspy voice, asking me "What do you know about recent Peruvian history Clint?"

"Practically nothing," I replied, "like most Americans."

He smiled wryly, nodding his head. "Well, bear with me. To understand your sister's disappearance and our efforts to find her, you are going to need a brief history lesson. First, have you ever heard of *Sendero Luminoso?*"

"Shining Path? No, I don't think so."

"Well, let's start there. Shining Path was a homegrown terrorist organization that began in the Andes in the late seventies and early eighties and eventually moved down to threaten Lima. They used extreme violence to achieve their ends – bloody massacres, targeted assassinations, attacks on infrastructure, car bombs - you name it. By the early nineties they threatened to take over the entire country. In fact, the embassy was preparing to evacuate all U.S. citizens when the Peruvian government finally got the upper hand after capturing the supreme leader of *Sendero*, Abimael Guzmán. But the cost was terrible; tens of thousands of dead and much of the country in ruins. Since then, thankfully, things have stabilized and improved. Peruvian democracy still leaves a lot to be desired, but they have had a series of elected presidents and the economy, fueled by commodity exports, has boomed. But the memory of that time persists, like a psychic scar. And small bands of guerrillas still operate in the mountains and the jungle. Nothing like the threat of thirty years ago, but worrisome nonetheless."

"But what does this have to do with…"

He held up his hand. "Bear with me Clint. I'll get to the connection with your sister's disappearance in a moment."

"Okay. But you mentioned car bombs. My driver told me he couldn't park in front of the embassy because of that threat. Is that why this building seems like a fortress and all the security?"

"I'll let Charles answer that," Hogan said.

"You're right Clint. While the threat is not nearly what it was in the eighties and nineties, we are still a prime target. We used to be downtown, but outgrew the space and needed somewhere with more protection. Hence, what you see here. Not what we would prefer but it is what it is. And we are not alone. Back in the mid-nineties, another terrorist group occupied the embassy of Japan and held scores of important people hostage for weeks until the Peruvian special forces tunneled in and rescued them. After that, Japan built a brand-new embassy so fortified it would take a full-fledged military assault with tanks and mortars to breach it – and even then, it would be a tough go."

I nodded and thought again – *not in Kansas anymore!* "And what about drug-related violence? I met a guy on the plane down here who said it was pretty severe."

Hogan picked up the ball. "Yes, that's true. A lingering problem that's been troubling us and the Peruvians for decades. In the past, there were links between the political terrorists and the cartels. They are less important nowadays, but the cartels are still present and active and drug-related street crime is on the up-tick?"

"How about in Cajamarca?" I asked.

"Not a major problem – yet," Hogan said.

I reached for my water bottle sitting on Macalister's desk and took some swallows. Hogan continued his lecture.

"Here's another question for you Clint. What do you know about Lori Berenson?"

I drew a blank. "Nothing at all," wondering where all this was going.

"Lori Berenson was an idealistic and naïve young woman from the States who in the eighties fell into a romance with a member of one of the terrorist groups here. She wasn't exactly Patty Hearst, but she was an active participant in their violent activities. She was ultimately captured by the police, tried, convicted, and jailed for terrorism. She had a rough time of it in prison and her parents and friends in the States applied a lot of pressure on us to try to get her released and returned. It put us in a very tough spot. We wanted to help out an American citizen in trouble, but the Peruvian government – and public – was not at all sympathetic. She ultimately was released from prison and put under house arrest, but her case remains a touchy issue between us and the Peruvian government up to this day."

I was embarrassed to ask who in the hell was Patty Hearst, but didn't want to display any more of my ignorance. "So again," I said, "what's the connection? Are you implying that my sister has gone underground with some terrorist group? That's absurd. I know Mel and…"

Hogan again held up his hand. Exchanging looks with Macalister, he said, "No Clint. That's not what *we* are implying. That's what the local authorities in Cajamarca are suggesting."

I was getting angry. "Well that's just absurd. We need to go there and get them straightened out. What evidence do they have? What the hell is going on?" I could feel myself on the edge of pounding the desk and demanding we send a squad of Marines to Cajamarca, if necessary, to get things straight. I took a deep breath and tried to control my temper.

Hogan looked at me sympathetically. "I can appreciate your anger and frustration Clint. From all we know we don't think your sister has pulled a Berenson, *but* we also don't have all the facts. There's a slim possibility, and only that, that there might be something to it. We just can't dismiss it out of hand until we have all the facts."

I was clenching and unclenching my fists. I was tempted to lash out but realized that would be the ultimate stupidity. Hogan was just giving me the facts. I envisioned Jack Nicholson yelling at me that I couldn't handle the truth.

"Well," I said, trying to keep the anger from my voice, "why don't we go and get the facts?"

Again, the exchange of looks. This time Macalister responded. "Well, Clint. That's more complicated than it seems. Very complicated, in fact. The regional governor of Cajamarca, who has almost absolute control, is a radical leftist who is profoundly anti-U.S. and allied philosophically with Cuba and Venezuela."

Despite not paying much attention to the news, I had some inkling of what that meant. I also remembered John telling me something the State Department had told him about the governor.

"When we got in touch with him about your sister's disappearance, he was immediately dismissive and suggested that we had some ulterior motive in asking his permission to investigate the matter. He made it clear that we would not be welcome and he would not lift a finger to help. He did, however, give us the name of a local police inspector who could look into the matter for us. We contacted him and he promised to find out what he could. He got back to us a couple of days later and what he told us was not good news. He claimed to have spoken with your sister's colleagues, who told him that she had established a romantic relationship with a local university student with leftist sympathies and had run off with him. In other words..." I interrupted. "In other words, the Lori Berenson scenario."

He looked at me with a dour expression on his face. "Yes. I'm afraid so."

"I don't buy it," I said. "That doesn't sound like my sister. She is not impulsive," *like me.* "I cannot imagine her doing something so rash and out of character. And even in the most unlikely case she did, she would somehow let us know she was all right and not to worry."

Macalister viewed me skeptically. "Look Clint. We know that you and your family are suffering right now. But when was the last time you were in close touch with your sister? Maybe she changed. Maybe she's like a lot of young Americans who come to Latin America and are appalled by the poverty they see and want to do something about it, maybe even to the point of supporting revolutionary solutions. Believe me, it happens a lot more than you might think. Then she meets some charming and committed leftist guy and goes the whole nine yards. It's not impossible. We have to look at all angles."

I tried to control my anger. "That might be true. But Mel is too level-headed to do such a thing. And under no circumstances would she put our family through such anguish."

But in the back of my mind there was a nagging doubt. Mel had been distant over the past few years and, even though I didn't want to admit it, maybe Macalister had a point. Then I thought of something. "What about the Ingrid Betancourt scenario? What if Mel has been kidnapped and is being held hostage for future leverage. That might explain why we haven't gotten any ransom demands."

They both looked surprised. "How do you know about Ingrid Betancourt?" Hogan asked.

I was about to reveal my conversation with Blake Anderson but thought better of it. He had made it clear he needed to maintain a low profile while in Lima and I didn't want to get him into some kind of bureaucratic entanglement. "John had mentioned it to me as a possibility," I lied.

Hogan looked skeptical. "Well, it's not totally out of the realm of possibility, but not very probable. As I said, Cajamarca is not a major center of drug trafficking and it's unlikely that if there were any gangs around, they would target your sister for kidnapping."

Macalister chimed in. "Yes, unlikely. But still worth checking out." Then he shifted gears. "Here's another possibility. What if her disappearance had nothing at all to do with politics or drugs? What if she and this local university student decided to run off and get married? Maybe his parents disapproved of him marrying a gringa so they had to skedaddle to some other place to get hitched? And maybe they are off on a honeymoon in some remote location in the Andes and Mel has not been able to contact you?"

That seemed even more off-the-wall than the other scenarios, but I simply nodded. Far-fetched, yes. But again, not entirely impossible. Meanwhile, I was getting antsy. "Look gentlemen," I said. "We can sit here all day discussing possible scenarios. But the clock is ticking. We need to get to Cajamarca to pick up the trail, and the sooner the better."

Macalister shifted uneasily in his chair and cleared his throat. *Here it comes,* I thought to myself. "Well Clint. Here's the story. The governor in Cajamarca has made it crystal clear that embassy staff are not welcome in his bailiwick. Even if the ambassador defied the governor and let us send a team to Cajamarca with you, it could well make things even worse, especially if the Lori Berenson scenario is a possibility. That is still an extremely sensitive issue. Even though the governor is a leftist and theoretically might be sympathetic to someone committed to his way of thinking, he is also a nationalist more than ready to play the anti-American card." He saw my face fall. "I know this is a disappointment, but here we have to look at the bigger picture."

I sat back in my chair, momentarily stunned but not totally surprised. John and Blake Anderson had warned me the embassy might not be helpful and they had been right. *The bigger picture!* What a load of crap! But what could I do? I had no cards to play.

"Then I'm on my own," I said, trying to keep the bitterness out of my voice.

"I'm afraid so," Macalister said. "Our hands are tied."

"Well, can you at least give me the name of the university student Mel supposedly has a relationship with. I can try to track him down. Has anybody tried to reach him?"

Hogan responded, shaking his head. "We have only had contact with the local police investigator." Reaching into his shirt pocket, he dug out a card. "Here is his name and contact information. When you get to Cajamarca, you can look him up. But a warning; he probably won't be very helpful. He wouldn't give us the name of your sister's local boyfriend, citing privacy issues. And he clearly did not extend himself to gather information when we asked him to look into the disappearance. I'm not sure whether he's lazy or just following orders from higher-up, or both. But his reluctance to carry out a thorough investigation was palpable. Maybe meeting him face-to-face will produce better results, but I wouldn't get my hopes up."

Wonderful. What encouraging words. But again, like it or not, Hogan was giving me the hard facts and if I were to be successful, I needed to

117

hear them. I glanced at the card: *Felipe Calderón, Inspector de la Policía Provincial,* along with an address and phone number. I tucked it into my pocket to add to my growing collection.

I struggled to control my growing anger and frustration. I felt like ripping into both of them. *You guys are the professionals. It's your job to help Americans abroad who are in trouble. And you are leaving it up to me? Some flawed guy who doesn't know the country and who never has had to deal with a situation like this? Come on!* But then I remembered some advice from the therapist my father forced me to see. Try to take your anger and frustration and turn it into something positive. I thought it was bullshit at the time but right now it seemed spot on. *What good would it do to explode?* It would just make things worse. I needed to grow up. No more temper tantrums. The stakes were too high. And if I had to deal with the situation on my own, so be it.

I grabbed the water bottle and drained it. Putting the empty back onto Macalister's desk, I said, "I see the bind you guys are in," still not sure I bought their excuses. "Unless there's something else, I'd better get going."

Macalister nodded and got up to see me out. Hogan rose, shook my hand, and wished me luck. Macalister put his hand on my back as he led me to door. Resisting the temptation to brush it off, I turned and we shook hands. "Sorry we can't be of more help Clint. Keep in touch and let us know how things go."

I chocked back the smart remark that was on my lips and said, "I'll do that." Then, unable to resist the dig I added sarcastically "And thanks for all the help."

His expression remained stolid and he shut the door behind me without another word. I would have loved to eavesdrop on the conversation between Macalister and Hogan after I was gone. Did they shake their heads in remorse and regret that they couldn't do more? Or did they heave sighs of relief that one more problem had been taken care of? In the last analysis, of course, what difference did it make? It was up to me to carry the ball and to accept the kind of responsibility that I had avoided most of my life. In some strange way, I was looking forward to the challenge.

Twenty-One

I GOT BACK TO THE Sheraton at around four thirty. During the ride from the embassy, I told Manuel that I hoped to be in Cajamarca the next day. He gave me some suggestions about the city and warned me that I should be careful upon arriving to take it easy since the altitude was at about 7500 feet. He also asked me to call him when I got my flight details so he could drive me to the airport. I thanked him and gave him a generous tip on top of what seemed to me a pretty reasonable fee.

At the desk, I asked the concierge to book me on the next flight to Cajamarca as well as a hotel. He promised to call me in my room when it had been arranged.

Back in my room, I immediately called my brother on the cell-phone he had given me to up-date him on recent developments. He answered on the second ring. "Hey Clint. How are you? How are things going? Any news about Mel?"

I spent about five minutes recapping my conversation with Macalister and Hogan. He didn't interrupt but I could hear gasps of exasperation as I spun the story.

When I had finished, he exploded: "What a couple of jerks! Kind of what I expected. Sorry to have you in this spot Bro. I was hoping they would be more help." Then he added, "Listen. Try to get in touch with my buddy Lamar Jenkins. He's a real straight shooter and won't give you any of that bureaucratic bullshit."

"Thanks John. I'll do that."

"So tomorrow you'll be in Cajamarca. That's great, but watch your step. I don't like the sound of the situation there. You may be on very unfriendly turf." Then, with a catch in his voice, he said "Take care of yourself Bro. And keep me posted."

"Will do John. Call you tomorrow."

Seconds later, the house phone rang. The concierge said my ticket for the 8 am flight to Cajamarca was on its way up to my room along with the hotel reservation. Two minutes later, there was a knock on my door and a bellboy was there with my ticket. I called Manuel and asked him to pick me up in the morning for my ride to the airport.

With that confirmed, I dialed the number for Lamar Jenkins John had given me. The phone rang for some seconds with no answer – and no prompt to voice mail. Finally, I heard a voice on the other end utter a cautious "Hello," and then with a hint of suspicion, "Who's this?"

"Hi Lamar. It's Clint Jackson, John's brother."

"Hey. Good to hear from you Clint. John said you might try to get in touch. I presume you are in Lima." He spoke with a decided southern drawl.

"Yes. But not for long. I leave for Cajamarca tomorrow to look for my missing sister."

"I figured you would. John told me what had happened to her. Any way I can help?"

I filled him in on my conversation at the embassy. I could hear him mutter "assholes" under his breath. A man after my own heart. "So," I finished, "I'm going it alone. Any advice?"

"I can offer more than that. But before I do, let me add some context as to what you might run into in Cajamarca. The embassy guys could have been more helpful, but they are right that things are complicated there. Right now, it's the center of major protests over the rights to a gold-mining operation near two lakes outside of the capital. Indigenous groups are arguing that the land involved is theirs. They and environmental activists are warning about the polluting effects both above ground and underground. In the meantime, the governor is stirring the pot for his own purposes. He is siding with the protestors to bolster his claim to be 'a man of the people,' while more quietly playing cozy with the mining companies who will bring jobs and money to the region. My guess is, based on past experience, that his Marxist posturing notwithstanding, he is expecting to benefit personally from whatever contracts are ultimately signed. I've been involved in the mining business here, mostly copper and natural gas, for about five years and seen that dynamic operate more than once. And when you're talking gold mining, you're talking really big bucks. There already is a large gold mine in Cajamarca, Yanacocha, that has been in operation for some time and has churned out billions in profits. I don't know if any of this has to do with your sister's disappearance. But it's useful information to have."

"Thanks, Lamar," I said. "I appreciate it. I really am flying blind here and every bit helps."

He paused for a minute, and I pictured him debating what to say next. "Listen, Clint. We have guys on our payroll who are experts in things like kidnappings and hostage rescue. Part of doing business in this part of the world. I'll need to check with my boss, but I think I can get him to agree to send a couple of these guys to Cajamarca to help you out. Where are you staying?"

I opened the packet with my reservations and pulled out the voucher for the Hotel Costa del Sol, located on the main square. I relayed this information to Lamar. "Okay Clint. Got it. And I have your cell-phone info. I'll give you a call tomorrow. I can't promise anything, but I think I can convince my boss to help you out."

"Lamar, if you can get them to help me, that would be great, just great."

"Glad to be of assistance Clint," he said. "And how is John doing? Is he holding up okay?"

"He's hanging in there, but is under a lot of stress." I didn't elaborate. No sense going into the gory details as to why I was in Peru looking for Mel instead of my brother.

"Well, I hope things work out," Lamar said. "John is a good friend and I hope y'all can find your sister and put this behind you."

"Thanks Lamar. I'll look forward to hearing from you tomorrow."

"No problem. I'll be in touch," and we ended the call.

I was encouraged by Jenkins' promise to get me some help. I certainly needed it, especially after the disappointment of the embassy's response.

It was almost six o'clock and I was suddenly starving. The hamburger and fries had tided me over through a rough afternoon. But now I needed something more substantial. I thought about eating in the hotel but decided I might try something more adventuresome and hunt out a restaurant that specialized in the local cuisine.

Grabbing my cap and my jacket, I took the elevator down to the lobby. Luckily, my buddy Mario was still on duty. I asked him for a recommendation. He responded quickly. "You should try the Restaurant José Antonio in Magdalena del Mar. It's very popular with natives and tourists alike. It's about a half hour from here, depending on the traffic."

"That sounds great Mario. Just what I'm looking for."

We went to the door and he signaled for a taxi. As he opened the door for me to exit, he added "There are lots of taxis at the restaurant waiting for passengers. You shouldn't have any trouble getting back to the hotel."

I thanked him and slipped him a ten *sol* note that he gratefully pocketed.

The traffic was the usual nightmare. But my driver got me to our destination within the estimated half hour by taking a route that involved so many twists and turns, sudden accelerations, sudden braking, and near misses that I considered it a minor miracle we arrived at all. He assured me that there was nothing unusual about the experience and noted with pride that so far, after years of maneuvering through Lima's traffic, his vehicle had nary a scratch.

The restaurant was in a kind of cul-de-sac off a main avenue, surrounded by commercial and residential buildings. It had a red-tile roof and white stucco walls with a Spanish colonial feel to it. When I entered through the heavy oak door, the maitre'd' greeted me with a welcoming smile and led me to a table for two in a back corner. It was, I assumed, a bit early for locals to have dinner, but there was a smattering of foreign tourists babbling in various languages at the surrounding tables.

When the waiter took my order, I chose a dish that included two out of three of the items the guys in the barbershop had recommended: *ceviche* and *anticuchos*. Guinea pig was not on the menu, and even if it had been, that was a step too far for me. The side dishes were potatoes *and* rice, which the waiter assured me was typical of Peruvian meals. When he asked what I would like to drink, I was sorely tempted to try the much-heralded *pisco sour. Just one wouldn't hurt, would it? Yeah, right,* my little voice said in a familiar refrain, *followed by a steady succession that would leave you sloshed.* I had an early flight in the morning and could not afford to be fighting a hangover. I told the waiter just water. *Wow,* the little voice said, *almost twenty-four hours without a drink! Way to go guy!* Enough with the self-pity. One step at a time.

When the food arrived, I attacked it eagerly. It was all delicious. The reviews had been right. I cleaned my plate and then ordered dessert, a slice of *pio no-no,* a kind of sponge cake with caramel, and an espresso coffee. I paid with John's credit card, promising myself that I would reimburse him, and headed back to the Sheraton. At the hotel, I hit the sack at the ungodly hour of nine o'clock. I was exhausted and keyed-up at the same time. As I began to unspool the events of the past two days in my mind, exhaustion prevailed and I fell into a deep sleep, the first in many years that had not been preceded by copious amounts of alcohol.

Twenty-Two

OUR *LAN PERU* FLIGHT began its descent into the Cajamarca airport at a quarter to nine. I had a window seat and could see the intermontane valley in which the city was located unfold below me. A bright sun and brilliant blue sky, a welcome relief from the cloudy gloom of Lima, highlighted the green and gold landscape below that reminded me of California. Most of my fellow passengers were dark-skinned Peruvians with a smattering of foreign tourists mixed in.

The flight had taken a little less than an hour. Manuel, who had driven me to the Lima airport, told me that going by land would have taken at least twelve hours, climbing the steep peaks of the Andes over winding roads. A beautiful scenic trip, if sometimes white-knuckled, but one I did not have time for.

I stepped off the plane into the blinding sunlight and immediately felt a chill breeze. When my duffel arrived, I immediately pulled out my leather jacket and shrugged it on. I did not feel light-headed but could tell that the air, while cleaner than Lima's, was also lighter.

There was a line of taxis waiting and I took the first one in the queue. I directed the driver to my hotel, which he informed me was only ten or fifteen minutes away. Manuel had told me that the population of Cajamarca, which had nearly doubled over the past decade, was still only about two hundred thousand. Many of the streets were narrow, but there was nothing like the traffic, noise, and confusion of Lima. Along the way, my driver asked the usual questions, including what brought me to Cajamarca? "Tourism," I replied, even though business might have been closer to the truth: the business of finding what had happened to my sister. To my ear, the driver's Spanish seemed a little halting, probably because his first language was the Indigenous Quechua. Another bit of information Manuel had provided.

As promised, after ten minutes of driving through the narrow streets of the city, we arrived at the Hotel Costa del Sol. My driver insisted on carrying my duffel up to the hotel lobby. I would have preferred doing it myself, but he told me that recent arrivals often experience light-headedness and it was best not to over-exert myself. I felt fine, but didn't see any sense in making an issue of it. He led me into the lobby and to the reception desk. We had negotiated the fare before leaving the airport, which Manuel assured me was the custom when taking a street taxi. After the driver had deposited my duffel, I gave him the agreed-on amount along with a generous tip. Manuel had also told me that tipping was not as nearly as common a practice as in the States, but to me the amounts involved were trivial and I figured it was one gringo custom I could adhere to.

When I checked in, the clerk informed me that while my reservation was okay, my room was not yet ready for occupancy. I would have to wait until noon. In the meantime, I could check my duffel and place my valuables in the hotel safe. I checked the bag, but kept most of my valuables and my backpack. In Lima, I had purchased a money-belt for my cash as well as a cloth holder around my neck for my passport, which I tucked under my shirt and sweater after showing it to the desk clerk. However, I handed over my wallet for safe-keeping. Even if Cajamarca was not Lima, I assumed that pick-pockets were a problem, especially in the narrow streets.

After these matters were resolved, the clerk suggested I have some complimentary coca tea available in the lobby. "It's a good remedy for altitude sickness," he said with a knowing smile. I still felt fine, but decided to follow his advice. After preparing a cup with plenty of sugar, I took a seat and began to sip the brew. Not bad. From what I had read in a travel magazine on the plane, *té de coca* had been an Andean staple for centuries. Much of the Indigenous highland population not only drank the tea but chewed the leaf to deal with the altitude. So, some actual health benefits beyond getting stoned.

When I finished my tea, I decided to get moving. I couldn't just wait around the lobby until my room was ready. I had too much to do and time was precious.

Shrugging on my jacket, I slung my backpack over my shoulder and headed out into the street. The first thing I had to do was go to the site where Mel had been working. John had told me that it was about fifteen miles southwest of the city, higher up in the Andes. He also had provided the name of the professor in charge of the project, Jeremy Cartwright.

Outside, there were several taxis waiting patiently for passengers. I spotted the same one that had driven me from the airport and headed toward it. The driver, whose name was Daniel, got out of his car to greet me with a smile. "Good morning again, Señor. Where can I take you?" When I told him my destination, he nodded in recognition. "Where the young *norteamericanos* are working. I know the place." We negotiated a price that seemed more than reasonable. It covered the trip to the site, wait time, and the trip back.

I got in and we began to navigate our way out of the city. Soon, we were on a narrow, paved road that headed up the mountains to our west. There were plenty of twists and turns and the engine of Daniel's beat-up sedan groaned as we ascended the incline. Where we were going was an area more than 12,000 feet above sea level and I began to feel a slight shortness of breath. The air was still crystal clear and the sky a deep blue. Looking back during one of the turns, I got a spectacular view of the city of Cajamarca and its surroundings.

After half an hour of steady climbing, we reached a place called Cumbe Mayo. Daniel explained that it was a major tourist attraction containing interesting pre-Incan ruins and striking natural rock formations. When he asked if I wanted to visit, I demurred. Under normal circumstances, I would have agreed. But the circumstances were not normal and I had more important things to do.

About a mile past Cumbe Mayo, we turned onto a gravel road that led us even higher into the mountains. Soon, the gravel gave way to dirt and we slowed. Daniel navigated as best he could to avoid the numerous pot holes. He wasn't always successful and we bounced around quite a bit and I worried about what the rough ride would do to his already shaky suspension.

By this time, I felt a slight headache forming and some queasiness in my stomach. Luckily, I had stashed a couple of water bottles in my backpack. I took one out and began to quench my thirst, immediately feeling better.

After about twenty minutes of bumps and rattles, we arrived at our destination. "Here we are Señor Jackson," Daniel said as he parked in a cleared area near a dust-covered jeep and a battered pick-up truck. "I'll wait for you here."

"Thanks Daniel. I don't know how long I'll be, so make yourself comfortable."

"No problem Señor. I'll be waiting right here for you. Don't worry."

Getting out of the car, I had a brief moment of dizziness. I steadied myself with deep breaths and took more swallows from my water bottle.

Stretched in front of me was a large plain, mostly bereft of vegetation aside from some bushes and tufts of brown grass. In the distance, I could see some rock formations. Further on, the mountains rose up like a massive barrier. If I was at about 14,000 feet already, the peaks ahead must reach 20,000.

There was a beaten path that led from the parking area westward, where I would find the archaeological dig. I was tempted to hurry along but my body said "hold it." No sense risking a dizzy spell and maybe passing out. After five minutes of carefully-paced walking, I came upon a campground with half a dozen tents arranged in a semi-circle around a fire pit. To one side was a canvas cover attached to eight-foot poles at the four corners. Underneath were a rough wooden table and a cluster of folding chairs. I assumed that was where the group had its meals. As I approached the camp, I saw that it was empty, not a soul in sight. The team, I assumed, was further on, working the site.

I paused for a moment to catch my breath. Looking at the tents, I wondered which one was Mel's. There was the possibility that since she had gone missing, they had packed it up. But my gut told me that it was still there, awaiting her return.

The whole scene was spooky and a little unreal. I scanned my surroundings and looked up at the sky, where I saw some large birds circling in lazy fashion. I wondered if they were condors, native to the region, but couldn't tell from a distance. The only sounds I heard were some insects chirping and the wind whistling.

I tried to imagine what it was like for Mel to be at a place like this, almost another world. Of course, she had her friends and her work to keep her busy and was used to working in remote locations. But still...."

Just then, I heard some indistinct voices in the distance and headed along the path in their direction. About a hundred yards on, after passing through a passage-way between massive slate-gray boulders, I saw the digging site ahead. It looked almost like a construction zone before the foundation was poured. The entire area was about thirty yards by thirty, divided into separate lots marked off with stakes, cords, and bright-colored ribbons fluttering in the breeze. There were piles of dirt and rocks at the sides of the holes from which the voices I had heard emanated. At each lot there were an array of digging tools along with tripods containing surveying gear and cameras. It all looked quite professional and well-organized. To my immediate right was a large silver trailer with an extended awning. Just how they managed to get a trailer to this location was something of a mystery. They certainly couldn't have squeezed it through the narrow passage-way by which I had entered. A mystery for another time. I had a more serious and immediate mystery to untangle.

As I was about to head for the trailer, where, I assumed, I would find Professor Cartwright, I heard a voice behind me say in an authoritative tone, "Stop where you are and turn around."

I did as I was told, finding myself confronting a Peruvian in uniform with a holstered sidearm and, more disturbingly, an automatic weapon on a sling over his shoulder. He wasn't aiming it directly at me, but he had his finger on the trigger ready to fire. We were less than a yard apart and he couldn't miss.

Recovering from the shock, I stood still and raised my hands to shoulder level, palms out. He looked at me with suspicion and still kept his finger on the trigger.

"Who are you? What are you doing here? Don't you know this is a restricted area? No visitors allowed."

I did my best to keep calm. "My name is Clint Jackson," I said. "And I'm here to find out what happened to my sister Mel, who was working at this site and disappeared about a week ago. I need to speak to Professor Cartwright to find out what happened to her."

His expression changed from hostile to sympathetic. Much to my relief, he took his finger off the trigger. "Sorry Señor Jackson. I was just doing my duty. No one told me you were coming."

I heard footsteps behind me. "It's all right Gustavo." A reassuring voice said, "Señor Jackson is most welcome here."

"Sorry Professor. I was just following procedure."

"I know Gustavo. I know."

It now seemed safe to turn around without risking a bullet in the back. Facing me was a much friendlier face. Cartwright was a trim and fit guy I judged to be in his fifties. He had a full head of black hair, graying at the temples, and a full beard. He was dressed in jeans, a flannel shirt covered with a fleece vest, and work boots. He extended his hand, "Clint, is it? Jeremy Cartwright here. Pleased to meet you, although I wish it were under more pleasant circumstances."

Where had I heard that before? "Same here," I replied.

"Sorry for the unfriendly welcome. We thought it was likely that some family member might show up looking for Mel, but we didn't have any prior notice. The embassy, I'm afraid, really has not been helpful. I don't think the ambassador wanted us here in the first place. And now that your sister has gone missing, probably sees us as more trouble than we're worth." He shook his head ruefully. "But enough about that. Come on over to the trailer and we'll talk."

I followed him to the trailer, which I presumed to be the command center for the operation. Under the awning, there was a wooden table similar to the one I had seen at the campground with the same kind of folding chairs. Along the side of the trailer was a long bench, which contained some tools along with shards of ancient pottery and parts of bones.

"Have a seat," Cartwright said. "How about some coca tea? You look like you need it."

Just two days ago, I would have said, "I really need something stronger." But the thought barely crossed my mind.

"Coca tea sounds great."

"We live on the stuff up here," Cartwright said, as he poured some hot water from a thermos into a tin cup with the coca leaves floating on the surface. I added a spoonful of sugar from a jar on the table and began to sip, almost immediately feeling better.

"Don't rat me out," Cartwright said with a conspiratorial smile, "But I let some of the kids chew the leaves. They burn up a lot of energy at this site and getting a direct infusion of coca helps. Not an issue up here, but it would probably freak out the embassy and maybe even some of the parents. And, if I thought it might become a habit, I'd stop it," he said, anticipating a question I had on my lips. I wondered, too, if Mel had taken up the custom. But if so, we had bigger fish to fry.

Even though it was early in the day, Cartwright looked tired. There were worry lines on his face and his gray eyes drooped. He rubbed them and then stifled a yawn. "Sorry," he said. "I haven't been getting much sleep lately." He let out a sigh. "I've been working on sites like these throughout the Andes for about thirty years, first as a student and then as a professor taking the lead. I've had kids get sick. I've had them suffer broken bones. A few of them got bored and lonely and quit in the middle. But I've never had one just go missing. We're all devastated by your sister's disappearance. Everybody loved Mel. She was – is – a joy to work with." Tears began to form, and he wiped them away.

I just nodded. I wasn't surprised. Mel *was – is* special. I didn't want to think of her in the past tense either.

Recovering, he continued. "Frankly, after a couple of days and no sign of Mel, I considered shutting the whole operation down. Close up business. I probably would have, but the kids convinced me that was the last thing Mel would have wanted. We've all gone to too much trouble and put too much effort into the project to give up now. But I still have my doubts. It somehow doesn't seem right to me to go on and just ignore that one of my kids isn't here."

"Well, for whatever it's worth, knowing my sister I think your students are right. It's what she would want."

"Thanks for that Clint. That helps a lot."

"What do you think happened to her, professor? I've been hearing a lot of theories, none of which seem very plausible to me right now. Yesterday, at the embassy, two guys there suggested what they called the "Lori Berenson scenario." That somehow Mel had fallen in with a left-wing guerrilla group and had run off to join their ranks."

I knew I didn't have to explain what that name meant to the professor. He nodded in recognition but looked skeptical. "Well, I suppose nothing is impossible, but I saw no hint of that in Mel or any of the others." He took a pause, "They know why they are here and the commitment they have to make to their work. They have been warned in no uncertain terms *not* to get involved in local politics. And as far as I know, they haven't." He looked up at the sky, then back to me. "But I'm not with them all the time. They take breaks and go to Cajamarca on their own. They have some favorite bars and restaurants there and I'm sure they do some of the normal stuff college students do in their free time. Several sleep in later than usual after those visits to the city."

He again looked up at the sky, as if for inspiration. Then leveled his gaze. "Even though they are strictly prohibited from any involvement in local politics - no meetings, no demonstrations, not even signing petitions – they have their political sympathies. From what I can gather, all six of them, including your sister, are on the left of the spectrum. And as anthropology students, they have a natural interest in environmental issues and matters related to Indigenous rights, both pretty hot topics around here."

"I know. The embassy guys filled me in."

"So, it doesn't take much imagination to think that during those social trips to town, they meet up with Peruvian contemporaries who were deeply involved in these issues and probably expressed their sympathies and support. But, actually getting involved, going to the extreme of joining up with some left-wing eco-warriors or even Marxist-inspired groups á-la Lori Berenson seems too much of a stretch. Especially for Mel, who I consider among the most level-headed in the group. But," he added with a shrug, "I couldn't say with one hundred percent certainty that is totally out of the question either."

I nodded my understanding. "Besides meeting with young Peruvians in town," I said, "I understand that some local university students have worked at the site. At the embassy, they told me that Mel had become especially friendly with one of the young men, friendly to the point she might have run off with him without informing anyone."

Cartwright gave a slight smile and shook his head dismissively. "I really doubt that one. We do have local anthropology graduate students join us about once a week to help with the dig, part of our community outreach. They seem like nice kids, thrilled to be involved in a project that is of particular local interest and importance and eager to become familiar with the advanced technology tools we have. But I've seen no signs of any romantic attachments being formed." Then, scratching the back of his hand, he added, "I'm pretty close to the kids. However, I sure don't know everything they are thinking and doing 24/7. Maybe you should talk with them when they take a break in…" glancing at his watch "…about thirty minutes from now. I'll make myself scarce and you can talk to them freely. They may have some helpful insights that they don't necessarily want me to hear. And they would know more about the romance angle than an aging bachelor like me, married to his work."

"Thanks. I appreciate that. I would like to speak with them. And that reminds me. One of the things that popped into my mind when I got the news that Mel was missing was the possibility that there was some bad blood in the group. I hate to say it, but maybe one of the team had a hand in her disappearance."

He looked taken aback, then recovered. "I can see why, from afar and with the shock, you might think that. But I saw absolutely no signs of that. Of course, they are competitive and highly-motivated, some even high-strung. And, in a situation like this, where they are together all the time in a constricted environment, there are bound to be some frictions and petty annoyances that are blown out of proportion. In fact, I had to disband a project once because the internal tensions got out of hand. But that has definitely not been the case here. They all seem to like each other, enjoy working together as a team, and have shown no telltale signs of disharmony. After decades in this business, I've gotten pretty good at reading the signs and gauging the emotional temperature of the team working on my projects. But again, maybe this is something you should try to bring up when you meet with them. It'll be a bit touchy, but you might get a different temperature reading than I do. Maybe you'll pick up a vibe I've missed."

"I'll do that," I said.

We then moved on to the Ingrid Betancourt scenario. Again, I didn't have to explain the name. "Not very likely," he said. "There is no major drug activity here and I keep my ear pretty finely-tuned to what's happening locally. Besides, there were no signs that Mel had been forcibly removed from the camp. It looks as though she left on her own. Her tent, when we looked inside, was, as usual, neat as a pin. The only thing missing was her parka. If she had been planning on leaving for good, she would have packed more gear."

I mulled that over for a few seconds. "No signs of a plain, straightforward kidnapping either?"

"Nope. Have you received any ransom demands?"

"Not as of this morning." I took out my phone and turned it on. As I expected, no service. It was possible that John might have called to let me know that he had heard from kidnappers. But the odds seemed long and I returned my momentarily useless phone to my pocket.

Cartwright's concerns seemed genuine and was a likeable guy. Maybe a little full of himself, like most academics, but also down-to-earth and no-nonsense, at least from what I could tell. Maybe his students had a different opinion. I'd find out. So far, he hadn't done much to bolster my spirits or offer any clues for avenues I might pursue.

He sensed my frustration. "Clint. I know this is a terrible situation for you. I wish I could be of more help, but I'm as stumped as you are. If it's any consolation, and it probably isn't, Cornell is applying as much pressure on the State Department as it can to get to the bottom of Mel's disappearance. Our congressional liaisons are also demanding action. But…"

"I appreciate the efforts," I interrupted. "But after my talk with the embassy guys yesterday, I'm not expecting help from any officials. They are going to sit on their hands and cover their asses," I said bitterly.

Cartwright chuckled. "A lovely image. You are undoubtedly right. More tea?"

"Sure. Thanks," I said, extending my cup. He put in some fresh leaves, poured in the hot water, and handed the cup over for me to add the sugar. He then did the same for his own cup.

We remained silent for a time, sipping our tea. "I'm not surprised by the embassy's lack of action," he said, putting his cup down. "I have to deal with them a lot as part of this project," he said, waving toward the site. In the background, I could hear the mutter of low voices as the team went about their chores. It was, I thought, almost like being at grave site with mysterious sounds coming from the holes in the ground. And, looking at some of the bones on the bench next to the trailer, maybe it literally was a kind of cemetery. "And they have not been particularly helpful."

He settled back in the chair. "The ambassador is a political appointee, not a career man. He's new to the job and doesn't seem to have a firm grasp of what it entails. Nor does he understand much about Peru. To top it off, he hasn't learned Spanish and shows no inclination of trying to learn." Cartwright's face showed his disapproval. "But he *does* understand politics. What do you know about the political situation here in Cajamarca?"

I told him what Macalister and Hogan had told me. "That's the gist of it, Clint. And the ambassador doesn't know what to do. He can't abide the governor, but knows he has to deal with him to protect and promote U.S. interests here. And that means mining interests, which are the most prominent. So, that translates into 'don't rock the boat.' If the governor says stay out, even if it means not trying to find out what happened to a missing American citizen, then that is what the ambassador is going to do. I'm sorry, but that's the way it is."

What he said came as no surprise, but it did nothing to lift my spirits.

"I've had my own problems with the governor."

"How so?"

That look into the sky again, then back to me. "I hope I don't bore you with the story, but it will help put you into the picture here."

"Sure. Go ahead," I said, figuring the more information I could gather the better.

"I had been working at Cumbe Mayo down the road," he nodded in a southerly direction, "for about five years. One day, a Peruvian colleague told me he had heard about a site several kilometers to the north that Indigenous sources told him might have antedated where we were currently working. I immediately checked it out and saw signs that it might be a promising place to investigate. After some preliminary survey work using drones and infra-red technology, we thought that the site you see here was worth a deeper look. But you can't just start turning the earth. You have to get permission, first from the national government, then from the locals. It can be a lengthy and laborious process, sometimes moved along with some inducements." He rubbed his forefinger and thumb together and I got the message: some cash to grease the wheels.

"It's a pain for researchers. But you can understand the Peruvian point of view. This is their land and their patrimony. They appreciate the foreign interest in their culture and the advanced tools they can bring to any archaeological project. But they want to keep tight control. They've been ripped off too often in the past and don't want history to repeat itself."

He shifted in his chair. "Have you heard of Hiram Bingham?"

I shook my head and Cartwright looked a bit surprised. Presumably, this Bingham character was somebody any well-informed individual would be familiar with. Well, I'm afraid I didn't qualify.

"Hiram Bingham was an American who in the early twentieth century 'discovered' Machu Picchu."

"That, I've heard of."

Cartwright chuckled. "Well, Bingham deserves a lot of credit for the discovery. Or more precisely, 're-discovery' since locals had known of the site for some time. But Bingham was a glory hog and didn't do much to acknowledge the help he had gotten from several Peruvians. More seriously, he took back to the States many of the precious artifacts he had found and donated them to the Library at Yale, where he was teaching. Recently, the Peruvian government has demanded these items be returned and some of them have been. They are not only culturally important but have significant monetary value. The same sort of dynamic is at play in various other countries around the globe who feel that archaeologists, explorers, colonial officials, and just plain tourists have robbed them of their cultural heritage. They have tried in recent years to stem the flow through tighter customs controls but a lot of the trade continues."

This was all interesting, but I wondered what it had to do with Mel's disappearance. Cartwright read my impatience. "Bear with me Clint.

This may be helpful information, or maybe not. We'll see. At any rate, anyone involved in a project like this has to jump through numerous hoops. Getting permission from the national authorities went pretty smoothly. I had gotten it many times before, had the right contacts, and knew what buttons to push." I wondered if that included "knowing the right palms to grease" as well.

"But getting permission from the local governor was a different story. He is adamantly anti-American and…"

I interrupted: "Yeah, the embassy guys gave me the picture."

"Yeah. A real tough nut to deal with. At first, he didn't even want to allow us to set foot in his territory much less begin operating an archaeological site. I don't know how much his reaction had to do with a genuine nationalist position and how much to do with political posturing, but it left me in a bind. I had already done the preparatory work and assembled the team. I also am absolutely convinced that this is a valuable enterprise, one that will make an important contribution to our knowledge of the pre-Incan world."

He paused for a moment. "Sorry, Clint. That probably sounds pompous and self-important, doesn't it? A common academic affliction. But I sincerely believe it."

I smiled. I could see how Cartwright could be an effective leader of his young team. He was committed and passionate. He almost had me ready to volunteer and start digging.

"So, I wasn't about to give up. As I said, I had worked at Cumbe Mayo and as a result had a lot of contacts with Cajamarca archaeologists and anthropologists along with some local officials. I prevailed on them to intercede on my behalf and they were able to arrange a meeting for me with the governor." He looked up at the sky in the by-now familiar manner. "Not the most pleasant encounter I've ever had. He was hostile, suspicious, and all-around unpleasant. He harangued me about Yankee Imperialism in a ten-minute rant, trying to get my goat. I kept my cool and let him wear himself out. When I had a chance, I laid out my case, stressing the advantages we had in terms of technology and expertise to make the most of our dig and promising to coordinate as much as possible with my Cajamarca colleagues. I tried to stress that what we were doing was of international significance. And, laying it on a bit thick, I argued our site might become as much of a tourist attraction as Cumbe Mayo. Maybe even more so if what we turned up proved to be as unique as we hoped. That finally brought a smile to his face. Foaming at the mouth about Yankee Imperialism was one thing. Raking in Yankee tourist dollars, as well as money from global tourists, was quite another."

I was enjoying the lecture. Cartwright must be dynamite in the classroom.

"Eventually, we came to an agreement. I promised to follow all guidelines to the letter and to coordinate closely with local colleagues. That meant, as I mentioned, including graduate students from the local university participating in the project on a regular basis. In addition, I agreed to surprise inspections from government officials, who could show up at any time. They would have free rein to look at everything we were doing, chart our progress, and review the daily log I kept of our activities. Actually, that has become pretty standard practice throughout the country and I have no real problem with it. In fact, most of the inspectors, who have some training in archaeology, enjoy the visits. But I have no illusions. If they found something amiss, they would not hesitate to inform the governor, who would like nothing better than to make headlines by kicking us out."

"That must make things pretty tense," I said, belaboring the obvious.

Cartwright nodded. "Yeah. Unusually so. In addition to dealing with all the physical and emotional challenges that come with a dig like this in these surroundings," he said, waving his hand toward the site and beyond, "we have to put up with an aura of hostility and suspicion. Most of the burden falls on me," he said in a matter-of-fact manner, "which I accept as the price of doing business. But it also affects the kids. They don't often express their worries, but I can sense it cropping up from time to time."

"And I suppose Mel was not immune from those concerns."

"You assume correctly. Although she was often hard to read. I always suspected that behind her calm exterior lay something else. But I didn't know what and never pried."

I was not surprised. Just like my brother John, Mel had steeled herself against our family turmoil by putting up a barrier of self-discipline and self-control. I was the only one of the three siblings who had gone in the other direction.

Cartwright seemed to have ended his lecture but another question came to mind. "What about the armed guard? Is that part of the arrangement with the locals as well? He nearly scared me out of my wits."

With a rueful look, Cartwright said, "It seems I'm doing nothing but apologizing. Sorry about the scare. To answer your question, it is part of our arrangement with the government and is standard operating procedure at any archaeological site in Peru. In a poor country like this one, buried treasures found at sites like these, are tempting targets for thieves. If they find the right artifact, they can sell it on the black market for enough money to feed their families for several years. It's almost akin to a gold rush. The government pays for the guards, who are supposed to protect the cultural treasures from outsiders as well as to monitor diggers like us to make sure we don't do anything hinky."

"Another layer of intimidation, then?"

"In theory, yes. In practice, at least here, not so much. When he was first posted here, Gustavo was stoic and stand-offish. And he made us more than a little nervous when he practiced firing his weapons. But he is here almost all the time, day and night. He gets a weekend off every two weeks, when they send a replacement. So, we always have a guard. Gustavo lives in that little hut across the way." He pointed his finger to the other side of the digging area where I saw a dun-colored adobe structure with a thatched roof. I had missed it before since it blended almost completely into the surroundings. "Gustavo spends most of his time there, listening to Andean music on cassettes and reading popular magazines. We buy him a new supply whenever we make a provision run to town. But he is bored out of his gourd. We think he has a girlfriend, who he apparently sees on his time off. But he is private about such things and we don't press him. It didn't take long for us to see how lonely he was. I even thought about getting him a dog for company. But he told us that would be against the rules unless it was some kind of vicious guard dog, something he didn't want to deal with. More trouble than it was worth."

"I'm glad," I said. "It was scary enough dealing with a human. A big dog with its teeth bared would have sent me off the deep end."

"I know what you mean. But if Gustavo would agree, it might not be a bad idea to have a guard dog around. In addition to discouraging any would-be robbers it also would help to ward off animal predators, especially mountain lions. I once had to abandon a site because of their presence."

I was beginning to see what a challenge Mel had accepted – and probably welcomed – in joining the team.

"To get back to your question. After the first week of eating alone in his hut, we invited Gustavo to join us for our meals. He was reluctant at first, maybe afraid of breaking some rule that would get him in trouble. But who was to know? He became a regular at our table and gradually began to loosen up. We even managed to coax a smile from him from time to time. He began to ask us questions about where we came from in the States and why we were in his country. By now, we consider him as part of the group, more a friendly presence than a hostile threat. Of course, he still carries those weapons and if push came to shove probably would not hesitate to use them."

"Do you think he knows anything about what happened to Mel?"

Cartwright pondered the idea for a moment. "He was very upset, as we all were, when she went missing. He seemed to think somehow it was his fault. We assured him it wasn't. As you can see, the campsite for the kids is pretty far away from Gustavo's hut and unless Mel had screamed, which she didn't, then he wouldn't have heard a thing. He probably also sleeps like a log. Another argument for a guard dog. But even when we pointed this out to him, he still seemed disconsolate. And the visit from the local police investigator looking into Mel's disappearance didn't help brighten his mood."

"You mean Felipe Calderón? The embassy guys gave me his name. Said I should contact him when I got to Cajamarca."

"Yeah," Cartwright replied with a look of disgust, "Yeah, well I wouldn't expect much help from Inspector Felipe Calderón. Now *there* was intimidation. He came swaggering into camp with an attitude that bordered on contempt. He questioned each of us as though we were all suspects. I had the distinct impression he was simply taking the opportunity to berate us for causing him an inconvenience rather than seriously gathering information. After talking to some of the kids, he told me that Mel had probably run away with one of the local university students and that we'd hear from her eventually. Since there was no sign of foul play at her tent, he dismissed the kidnapping possibility out of hand."

I nodded. "That's what the embassy guys told me he had reported."

"After questioning us, he met privately with Gustavo in his hut. I don't know what was said, but I imagined he delivered a dressing-down, adding to Gustavo's feelings of guilt."

"Has Calderón reported back to you?"

"Not a peep. My guess is that his interviews with us was the beginning and the end of his investigation." He paused for a moment, then added "He's a real jerk."

"Do you think he's operating under the governor's orders?"

"Undoubtedly. The police are like his local gestapo. I wouldn't trust them an inch."

Great, I thought to myself. *One more obstacle in front of me if I hoped to find Mel.*

Twenty-Three

"LET ME GET THE kids together so you can talk to them. I'll take a hike so you can be alone with them," Cartwright said. "I have a pretty good relationship with all of them, but I'm still the authority figure. They might feel freer talking to you, someone closer to their own age, without me lurking in the background."

"Thanks. I appreciate that."

Cartwright pushed his chair back, then grabbed a broad-brimmed canvas hat and placed it on his head, adjusting the chin strap so it was firmly in place. "If you plan to be here for any length of time, Clint, you should get one of these," pointing to his hat. "The sun up here is fierce. You can get badly burned in no time. Sun block is also essential. Your baseball cap is not going to do the trick."

I wasn't going to reject his advice. I had a good tan from my construction work, but this was a whole new ball game. No sense taking chances. "I'll try to get properly equipped as soon as I get back to Cajamarca," I promised.

With that, I got up and accompanied Cartwright to the digging sites. "We are exploring six places we have determined most likely to contain the most useful material to reconstruct what this place was like one maybe even two thousand years ago," he explained. "Each student is responsible for the excavation of their respective sites, which you can see are marked off and identified."

"Yes. I noticed that when I arrived. I do construction work," I explained, "so it looked familiar."

He chuckled. "Well, what we do is more like 're-construction. But the principles are the same." Then, he said somberly, "That area over there, with the blue ribbons on the cords, is Mel's site. We've let it be, expecting to have her back soon and at work. But, if not…."

"Someone else will have to do the work."

"Yes. I'm afraid so." He shook his head. "Follow me," he said, clearing his throat and leading me to the closest pit. Standing on the edge, I looked down into a hole that was about ten feet square and ten feet deep. There was a wooden ladder descending to the bottom, where a guy wearing a hard hat with a light on top, gloves, and a mask, was on his knees slowly digging with a trowel. Next to him was a sieve to filter out whatever material he found.

He was absorbed in his work and didn't hear us at first. Cartwright cupped his hands and shouted "Hey Ken. Time to take a break." Somewhat startled, he looked up and saw us staring down at him. Standing, he waved at us and scrambled up the ladder. I couldn't read his expression behind the mask, but I imagined him thinking to himself, "Who's that other dude?"

At the top, Ken removed his mask to reveal a freckled face with a red beard. His face was covered with dust, except for where the mask had protected it. It reminded me of coal miners emerging from their tunnels, their faces streaked dark. "Ken," Cartwright said. "This is Clint, Mel's brother. He's come to Peru to find out what has happened to her."

A smile split Ken's face and he extended his hand. "Great," he said, as we shook. "Pleased to meet you and happy you are here." Then squinting, he added, "I can see the family resemblance. You're the younger brother, right? Mel talks a lot about you."

That rocked me a bit. I couldn't read anything in his expression but had to wonder how much of my sordid story Mel had revealed.

"Ken," Cartwright interjected, "Why don't you round up the rest and meet us at the trailer? Clint would like to talk with all of you while I make myself scarce."

"Sure thing Jere…Professor Cartwright." He turned to get the others and we returned to the trailer and waited. While we did, Cartwright said in a low voice, "Ken – Ken O'Malley, is the most gregarious and outgoing of the bunch. The others, as you'll see, are a bit more low-key and might be more reticent to talk. You may need to keep Ken under control as he tends to dominate the conversation."

"Thanks for the tip. I'll keep that in mind."

I turned to see Ken making the rounds of the sites as the four other students emerged one-by-one. Again, I was reminded of miners coming to the surface and taking a moment to adjust to the light. The image was reinforced when one of the males approached with a big wad stuck in his cheek, discretely spitting on the ground before arriving at the trailer. In this case, chewing coca rather than tobacco. I wondered if it might be a healthier choice.

When they arrived at the awning, Cartwright made the introductions. In addition to Ken, there were two other males, Barry and Woodrow, and two females, Linda and Serena. If Mel had been present, that would have meant an equal gender balance. I wondered if that was by chance or on purpose. When they removed their hard hats and lowered their masks, I saw that Barry, who had the chaw in his mouth, which he discreetly removed and placed in his handkerchief, had blonde hair, blue eyes, and a beard. Woodrow, or "Woody," as he preferred to be called, had dark hair, dark eyes and a beard as well. Maybe they were imitating their mentor, I speculated, or maybe it was easier to have a beard than try to shave under these spartan conditions. Linda was a willowy blonde with cornflower blue eyes while Serena was dark-haired with startling green eyes. I guessed from the name and the looks that she was a Latina. All seemed in very good physical condition, a basic requirement for the arduous work they did. I knew Mel did not lag behind in that department. They were uniformly dressed in jeans, sweatshirts, heavy boots, and knee pads to cushion the strain of their digging.

We shook hands and took seats around the wooden table. Cartwright excused himself and took off, saying he'd be back in about half an hour. I watched him disappear around an out-cropping before I asked, "Well, you all know why I'm here." They nodded in unison, concerned looks on their faces. "What can you tell me about Mel's disappearance? I need all the information and help I can get."

As I expected, Ken spoke first. "Before we begin Clint, can we get some water? It's important we stay hydrated."

"Sure. Sure," I replied. "I could use some myself."

He grinned, got up from the table, and entered the trailer. After a few seconds, he emerged with six bottles of water. He handed me one. It was surprisingly cool. Noting my surprise, he explained, "The trailer has a generator that powers a small refrigerator. It's like our oasis up here. Jeremy – Professor Cartwright – somehow managed to get a water line from the trailer attached to an underground spring so we can even take showers. As you can tell, that's something we badly need at the end of a day of digging."

"I can only imagine," I said, opening my bottle and taking a thirsty swallow. "I work construction. Same need."

That produced some nods and smiles, although I noticed Serena not joining in. She had a somber and preoccupied look on her face. I wondered why.

Again, Ken took the lead. "Well, Clint. We are ready to help in any way we can. Before we do, however, so as not to waste time, can you tell us what you already know?"

He sure was the take-charge guy. I laid out the story from the time I had gotten the phone call from John to my arrival in Cajamarca. I went over the various scenarios I had discussed with the embassy guys and could see the skeptical looks on their faces. Several shook their heads as I brought up Ingrid Betancourt and Lori Berenson. I mentioned the kidnapping possibility, letting them know we had received no ransom demands.

Serena, somewhat to my surprise, spoke up. "Did you see our tents when you came in?"

"Sure," I said. "Six arranged in a semi-circle."

"My tent is right next to Mel's. I'm a light sleeper. On the night she disappeared, I didn't hear a sound. I can't imagine that Mel wouldn't have put up some kind of a fight if she were being kidnapped. At least let out a scream for help. But there was nothing. You can check out her tent. We couldn't find any signs of a struggle, either inside or outside. From all we can tell, Mel snuck out of camp on her own accord."

"Did any of you hear anything?" I asked.

They all shook their heads. I wasn't about to dismiss the kidnapping possibility altogether, but had to admit that the evidence seemed to be against it. *Then what was the explanation?*

"So, what do you guys think? You were the closest to her. Was she unhappy? Was the work and the isolation getting to her? Did she show any signs that she might split without telling anyone? I just can't wrap my head around that. That's not my sister."

This time, Barry spoke. He had a thick New York accent. "We're as stumped as you are. Mel was doing great. She was really into our project and her site was turning up some of our best evidence. She was pouring her heart and soul into the whole effort. When we had dinner the night before she disappeared, she was laughing along with the rest of us at Woody's corny jokes and Ken's wild stories. It just doesn't make any sense," he said, shaking his head sadly.

"Well, there is another explanation. The police investigator, Calderón..."

"That creep," Ken said, the others nodding in unison.

"Yeah," I said. "I get that. At any rate, he told the embassy he thought Mel had formed a romantic relationship with a local university student and they had run off together. That would explain why she seemed to have left voluntarily. But even if that were the case, I can't imagine her doing something that rash, and in the process putting her family through hell. On the other hand, I can't rule anything out at this point. Professor Cartwright suggested that if Mel had been involved in some kind of relationship with a local, you would know more about it than he would. And even if Calderón is a creep, maybe he knows something we don't."

I looked around the table for a response, trying to read their expressions. Most of them again appeared skeptical, but I noticed Serena looking down at her hands, avoiding eye contact. This time, Woody was the first to respond. "We do have local university students working with us on the site. They usually can't make it more than once or twice a week. They're a mixture of males and females and usually rotate so that they can get a feel for each site and how we approach it. They have lunch with us, but go home for dinner, so there's not much of a chance to engage on a social basis. There is an opportunity to meet them informally when we go into town on the weekends. Right Barry?" he said with a wicked smile.

Barry blushed. "Barry does have a relationship with a local. Or at least a budding relationship," Woody explained, a mischievous look on his face.

"When we're in town, we stick together, Woody continued, "Of course, when we go, I don't keep my eye on Mel all the time...."

"Oh, no?" Barry retorted. "Could have fooled me."

Now it was Woody's turn to blush and the rest of the group laughed although once again excepting Serena. So, Woody had an obvious crush on Mel. I wondered if it was reciprocated. I also wondered what that might have to do with her disappearance. Probably nothing, but worth filing away.

"As I was saying," Woody resumed, overcoming his embarrassment, "If she had any kind of relationship with a local, I saw no signs of it."

"And you would know," Barry said, sticking the needle in again.

That brought a collective laugh, Serena once more excluded. In fact, she looked more somber than ever. "Sorry Clint," Linda said, noticing the look on my face, "Not the best time for us to be joshing one another. It's just that we've been so worried about Mel we need to let off some steam once in a while."

"No problem," I said. "I can understand." *At least you're not hitting the bottle, which is probably what I would have been doing in your circumstances.*

Switching the subject, I asked, "How do you guys get along with Professor Cartwright?" I asked, more out of curiosity than anything else.

"He seems like a nice guy."

"Yeah. He's great," Ken said, the others nodding in agreement. "Pretty demanding, but also inspiring and caring. We are privileged and lucky to be learning from the best."

Then a funny thought hit me. "Listen, I've heard about professors and their graduate students getting involved romantically. Any possibility that he and Mel might have had something going?"

Their faces shouted *Are you kidding us? What planet are you from?*

Befuddled, I said eloquently, "What?"

They tried hard to muffle their amusement. "Clint," Linda said, "You live in San Francisco, right?"

"Sure, but what..." Then I got it. "Okay. Understood. Sorry to be so dense."

"It's okay," Ken said. "The prof is very discrete. And students are definitely off limits."

A few moments later, we saw Cartwright walking in our direction from the other side of the dig. I sure hoped the wind hadn't carried our discussion his way. From the look on his face, I guessed he hadn't heard anything.

As he neared us, he asked, "Not interrupting anything, I hope? How's it been going, Clint?"

I waited until he took a seat at the table to respond. "What I've heard helps in filling out the picture, but I guess it also raises more questions than answers."

He nodded. "Yeah. I kind of figured as much." Then, leaning toward me, he asked, "Anything else we can help you with? You want me to take another hike?"

I tried to think of more questions to ask without him present. If I had been a professional investigator, I probably could have come up with something. But I was just an out-of-his depth amateur, stumbling around in the dark. One thing I had learned was that the team seemed to be pretty close, no serious divisions or rivalries that I could detect. At least on the surface. I thought that I could safely discount any foul play from her teammates as related to Mel's disappearance. "No. I can't think of anything else at the moment. Time for me to get going and let you all get back to work."

We all rose and I thanked them for their time. Ken said, his voice raspy, "We sure hope you can find Mel and bring her back to us. Anything we can do to help, let us know."

There was a chorus of amens and a few tears began to glisten. This time, Serena was included.

"I'm going to do my best," I promised.

Cartwright took me aside and slipped me a piece of paper. "There is no cell-phone service up here, but I have a satellite phone in the trailer. If you have any further questions or if you have any news about Mel, please give me a call anytime, day or night."

I shook his hand again and turned to head back to my waiting taxi when a thought struck me. "I'd like to take a look at Mel's tent before I leave, if that's okay?"

Before Cartwright could answer, Serena, who was hovering nearby, spoke. "I'd be glad to show Clint the way Professor."

It seemed a little weird. I could easily scout out the tent on my own. She seemed to sense my skepticism, which was probably shared by Cartwright. He was about to say something, when Serena added, "I know the details of her tent like the back of my hand. We spent a lot of time together engaging in girl talk, kind of 'we-time' without the guys around. I'd be happy to show it to Clint. Maybe he and I can spot some things we might have missed before."

I'm not sure whether either of us bought what she was selling. But it was clear to me that she had things to tell me that she had been reluctant to share with the group. Cartwright seemed ready to object when I said, "That would be great Serena. I appreciate the offer. Let's get going."

Cartwright nodded his blessing, a troubled look on his face, and off we went. Once we had passed through the narrow passageway between the rock formations on the way to the campsite and were out of earshot, Serena asked, "Clint. Can we stop for a minute?"

"Of course, Serena." When I saw the look of utter desolation on her face, I asked "What's wrong? What...? Before I could finish, she began to sob uncontrollably, unleashing a torrent of tears that probably had been building up since Mel had gone missing.

I was befuddled but not totally surprised. I had been puzzled by her reactions at the table with the rest of the team and guessed that she was hiding something. That she knew more about Mel's disappearance than she let on.

I tried to comfort her. I patted her shoulder, then pulled her to my chest with my arms around her as she shook with sadness. Gradually, the sobs and tears subsided and she regained her composure, pulling away from me with a look of embarrassment. I gave her my handkerchief to dry her eyes. After a few seconds, I asked, "What's wrong Serena? What's going on?"

"I'm so, so sorry, Clint. I think I know what happened to Mel, but I've been afraid to tell anyone until you appeared on the scene." I wanted to learn more, but she held up a hand. "Could we go to the campsite, please? I need to sit down. I'm feeling a little dizzy."

It only took us a couple of minutes to reach the campsite. I held

Serena's arm to steady her and she remained silent until we reached the wooden table under the tarp. I pulled out two chairs and unfolded them, guiding Serena into one while I took the other next to her. Dumping my backpack onto the table, I pulled out my remaining bottle of water, unscrewed the top, and handed it over to Serena. She took some deep swallows, a little water dripping onto her chin, which she wiped off with the back of her hand. I gave her time to recover, controlling my impatience. *What did she know? Would I finally get some answers?*

She gathered herself and looked me in the eye. "Mel and I were very close, BFFs from undergraduate days." I probably should have known this. That is, if I had been any kind of responsible brother, which, of course, I was not. And if the two girls were close, Serena probably knew the whole depressing story. I could read her mind, *and this is the guy who's going to rescue Mel from whatever mess she is in? Good luck with that!* But I was getting ahead of myself. I needed to hear what she had to say first and go from there.

"Mel and I shared things that we did not share with the others." She looked down at her hands twisting in her lap, then back up to eye level. "You asked about the possibility of a romantic relationship with one of the local university students. Well, that's not *exactly* the case, but not too far from the truth either. It *was* a relationship, but so far as I know it was not romantic. at least so far as Mel was concerned. From her point of view, it was a close friendship based on mutual concerns, nothing more. What the guy felt, I couldn't say. Mel hinted that he might be falling for her, but if so, she wasn't about to reciprocate."

I was tempted to interrupt with questions: *Who is this guy? Where can I find him?* But I thought it best to let her continue. "They met several months ago when he, Jaime is his name, came to work on the dig. By chance, he started out with Mel and even though Professor Cartwright makes it a point to rotate the visitors so they get the full gamut of the operation, Jaime seemed more often than not to find a way to be with Mel."

She took another gulp of water, then went on. "As you can imagine, working in such close quarters in an intimate space, you get to know your fellow digger pretty well. And we like interacting with the Peruvian students, teaching them what we know, showing them how to work the new equipment we have, and also learning a lot from them about their culture and outlook. From what Mel told me, she and Jaime spent a lot of time talking not only about that kind of stuff but also about local politics."

"From what Professor Cartwright told me, that's dangerous territory."

She nodded. "Yeah. But we are all curious about what's been going on in Cajamarca. When we go into town, we really get a feel for it. We can't ignore the demonstrations we see, although we do stay clear of any overt participation."

"Demonstrations over the gold-mine controversy, I assume."

She was surprised. "So, you know about that?"

"Yeah. The embassy guys filled me in yesterday. Sounds complicated."

Serena nodded. "Yes. It is. Well, to get back to Jaime and Mel. Mel told me that Jaime was deeply involved in a student group that was fighting the concession allowing for the operation. Mel said he was front and center at some of the protest rallies and once had been roughed up by the police. She had tried to warn him to tune it down, but he persisted in his activism. She became increasingly worried about his safety. The protests have been increasing in size and intensity lately, and the repression has ramped up as well. Up until now, protestors have only suffered tear gassing and beatings. But it's only a matter of time before there are some fatalities. Jaime, on the front lines, could well be one of them."

She paused for a moment to drink some more water. "The evening before she disappeared, Mel told me that she was meeting with Jaime that night to try to convince him to at least adopt a lower profile. She didn't want me to tell any of the others since what she was doing was way outside our guidelines. If Professor Cartwright knew, he would throw a fit. He is very protective of us and does his best to make sure we don't get into trouble. He also is sensitive to the fact that if any of us openly associated with the protests in any way, the local authorities would immediately shut down the project and kick us out of the country."

"He told me how difficult it was for him to get permission for the project," I said.

"Yes. And Mel knew this as well. She knew the risks, but felt she owed it to Jaime to take the chance. Swearing me to secrecy, she told me she planned to sneak out of the camp after we were all asleep. She had arranged to meet Jaime on the road from Cumbe Mayo to our camp, about three hundred meters from here," she said, pointing past the parking lot where my taxi was waiting for my return. "She planned to meet Jaime and do her best to convince him to lower his profile. Mel said she would be back well before dawn and not to worry. She knew what she was doing."

I shook my head. *My headstrong sister. A family trait.*

"I did try to talk her out of it, Clint. But it was no use. She was determined. If only I had been more insistent, maybe even threatening to tell Professor Cartwright, all of this wouldn't have happened," she said with remorse.

"Don't blame yourself Serena. Once my sister determines to do something, nothing short of actual physical restraint will stop her. And sometimes not even that. So, what do you think happened to her and Jaime?"

"I don't know. I've been working it over and over in my mind for days. The one thing I'm positive did not happen is what that police investigator, Calderón, implied," a look of disdain on her face. "As I said, Jaime might have had a crush on Mel, but her feelings for him were more like a big sister looking after a brother who was heading for trouble."

I winced. The parallel hit home. Serena picked up on it. "Sorry, Clint. She told me a lot about you. I think I know your family almost as well as I know mine."

"That's okay, Serena," I said reassuringly, "Then you don't buy the elopement theory?"

"Not for a minute. It's bullshit," she said with some vehemence.

"Then…?"

"I don't know. I can imagine all sorts of possibilities, most of them things I'd rather not think about."

"Such as?"

"Well, this may be going into tinfoil hat territory. But suppose Jaime was a plant, sent to sabotage our project? Working for the governor to smear us and get us out of *his* territory. Jaime lures Mel to his car, which is then surrounded by the local police. Mel is caught 'consorting with the enemy' and we are booted out."

"But wouldn't that have been made public immediately?"

"Yeah. There's the flaw. But what if things went terribly wrong and…" She couldn't continue.

"And Mel got hurt – or worse – resisting the trap. And the police are covering everything up?"

Serena nodded in agreement, tears again clouding her beautiful green eyes.

"I don't like thinking along those lines myself, Serena. But we need to consider all possibilities." Then, I asked, "Any word from Jaime since Mel's disappearance?"

"No. Not a word. I wanted desperately to get in touch with him. But that's not easy. For one thing, I don't know his last name. I would have to get that through Professor Cartwright, who in turn would need to get it from his colleague at the University of Cajamarca. And then I would have to use the satellite phone to call him, which means telling Professor Cartwright the whole story."

That brought up a question I had had on my mind from the beginning of Serena's story: "Why *not* tell Professor Cartwright the whole story?" I asked with some bite in my voice. "Maybe if he had the full picture, he could take some action that would help solve the mystery."

My scolding tone didn't help. Serena seemed on the edge of another meltdown. She looked at me with anguish, ready to break down in sobs. She put her hands to her face, took deep breaths, dropped her hands, gathered herself and looked me square in the eyes. "Don't you think I've wrestled with that for days? It's driving me nuts," she said with some bitterness. Then, in a calmer tone, "I actually considered spilling the whole story when we found Mel had gone missing from the camp. But she had sworn me to secrecy and I thought, foolishly perhaps, that there had been some hitch in her plans and that she would show up sometime that day with an excuse of some sort that would keep her and me out of trouble. I kept that hope going for the next few days, rationalizing that if I spilled the beans to Professor Cartwright, Mel's future at the site and perhaps her career would be toast."

I could see her reasoning and nodded in understanding. She was wrestling with a real dilemma and I had to refrain from being judgmental.

"When three days had passed and still no Mel, I was on the verge of talking to Professor Cartwright when he informed the group that we would be visited by a local police investigator that morning and we all should be prepared to be interrogated. I was terrified. I grew up in Guadalajara, Mexico and had learned that most policemen were our enemies, not our friends. I assumed that the one coming to interrogate us was as cruel and corrupt as those in my hometown. I swore to keep my cool and tell him nothing."

After draining her water bottle, she continued. "When I saw Calderón, I immediately knew he was just what I feared – arrogant, bullying, and not likely to lift a finger to help us find out what had happened to Mel. We were each interrogated separately in the trailer. Luckily, Professor Cartwright demanded to be present. I still felt uncomfortable, not only because I had something to hide but also because that pig kept undressing me with his eyes. I knew that if I told him what I knew, it would only make matters worse, putting Jaime in danger and spelling the end of the project. I did keep my cool, but afterward had to hide behind some rocks and vomit all that had been in my stomach."

I nodded in sympathy. I had had my own run-ins with the police in Mexico and could understand her distrust of them. I had even been their guest for one night in a Mexican jail, an experience I was not anxious to repeat.

"What about Calderón spinning the elopement theory? From what you tell me, it seems he arrived with it already formed. Maybe he knows something about her connection with Jaime?"

She nodded. "Yes. I think that may well be the case. The police undoubtedly have agents inside the protest groups who keep track of leaders like Jaime. They could be aware of his relationship with Mel and have put two and two together. But the elopement theory is still bogus. For my money, they are using it to cover up something else. Maybe my worst-case scenario theory," she said grimly.

I nodded. I didn't want to dwell on that somber possibility. The image of Mel's body abandoned in some isolated spot flashed through my mind. But I couldn't dismiss it either. Another reality check. "I'll do what I can to look into that," not at all sure how to go about finding out the possible extent of police involvement in Mel's disappearance, but vowing to try. "Getting back to my question, Serena, why not let Professor Cartwright in on what you know?"

"Yes, why not? I've asked myself the same question a million times. Maybe it's just a rationalization, but I still want to protect Mel and Jaime if I can. Furthermore, Professor Cartwright told us that about all the local authorities are going to do will be done by Calderón, and we all realize that will add up to a big nothing. He also told us that the State Department's hands are tied and they are not going to be any real help. So, if I spilled to Professor Cartwright, what good would that do? Then, he told us that you were on the way, so I decided to wait until I had a chance to tell you the full story. And I guess by now I have done that."

Another sobering moment. A lot was falling on my shoulders, I was making some progress, but faced many unanswered questions. My next step seemed clear: "How can I get in touch with Jaime?"

"As I said, I don't even know his last name. You'll need to contact his professor in the University of Cajamarca's anthropology department. He should be able to help you locate Jaime. If he hesitates, just tell him you are seeing him at the suggestion of Professor Cartwright. Not exactly the truth, but I doubt if he'll question you. If you give me your phone, I'll enter his name for you."

I unlocked my phone and handed it over. "His name is Justinio Quispé," Serena said, her fingers flying over the key-pad. Returning the phone to me, she said, "He is Indigenous, from a small town about fifty miles from Cajamarca. He did his advanced studies in France and is multi-lingual, although his native language is Quechua. How's your Spanish?"

"A lot better than my Quechua."

That brought the first laugh I had heard from her, a nice melodious one. "I'm not surprised. We are all required to have fluency in Quechua to be part of the project. Not all that easy to learn. But if your Spanish is serviceable, you should have no trouble communicating with Professor Quispé."

"I'll do my best," I said with a smile.

She answered my smile, then said, "Unless there's something else, I better head back before the guys get suspicious."

"Just one more thing," I said, "I'd like to see Mel's tent before I leave."

"Certainly. Let me show you," Serena said. We walked to the tent in the semi-circle that was farthest from the table. Serena lifted the flap, and gestured for me to enter. I crouched down and peered in. "Everything is in place." Serena said. "We haven't touched a thing. Just waiting for her to return."

"Did Calderón check it out? Look for clues?"

She scoffed. "Of course not."

I backed out and stood upright. Suddenly, I felt light-headed and for a moment staggered. Serena grabbed me by the arm. "Are you all right, Clint? The altitude getting to you? Want to sit down?"

I took some deep breaths and steadied myself. "I'm okay, thanks. Seeing where Mel spent so much of her life these past months and realizing that...." I couldn't finish, afraid I would start sobbing.

"I know. I know," Serena said, close to tears herself. "But I'm so glad you are here, Clint. You give me hope that Mel will be found and we can all get back to normal."

"I'm going to do my best," I promised. I kept my doubts that my best would be enough to myself. The fact that I had a lead to follow gave me some comfort. And if Lamar Jenkins' professionals showed up, there would be some additional manpower to deal with what was clearly a complicated situation in a difficult environment. I could sure use any help I could get.

Serena and I hugged goodbye as she wished me luck. I watched until she disappeared behind the rock outcropping fighting the irrational fear that she might be in danger because of the secret she held. When she was out of sight, I walked briskly to my waiting taxi, eager to get back to town and try to find Jaime, someone who might have the answers to the mystery of Mel's disappearance.

Twenty-Four

B Y THE TIME DANIEL delivered me back to the Costa del Sol, it was almost one o'clock. I had considered going straight to the university but was feeling light-headed and a bit disoriented. Better to get some food in my stomach. I hadn't had anything to eat since a light snack on the plane and couldn't keep going just on water and coca tea.

I arranged for Daniel to pick me up at two o'clock for my trip to the university. He was happy to oblige. He probably was making more money off of me in one day than he usually earned in a week. Moreover, we had talked a lot about what was going on in Cajamarca during the trip to and from the digging site. He had some strong opinions on local matters and did not hesitate to share them. He helped me get a clearer picture of the current situation and added to the information I was accumulating.

At the desk, the clerk told me my room was now ready and handed over the key. I retrieved my duffel from storage but left my wallet in the hotel safe. I lugged my duffel up the one flight of stairs to the second floor and walked down the corridor to my room. Unlocking the door, I stepped in. It wasn't the Sheraton, but it had all the basics. I unpacked the essentials and used the bathroom to brush my teeth and take care of other needs.

I thought about going to a local restaurant, but decided it would be easier and quicker to eat at the hotel. When I arrived at the dining room, there was a fair-sized crowd but I found a seat at a small table in the corner and a waiter appeared immediately with a menu. I told him to wait while I scanned it, then ordered a sandwich, a salad, and water and told him I was in a hurry. He promised to bring me my order as quickly as possible.

While I waited, I began to scribble some notes on hotel stationery from my room. I had read a fair number of mysteries and recalled that police investigators and private detectives frequently kept a log of their activities, jotting down pertinent names and events and trying to establish time lines for the crimes they were trying to solve. I sought to do the same. I had a pretty good memory, despite the ravages of alcohol abuse, but things were happening so fast I knew I couldn't trust my recollections to be unerringly accurate and on target. I began with what John had told me in St. Louis and followed that with as much as I could recall subsequently, including my conversation with Blake Anderson, the meeting at the embassy, and my recent discussions with Cartwright and his students. As I was jotting down this information, the waiter delivered my meal and I continued writing while I wolfed down my sandwich.

By the time I got to my salad I had finished writing. Reading over what I had so hastily jotted down, I didn't have any epiphanies. I still had many more questions than answers. But at least I was doing something to try to organize my thoughts. It was a work in progress and hopefully at some point the separate pieces would fall into place.

The lunch had done me good. The light-headedness was gone and I could feel my energy level begin to return to normal. I put the cost of the lunch on my hotel bill and looked at my watch. Almost two o'clock. When I exited the hotel, there was Daniel waiting for me, right on the dot. Blake Anderson had told me that Peruvians considered appointment times more aspirational than actual and were notoriously late for things ranging from business meetings to social engagements. If so, Daniel was an exception to the rule. Perhaps it was because he didn't have much else to do. But I appreciated his promptness. The last thing I needed at the moment was to waste time needlessly.

The university was on the southern outskirts of the city, a fifteen-minute drive from the hotel. When we arrived at the campus, Daniel asked a passing student where the anthropology department was located. I didn't catch the words that were exchanged but saw the gestures that pointed to a building about fifty yards away. Daniel thanked the student, then told me, "The Department of Anthropology is part of the university museum, straight ahead. The museum is on the first floor and the department offices are on the second."

Daniel drove to the small parking lot at the side of the museum and let me out. "I probably won't be too long Daniel."

"No problem, Señor. Take all the time you need. I'll be here."

When I approached the entrance to the museum, an armed guard asked for my credentials. I pulled out my passport and showed it to him. He scanned it, handed it back, and gestured for me to pass through.

"Where can I find Professor Quispé?" I asked.

"Second floor," he said in a tone that bordered on hostility. "Take the stairs on the other side of the exhibits."

My "thank you" elicited only a grunt. As I walked through the exhibits of what I took to be pre-Inca artifacts as well as models of ancient villages, I could feel the guard's eyes on the back of my neck. I presumed that he, like Gustavo, was assigned to make sure that nobody tried to make off with any of the valuables displayed in the cases I was passing.

When I got to the second floor, I entered a dark corridor lined with bookcases filled with more artifacts. There were hundreds of them. Halfway down the corridor, I saw two young people, a girl and a guy, sitting on a bench. They were deep in conversation, their foreheads almost touching.

When I approached, they looked up. "Excuse me," I said. "Can you tell me where I might find Professor Quispé?"

They didn't seem all that surprised by my appearing before them. I presumed that a fair number of foreigners came to see the head of the department.

The guy stood up and pointed to a door directly across from where they were sitting. "You'll find Professor Quispé's office right through that door."

"Thanks," I said, crossing the corridor. As I got closer, I saw a plaque that read *"Professor Justinio Quispé, Jefe, Departamento de Antropología."*

I knocked and heard a voice on the other side say, "One moment, please." Then footsteps, the turning of a dead-bolt lock, and the door opening just wide enough to reveal half a female face staring at me.

Weird, I thought. What's going on? "Yes," the woman said, "How can I help you?"

"I would like to see Professor Quispé. It's rather urgent," I added.

"I'm sorry *Señor*, but Professor Quispé is scheduled to have conferences with students all afternoon. Perhaps you can return…"

"I'm afraid I need to see him immediately. Time is of the essence. Please tell him that Clint Jackson, Melanie Jackson's brother, needs to talk with him. Tell him that it is literally a matter of life and death. Professor Cartwright…."

I didn't need to tell the little fib. She opened the door wide and I had the full picture of a dark-haired, middle-aged woman, dressed in a white blouse and black skirt, wearing thick black-rimmed glasses with a concerned look on her face. I assumed she was Quispé's secretary-cum-watchdog.

"Please come in, Señor Jackson. I'll tell the professor you are here."

I was in an outer office, with the usual accoutrements: desk, phone, chairs, photos on the wall. Directly in front of me was the door to Quispé's office, firmly closed. I could hear faint voices behind it.

I fully expected the secretary to knock on the professor's door at once. Instead, she said "excuse me," gesturing for me to move away from the door to the corridor while she closed it and re-did the locks.

"I apologize, Señor Jackson. We have to be careful."

I nodded as though I understood, even though I didn't.

She moved to the professor's door and knocked tentatively. There was no immediate response but the voices stopped and I could hear footsteps behind the door. When it opened, I saw the man I presumed to be Professor Quispé, who looked decidedly annoyed. "Mariana. How many times have I told you not to interrupt me when I with a student?"

"I'm sorry, professor. But…"

Before she could get the rest out, Quispé looked over her shoulder and saw me. "Who are you?" he asked in a decidedly unfriendly manner.

"I was about to explain, professor," Mariana said. "This is Clint Jackson, Melanie Jackson's brother. He said it was urgent that he see you."

Qispé softened a bit, but I still saw skepticism and maybe a little fear on his face. I got the distinct impression he wasn't about to welcome me with open arms. "Very well," he said, in English. He extended his hand, and I took it. "Please come in, Señor Jackson."

I followed him into his office, which contained a desk surrounded by crowded bookshelves. Two chairs were opposite the desk, one of which was occupied by a young woman, the student he had been advising I presumed. "Excuse me, Carolina," he said in Spanish. "We need to interrupt our session while I speak with Señor Jackson, Melanie Jackson's brother. Please wait outside until we are finished. Then we can continue."

When I had entered the office, Carolina had turned to look at me, surprise on her face. When she heard my name, surprise was replaced with concern and, like Quispé, a hint of fear. She was petite with dark hair, dark eyes, and Indigenous features, and dressed in what I took to be the informal student uniform of sweatshirt and jeans. "Of course, professor," she said in a low, shy voice. As she got up to leave, I thought she was going to say something to me, but she walked out of the office without a word, closing the door quietly behind her.

Quispé settled into a comfortable leather chair behind his desk and I sat down opposite. "Now, Señor Jackson," he said in English. "How may I help you?"

I wasn't exactly sure how to proceed. The vibes I was getting from him were not positive. He seemed nervous and I sensed a defensiveness in his attitude. Maybe it would put him at ease, I thought, if we conversed in Spanish. "Well, professor, I assume you know that my sister, Melanie, has gone missing and..."

"You speak Spanish, Señor Jackson."

"Yes, although I wouldn't call myself fluent," I said with a self-effacing grin.

"Let's try conversing in Spanish. I am trying to improve my English, but it is, how do you say? 'A work in progress.'"

He seemed to relax a bit. As he spoke, I took in the details. He appeared to be Cartwright's age, somewhere in his fifties. He was short and stocky, with dark skin, black hair, and black eyes. He was dressed more formally than his students in a brown crew-neck sweater over a white dress shirt and dark slacks. I guessed this was his office gear. Out in the field, he probably dressed more like Cartwright.

"Yes, Señor Jackson…"

"Please call me Clint, professor." One more step in building some rapport.

"Whatever you say, Clint," he said with the beginnings of a smile. "I do know of your sister's mysterious disappearance. Jeremy told me about it soon after it happened and I immediately relayed the news to my students who had worked with her. They are, as you might expect, extremely upset. They are very, very fond of her and devastated that something seems to have happened to her while in our country." He shook his head, a remorseful look on his face. "How can I help you?"

Now came the tricky part. "I have heard that Melanie had established a close relationship with one of your students. A young man by the name of Jaime. I don't know the last name…"

He seemed startled, but recovered. "Yes. Jaime Mendoza. Who told you about him?"

"I was at the embassy in Lima yesterday. The officials there told me that a local police investigator, Felipe Calderón, had concluded that Mel and a local student might have eloped without telling anyone."

At the mention of Calderón's name, Quispé's reaction showed none of the disdain of Cartwright and his students. Instead, he blanched and discomfort was etched all over his face. He picked up a pencil and began to tap the eraser end nervously on his desk.

"Has Calderón spoken to you, professor?"

He swallowed and took a deep breath. "Yes. He came here the day after your sister disappeared and questioned me and some of the students who had worked with her."

"Was Jaime among them?"

"No," Quispé replied, his pencil tapping an ever-increasing rhythm on his desk, "He was not at the university that day."

"What do you think of that theory? Any possibility that it might be true?"

Quispé looked agonized, staring down at his lap for a moment, wrestling with how to respond. I began to think maybe it was true. That Mel had taken off with Jaime. That would be good news. It meant we would hear from her at some point and that she was safe. But it still seemed far-fetched. Quispé confirmed my suspicions. "No, Clint. I am *positive* that was not how your sister went missing. Jaime was not involved in any way with her disappearance."

I was rocked. I didn't want to betray Serena's confidence and reveal that she had assured me Mel was planning to meet with Jaime the night she disappeared. I tried to phrase my question in more general terms. "Well, professor, I have heard from a pretty reliable source that Jaime *was* involved. And I need to speak with him as soon as possible. It could be a matter of life or death," I said, my voice cracking.

The pencil continued its frantic dance. Quispé saw my anguish and looked at me with sympathy and what I thought was a tinge of regret. "I need to tell you something in the strictest confidence, Clint. I don't want word to get out concerning what I'm about to tell you. Agreed?"

What choice did I have? "Sure. Agreed." *Anything to get to the bottom of this mystery.*

"I don't know how much you know about the current political turmoil here…"

"I've gotten a pretty good picture from the embassy and from Cartwright and his students. Protests over letting contracts for a gold mine, with young people prominently involved. And I understand that Jaime was one of the leaders."

"Yes. That's the general picture. Most of my students have been active in the protests, naturally concerned with the environmental impact of the proposed mines and the consequences for the nearby Indigenous population. And you heard correctly. Jaime is a prominent figure in the protests. In fact, he has been singled out several times as a ringleader and roughed up by the police."

He paused for a moment, then continued. "I have had to walk a fine line. I am sympathetic with my students' position and their desire to mobilize to defeat the project. But I also don't want them to get hurt. These protests can become very violent, with tear gas, attacks with batons, and shots fired either as warnings or sometimes directly into the crowd. We have already had dozens wounded and several deaths. Fortunately, so far, not touching any of my students. But it's only a matter of time when something serious does happen to one or more of them."

At that point, he seemed to realize the pencil-tapping was revealing both his nervousness and serving as something of a distraction. He purposely let it fall to the desk and folded his hands in front of him.

"Sorry," he said. "A nervous habit. Some years ago," he resumed, "we had similar protests over the Yanacocha Mine. I presume you've heard of it? One of the biggest such operations in the world."

I nodded. "Well, during one of those protests a student of mine was beaten to death by the police. It was heart-wrenching for me and the entire university. The last thing I want is for history to repeat itself. I feel it is my responsibility to protect my students as best I can."

He sensed I was becoming impatient. *What does all this have to with Jaime and Mel?*

"And that's where we come to Jaime. After Calderón's visit, I immediately got in touch with Jaime and called him to my office. I repeated what Calderón had said about him and Mel eloping. It was clear just from his presence that it was a preposterous speculation. He assured me that he had absolutely nothing to do with Mel's disappearance."

Quispé absent-mindedly reached for the pencil again, but caught himself in time. "But, to be frank, I don't think Jaime was telling me the whole story. He seemed to be hiding something, but I didn't press him at the time. Maybe I should have, but I didn't."

I was sure the professor was right. Jaime was hiding something. *But what?* Again, I couldn't reveal Serena's confidences so I just nodded.

"Whatever Jaime's involvement, I knew he was in real danger. Calderón didn't seem in any great hurry to find out what happened to your sister, but I knew he had Jaime in his sights. At some point, sooner rather than later, he would interrogate him. And he would use any excuse to throw Jaime in jail. If they had eloped, as he had theorized, and he found Jaime alone without Mel, he would charge him with kidnapping, maybe even murder. It would all be circumstantial and trumped up, but that doesn't make much difference here in Cajamarca. One more trouble-maker removed from the scene."

I understood Quispé's concern. I was about to interrupt with a question, but decided to let him go on.

"Another thing, Clint. We are a public university, dependent almost entirely on government funding. And the government is already unhappy with student participation in the protests. Charging Jaime with a serious crime would have other, larger repercussions. So, I was in a real bind. The only solution I could think of was to have Jaime disappear for a while. I told him to pack his bags and head for one of our project sites. He left that afternoon."

I was staggered. "Listen, professor. I appreciate your concern for your students. But I *have* to talk with Jaime. He's the only real lead I have at this point."

He looked at me quizzically, caught off guard by my insistence. *Why so determined to talk with Jaime?* I was sorely tempted to tell him what I knew of the clandestine meeting with Jaime and Mel the night she disappeared, but still held back, not wanting to get Serena in trouble.

"You have got to tell me where he is. I swear that I won't reveal his whereabouts to anyone else."

He had a look of sympathy on his face, but he shook his head. "I'm very sorry, Clint. But I just cannot do that. I have to look after the well-being of my students. It is my duty to protect them at all costs. I must keep Jaime safe. I'm afraid he is in real danger. If Calderón locates him, I'm sure he will make him the scapegoat in your sister's disappearance. There is a good chance he has his men already following you. If I told you where Jaime is, you could lead Calderón right to him."

I thought that was unlikely. Quispé seemed to be laying it on a bit thick. How could Calderón be on to me? I had just arrived in Cajamarca. But what did I know? Maybe he had the hotel inform him of any new check-ins and noted the name Jackson on the register. Putting two and two together, he figured that I was Mel's brother and had assigned a tail. If so, they were pretty good. I hadn't noticed anybody following me up to the site or to the university, not that I had been keeping close tabs. I vowed to keep a closer eye on any would-be followers from now on.

I concluded that I could not dismiss Quispé's fears out of hand. But I was frustrated and could feel the old Jackson family anger begin to build. Maybe I should reach across the desk, grab Quispé by the neck, and shake Jaime's whereabouts out of him. But I stifled the urge. Physical force would do no good in this situation, only make matters worse. And even if I did resort to force, who's to say that Quispé wouldn't send me off on a wild goose chase? I had to think of another way to locate Jaime, although I couldn't immediately think what that might be. Quispé had slipped me a clue, perhaps inadvertently, perhaps not. He had sent Jaime to one of the university's digging sites. Now, I had to figure out which one, and where.

Controlling my anger and trying to keep my voice steady, I said, "I understand professor. I'm operating in foreign territory here. Just feeling my way. From what I can tell, I am the only one in Peru who is actively looking for my sister. The more time that passes, the more the odds seem against me finding her. I appreciate your concern for your student, but I'm sure you can appreciate my concern for my sister."

He looked sympathetic, but he wasn't about to budge either. "I do appreciate that, Clint. But my hands are tied." *Where had I heard that before?* "I cannot put my own student in danger."

"Well," I said, "I guess that's that," and got up to leave. I reached my hand across the desk and thanked Quispé for taking the time to see me. When I took his hand, I involuntarily squeezed harder than I intended and he winced. I thought about apologizing, but then thought 'What the hell?' It was better than wringing his neck, which still lingered as a possibility in the back of my mind.

Quispé didn't seem to take offense. "A word of advice, Clint, if you don't mind. If you run into Inspector Calderón, don't trust him an inch. In Peru, unlike in your country, the police, with some exceptions, are corrupt and among the last to call if you need their help. And Calderón is no exception."

"I've already gotten that impression, professor. But thanks for the advice."

Quispé came around his desk to escort me out. Opening his door, he said to his secretary, Mariana, "Please have Carolina come back in."

"Very well, professor. She is waiting outside in the hallway. I'll call her in."

Quispé put his hand on my shoulder. "Best of luck to you, Clint. And please let us know if you get word about Melanie. We are all praying for her safe return."

I was tempted to make a wiseass remark, but refrained. "Thanks, again, professor. I'll do that."

Mariana opened the office door to the corridor and let me exit first before she called Carolina, who was talking with the couple I had seen on the bench on my way in. I presumed they were also Quispé's students waiting for their session with him. Carolina gave me a shy, sympathetic look as she passed by on her way into the office. As soon as the office door closed, the couple approached me, the guy saying in halting English, "Excuse me, Señor. Are you Melanie Jackson's brother?"

I responded in Spanish, "Yes, I am. Did – do -you know my sister?"

They both nodded and then introduced themselves; Aníbal and Rosario. "My name is Clint," I said, shaking their hands.

They looked nervous, glancing over their shoulders to make sure nobody was nearby. "Can we invite you for a coffee, Clint?" Aníbal asked. "There is a little café at the end of the corridor."

I was tempted to decline, anxious to get back to the hotel and make some calls. But I sensed they wanted to tell me something, something they wanted to keep out of the earshot of any passersby. "Sure," I said with a grin, "That sounds like a fine idea."

As we headed down the corridor, my eye caught a large map on the wall. "Hold on a minute," I said. "I'd like to look at that map." We drifted over for a closer inspection. It was a map of the Department of Cajamarca with red pins stuck into it and red ribbons radiating out to little tags with writing in what I assumed was Quechua.

"What's this?" I asked.

"That shows the location of all the sites in Cajamarca Department where the university has projects," Aníbal explained.

I took a closer look and my heart sank. There were at least a dozen sites, scattered throughout the region, all, I presumed, in remote locations. I had hoped that I could follow the clue Quispé had let slip, tracking Jaime down at a digging site. Now that I faced the reality staring me in the face, I realized the impossibility of trying to pick the needle out of the haystack. I could spend days if not weeks on a fool's errand. Nonetheless, I took out my phone and snapped a picture of the map. If going to each site one-by-one was my only choice, then so be it.

"A lot of activity, isn't it?" Rosario said.

"Are there students at each one of these?" I asked.

"Almost all," she replied.

"Impressive," I said as we resumed walking to the café. When we arrived, I saw that the "café" was little more than a small break room. There were two tables, some chairs, a stand containing a coffee maker and some plastic cups, a small dorm-style fridge, and a kitchen sink. We were the sole occupants, which I considered a plus. If I were to get any useful information from the two students, some privacy was essential.

Aníbal gestured for me to take a seat while Rosario went about brewing a fresh pot of coffee. "Well, Clint," Aníbal said, "we want you to know that all of the students here are very concerned about what happened to your sister. If we can help you in any way, we are all ready to do so." In the background, Rosario added her assent.

The coffee was beginning to brew, and the aroma filled the room. I was ready for a healthy dose to perk me up. The tension of the day, plus the altitude, had left me drained. A caffeine jolt would hit the spot. I pushed aside the desire for something stronger than coffee.

I waited while Rosario poured coffee into three plastic cups. She set them down in front of us and took a seat at the table. I added some sugar from a bowl on the table and took a tentative sip, not expecting Starbucks quality. But it was surprisingly good and after a few more swallows, I began to feel its beneficial effects take hold.

"I appreciate your willingness to help. I need all I can get," I said frankly. "But before I begin, could we close the door? I want to keep this conversation confidential."

"Sure," Aníbal said. He got up, grabbed a sign that said "occupado," and hung it on the outside of the door before he closed it. "Sometimes we have private meetings in here, so it's not unusual to see the 'occupied' sign. We shouldn't be disturbed." I guessed that those "private meetings" had something to do with student involvement in the gold mines protests.

I laid out the story, much as I had with Quispé, again leaving out Serena's revelations about Mel's plan to meet clandestinely with Jaime. When I got to the part about Quispé refusing to give me the exact location where he had sent Jaime, I said, "That's where you can really help me out. I desperately need to talk with Jaime. Do you have any idea where he might be? Where I can find him?" The two exchanged knowing looks and nodded in unison.

Rosario spoke first. "We sincerely appreciate Professor Quispé's desire to protect us. But sometimes, he goes too far. We are all adults, willing to take full responsibility for our actions. We are okay with submitting to the professor's authority when it comes to our academic work. But he steps over the boundaries when it comes to our non-academic activities."

"You mean, like participating in protests, getting politically involved?"

"Exactly," Aníbal added. "We greatly respect the professor, but we have our own individual beliefs and sense of commitment. We don't want him telling us what to do outside of the university."

"To be fair," Rosario interjected, "The professor is under a lot of pressure from the university administration to rein in our activism. I've heard, too, that the police have been threatening him and his family if he does not cooperate in trying to stop us from protesting. He's in a tough spot."

I nodded my understanding. Not a happy situation to be in. "Professor Quispé mentioned the police investigator, Calderón, who is supposed to be looking into Mel's disappearance. Could he be the one issuing the threats? The professor advised me to stay well clear of him."

"That's good advice, Clint," Aníbal said. "Calderón most likely is the one making the threats. He is, how do you say it? Bad news."

"So," I asked, "Where do I go from here? How do I find Jaime? That's how you can help me the most."

They exchanged looks again, nodded, and seemed to come to a common agreement. "I might be totally wrong," Aníbal said, "but I don't think Jaime went into hiding willingly. He is very strong-willed and determined. He takes his responsibility as a leader of the protests very seriously and would not abandon us without a good reason or without undue pressure being applied."

"He also would do everything he could to help find Mel," Rosario added. "He was very fond of her. I'm sure that if he were here, he would be more than happy to assist you anyway he could."

They probably read my expression: *Hypotheticals and good intentions aren't going to get the job done.*

Reading my mind, Aníbal said, "But he is not here, Clint. And we don't know for sure where he is hiding. But we do have a pretty good idea. I saw you take a picture of the map of our sites on your phone. If you bring it up, we can show you where we think Jaime is."

I took out my phone and recovered the photo of the map. I gave it to Aníbal, who moved his fingers to enlarge a part and returned it to me. "Do you see the site near a place called San Ignacio?"

I squinted. "Yes. It looks to be in the far north of the department, near the border with Ecuador."

"Exactly. It is the site farthest from here and the most difficult to reach. It's at least a seven-hour drive over mountainous terrain. To get to the site you need a four-wheel vehicle. And, if somehow the authorities were able to track Jaime down, he could flee across the border. It's the only one of our sites that would allow for that possibility. There's no guarantee I'm right, of course, but it's where I would have sent Jaime if I had been in the professor's shoes."

"I agree with Aníbal," Rosario said. "It's the logical choice."

I felt a stir of excitement. What they told me made sense and I was eager to follow the lead. But some doubts percolated below the surface. Could I really trust my two informants? They seemed like nice kids and I tended to believe their genuineness. But suppose they were just sending me on a wild-goose chase, looking to protect both Jaime and the professor? Such speculations, however, were a waste of time. What choice did I have but to believe them and follow the lead they had given me, probably at some risk to themselves? I thanked them for their help and promised to keep my conversation with them confidential. They wished me the best of luck in finding Jaime and unraveling the mystery of Mel's disappearance. As I left the museum building and headed for my waiting taxi, I did so with renewed hope that I was on the right path. There were a lot of unknowns ahead, but I felt I had accomplished a lot in the relatively short time I had been in Cajamarca. I had made progress and was beginning to feel a sense of optimism that I could indeed live up to the expectations my family had for me. That was a rare feeling and I hoped it would not be a fleeting one.

Twenty-Five

THE EVER-FAITHFUL DANIEL WAS waiting patiently for me. When I was settled in the passenger seat and had put on my seat belt, I told him to take me back to the hotel. He started up and we began to make our way out of the campus and on to the main highway. Mindful of the warning that I might be followed by the police, I checked the rear-view mirror and saw nothing suspicious. Of course, all I knew about clandestine surveillance I had gleaned from detective and spy novels. They gave me some ideas of giveaways, but I certainly was no expert. Far from it. I made the decision to relax and do the best I could to spot and evade would-be pursuers.

On our way back to the hotel, I asked Daniel if he knew of anyone with a four-wheel drive who could take me north toward Ecuador the next day. "Certainly, Señor Jackson. I would be happy to do it. I can borrow my uncle's heavy-duty SUV, no problem. Where, exactly, are you planning to go?"

"To a place near San Ignacio. It's in difficult terrain. I can show you on my phone when we get to the hotel."

He nodded. "Wherever it is, I can get you there," he said with confidence.

I expected him to ask why I wanted to go to such a remote location, but if he was curious, he didn't show it. If that's where a well-paying customer wanted to go, why ask questions?

When we arrived at the hotel and parked, I took out my phone and used my fingers to enlarge the map that identified the exact location of the archaeological site. From what I could tell, it was about five miles north of San Ignacio. Daniel looked at it carefully. "Yes," he said.

"We shall definitely need a four-wheel drive vehicle to reach that site. But don't worry, Señor Jackson, I can drive you there tomorrow. No problem."

"How long do you think it will take to get there?"

"Five, maybe six hours, depending on conditions. Sometimes there are accidents or wash-outs. Maybe even check-points and road-blocks. Are you planning to stay in San Ignacio?"

I really didn't know. It depended on how quickly I could find Jaime. "I'm not planning on it, Daniel. If possible, I would like to return to Cajamarca the same day. But it may be that I'll have to find lodging there for the night. We'll just have to see how things go."

He must have been curious. And maybe even a little suspicious. *What things? What was this gringo up to? Something criminal?* If so, he didn't show it. To assuage any misgivings, I gave him a hundred-dollar bill as an advance with the promise of another once the trip was completed.

We agreed on an early start; five-thirty in the morning. He gave me his card with his phone number in case there were any changes. We shook hands to seal the agreement and I got out of the taxi and headed to the hotel. Before I got to the door, I stopped as though I had forgotten something, and turned around. I scanned my surroundings and saw nothing that indicated I was being watched. Just because I couldn't spot anything didn't mean there wasn't somebody on the streets or in the plaza keeping an eye on me. Once again, I thought, *we're not in Kansas anymore,* turned, and walked into the hotel.

As soon as I got into my room, my phone vibrated. The screen said it was Lamar Jenkins. *Just in Time! Maybe the cavalry was on the way.* While I was making progress on my own, it was increasingly clear I was out of my depth operating alone. Having some professionals on my side was something I badly needed.

"Hello Lamar," I said, "Clint Jackson here. What's up?"

"Hey, Clint. How's it going? Any luck in finding out what happened to your sister?"

"I made some progress today and plan to follow a lead tomorrow. But I sure could use some back-up. Things are a little hairy here."

"Are *you* in any danger?"

I waffled between macho bravado and the truth. "I don't think so.

But I've gotten a little paranoid. It's complicated up here and some of the people I've spoken with have warned me I might be on the radar of the local police. There's a lot going on behind-the-scenes that makes me uncomfortable. I sure hope you can send some guys here who are trained to deal with this kind of situation. I'm feeling a bit like a babe in the woods."

He was silent for a minute. "Well, Clint, I'm afraid I have bad news on that score. Last night, my boss informed me that several of our operations in Peru have experienced what seems to have happened to your sister: mysterious disappearances of key personnel, with no signs of by whom or for what purpose. The best guess is that some eco-terrorist group is taking hostages to force us to stop operations. So far, we haven't gotten any demands. It's just speculation at this point. I'm not sure how your sister's case fits into this scenario, but her disappearance seems to fit the pattern."

My heart sank. I knew what he was going to say before he said it. The cavalry was *not* on its way. "I waited until now to call you," Lamar continued, "to see if we could send a couple of guys, like I promised, to help you out. But, I'm afraid it's 'all hands on deck.' We can't spare anybody. In fact, we're planning to fly in more guys tomorrow to provide reinforcements. I'm *awfully* sorry, Clint. I know you are in a tough situation, but we have to look after our own. That has to be our main priority."

My twin demons – anger and frustration – raised their ugly heads again. But Lamar was right. I expected more from the embassy guys. It was their responsibility to look after Americans abroad. And I found their excuses for not helping look for Mel lame in the extreme. But Lamar and his company had no such responsibility. I might not like it, but I could understand the rationale. They had a business and their own personnel to protect. They couldn't afford at the moment to do a favor for the brother of a college buddy.

I did my best to hide my disappointment. "I understand, Lamar. And, I appreciate your concern and willingness to help." I was tempted to say something like, "I'll just soldier on alone," but resisted the self-pity. Time, once again, to man-up. "I hope things work out for your company, Lamar. Sounds like a nasty situation."

"Thanks, Clint. We'll manage. We've been through this kind of thing before. Sorry, again, that I can't help. Keep in touch, will you? Maybe we'll get some kind of break that will help you find your sister."

"Thanks, Lamar. I'll do that," and with that I ended the call.

I sat down on the bed and pondered what to do next. My eyes landed on the mini-bar and I felt the irresistible tug. Getting up, I went over and opened the door. There were several cold beers just begging to be opened and gulped down one after the other. There were also small bottles of whiskey on top of the bar calling my name. But my better angels prevailed, at least for now. I took out a bottle of cold water, twisted the cap, and drained most of it in a single swallow, causing my eyes to burn for a moment. Disaster avoided, or at least postponed.

The next item on my agenda was to call my brother John. When he answered, I could hear some strain in his voice. "Hi, Clint. Great to hear from you. How are things going?"

I gave him a summary of my day and what I had discovered so far. "So, tomorrow you are going to look for this guy Jaime, who may have some clue as to what happened to Mel?"

"Yeah. That's the plan."

"You going alone, or did Lamar send some reinforcements?"

"I forgot to tell you. I just got off the phone with him and the news is not good. He says that there has been a recent spate of kidnappings of his company's personnel and they can't spare any professionals to help me out. Sounds a little fishy to me. Maybe a convenient excuse not to get his company involved in our problem."

There was a pause. "I don't think so, Clint. Lamar is a very trustworthy guy. Tell you what. Let me do a little digging. I have some sources I can check to see if what he told you is on the up and up."

"Okay, Bro. By the way, how are Mom and Dad doing?"

After another pause, he said "Mom is okay. Seeing you really brightened her mood. She's confident you can find Mel." I wished I shared her confidence. "But Al continues to deteriorate." Then, his voice cracking, he added, "I don't think he has many more days left, to be honest. The doctor saw him yesterday and the prognosis was not good. The only thing that seems to keep him going is…"

"That I'll find Mel and bring her home," I finished.

"Yeah. I'm afraid so." *Nothing like a little added pressure to add to my guilt.*

He must have sensed my unease. "I know you are doing the best you can, Clint. I wish I could be there to help you out, but…"

"That's okay, John. Actually, I feel pretty good about the progress I've made. If I can locate this Jaime guy, we should have more answers."

"Let's hope so, Bro. Keep in touch, okay?"

"Sure thing," I replied. "Talk to you tomorrow, hopefully with good news."

After I disconnected the call, I could feel the beginnings of a dangerous slide into self-pity. The bravado I had felt about making progress gave way to an overwhelming sense that I was way out of my depth. I had been counting on Lamar Jenkins to provide back-up. Now, that option was off the table. While I *had* made some progress, everything I had learned today underscored how complex the situation was and how little I really knew about the environment I was operating in. I was particularly concerned about the police. And not for the usual reasons. Maybe Calderón was dismissing Mel's disappearance with some phony story because he couldn't be bothered. But maybe he or somebody else had been involved in whatever happened to her and were trying to cover it up. If so, what could I, a naïve gringo, do about it? I tried to dismiss these fears as excessive paranoia, but they lingered in the back of my mind nevertheless. Add to that the pressure of family expectations, *please find Mel so Al can see her before he dies,* did little to ease my burdens.

Once again, my eyes drifted to the mini-bar. The usual rationalizations appeared: *Just one beer couldn't hurt. I can handle it. Besides, I need something to calm my nerves.* But, again, I resisted. Reality set in. I had a long trip ahead of me in the morning. The last thing I needed as accompanying baggage was one of my notorious hangovers.

I looked at my watch. It said six-thirty, reminding me that I was hungry. Time for dinner. Daniel had recommended a restaurant a couple of blocks from the hotel, just off the main plaza. I went down to the lobby, which was crowded with a tour group just checking in. As I made my way to the exit, one of the staff approached me. "Where are you going Señor?"

It threw me off. *What business was it of his where I was going?* I stifled my annoyance. "Just out to get some dinner."

"Some place nearby?"

"Just a few blocks away. Why do you ask?"

He could sense my annoyance. "I'm sorry, Señor. It's just that we are expecting a demonstration in the plaza to begin in about an hour. It can be an...ah, inconvenience. Lots of people, lots of noise, lots of police. We don't want you to be caught up in something unpleasant," he explained, with an apologetic look on his face.

"I appreciate the warning. I'll try to be back before any trouble starts."

"Very good, Señor. Enjoy your meal."

When I exited the hotel, I saw small clusters of people in the plaza, presumably preparing for the demonstration. I skirted the edges of the plaza and entered the restaurant, Las Tullpas, Daniel had recommended. Most of the tables were empty and I seated myself at one near the back. A waiter appeared, handed me a menu, and returned in about a minute with the bottled water I had requested. I ordered lamb with potatoes and rice, the dish that Daniel had suggested. When it arrived, I took my time eating. A few other customers trickled in. I recognized some of the tourists who had been checking in at the Costa del Sol. I assumed they had been warned as I had about the up-coming demonstrations and were anxious to eat and get back to the hotel.

I decided to take my time. Despite the warning, I was curious to see the demonstration. I ordered some dessert and coffee and lingered over both until it was almost eight o'clock. Paying the bill, I left a generous tip. Outside the restaurant, I could see that the plaza was now full of people shouting slogans, waving signs, and banging on drums. I estimated the crowd to be in the hundreds. Several were shouting through bullhorns. I had some difficulty making out what the speakers were saying, but the crowd seemed to be following their lead shouting out phrases like "Profits, no. People, yes" and "No to gold, yes to mother earth," or something along those lines.

Surrounding the crowd on all sides of the plaza were scores of uniformed police, many with body armor and protective shields, armed with tear-gas guns. They stood stoically but their body language indicated they were eager to confront the crowd at the slightest provocation.

Many of the protestors wore colorful Indigenous garb. While all ages seemed to be represented, the great majority were young people, dressed in the familiar jeans and sweatshirts. I wondered if the students I had spoken with this afternoon were at the demonstration. I couldn't see any of them, but I wouldn't have been surprised if they were present. I could picture the mysterious Jaime as one of the leaders, using a bullhorn to stir up the crowd. I also tried to picture Mel at his side, perhaps trying to restrain him, perhaps urging him on.

I strolled casually behind the police lines back to the Costa del Sol. Standing on the steps to the hotel, I took about five minutes to absorb the scene in front of me. I had witnessed some protests in San Francisco, mostly over homelessness or gay rights. But this was something new and a bit surreal to me. I took a few pictures of the crowd with my phone and then entered the hotel.

I saw the guy who had warned me about the protestors and approached him. "Thanks for the warning," I said. "Are these protests common?"

"Yes, Señor. Almost every night now for the past several months."

I was about to say something flippant along the lines that it added to the tourist experience, something to tell the folks back home, but kept my mouth shut. Who knew what he thought?? Maybe he was all in favor of the protests. Or, on the other hand, maybe he found them a troublesome nuisance bad for business. I bid him a *Buenas Noches* and took the stairs up to my room. I thought about trying to catch the local news on TV to see how they were covering the demonstration, but decided to hit the sack instead. It had been a long and tiring day with another one on the horizon. It didn't take more than a few minutes after my head hit the pillow for me to fall into a deep sleep. Just before I did, the thought hit me that this was the second night in a row I had fallen asleep without the aid of alcohol. Hopefully, it was something I could get used to.

Twenty-Six

D ANIEL WAS WAITING FOR me in the lobby when I descended at five-thirty on the dot. I was beginning to question Blake Anderson's assertion that Peruvians were notoriously unpunctual. So far, Daniel had proved the exception to the rule. Of course, he had a financial incentive to make sure he was prompt.

We shook hands and wished each other good morning. Outside, Daniel guided me toward a late-model black Nissan SUV. We got in, buckled our seat belts, and made our way out of the plaza. I saw ghostly figures cleaning up the debris from last night's demonstration as we headed through deserted streets to the main highway north. It was still dark, but the sky was lightening to the east as the sun began its rise over the Andes.

It didn't take us long to begin a series of ascents into the mountains to our west. While San Ignacio was about 150 miles from Cajamarca as the crow flies, we were not crow's and had to take a series of twisting roads that wound up and down through the mountains. Fortunately, there was little in the way of traffic, the road was paved, and Daniel was an excellent driver.

After two hours, we stopped for breakfast at a roadside café. Outside, several trucks were parked. Inside, we enjoyed a hearty breakfast of ham, eggs, rolls, and coffee. As we were leaving, Daniel asked several of the truckers what road conditions were like on the way to San Ignacio. No problems, they told him and we resumed our journey.

Up to this point, I hadn't said much, not wanting to distract Daniel while he was focusing on keeping us on the road and navigating one hairpin curve after another. But when we reached a flat stretch, I opened up the conversation. "Tell me, Daniel. What do you think of these protests over the gold mines?"

He seemed a little startled. Maybe I had put him in an uncomfortable position, although it was a pretty natural question for a visitor to ask. After some hesitation, he said, "Well Señor Jackson," - I had asked him to call me Clint, but he had steadfastly ignored that request and I didn't push it – "I don't like them. They are bad for my business. Foreign tourists don't want to visit a place that has so much trouble. Too much violence."

"Have you seen a decline in tourism as a result of the protests?"

He thought about it for a minute. "Not so much, Señor Jackson. But many foreigners don't know about the dispute until they get here. I'm afraid once the word gets out, others will hesitate to come to Cajamarca."

"Have any tourists been hurt because of the protests?"

"No. Not really. A few have suffered from the tear gas, but nothing serious – yet."

What he said made a lot of sense. He depended on tourists for his livelihood and when tourism dried up all he had to fall back on was local passengers. Probably not enough to keep him and his family afloat. "So, you are in favor of opening up the new mines?"

"That is a more difficult question, Señor Jackson," he said, glancing at me quickly, then returning his eyes to the road. "Let me explain. I come from one of the small towns outside of Cajamarca. It is mostly Indigenous. I am, what do you call it? A half-breed. A mestizo, or as we say in Peru, a *cholo*. My mother is Indian, my father white. Most of our town is Indigenous and I am often torn between the two worlds, if you know what I mean."

"I do, Daniel."

"So, I can sympathize with those Indigenous communities who are afraid the new gold mines will destroy their sacred grounds and contaminate the land. On the other hand, the gold mines will bring wealth to Cajamarca and provide good-paying jobs for many in the community, Indigenous and white. You have heard of the Yanacocha mine?"

"Yes, I have. And if I have time, I'd like to visit it."

"Well, there was a lot of objection to that mine when it opened. We went through some of the same protests. And while Yanacocha's record has not been perfect, it has greatly benefitted Cajamarca. It's one of the main reasons the city has grown so rapidly over the past ten years. The mine provides very good jobs for many locals, often paying ten times what you can earn in an average occupation. My uncle has worked for Yanacocha from the beginning and does very well." Tapping the steering wheel, he said, "We are riding in his SUV, which he loaned me for the trip to San Ignacio."

"I guess there are two or more sides to every issue," I said.

"Yes. It's complicated." Then, he chuckled. "It seems as though throughout our history we here in Peru have been cursed by the good fortune of having great quantities of gold and silver."

"What do you mean, Daniel?"

"I don't know how much of our past you are familiar with."

"I'm learning more every day."

"You do know that we once had a great empire, the Incas?"

"Sure. I learned about it in high school, although I'm not sure I remember all the details."

"Well, the Incas ruled supreme over what is today Ecuador, Peru, Bolivia, and parts of Chile for centuries. Then, in the early sixteenth century the Spaniards arrived under Francisco Pizarro and..."

I interrupted, "And, didn't they capture the Inca Emperor and hold him hostage? What was his name?"

"Atahualpa. Yes, they captured Atahualpa, who was passing through Cajamarca to take advantage of our thermal baths. You can visit them. They still exist, right on the outskirts of the city. They kept him locked up near the town square and demanded he fill two rooms with gold and silver if he wanted his freedom. So, he did what he was told and in return, the Spaniards executed him. After that, they conquered the rest of the empire and absorbed it into that of Spain. You can visit the rooms where Atahualpa was held prisoner and watch a recreation of the event. It is one of the city's main tourist attractions."

"So, the lesson is, for a long time, foreigners have lusted after Peru's gold. What is happening now with the mines isn't anything new."

Daniel chuckled. "Yes. Although, so far, nobody has been kidnapped or executed."

I felt a chill. "So far." Once again, I wondered: *Could any of this be related to Mel's disappearance?*

I was suddenly thirsty and reached into the backseat to grab a bottle of water from my backpack. "Want some water, Daniel?"

"Yes, Señor Jackson. Thank you."

As I pulled out two bottles, I noticed a local newspaper on the seat. Daniel had been reading it while waiting for me yesterday at the Cumbe Mayo site. It gave me an idea. I opened both bottles, passing one to Daniel. "By the way, I see you read the local newspaper." He nodded. "have you seen anything in it over the past few days about an American student who has gone missing in Cajamarca?"

He looked at me quizzically. So far, he had been discreet, not asking a lot of questions about why I was in Peru. He probably assumed that I was just another tourist. And one who paid him well. But he must have been curious as to why I had been at the archaeological site near Cumbe Mayo, then to the University, and now on the way to another site. I debated what to tell him. The easiest course would be to lie and tell him I was an amateur anthropologist with an interest in ancient Peru and was talking with professors and students about sites they were working on. If so, why the question about a missing American student? How did that fit? I decided to level with him, making sure I did not reveal too much and get others in trouble.

"No, Señor Jackson. I haven't." He hesitated. "Why do you ask?"

"Well, Daniel, I am here in Peru looking for my sister, Melanie. She was working at the site near Cumbe Mayo and disappeared without a trace about a week ago. No one seems to know how or why and I am trying to track down any possible leads. I thought maybe her disappearance had been reported in the newspapers. It's the kind of event that would be reported widely in the newspapers and on television in the United States. I thought it might be the same here in Peru."

Daniel shook his head. "I am very sorry to hear about what happened to your sister, Señor Jackson. But I have not seen or heard anything about it. Sometimes foreign tourists go missing in and around Cajamarca, but they usually turn up eventually. Maybe the same will happen with your Melanie."

"What about those who do not turn up?"

He shrugged. "You will not read about it in the newspapers. The local authorities do not want to discourage tourism."

"What about the police? A local investigator, Felipe Calderón, has been assigned to my sister's case." At the mention of the name, Daniel grimaced and his grip on the wheel tightened. "In the United States, there are specialists assigned to missing persons cases and they publicize the disappearance as widely as possible. Often, they offer rewards for any information." I didn't mention that many of these cases went unsolved.

"Peru is not the United States, Señor Jackson. The police in Cajamarca do not take disappearances very seriously, unless it involves someone with political connections. And this officer you mention…"

"Calderón."

"Yes, Señor Jackson. Inspector Calderón. He is a very dangerous man. If you speak with him, be very careful."

"I'll keep that in mind, Daniel. Thanks for the advice." I didn't add that virtually everybody I had met had told me the same.

"So, Señor Jackson. Our trip to San Ignacio is part of your effort to find your sister."

"Yes."

"Do you expect to find her here in San Ignacio?"

I really hadn't thought of that possibility. *Could it be she was hiding out with Jaime?* I felt a surge of hope. But it faded. If that were the case, Quispé and the students at the University would have told me so. "I'm not sure, Daniel. I hope so. But we'll just have to wait and see."

We then lapsed into silence as Daniel navigated some tricky parts of our route up and down mountain passes.

Ever since we had left Cajamarca, I had made it a habit to check if we were being followed. To my unpracticed eye, I couldn't detect anyone on our heels. For many stretches, we were the only vehicle in sight for miles in both directions. Then, some paranoia kicked in. *Suppose the police had placed a tracking device in our vehicle? What if Daniel himself had allowed it? Perhaps he was in cahoots with the police? Maybe not willingly? I was sure they had the means to coerce him to do what they wanted. Maybe they paid him more than I was paying him to let them follow us and lead the way to Jaime? Maybe…?* I could feel my pulse pounding and took a deep breath. These speculations were getting me nowhere. I had to keep alert. But I also had to keep a steady grip on my fears, not letting my imagination getting the best of me.

Twenty-Seven

WE ARRIVED AT SAN Ignacio a little before noon. We were greeted by a gigantic statue of a peasant woman in typical garb astride a globe of the world. I asked Daniel what she symbolized, and he just shrugged. We drove through the town, heading in a westward direction. San Ignacio was a bit off the beaten track but nonetheless attracted a smattering of tourists. It was located near a national park, with the mouthful name of Santuario Histórico Tabaconas-Namballe. The park attracted naturalists and those drawn to eco-tourism.

On the far side of town, we stopped at a gas station with an adjoining café. Daniel had the tank, which was almost on empty, filled. It had been some time since I had seen an attendant do the full honors of pumping the gas, cleaning the windshield, and checking the oil and tires. Soulless self-service had yet to make its presence felt in San Ignacio. Probably only a matter of time.

After Daniel had gotten instructions to the University's archaeological site, we adjourned to the café for a quick lunch. I was anxious to keep moving, but realized we both needed some nourishment for what could be a grueling afternoon. We gobbled down some sandwiches and then hit the road. By this time, the sun was at its height, the sky was a crystal blue, and the temperature had warmed to the point where I shed my leather jacket.

It didn't take more than five minutes after leaving the café in the direction of the national park that we ran out of paved road. We crunched onto gravel as we began to wind our way again upward, cresting several ridges with the road narrowing along the way. If we met somebody coming in the other direction, we would have to pull over to the side to let them pass, or vice-versa.

Crossing a ridge, we could see a valley ahead of us with a lake glittering blue in the distance. The vegetation was lush as we entered an area that seemed one part granite mountains and one part tropical forest. As we descended, we spotted a sign that indicated the Santuario was fifteen kilometers ahead. Passing the sign, Daniel made a right turn onto a dirt road that wound upward again. The road soon deteriorated into no more than a beaten path that barely accommodated our vehicle. Tree branches began to brush both sides of the SUV as we bumped our way up the hill. Daniel engaged the four-wheel function, which helped smooth our ride. After about fifteen minutes of a slow grind, we reached an open area where several jeeps were parked. Daniel pulled to a stop and I got out. The rest of the way, I would have to navigate on foot.

I grabbed my backpack and got ready to hike to where I hoped to find Jaime. Remembering Cartwright's warnings, I lathered on sun block and adjusted the straps on the broad-brimmed hat I had acquired at the truck stop cum tourist shop. Daniel provided me with some insect spray, which I applied liberally. I checked to make sure I had plenty of water along with some energy bars in my backpack. The site was about three kilometers away, uphill. Even though the altitude was a more reasonable 6,000 feet or so, it was going to be a tough go and I didn't want to be another Jackson in need of help in Peru.

Daniel wished me luck and assured me he would be at his post when I returned. I thanked him and turned to head up the mountain path that led to the site. Just beyond the parked jeeps, there was a sign on a post with the University seal and an arrow pointing in the direction of the site. I stopped to read the writing on the sign, which indicated the University had received official permission to operate. I tried to ignore the bold-faced lettering in red: **NO VISITORS ALLOWED WITHOUT PERMISSION.** I didn't bother to read the fine print. I had come this far and was not about to turn back.

Reassured I was indeed in the right place, I began my ascent. The path was generally smooth, although occasionally rocky. In wet weather it would have been slippery, but today was sunny and cool, not a cloud in the sky. It was a steady slog up hill and after about a mile I was beginning to work up a sweat. By this time, I had become acclimated to the altitude but still began to huff and puff as I made my way upward.

Finally, after about thirty minutes at a healthy pace, I crested a ridge and saw the archaeological site spread out before me. It was similar to the one I had visited the day before: a semi-circle of tents, a tarp on poles covering a table and chairs, and various instruments for measuring and photographing scattered about. There was no trailer, not surprising given the location, and the site itself, surrounded by stakes and cords, was above-ground, a circular clustering of well-arranged stones that reminded me of pictures I had seen of Machu Picchu.

Sitting around the table were seven students, three females and four males. They were engaged in an intense conversation of some sort and didn't notice me until I was about fifteen feet away. I made my presence known with a loud "Hello," that startled them. I saw looks of surprise and some fright as they turned to face me, a sudden apparition from out of the blue.

One of them, a tall muscular fellow rose from his chair. "Didn't you see the sign, idiot? No visitors. What the hell are you doing here?"

He began to advance toward me, his fists balled. I held up my hands, palms out in a gesture of reassurance. "I'm not a tourist just out exploring. I'm Melanie Jackson's brother, Clint. I'm here because I think one of you may have information about my sister's disappearance. No other reason."

The tall guy uncurled his fists, but still looked at me with suspicion. He got closer and said, "What proof do you have that you are who you say you are?"

I kept my left hand raised and with my right I dug under my shirt and pulled out my passport. I handed it over to the guy without a word. He took it, eyeing me skeptically, and opened it to the page with my photo. He glanced down at it then at me several times. "That was before I had my hair cut and shaved my goatee," I explained. That produced a flicker of a grin.

Nodding, he returned it to me. "So, Señor Clint *Eastwood* Jackson. Why do you think *we* can help you find Melanie?" Throwing a glance over his shoulder, he gestured to the group, "We have been up here for weeks. We weren't even in Cajamarca when she disappeared."

"Then, how do you know she's missing?"

He looked uneasy. "We do go into San Ignacio for supplies and to use our phones. That's how we learned she was missing. But we don't know anything more than that. So, you might as well turn around and head back. We can't help you."

Behind him, all faces were turned toward me. I couldn't read the expressions, but I sensed some sympathy. I didn't think everybody agreed with the guy. At any rate, I hadn't come this far to give up easily.

"Okay, I understand. But before I leave, do you mind if I sit down and rest for a minute? It was a pretty tiring climb to get here."

I thought he was going to refuse, but one of the females at the table stood up. "Come over here Señor Jackson. There is an empty chair right here," she said, pointing to her right.

The guy didn't look happy, but he relented and I walked over and sat down. "Thank you." Then, turning to the girl who had offered me a place at the table, I said, with a smile, "So, you all know that I am Clint *Eastwood* Jackson," a line that was sure to produce some chuckles as it did this time, "but who are you?"

A perfectly natural question, but it made them uneasy and I was beginning to suspect why. "My name is Mercedes," the girl next to me said. The tall guy, who had pulled up his chair next to mine as though ready to intercede if necessary, was Rodrigo, clearly the leader of the group. As we went around the table, I did my best to remember all the names. But I was most interested in the males. Two of the guys answered quickly and naturally, but the third, who was staring down at his lap most of the time, mumbled the name Rafael – but I had my doubts. It was, I was pretty sure, Jaime.

I spent the next ten minutes trying to set the group at ease. I asked them questions about the site and their work and told them about myself and my life in San Francisco. They relaxed a bit. The three females, in particular, made it a point to emphasize how upset they were by Mel's disappearance and expressed their sympathy for what me and my family were going through. Nonetheless, under the surface, there remained a palpable tension. I noticed, too, that "Rafael" did not utter a single word, continuing to find whatever was in his lap of endless fascination.

The time now seemed right, to take the plunge. "Listen," I said. "I

185

have learned that one of your fellow students, a guy named Jaime, was probably the last person to see Melanie before she disappeared. I also know that he is here, among you. That he came here because he is afraid the police will blame him for whatever has happened to my sister. And I need to talk with him, find out what he knows. It's the only real lead I have at the moment. And I can assure you…"

Rodrigo interrupted, grabbing my arm in a tight grip. The group fell silent as he said, "Listen, Clint. I don't know where you got this information, but it's not true. Jaime is not here. We haven't seen him in weeks. Your trip here has been for nothing. It's time for you to leave."

He began to pull me up from my chair. I prepared to resist, violently if necessary, when a voice spoke up. "No, Rodrigo, please no." It was "Rafael." "You are right, Clint. I am Jaime."

Rodrigo reluctantly loosened his grip. The rest of the group remained silent. "My friends were just trying to protect me, Clint. Maybe I can help you, but do you mind if we talk alone?"

"Sure thing, Jaime," I said, rubbing my arm. "How about we head to those rocks over there?" pointing to the arranged stones of the site

"That will be fine, Clint," he replied. Leaving the group, we headed for the stones until we were well out of earshot. However, I could feel all eyes on us. I felt certain that if they believed I posed any physical danger to Jaime they would be on me in no time.

When we stopped and faced each other, I took a closer look at Jaime. He was maybe five and a half feet tall, maybe 150 pounds, with a mop of curly brown hair and thick-rimmed glasses behind which were sad-looking brown eyes that reminded me of a puppy we once had. He was probably in his mid-twenties but looked to be a kind of nerdy teenager, gentle and shy. I could see how Mel might have felt protective of him, particularly if he had fallen for her. Physically and from his body language, it was hard to believe he was the firebrand rabble-rouser who so concerned the local police. But when he spoke, he had an unexpectedly deep and powerful voice. We were almost whispering, but I could well imagine that before a crowd that voice could stir deep emotions.

He glanced nervously over my shoulder, back toward where the group was clustered. "How did you find me, Clint? Who told you I was here? Professor Quispé?"

I wasn't about to betray confidences. I shook my head. "I can't tell you, Jaime. The important thing is that I am here."

Still looking over my shoulder, worry lines deep in his face, he said, "Is it possible that the police have followed you?"

That put me on the spot. "Possible?", yes. I waffled. "I've been warned that they might. But I've been careful. There are no signs that they have followed me. I've been checking regularly."

He looked dubious. "I hope you are right, Clint. You understand that if the police find me, it means trouble, serious trouble, for everyone who has been involved in hiding me. Lives will be endangered."

What he said sobered me, although I did my best not to react. I really hadn't thought through all the consequences of my actions. I was so focused on finding Mel, I hadn't considered the possibility I was putting the lives of others in danger. The typical naïve American stumbling around in a foreign country, causing harm with the best of intentions. But, no sense dwelling on that now. I had Jaime in front of me and needed for him to tell me what he knew. "All I can say, Jaime, is that I won't say a word to anyone about your whereabouts. I don't want to put anyone in danger. *But I have to find out what happened to my sister.* I'm sure you can understand that. I've been told that you and Melanie were close. You must want her to be found safe and alive as much as I do. And right now, I'm about the only hope she has. I'm not getting any help from the embassy and the local police, I'm told, are useless." He nodded in agreement. "So, that leaves me."

I was laying it on a bit thick, but it was the truth. "I've been told, Jaime, that you were planning to meet Melanie the night she disappeared. A secret meeting that had something to do with your leadership of the protest movement. What happened that night?"

His eyes widened. "Who told you that?"

Back to that, again. "Look, Jaime," my voice taking on a sharper tone, "To repeat. I am not going to betray any confidences. And that should show you that I'm not going to betray you either." Then, deciding to apply a little additional pressure, "Of course, if I think you know something important and won't tell me what is, well then...." I let it trail off. Not an explicit threat, but he got the message.

He looked down at his shoes. I wondered if he was thinking of bolting and prepared to grab him before he did. But when he looked up, his eyes were moist and there was a look of anguish on his face. "Yes, Clint. It's true. I was planning to meet Melanie that night. She was sympathetic to our cause, but believed that we were going too far. That we were escalating the confrontation to the point of inciting real violence. She knew that the police were following me and wanted to meet secretly so we could discuss the future of our movement. I didn't want her to be involved or get into trouble herself, so that night I made sure I was not followed and drove to a point past Cumbe Mayo where we had arranged to meet. But, Clint, the thing is..." He began to sob, "...the thing is, she never showed up."

He wiped his eyes and regained control. "I waited for hours. I even got out of the car and walked toward her campground. But there was no sign of her. I thought she had changed her mind or maybe couldn't get away without being seen. It wasn't until the next day that I discovered she had gone missing. Then, Professor Quispé sent me here.

"Believe me, Clint. I have been in agony. There is nothing I want more than to help you find Mel. But," he shrugged, "the minute I appear in Cajamarca, I'll end up in jail."

I nodded my understanding, but I could not hide my disappointment. *Was Jaime telling the truth? Who knew for sure?* I thought he probably was. All the signs pointed in that direction. If so, the mystery of Mel's disappearance only deepened. But I couldn't shake the nagging sense that Jaime wasn't telling me everything. Maybe it was because I didn't want to accept the fact that he had no idea what had happened to Mel. But maybe, too, somewhere deep in my gut I felt there was something he was hiding from me. There was something a little off in his performance that I couldn't quite put my finger on. But I was stuck. As with Quispé, I couldn't try to beat the whole story out of him. For one thing, Rodrigo and the others would be on me in a second. Finally, I just had to accept what he had told me and go on from there.

"Well, Jaime, I appreciate your difficult situation. Rest assured I won't tell anyone where you are." He didn't look totally convinced.

Looking past him, I asked, "Just out of curiosity, how far to the border with Ecuador?"

Turning around, he pointed northward. "Only about ten kilometers that way. On the other side of that lake."

I was about to suggest that he get going in that direction as soon as possible. I couldn't guarantee that somehow the police might not have tracked me and that I had put him in danger. I didn't want that possibility weighing on my conscience. Maybe he wasn't telling me the whole story, but Mel clearly had protective feelings for him and I owed it to her to try to keep him safe. I hoped he got the message.

"Well, I guess I better get back to Cajamarca," I said. "And thanks for telling me what you know, Jaime."

I extended my hand and we shook. "I hope you can find Mel, Clint. She means a lot to me. To all the students. I only wish I could be of more help." He seemed sincere, but I still had my nagging doubts.

Passing by the group at the table, I pulled Rodrigo aside. In a low voice, I said, "Maybe it is better that Jaime try to cross the border soon." I explained my reasoning and he nodded in agreement.

As we parted, he wished me good luck on finding my sister. I thanked him, then turned and headed back down the trail. While my trip to see Jaime had not been a totally wasted effort, it was clearer than ever that I would need a lot of luck if I was to solve the mystery of her disappearance.

Twenty-Eight

WE DIDN'T GET BACK to Cajamarca until well after nine o'clock. Both Daniel and I were beat. When we arrived at the hotel, Daniel asked me if I would need him tomorrow. At that point, it wasn't clear what I would be doing the next day. "I'm not sure, Daniel. But if I need you, I'll call."

I handed over the rest of his fee and added twenty extra dollars. Entering the hotel, I went straight to my room to clean up, planning to head down to the restaurant for dinner. By this time, I was starving. But as soon as I closed the door to my room, my phone buzzed. Looking at the screen, I saw that it was Lamar Jenkins. "Hello, Lamar," I said, "What's up?"

I was hoping that he had found some guys who could come to Cajamarca and lend me a hand. But that was not to be. "Hi, Clint. Any luck on finding your sister?"

"Not really, Lamar. I followed a promising lead today, but it turned out not to be of much help."

"Sorry to hear that. Listen, the reason I called was to let you know what's going on with our kidnappings. We got word today that our men are being held by an eco-terrorist outfit that calls itself the 'Atahualpa Brigade.' I'm not sure you know the significance of the name, but..."

"Actually, I found out today about Atahualpa being held by the Spaniards for ransom. It took place right here in Cajamarca."

"Yeah," he said, a dismissive tone in his voice. "Well, they don't want gold this time. What they want is for us to stop our mining operations throughout the country. If we don't, they plan to execute the hostages one by one until we agree to their demands. They are giving us forty-eight hours before they start killing our guys. We don't know much about this outfit, but we have to assume they mean what they say. The embassy has mobilized all its forces – FBI, CIA, DEA – to help us and the Peruvian government has offered its full cooperation. So far, we have few leads and the clock is ticking. We can't realistically give in to their demands. The costs would be enormous. On the other hand, we want to protect our guys. The pressure, as you can imagine, is intense."

Yes. I could realize that. But I also felt my resentment begin to swell. Sure, when powerful capitalist enterprises were involved, it was the full force of the U.S. and Peruvian governments riding to the rescue. But when it came to the fate of an American graduate student, *who cares?* A bitter reality, but reality nonetheless. I didn't much sympathize with the radical lefties who found the Bay Area their Mecca, but I was beginning to see their point.

"I can imagine, but..."

"But what does this have to do with your sister's disappearance? Well, I was wondering if you had picked up any indications that maybe she has been abducted by the same outfit? If so, maybe I could do a little prodding to get you some help."

I was sorely tempted to lie. *"Well, yes, Lamar. Some of the local students I met suggested that Mel had been taken by an eco-terrorist group."* But I couldn't. "No, Lamar. I have floated the possibility, but the professors and students who worked with her and with whom I spoke pretty much dismissed that possibility." *"Pretty much,"* I thought to myself. But it could not be completely discounted. Maybe there was enough ambiguity so that I could tell Lamar honestly that it was a possibility, no matter how slight? But again, I decided against it. Suppose he went the extra mile to send the cavalry, diverting resources he and his company desperately needed to deal with their own crisis, only to find out that Mel's disappearance had nothing to do with the 'Atahualpa Brigade'? Not only would I have egg on my face, but I could easily make everything worse. My credibility would be shot. "The brother who cried wolf."

"Well, Clint. If you hear anything that connects your sister's disappearance with our situation, let me know, will you? I want to help if I can."

"Thanks, Lamar. I'll be sure to get in touch. So long. And good luck."

"Same to you, Clint," he said as we disconnected.

I sat on my bed, various thoughts whirring through my mind. *Had Jaime told me the whole story? Was Mel's disappearance somehow tied up with the 'Atahualpa Brigade'? What should I do next?*

The last question was easy. Time to call John. He picked up on the second ring. "Hey, Clint. How was your trip north? Any luck?"

Before I answered, I asked him, "Any word from your end? Any message from kidnappers?"

"No. Not a word," he replied. Then I filled him in on my trip and its results. "So," he said, when I had finished, "We're back to square one," doing little to hide his frustration and disappointment.

"I'm afraid we are. And I'm running out of ideas and leads to follow. One thought I had was to go to the local newspaper and place an ad offering a reward for anyone who can provide information as to Mel's disappearance. So far as I know, there has been no mention of it in the press or on the air. What do you think?"

He mulled it over for a moment. "It might be worth a shot. But you'll need to watch out for grifters who will take advantage of you and provide you with false information and false hope just to get a reward. Unfortunately, we don't have the FBI helping us out to filter the responses you might get, separating the greedy and the loony from those who might have genuine information."

"You're right, Bro. Let me sleep on it. Oh, and I almost forgot. Have you heard about the kidnappings of Americans working for mining companies here? It's been carried out by an outfit called the 'Atahualpa Brigade.' They are demanding that the companies cease their operations in forty-eight hours or they will start executing the hostages. I spoke to Lamar Jenkins just before I called you and he explained that his company, the embassy, and the Peruvian government are going all out to try to rescue the captives. I wish they showed the same concern for Mel."

"Yeah, Clint. It's been on the news here. You think there might be any connection with what happened to Mel?"

"That's hard to say. Since you haven't heard from any kidnappers with demands, it seems unlikely she is part of the scheme. She's not associated with the mining companies in any way. In fact, she probably has some sympathy with the 'Brigade,' although I can't imagine her approving of their tactics. But at this point, I'm not ready to rule out any possibility. By the way, how are Al and Mae? Any changes?"

He hesitated. "No. Not really. Pretty much status quo."

I had my doubts, but didn't want to press it. I suspected my brother was protecting me, realizing I had enough to deal with as it was.

"Well, Bro. I've had a long day. I need to get something to eat and then get some sleep. I'm bushed."

"Okay, Clint. Hang in there. Keep in touch." Then a pause. "I hate to bring this up, Bro. You're under a lot of pressure. How are you handling it? I worry about you."

The message was far from subtle. That was a polite way of asking, "Are you still hitting the bottle?" Given my history, that was a perfectly legitimate question, but I was still irritated. "Thanks for the concern," I answered, some sarcasm in my voice. "But I'm holding up okay." I took a glance at the mini-bar. "So far, resisting temptation. And, to tell you the truth, in some kind of weird way I'm enjoying myself. It's kind of like living a real adventure, trying to unravel a deep mystery. Of course, the fact that my sister's life lies in the balance hangs over everything I'm doing undermines the enjoyment. Still, if you get what I mean..."

"I think I can, Clint. Maybe that's the best way to look at it and keep your sanity. Just take care of yourself, Bro. I don't want to lose two siblings," he said somberly.

"I'll watch my step, John. Talk to you tomorrow."

After hanging up, I went down to the hotel restaurant. Even though it was almost ten o'clock, it was crowded with tourists returning from their daily expeditions. I found an empty table and took a seat. A waiter appeared immediately and handed me a menu. I told him to wait while I scanned it, ordering something with chicken, fried potatoes, and, of course, rice. He poured me some water from a plastic bottle into a glass and I told him to bring me another with my meal.

While I waited, I looked up at a big screen television in the corner. None of the tourists seemed to be paying much attention to what was on the screen, but I noticed the servers glancing at it whenever they could. I had some difficulty in understanding every word, but I saw immediately that the big story was the action by the 'Atahualpa Brigade.' Interspersed with interviews with various officials were shots of helicopters hovering over unspecified locations while SWAT teams descended from ropes to the ground below. From what I could tell, this was stock footage, not a current operation.

When my waiter returned with my meal, I gestured toward the screen. "What's going on? *Qué pasa?* It seems serious."

He nodded and explained what I already knew. The government was gearing up to deal with this latest hostage crisis. I asked him what he thought of it, and he shrugged. "Crazy things are always happening in Peru," he said. "This is just one more." Then, appearing to realize that tourists would not see kidnappings of foreigners as "just one more crazy thing," he assured me that I had nothing to worry about. "There is no 'Atahualpa Brigade' in Cajamarca."

After he left, I began to ponder what he said. "No 'Atahualpa Brigade' in Cajamarca." If that was true, *why not?* There was already a major mining operation in the area and more planned for the future. In terms of symbolism, what better place to exert some revenge in the name of the Inca Emperor? What about those protests in the plaza? No connection to eco-terrorist groups? Or, at least, some sympathizers? It didn't make much sense to me, but a lot of things I'd been stumbling over the past two days didn't make a lot of sense.

Halfway through my meal, the U.S. ambassador appeared on the screen. A slick-looking guy who might have been central casting's idea of the typical diplomat, he spoke in English. I saw some of the tourists turn their heads toward the screen as he began to speak. His jaw set firm, he pledged an all-out effort to free the hostages, repeating the by-now familiar refrain that "We do not negotiate with terrorists." His tone was firm, but I could see some fear in his eyes. Not inclined to be very charitable toward him given how he had failed to respond to Mel's disappearance, I wondered how much of the fear had to do with concern for the lives of the hostages and how much a failure to rescue them would tarnish his own reputation.

When the ambassador was done, a spokesman for Amalgamated Mining, the main company affected by the crisis, appeared along with some of his assistants. I wondered if Lamar Jenkins was among them.

He thanked the ambassador for his support and pledged to do "whatever it took" to resolve the crisis peacefully. "Looking after the safety of our personnel," he proclaimed, "Is our number one priority." It sounded like boilerplate to me. Personnel above profits? I wasn't so sure. But I momentarily gave him the benefit of the doubt.

After that interview, two Peruvian commentators discussed the current crisis. They began by pointing out that Peru had a very long history of kidnapping and hostage taking. In the great majority of cases, the negotiation was pretty straightforward: Release of hostages once a ransom was paid, although. I thought, that hadn't panned out too well in the case of Atahualpa, or an exchange of prisoners. In this instance, however, major multinationals were expected to shut down operations in which they had invested tens of millions to save the lives of a few. The financial losses would be substantial. And who would assure that the terms negotiated would be carried out on both sides? It was not clear, the commentators speculated, that the Brigade leaders had thought through all the complexities of their demands. They were driven, they implied, more by idealistic romanticism than a full understanding of the realities.

While I was having my dessert, one of the tourists came to my table and asked me in English, "Excuse me, sir. Are you an American?"

"Guilty as charged," I said with a grin.

"Can you tell me what's going on? My Spanish is pretty rudimentary. I saw the ambassador on the screen, but couldn't hear him very well. Some kind of trouble, I presume."

He was a middle-aged guy decked out in trekking gear. I invited him to take a seat. "My name is Brad," he said, extending his hand.

I took it. "Clint." I then explained what was going on with the "Atahualpa Brigade."

His brow wrinkled. "Anything for us to be worried about? I'm here with my wife and two kids," he said, pointing to a table near the window where a blonde woman with two equally blond teenagers, a boy and a girl, sat. "I don't want to put them in any danger. We're booked for a couple of days here, then on to Machu Picchu. Maybe we should consider cutting the trip short and getting back to the States."

"Well," I said, "from all I know the kidnappings are targeted specifically at employees of American mining companies, not at tourists. I think you should be safe enough."

"Are you planning to stay?"

"Yes, I am," I said, without explaining why.

He nodded and got up from the table. "Thanks for filling me in, Clint. I'll talk things over with my family and we'll decide where to go from there."

"No problem," I said. "Hope things work out."

After Brad left, I finished my dessert and returned to my room. It was almost midnight and I was dead on my feet. Seconds after my head hit the pillow, I was fast asleep.

Twenty-Nine

I AWOKE WHEN SUNLIGHT BEGAN to filter through the window shade. My watch said seven-thirty, time to get moving. As I shaved and showered, I pondered my next steps. I sketched out a plan of action, then headed down for breakfast with the sheets of paper on which I was trying to establish a narrative and a time line. I should have done it before I had gone to bed, while the details were still fresh. But I was too tired. I felt confident that I could remember clearly the details of yesterday's trip and enter them into my diary.

When I got to the restaurant, it was about half full. Again, mostly tourists with the occasional single male who I guessed to be businessmen. I sat at the same table near the TV. The screen was once more filled with news about the hostage crisis. So far as I could tell, things stood as they had last night. No new major developments. On the upper right-hand corner of the screen was a clock ticking down the forty-eight-hour deadline. It showed thirty-five hours, twenty minutes to go.

While I was eating my breakfast and scribbling my notes, Brad came by to say hello.

"Hi, Clint," he said. "Just wanted to thank you again for the information last night."

"Glad to help. What have you decided?"

"We're going to stay, stick to our schedule. This morning, we have a tour to Cumbe Mayo. Have you been?"

"No, I haven't. Not yet."

"Well, maybe you would like to join us. There's plenty of room."

"Thanks for the invitation. That's very kind of you. But I have a lot of work on my schedule today. Perhaps I'll get up there some other time."

I could see him get ready to sit down and continue the conversation. He was a nice guy and I didn't want to be rude. "Right now," I said, pointing at the sheets of paper, "I need to prepare for an important meeting." Looking at my watch, "In about half an hour."

I'm not sure he believed me, but he drew back. "Sorry to interrupt, Clint. Maybe you can join us on another tour, maybe tomorrow?"

"We'll see, Brad. And thanks again for the invitation. Have a nice excursion."

"Sure, Clint. You have a good day." He turned and rejoined his family and I returned to my writing. By the time I was on my second cup of coffee, I had filled three pages with a chronology of my trip to San Ignacio. Reading over what I had written, I tried to tease out any clues that would give me some solid answers. So far, not much. I had eliminated some possibilities, but there still seemed nothing tangible that I could hang on to that would lead me to Mel. Right now, I seemed to face nothing but dead ends.

I signed the chit for my breakfast, assembled my papers, and headed for my room. Once there, I sat on the edge of the bed and pondered my next steps. Looking at the top of my bureau, I saw the pile of business cards I had accumulated since my arrival. Picking them up and sifting through them, I came upon the one I had gotten from my driver in Lima, Manuel Rodríguez. I'd almost forgotten it even though it was only a little more than two days ago that he had given it to me. On the back was the name of his brother, Enrique, who I remembered was some official in the mayor's office in Cajamarca. Manuel had urged me to contact him, but in the whirl of activity since my arrival I had forgotten all about him.

I didn't know what help Enrique could be, but it was worth a shot. I dialed the number, expecting to be put on hold by a secretary. But instead, Enrique himself picked up. He must have had caller ID because he spoke before I had a chance to introduce myself. "Hello, Señor Jackson. I've been expecting your call. Manuel told me you would be arriving in Cajamarca. How can I help you?"

A pleasant surprise. I had expected bureaucratic caution and a polite brush off. But the tone seemed genuine. "Hello, Enrique. Sorry that I didn't contact you sooner, but I have been very busy the past two days. I suppose that Manuel told you that I am looking for my sister, Melanie, who disappeared from an archaeological site near Cumbe Mayo more than a week ago. So far, I have not had much success in finding out exactly what happened to her. I thought that perhaps you might have some insights into how I might continue my investigation. I know you must be busy, but I would appreciate any help you can provide." I was about to add that I was getting desperate, but he could probably discern that himself from the tenor of my voice.

"Yes, Señor..."

"Please call me Clint."

"Yes, Clint. Manuel told me about your predicament." He paused for a moment, "I am very busy this morning. What about lunch? Can you meet me for lunch, say around one o'clock?"

"Certainly. That sounds fine to me."

We arranged to meet at a restaurant a few blocks from the hotel. When I hung up, I felt a surge of optimism. Enrique's willingness to help seemed genuine. At the least, he could provide me with a clearer picture of what I was up against as I tried to navigate the complex reality of the local scene.

My next step was to go to the offices of the local newspaper and place an ad offering a reward for information about my sister's disappearance. John had been right to warn me that it could produce a lot of falsehoods from people looking to make some easy bucks and could well be a waste of time and money. It was like playing the lottery, hoping you got the winning ticket. At this point, I thought it was a gamble worth taking.

I went down to the business center just off the lobby and, using a computer, drafted the notice to be placed in the newspaper. I kept it brief, providing details on where and when she had gone missing but nothing more. I had a picture of her on my phone that I could transfer to the printer and added the basic facts of age and nationality. I debated over the amount of the reward, finally settling on five hundred dollars in return for verifiable information on her disappearance. In the States, it would be a laughable amount. But from what I had seen, five hundred dollars would go a long way in Cajamarca. I included my name and cell-phone number. I thought about mentioning the hotel, but didn't want a steady stream of unfiltered respondents pounding on my door.

Printing out two copies, one for the paper and one for me to keep, I put them in an envelope and went to the front desk, asking directions to the newspaper office. The clerk raised an inquisitive eyebrow. I guessed not many tourists, especially gringo tourists, wanted to know the whereabouts of the *Eco de Cajamarca*. But he was too polite to inquire further. Grabbing a single-sheet map of the city, he drew a line that led me to the *Eco*, which, like everything else in Cajamarca, it seemed, was only a few blocks from the main plaza.

I thanked the clerk, pocketed the map, and walked out onto the street. It was another cool, sunny day. Outside, workers in blue coveralls were sprucing up the plaza, getting ready, I thought, for the next protest. As I walked toward the *Eco's* office, Indian women, dressed in white blouses, full skirts, and sporting derby hats, clustered on the steps of the Cathedral next to the hotel, held their hands out, begging for a few *soles*. Some were carrying babies swaddled in blankets and hanging from their shoulders. They had pitiable looks on their faces, looks and voices that pleaded for compassion. I was tempted to hand over a few coins, but that would begin an endless process. Instead, I hardened my heart and moved on, trying to ignore their pleas as best I could.

Five minutes later, I arrived at the office of the *Eco*. It was located in an unprepossessing two-story building. A window with the paper's name etched on it contained pages from the most recent edition, pasted so that the passing public could pause and scan the news free of charge. When I tried the front door, it was locked. Through the pane, I could see a counter and behind it a young woman, her head bowed, looking at her phone. I knocked loudly and she looked up, startled. She put down her phone and came to the door. Opening it a crack, she peered out and asked me somewhat suspiciously, "Yes, Señor. How can I be of assistance?"

"I would like to place an ad in your paper."

Ah-ha. A paying customer. "Yes, Señor. Please come in," she said with a smile.

I followed her to the counter and removed the ad I had drafted from the envelope, placing it face up and turning it so she could read it.

She took out a pair of glasses, adjusted them, and began to read. I had expected a quick and simple transaction. She would read the ad, perhaps not paying too much attention to the content, quote me a price, which probably included some editing of my rough Spanish, I would pay, she would give me a receipt and that would be that. I was wrong. Lifting her eyes from the draft, I saw excitement on her face. "Please wait here, Señor. I need to speak with my editor. Just a moment, please?"

What was this all about? It didn't take long for me to find out. Not sixty seconds later, she emerged with a fiftyish man in a white dress shirt with the sleeves rolled up and dark slacks. "This is the editor of the *Eco,* she informed me. "Doctor Roberto Martínez. He would like to speak with you."

He gave me a welcoming smile and extended his hand. "A pleasure to meet you, Señor Jackson. Won't you please come into my office," he said, pointing to the back of the room where I could see his name etched in glass on the door. I was a little uneasy. My simple transaction had suddenly become more complicated. Like any newspaperman, I belatedly realized, when Martínez heard about the content of my ad, he smelled a story. I should have figured. I thought about turning around and forgetting the whole thing. But something told me that I should at least hear him out.

I went with Martínez back to his office. There were no surprises there. His desk was piled high with papers, clippings, pens, pencils, paperclips, all scattered in a manner that looked like total chaos to me. There were file drawers against three walls, with newspapers stacked like kindling on top and drawers half open with folders jutting out at odd angles. It could have been the set for any number of Hollywood movies about the newspaper business.

Martínez took a seat in a well-worn swivel chair behind his desk, gesturing for me to take the chair opposite. Once I sat, he asked, "Care for any coffee, Señor Jackson? Coca tea, perhaps?"

"Coffee would be fine, thank you."

He grabbed the phone on his desk and hit one button. It was an inter-office connection. "Graciela," he said, in a pleasant voice. "Two coffees, please. Thank you, my dear," and put the receiver down.

Picking up the draft of my ad, he said, "I am very sorry that your sister has gone missing, Señor Jackson. Very sorry, indeed. And I would like to help you find her, if I can."

"I appreciate that. It's why I wanted to place the ad. Hopefully…"

He cut me off. "Yes, Yes. I understand. But there are some things you need to consider. I'm not sure if you have read our paper…?"

"I haven't had the time to do more than glance at it."

"Well, the fact is, we have dozens of ads like yours located in the back pages. Sadly, people – and animals – go missing here all the time, although rarely is a reward offered. And, in most cases, they stay missing."

"What about the police? Don't they…?

Again, he interrupted, although I knew what he was going to say. "The police, I'm afraid, cannot be bothered. Unless, of course, it involves a person of some local influence. That, however, is the rare exception."

"That's the impression I have gotten. From what I can tell, the local police haven't made much of an effort to find my sister. They seem more annoyed than concerned."

He nodded in understanding. Just then, Graciela knocked discreetly and entered with our coffees. She had gone to the nearby Starbucks and handed us each our respective cups, leaving packets of sugar and stirrers on the desk. She then quietly closed the door behind her.

"Let's drink these before they get cold," Martínez suggested.

We removed the lids, stirred in healthy amounts of sugar, and began to sip. I appreciated the jolt. "So, what you are saying Doctor Martínez…"

"Please, Roberto."

"So, Roberto. If I get your message, placing an ad about my missing sister among the many others in the back pages will not get much attention. Have I got that right?"

He smiled. "Exactly right, Señor." Then, leaning forward, his hands clasped in front of me, he gave the hard sell. "But if we make it a feature story on the front page with your sister's picture front and center and a banner headline reading," he spread his arms: "**American Student in Cajamarca Missing for More Than A Week**, we can really make a splash. That will be hard to ignore. It might even stir the police to action. It might even make the national news," he said, his eyes twinkling.

Yeah, my cynical side said, *and sell a lot of newspapers and make you a local celebrity. But,* I reasoned, *what was the alternative? An ad buried in the back pages and likely ignored?* I was silent for a moment while I gathered my thoughts. Martínez's offer was attractive, but I was worried that it might open a can of worms. I assumed that he or one of his reporters would go to the site near Cumbe Mayo to interview Cartwright and the students. They probably would check with the students at the University of Cajamarca as well. I didn't want to put any of them, Jaime in particular, in danger.

I was stuck between the proverbial rock and a hard place. I had run out of leads to follow. Publicizing Mel's disappearance might be the only way to pick up the trail. Still, I hesitated, not sure what to do. "Excuse me, Roberto. But I need to call my brother and get his advice. I can't make a decision right now without consulting him."

"Certainly, Señor Jackson. I understand completely." Getting up from his desk, he said, "I'll leave you alone to speak with your brother. Let me know what you decide."

After he left, I dialed John. He picked up immediately. "Hey, Clint. What's up?" There was a slight note of panic in his voice, having received a call from me outside of our normal framework. "Any news?", he said, as though bracing for the worst.

I tried to put him at ease, giving him the details of Martínez's offer. After going over the pros and cons, we agreed to go ahead with publicizing Mel's disappearance. We could only pray that it would produce positive results. As John argued, if we didn't take the risk and later found that it might have made the difference between finding her and not finding her, we would regret it for the rest of our lives. *More grim realities.*

I called Martínez back in and told him we had decided to go ahead. He smiled and rubbed his hands together. "Excellent, Señor Jackson. Excellent."

Sitting down, the editor pulled out a tape recorder and set it on the desk between us. "Now, let's start from the beginning. I would like to hear the full story." He then pushed the "record" button.

It took me about half an hour to trace what had happened from the first phone call informing us that Mel was missing up to the present. He generally let me run on with only occasional clarifying questions and quizzical looks. I omitted any mention of Jaime and only relayed what I had learned from Cartwright, Quispé, and the other students in general terms, not mentioning any names. Of course, I figured, if he wanted to pursue the story, he could easily retrace my steps and pin down the details. That was up to him. I didn't know how many reporters he had or how much he wanted to invest in the effort. I could only hope that I didn't get anybody into hot water.

When I had finished, Martínez stopped the recording. "Well," he said, "That's quite a story. Quite a story, indeed."

"So, where do we go from here?"

He thought for a moment. "Well, I am going to write up the story at once. I'll put in the information you have provided concerning the reward and include your sister's picture. Where did you get the photo?"

"It's from my phone."

"If you don't mind, could I borrow your phone for a few minutes? I think Graciela can enhance the picture so it will be clearer when we print the story."

I scrolled through my photos and isolated the picture of Mel. It was a head shot, with her smiling as though she hadn't a care in the world. My stomach clenched and I fought back tears as I handed the phone over to Martínez. He called in Gracielaa, who seemed to be lurking just beyond the door, and told her to make copies for what would be a lead story. "Right away, Señor Martínez. Right away." True to her word, she returned in a few minutes, handing over a photo of Mel that was clearer and sharper than the one I had been able to produce.

While Graciela had attended to her chore, Martínez and I discussed some of the particulars of what would appear in the paper. I told him that I was staying at the Costa del Sol Hotel, but was wary of having hordes descending on me there. He agreed, and recommended that not even my name be included in the article, just my phone number.

With that decided, I asked, "When will the story appear?" I didn't know whether the *Eco* was a daily or a weekly, whether it appeared in the morning or the afternoon.

I expected a delay but Martínez surprised me. "This afternoon, around three o'clock."

"That fast?"

"Yes. We have today's edition formatted and ready to run. We were going to feature these kidnappings by the 'Atahualpa Brigade' – you know about these?" I nodded yes. "Well, that's a national story, well-covered by the national press. Your sister's disappearance has more local interest, so we'll shift things around so it will be front and center on page one." He paused for a moment, then his eyes lit up. "Say, you don't think your sister's disappearance has anything to do with these other kidnappings, do you?"

"I don't think so," I said after a pause. "As I explained, we have not been contacted with any ransom demands. It seems unlikely. But who knows?" I said with a shrug. Then a thought hit me. "I was wondering why the 'Brigade' hasn't carried out an action here in Cajamarca. Of all the places in Peru, from what I understand, this would be the most logical target for them."

He nodded in agreement. "I've been asking myself the same question. In fact, I have one of my reporters working on that angle at this very moment. You know about the controversy over the proposed gold mines, I presume?"

"It's been hard to avoid, especially with the nightly protests in front of my hotel."

Leaning back in his chair, he reflected for a moment, then leaned forward. "Well, it's all very complicated and very Peruvian. You know about our governor?"

"Yes, both from the people at the embassy and from others I've spoken with. From what I can tell, he's a pretty slippery character. He wants to side with the 'people,' or at least appear to, but also realizes the economic potential of the mines."

"Exactly, Señor Jackson. You have, how do you say it? Hit the nail on the head." Lowering his voice, as though the room might be bugged, he said in a near whisper "I don't have all the facts yet. Nothing I can prove or print. But I'm willing to bet that the governor has some kind of secret arrangement with the 'Atahualpa Brigade.' I don't know what his game is, but you are right to find it strange that the 'Brigade' has not targeted Cajamarca. I'm also willing to bet that he is receiving bribes from the mining companies to approve the contracts. Again, I can't prove it. But it fits a pattern that is much too common in our history."

It all seemed bizarre. "So," I said, "It could be that the governor, being bribed by the mining companies is in turn paying off the radicals so they won't target Cajamarca. It reminds me of what I know of the Iran-Contra Affair in the eighties."

Martínez again leaned back in his chair, something of a twinkle in his eye. "Maybe, Señor Jackson. Maybe. Stranger things have happened. And," his journalistic instincts kicking in, "it would make quite a story. Quite a story, indeed. But for now, it's only in the realm of speculation."

"Well," I said, starting to get up from my chair, "I've taken up enough of your time. You need to work on your story."

He gestured for me to stay seated. "Don't worry, Señor Jackson. It won't take me long to write it up. But there is something I should warn you about. Once the story appears, you will not only be flooded with all kinds of false information but other journalists will try to contact you for interviews, including our local television station. And although the national outlets are absorbed with the 'Atahualpa Brigade' kidnappings, they may suspect a link between them and your sister's kidnapping, just as we have discussed, and descend on you like the plague. You may find yourself in the middle of, how do you say it? - A media frenzy. Prepare yourself for that possibility, Señor Jackson."

"Thanks for the warning, Roberto. I'll do my best to withstand the onslaught." Once again, I thought, *how could I have imagined, in my wildest dreams, this turn of events? If someone had told me a few days ago I might become a person of media interest in a political drama in a foreign country, I would have asked for some of what they were smoking. But, now, it seemed, that was a real possibility.*

Before I again prepared to leave, another thought hit me. "Say, Roberto. I've been told that a local police investigator, a guy named Felipe Calderón..." The name once more worked its magic. The newspaperman's face turned into a scowl that seemed to mix fear with disgust. "...is in charge of looking into Mel's disappearance. I've been told to avoid him and so far, I have. But what do you think? Should I go see him and sound him out? So far, I've only gotten second-hand accounts and impressions. Maybe it would be worth my while to go directly to the source. Talk to the man who is charged with investigating the case."

The expression on Martínez's face said it all. *Are you crazy? Calderón is the last person you should see. Naïve gringo!* When he spoke, however, he was more measured. "The people who have told you to avoid Inspector Calderón have given you good advice, Señor Jackson. He works hand-in-glove with the governor. He is a very dangerous man, not to be trusted. The police here," he said, "are not like the police in the United States. Sometimes, it is hard to separate them from the criminals they are supposed to protect us from. Very often, especially in places like Cajamarca, citizens take the law into their own hands rather than leave it to the police. We have learned from hard experience that relying on the police to solve crimes is a waste of time."

"I've heard others give me the same advice," I said. "But, still. I don't want to leave any stone unturned. If, by some chance, Calderón *does* have some information that would help solve the mystery of my sister's disappearance and I did not talk to him, I could well come to regret it."

He shook his head. "Well, Señor Jackson, I understand your sentiment and the position you are in. And, of course, I cannot order you *not* to talk with Inspector Calderón." His tone and his body language indicated that was exactly what he would like to do. "But if you do. Please be extremely careful. Approach him as you would a dangerous wild animal, careful not to arouse his anger. And, believe me, I know from hard experience that it does not take much to stir that particular beast. He may remain calm, but you can tell from his eyes that he is calculating just how far you can go before he strikes. And when he does, there is little you can do to stop him. People who have crossed Inspector Calderón have not come to a happy end," he concluded somberly.

I thought he was being over the top. Laying it on thick, trying his best to discourage me from going to see the policeman.

"Thank you, Roberto," I said, getting up from the chair and reaching out to shake his hand. "I appreciate the advice."

He took my hand and held it for a moment, looking me square in the eyes. He seemed to sense that I was not about to take his advice. That I was going to beard the lion Calderón in his den. The look on his face said *OK gringo. It's your funeral.* He released my hand, and said "Your welcome, Señor Jackson. And I wish you the best of luck in finding your sister. I only hope that our story provides you with the information you need to resolve the mystery of her disappearance. Please keep in touch. If there is anything we can, do not hesitate to ask. We want nothing more than to write a happy ending to this story."

I thanked him again and promised to keep him informed. I got the impression that he was sincere in his concerns. That he did want me to find Mel safe and sound. But I also realized that he was a journalist, intrigued by a story that would catch public attention and sell newspapers. And I couldn't blame him for that. In this case, our interests coincided. The more people who read or heard the story, the more the likelihood that it could produce leads to resolve the mystery of my sister's disappearance.

As I left the editor's office, I determined to take the next step: Try to talk to Calderón. I considered calling John, asking him if he agreed. But I decided that it was a decision I could make on my own. With the decision made, I asked Graciela to direct me to the local police headquarters, pulling out the hotel map so she could trace the route. She gave me an inquisitive look, but didn't ask any questions. Using a pen, she drew the route and wished me luck. I thanked her and headed to the street, preparing myself for yet another challenge – perhaps the most daunting of all.

Thirty

I HAD WALKED A FEW blocks east from my hotel to reach the offices of the *Eco*. To get to the police station, all I had to do was retrace my footsteps westward and go two blocks past my hotel. Graciela, a worried frown on her face, told me I couldn't miss it. She was about to say something, probably along the lines of *You definitely should not go there!* But refrained.

As I passed the Cathedral, the same cluster of Indian women were sitting on its steps, some in the process of feeding their babies. A few approached me, palms outstretched. Again, I resisted, feeling slightly guilty. I made a promise to myself that once things got settled, I would return to the steps and distribute some charity. But now, I had more urgent business.

Five minutes later, I was in front of police headquarters, located next to city hall. There were few people around, a lone guard at the door to the entrance. I took a deep breath and approached him. Like most other police I had seen, he had a pistol in a white holster at his side and an automatic weapon slung over his shoulder. When I got nearer, about five feet away, he held his palm up, signaling for me to stop. His expression was far from friendly. "What is your business here?", he asked in a hostile tone.

"I am here to see Inspector Calderón."

That seemed to set him back. I couldn't tell whether it was because it seemed a strange request from someone who was obviously a tourist. Or whether part of the reaction that the mere mention of his name seemed to induce. "Do you have an appointment?"

"No. But I need to talk with him about an investigation he is pursuing that involves the disappearance of my sister, Melanie Jackson."

He looked at me suspiciously. I guessed that he didn't know much if anything about Calderón's cases, but I could have been wrong. "Documents," he said, holding his left hand out while his right nestled on the trigger guard of his automatic weapon.

Careful not to make any sudden movements, I reached under my shirt and pulled out my passport. I handed it over. To my relief, he took his right hand from his weapon to hold my passport, while he opened it with his left. Scanning the photo page, he looked down, then up, squinting as he did so to make sure it was indeed me in the picture. I flashed back to yesterday with Rodrigo in San Ignacio and refrained from any smart remarks concerning how the hairy hippie in the passport picture was indeed the new, clean-cut version of Clint *Eastwood* Jackson. A small grin flashed briefly, undoubtedly when he read my name.

Pasting his hostile look back on, he closed the passport and handed it back to me. "Okay, Señor Jackson. You may enter."

I thanked him, as he held the door for me. I got a noncommittal grunt in return. But at least the first hurdle had been cleared. When he closed the door behind me, I spent a moment to take in my surroundings. I found myself in a good-sized, cavernous room, with a marble floor and a high ceiling. On my right, against the wall, I saw dozens of plastic police shields stacked alongside helmets with face coverings, ready for that night's protests. To my left were some benches for visitors. Recalling my own unhappy memories of the main reception area of the St. Louis Police Station, crowded with visitors, lawyers, policemen, some crying, some arguing loudly, producing a cacophony of noise and confusion, the same place in Cajamarca seemed eerily quiet. There was only one lonely couple, plainly dressed, who were huddled together, casting furtive looks in my direction. I shouldn't have been surprised. It was the unanimous opinion of everyone I had spoken with: The police in Cajamarca were not there to help; they were to be avoided at all costs.

My footsteps echoing off the floor, I approached the back of the room, looking for someone to give me directions. There was a solid wooden wall running the width of the room, with an open space and a counter in the middle. As I neared the open space, I saw a middle-aged woman dressed in a gray suit, her elbows propped on the counter, reading what looked to be a fashion magazine. I coughed discretely, not wanting to startle her. For all I knew, she had a gun ready for use under the counter. Putting down her magazine, she looked at me curiously. I assumed she didn't get many "customers," much less foreign ones.

"Yes, Señor. How can I help you?" The way she said it, in a monotone and without the usual smile I associated with receptionists, made me think she considered me more a nuisance than a welcome break from her boring routine.

"I would like to speak with Inspector Calderón."

That got a rise out of her. She was immediately on guard. I anticipated her next question. "Do you have an...."

I cut her off. "I don't have an appointment. But it is urgent that I see him as soon as possible." Handing over my passport, I said, "I'm Clint Jackson, Melanie Jackson's brother. Inspector Calderón is investigating my sister's disappearance. I need to find out what progress he is making. Please contact him and let him know I am here."

She didn't respond immediately. Going through the usual routine of glancing from the passport photo to the real me, she had a perplexed look on her face as though trying to decide the best course of action. I tried to read her mind. I guessed that she, like everyone else, was terrified of Calderón. Was it worth it to bother him with my request, coming from out of the blue? Maybe he was involved in weighty matters and had instructed her not to disturb him unless it was an emergency?

As she seemed to struggle, I tried turning on the charm. "I know the inspector must be busy," I said with the warmest smile I could muster, "but I would really, really appreciate it if you could call him. It would mean the world to me."

If charm didn't work, I thought to myself, I would threaten to call the embassy, imply that I had powerful friends and contacts, put on all the pressure I could, become a real nuisance. Maybe that thought had occurred to her as well. At any rate, she said, "One moment, Señor Jackson. I'll see if Inspector Calderón can see you. He is very busy, but perhaps he has the time for a brief visit. I'll call and see."

I felt relief. Another hurdle cleared. "Thank you very much," I said, pasting my smile back on. She didn't return it, but she did pick up the phone and punched in the numbers to Calderón's office. When someone answered, she covered the receiver with her hand so all I heard was a muffled conversation that lasted less than half a minute. Putting down the phone, she said, "Inspector Calderón will see you, Señor Jackson. You can wait on the bench over there and someone will be out soon to escort you to his office."

As I turned to take my seat, she said, "Do you have a cellphone, Señor Jackson."

"Yes, I do," I said, pulling it out and showing it to her.

"I'm afraid you need to leave it with me, along with your passport. Don't worry, they will be safe with me. You can pick them up here when you leave."

I wasn't entirely comfortable with that prospect. I was leaving valuable items with some official I didn't know. But, if I wanted to speak to Calderón, I had no choice. I gave here my phone, she placed it in a small gray plastic bucket with my passport, and tucked my items under the counter.

I sat on the bench and waited. The couple with whom I shared the bench paid me little attention, their heads close together in whispered conversation. I did my best to relax, but could feel my heart beat faster and my palms beginning to perspire. What was the old saying? *Be careful what you wish for?* I had determined to see Calderón and now here I was, about to have my wish fulfilled. Random thoughts ran through my head. *What if confronting him only made things worse? What if I lost my temper?* I began to imagine a scenario where I grabbed him by the throat, demanding answers. That rash action would surely end up with me in a jail cell. And it didn't take too much imagination to envision conditions in Cajamarca's jail making my night in the St. Louis counterpart seem like a stay at the Ritz-Carlton in comparison. Moreover, locked up in jail, I could forget about finding Mel.

Pushing these dark thoughts aside, I focused on my game plan. I discarded confrontation as a strategy. The sensible course was to be respectful, stay calm, and try to get some useful information. I wasn't expecting actual assistance, but hoped at a minimum Calderón could shed some light on what had happened to my sister.

Taking deep calming breaths, I tried to relax, expecting that I would be cooling my heels for a while. But then I saw a uniformed guard come out the door to my left and head in my direction. Without saying a word, a not too friendly look on his face, he gestured for me to get up and follow him down a corridor that led off the main hall. I got up, plastered a neutral look on my face, and did as indicated. Walking down the corridor, I saw portraits of various police officials on the walls, each with names and dates of service. We passed a row of offices, some with doors closed, others open, uniformed officers talking on the phone, typing on computers, or simply staring into space. At the end of the corridor, my guide held up a hand that said *halt*! I stopped in my tracks, while he knocked on a frosted glass door with the name 'Felipe Calderón, Inspector Principal' in large black letters. Without waiting for a reply, the opened the door and ushered me in, then closed the door behind me.

The room I entered was about the same size as that of Roberto Martínez. It also featured a desk and two chairs for visitors. Aside from that, it couldn't have been more different. In contrast to the cluttered chaos of the newspaperman, Calderón's office was a model of order and efficiency. There were bookcases and filing cabinets around the walls, with everything neatly in place – no half-open drawers, no books piled in disarray. The desk contained a laptop computer, a telephone, a reading light and nothing more other than an open folder laid out in front of the man behind the desk, who didn't bother looking up as I came in. Continuing to look at the contents of the folder as though they contained the secrets of the universe, Calderón gestured for me to take a seat while he absorbed whatever was on the written page in front of him. Finally satisfied, he closed the folder and stared directly at me.

"So, Señor Clint *Eastwood* Jackson. Why are you here?" *Man,* I thought to myself, *this whole crazy middle name stuff is getting on my nerves.* But I had bigger concerns. Calderón's tone and body language indicated he was going to be more hostile and suspicious than welcoming and helpful. Well, I had been warned.

I took a moment to register the details. He sat upright in his chair, his posture such as to win the approval of my Marine Corps Drill Sergeant. His dark blue uniform shirt was pressed and creased, his tie firmly in place. I couldn't measure his height, but I guessed he was close to six feet and looked to be in excellent shape. He was probably in his mid-forties, with glossy black hair, trimmed to precision. He had a narrow face, a beaked nose, and a jutting chin. The image of a bird of prey, a hawk or a falcon, formed in the back of my mind. His piercing black eyes stared into mine with an attitude intended to put me on the defensive. I could understand how many saw him as one scary dude.

I vowed to stay calm and measured. "Well, I am in Cajamarca to find out what happened to my sister, Melanie. She was working on an archaeological site near Cumbe Mayo when she went missing more than a week ago. Naturally, my family and I are extremely concerned and I have been dispatched to try to locate her. I have been told that you are in charge of the investigation into her disappearance and wanted to talk with you about what you have discovered." Then, to add a little pressure, I said, "And to learn from you first-hand how the investigation is proceeding."

If, as I had been told, Calderón had not taken the investigation seriously, that last comment might provoke him. Instead, the first words out of his mouth were "Your Spanish is very good, Señor Jackson."

How was I to respond to that? "Thank you, Inspector. But as I was saying…"

He held up his hand for me to stop. He glared at me for a moment in a stare that I could easily imagine turning the knees of anyone on the receiving end to jelly. I wasn't there yet, but it was early in the conversation. "And how long have you been in Cajamarca looking for your sister?"

"I arrived three days ago."

He looked at me with a sardonic half-grin, "And it is only now that you have come to see me? What took you so long? Most people in your situation would have contacted the police immediately on arrival."

So, that was how it was going to go. Avoid my questions, ask his own, and put me on the defensive. I really didn't have a good answer. I couldn't very well tell him that I had been advised by just about everyone I had met to avoid him at all costs. The best I could come up with was, "Well, to tell you the truth, as soon as I arrived, I thought it best to go to the site where Melanie was working to talk with the student team and her professor. I was hoping they had heard from her and all was well. Unfortunately, that was not the case. But they gave me some leads to follow and I've been busy trying to track them down. That's why it is only now that I have contacted you."

Skepticism was written all over his face. He was probably thinking, *in my experience, people who use the phrase 'to tell the truth' are planning to do the exact opposite.* But he just nodded and said in a clipped tone, "I see. And have any of those 'leads' proved productive?"

In some ways, I thought, but wasn't about to share anything with him. "Not really Inspector. That's why I am here with you now. To find out what you can tell me." My turn to ask the questions, "What has your investigation uncovered?"

He gave me the silent treatment, just staring at me for about thirty seconds. Finally, he pointed to the folder on the desk. "I have been reviewing my notes on your sister's disappearance. So far as I can tell, she left the campsite of her own volition. There were no signs of a struggle, no ransom demands that would indicate a kidnapping. Have you heard anything from kidnappers?"

I shook my head. "As best I can tell from talking to witnesses and other sources," Calderón said in a dismissive manner, "it seems that she had formed a romantic attachment with one of the local university students here. In my judgement, she has probably eloped with this young man without informing her family."

It was predictable. Everyone had told me that was the story he was peddling. I pushed back. "I'm sorry, Inspector. That just isn't like my sister. She is headstrong and determined. But she would never do anything like that, putting her family and friends through such anguish. There must be another explanation. You need to keep digging."

I might have crossed a line. His eyes narrowed and he spoke in an icy voice: "Are you trying to tell me how to do my job, Señor Jackson?"

I raised my hands in a placating manner. "Not at all, Inspector. It's just that..."

He cut me off. "I have more than twenty years of experience as a police inspector. I have been involved in hundreds of cases where family members don't want to accept the reality of what their children or their siblings might have done; committed a crime, run away from home because of abuse, become involved in terrorism. Believe me, I have seen it all. And unless some additional evidence emerges, your sister's case is closed," he said, slamming his palm down on the folder in front of him.

I struggled with what to say next. Maybe I should cut my losses and leave. It was clear he wasn't going to lift a finger to help. Case closed. But I decided to play a risky card. "I understand, Inspector. But I have one more question."

He looked annoyed, but didn't tell me to shut up and get out of his office. He simply waited. "You say that Mel had established a romantic relationship with a local student and they had eloped. Did you talk with the student's family? Have they heard anything from him?"

His eyes narrowed and I could see the gears turning. "Yes. I did. Of course."

"And what did they have to say?"

"They haven't heard from their son since the day your sister disappeared. They claim to have no idea where he might be," he said in a manner that indicated he thought they were not telling the truth.

I could picture Jaime's parents being grilled by Calderón. They must have been terrified.

I continued pushing. "Did they ask you to look into *his* disappearance?"

His fists clenched. I was beginning to piss him off. "No," he scoffed. "They did not. *They* believed he had eloped with your sister," implying that I was being unreasonable in my reluctance to accept that theory.

What to do next? Everything Calderón had told me was bullshit. I hadn't learned anything I hadn't known already. It was clear to me that he wasn't about to lift a finger to provide any real assistance. I mulled over telling him more, but figured it was a waste of time. The only thing I had gained was to confirm what everyone had told me. Calderón was a real son of a bitch. But maybe, just maybe, my showing up had put him on notice that not everybody was swallowing his story. Whether that realization was enough to stir him to further action remained an open question.

Calderón looked at his watch. "Well, Señor Jackson. I have a busy schedule today and am already late for my next appointment." He stood and extended his hand. I took it and he repeated what I heard so many times in the past few days, "Good luck on finding out what happened to your sister. I'm sure she will turn up safe and sound in the near future, most likely with a new husband in tow." He said it in a manner that was so smug and phony that I had to restrain myself from punching him in the face. He was clearly mocking me.

Despite the flush I felt rising in my face, I controlled my temper for the umpteenth time and thanked him for seeing me on such short notice. He touched a button on his phone, and the guard who had escorted me to his office appeared in two seconds, apparently stationed right outside the door. The guard accompanied me back to the main hall, where I collected my passport and cellphone. The couple that I had seen when I entered was still sitting patiently on the bench. If they were waiting to see Calderón I did not envy them. I had the advantage of being a foreigner, feeling, perhaps foolishly, that fact gave me some immunity from guys like him. But for the natives, it must have been a frightening prospect to deal with a man who oozed a sense of menace, eager to bully and intimidate. I felt like saying something to bolster their spirits, but couldn't think of anything useful and simply nodded as I passed by. Lunch with Enrique Rodríguez awaited me and I had every expectation that it would be a more pleasant and more productive encounter than the one I had just experienced.

Thirty-One

ENRIQUE AND I HAD agreed to meet at the Restaurante Salas on the main plaza. When I arrived, ten minutes past the agreed-upon hour, the restaurant was crowded with tourists. I scanned the room and at the back saw a man rise and wave to me. I weaved my way through the tables to where he beckoned, a broad smile on his face.

Extending his hand, he said, "Señor Jackson. It's a pleasure to meet you."

I really didn't need to ask if he was indeed Enrique Rodríguez. He was the spitting image of his brother, if a somewhat heftier version. He was wearing a crisp white dress shirt, his dark tie loosened, and his coat over the back of his chair. "Pleased to meet you as well, Enrique. And please call me Clint," I said, taking a seat.

"Very well, Clint." Then, pointing to a half-filled glass in front of him. "Would you like to join me with a pisco sour? It's the traditional drink of Peru. Have you tried it?"

Once again, I had to resort to a half-truth. "No, I haven't. I'm afraid I don't drink alcohol."

He looked at me skeptically. My eyes were clear of their usual bloodshot giveaway but he couldn't help but notice the broken veins in my nose. But he was discreet. "Well, that's a shame. What can I order for you? Water? Soda?"

"Water would be fine, thanks." For some reason, I was finding myself increasingly comfortable foregoing my old friend, alcohol. Of course, I had been through my periods of sobriety before, only to fall inevitably into bad old habits. Maybe, this time, I said to myself, it would stick, while a voice in my ear said mockingly: *Yeah, Right. Good luck with that!*

Enrique waved the waiter over. "Water for my friend here, Ignacio. And another pisco sour for me."

"Yes, Señor Rodríguez. Right away," he said, handing us our menus.

Up to this point, our conversation had been in Spanish. Enrique insisted, however, that we speak in English. "I badly need the practice," he explained. "Much of my duties involve dealing with businessmen from English-speaking countries, who are not always comfortable speaking in Spanish."

"I understand," I replied. "Whatever you would prefer is fine with me."

"English it is," he said, giving me another broad grin. "And don't hesitate to correct me if I get something wrong."

"Sure thing. No problem. Now, I don't know how much Manuel has told you, but…"

He held up his hand. "Let's get to know each other first before we get into the issue of your sister's disappearance. And I am starved. I do not perform well on an empty stomach," he said with a laugh, pointing to his paunch. "I won't be able to concentrate on what you have to tell me if my belly is crying out for food."

I curbed my impatience. I was anxious to get to the matter at hand, but he had a point. He really didn't know me other than the fact that his brother had recommended I speak with him. We were going to discuss some touchy issues. Being in the mayor's office, he was likely very attuned to the political environment, which, obviously, at the moment was tense. Here I was, a stranger, a gringo, asking for his help. If I had been in his shoes, I would be equally careful to get a good read of someone like me who appeared out of the blue and asked for help on a sensitive matter. I relaxed in my chair, gave him a grin and said, "My belly is sending me messages as well. It's been a long morning."

Picking up the menu, I looked it over quickly and then did the sensible thing. "What do you recommend?"

"Have you tried lomo saltado?"

I shook my head. "It's a typical Peruvian dish," he explained. "Strips of beef sautéed in onions with other spices. It comes with…"

"Rice and potatoes."

He laughed out loud. "You guessed it. Shall we order it?"

"Whatever you say, Enrique."

He called the waiter over and placed our order. I noticed that despite the crowd in the restaurant and the harried staff hustling to serve the demanding tourists, Enrique had no trouble getting the waiter's attention. My keen detective skills deduced that Enrique was a man of some consequence, whose needs had high priority. If that were true, I hoped it would work to my advantage.

While we waited for our food to arrive, we got to know each other. I told him about growing up in St. Louis, moving to San Francisco, and getting into the construction business. When it came to my family, I kept it barebones, skipping over the disagreeable parts. When I asked about his background, he told me that he came from what might be considered an upper-middle class family in the States. His father was a local judge and his mother taught in a private high school. He and Manuel were born only a year apart, Enrique being the older, and, he said with a chuckle, "wiser" brother. Both he and Manuel had studied at the Catholic University in Lima. Enrique had decided to follow in his father's footsteps, getting a degree in law. Manuel had dreams of being a teacher and had gotten his degree in Philosophy. Enrique rolled his eyes. "You can imagine, Clint, that there is not much demand for philosophers in a country like ours. Nor can you earn much of a living with such a degree. Manuel learned the hard way that his options were limited. He is not the only Peruvian with a college degree driving a taxi."

"And while he stayed in Lima," I said, belaboring the obvious, "you returned to Cajamarca."

"Yes. I thought about staying in Lima, but my family is here, my roots are here. So, I returned and married a local girl. How do you say it? My high-school sweetheart. We have three children. Are you married, Clint? Do you have a family?"

I had never even been close. "No, Enrique. Afraid not."

He didn't pry. He simply said, "Well, there is something very comforting about being part of a close-knit family. Of course, it can have its downsides as well. But on the whole, it gives me a feeling of security to know that my family is there for me. Especially, in times like these," he said, waving his hand in the air.

I could only nod. The picture he drew of family togetherness was about as far from my experience as I could imagine. "Well, maybe someday," I said, letting it hang there.

When our food arrived, we continued to talk while we ate. We both were hungry and it didn't take long for us to finish our plates. Enrique had ordered a third pisco sour and by the time we were done eating there was a glimmer in his eyes I had no trouble recognizing. We seemed to have settled into something of a comfort zone. I was still impatient to get down to business, but I thought it best to let him take the lead. When the waiter cleared our plates, we ordered coffee and dessert. While we waited, Enrique said, "Okay, Clint. Let's talk about what happened to your sister. What have you learned so far?"

I briefed him on the full story while he listened intently. I was still careful not to incriminate Jaime or any of the students who had helped me, speaking in generalities when it came to their contributions to the narrative. When I told him about the story on Mel's disappearance that would appear in the *Eco,* he nodded his approval. When I related my encounter with Calderón, his eyes narrowed but his face remained expressionless.

After I had finished, he took some time before responding. In the background, the TV in the corner was blaring up-dates on the kidnappings by the 'Atahualpa Brigade.' As far as I could tell, no real breakthroughs had occurred and the clock in the corner of the screen continued its merciless countdown.

"Well, Clint. I'm sorry this terrible thing has happened to your sister. And especially that it has happened here in Cajamarca. I know how you must feel. I can, how do you say it? Put myself in your shoes. If something similar happened to one of my family, I would be desperate to try to locate them."

He paused for moment to signal the waiter, who came scurrying over as if on cue. I thought for sure he was going to order another pisco sour, but instead he asked for more coffee. Raising an eyebrow in my direction, I nodded that I could use another cup as well.

"I think you have done the right thing in getting the *Eco* to run a story on your sister's disappearance. It might well produce some useful information. As to Inspector Calderón, well don't expect any action. Unless pressure is applied on him from above, he won't be of any help."

While we sipped our coffee, I gestured over my shoulder to the television screen in the corner. "You know, Enrique. I can't get it out of my head that Mel's disappearance might somehow be connected to these kidnappings by the 'Atahualpa Brigade.' It seems that they might be linked somehow, although I can't figure exactly how. Up to now, we haven't received any ransom demands. And, so far as I know, the 'Brigade' has not taken any action in Cajamarca, which seems strange to me given the symbolism and the current dispute over gold mining."

Enrique leaned forward and lowered his voice. "It's complicated, Clint. I don't know all the details, but I am sure there is an 'Atahualpa Brigade' active in Cajamarca. They just haven't taken any public action – at least, not yet."

I frowned. "Why not?"

He gestured for me to lean closer. Keeping his voice low, he said, "I work for a mayor who opposes the governor, so you need to understand that I need to be careful in what I say. Can I trust you to keep this confidential?"

"Of course."

He took a deep breath. "Well, I have gotten bits and pieces of information that indicate the governor has worked out a secret arrangement with the 'Brigade.' He will keep the mining companies at bay if they refrain from any violent action."

"Why would he do that? What's in it for him?"

He rubbed his thumb and forefinger together. "The same old story, Clint. Money. He can tell the mining companies that he is protecting them and they will keep paying him bribes to keep him in their pocket."

"And what's in it for the 'Brigade'?

"That's the tricky part. The governor is a genius at playing both sides, pretending to be a man of the people, defending Indigenous rights, while at the same time stringing the mining companies along that someday their concessions will be approved."

"I've heard that."

"Yes. Well, my best guess is that he has told the 'Brigade' that if they spare Cajamarca any violent action, he will make sure Indigenous rights are protected. In the meantime, he will delay any decisions on granting the concessions well into the future, assuring a steady income stream for himself. and keeping a lid on the popular protests."

I shook my head. All too Byzantine for me. "Interesting, Enrique. But I guess I'm still no closer to unraveling the mystery of my sister's disappearance."

He looked at me sympathetically. "I understand, Clint. And I wish I could do more to help you." He thought for a moment. "Listen. Let me talk to the mayor about your situation. We don't have much influence over the police, who are controlled by the governor. But we do have our own investigative unit. Maybe I can convince him to have them look into the matter. I can't make any promises, but it's worth a try."

"Thanks, Enrique. I appreciate that."

Enrique called the waiter, who appeared with the check. Enrique insisted on paying. As we left the restaurant and went our separate ways, he gave me an *abrazo* and patted me on the back. "It was a pleasure to meet you, Clint. And best of luck to you. Let's hope you find your sister safe and sound."

As I headed back to the hotel, I reflected on my lunch with Enrique. He had seemed sincere and I took his promise to get the mayor involved at face value. But how did I know? Maybe by the time he got back to City Hall, my plight would go to the bottom of his in-box as he dealt with more weighty matters. Even so, it had been reassuring to connect with somebody who was sympathetic and willing to lend an ear. And, maybe, just maybe, he could actually do something to get local officials involved in the hunt for my sister. Lost in those thoughts, I almost didn't notice a kiosk where the latest edition of the *Eco* had just hit the streets. I pulled out some coins and picked up a copy. Just as Martínez had promised, a banner headline blared the news of Mel's disappearance with her picture front and center above the fold. The seed had been planted. Now, I had to hope for a bountiful harvest of information.

Thirty-Two

I T WAS WELL PAST three when I returned to the Costa del Sol. With the *Eco* under my arm, I retrieved my room key. As the desk clerk handed it over, he gave me a brief quizzical look which he quickly replaced with his usual attentive smile. I wondered if he had read the paper already and begun to put two and two together. Melanie Jackson missing and Clint Jackson a guest. If he had, he didn't say anything.

I had turned off my phone while in the Restaurante Salas. Back in my room, I started it up, expecting it either to be ringing or my message box beginning to fill. But, so far, nothing. It was early yet, the story yet to circulate widely. And I had no idea how many people actually read the *Eco*, although the headline and the picture of a pretty blonde gringa would be hard to ignore. Better coverage, I presumed, would come from a TV interview. As though reading my thoughts, the phone buzzed. When I answered, it was a reporter from the local television station asking for an interview, just as Martínez had predicted. I didn't want the crew coming to the hotel and suggested we meet somewhere outside. We agreed on a location several blocks to the east of the hotel and I promised to be there in thirty minutes.

After disconnecting, I decided to call John to give him a status update. He answered immediately. "Hey Bro. Any news?"

I filled him in. As I relayed the details of my encounter with Calderón, he interrupted. "Geez, Clint. That was a dangerous thing to do. Be careful."

"Yeah. I know. But I figured it was worth a shot. At least rattle his cage a bit."

When I told him about my lunch with Enrique Rodríguez, he

agreed that it probably wouldn't lead to much. "Don't expect much from politicians," he said, "particularly in a situation as complex as you describe."

"I hear you. But who knows? He seems like a nice guy."

"Sure. But is he going to put himself out for a stranger recommended by his brother? Now if you were the executive of a big mining company, it might be a different story." He paused, "Speaking of that, Clint, there is something I should tell you. It's been gnawing at me ever since I got word that Mel had gone missing in Cajamarca. It seemed so improbable that I didn't think it was worth mentioning before. But now, maybe there is a connection."

"What do you mean?"

"You've heard of Amalgamated Mining, right?"

"Sure. They are the main target of the 'Atahualpa Brigade.'"

"Well, it so happens that Amalgamated is one of the principal clients of my law firm. I haven't been directly involved in their representation, but my firm's international division has been working on their case for concessions in Peru, notably in Cajamarca. It seemed far-fetched that the connection would have anything to do with Mel's disappearance. But now I'm not so sure."

I felt my grip on the phone tighten and my face flush. *Now you tell me! Thanks a lot!* I was about to let him know I was pissed off but that would only make things worse. I stifled my anger. Something I'd been doing a lot over the past few days. "You are probably right John. That seems like a long shot at best. All of the kidnappings so far have involved direct employees of the companies. Snatching the sister of a lawyer in the firm that represents Amalgamated seems a stretch." But I thought to myself, *not entirely out of the question either.*

"That's what I thought. Sorry I didn't mention it sooner."

I bit my tongue. "That's okay, John. Listen, I'll keep you posted. I have to go now. I'm doing a TV interview in about twenty minutes. Hopefully, that'll help stir the pot and give me some real leads to follow."

"Okay, Clint. I'll expect to hear from you later. Check in when you can."

"Will do, Bro. You can count on it."

After hanging up, I still had some time to kill. So far, there had been no phone calls with helpful tips. I took the opportunity to gather together all the business cards I had collected and enter the phone numbers in my contacts, something I had planned to do earlier but had never gotten around to.

When I finished that chore, I headed out for my TV interview. Passing the reception desk, I saw the clerk reading the *Eco*. It wouldn't take him more than a few seconds to connect the name of the missing gringa, Melanie Jackson, with her brother, registered at the hotel in the name of Clint Jackson. I stopped and went over to him. He was absorbed in his reading when I knocked on the desk to get his attention. He looked up, startled.

"Yes. Señor Jackson?"

"I see you are reading the article in the newspaper about the American girl who has gone missing. And you probably know it is not a coincidence that her last name and mine are the same. That Melanie Jackson is my sister."

"Yes, Señor Jackson. And I am very sorry to read about what happened to her. I hope that you find her to be safe and sound."

His name was on a tag on his shirt. "I appreciate that, Francisco." Leaning over the counter and lowering my voice. "And I would also appreciate it very much if you did not let others know that I am staying at the Costa del Sol. I presume you have a policy to protect the privacy of your guests?"

"Yes, we do, Señor Jackson. You can rest assured that I will not say anything about you being a guest at the Costa del Sol."

He seemed sincere. But I also suspected that the temptation to share the secret with others would be hard to resist. "Thank you, Francisco. And I'm sure you do not want a horde of reward-seekers crowding your lobby."

Apparently, he had not considered that likelihood. I didn't know whether it would be enough to guarantee his silence, but he nodded in agreement. "Certainly not, Señor Jackson. Certainly not."

I realized that even if Francisco did not let the cat out of the bag, there were other employees at the hotel who knew my name and that I was a registered guest. Realistically, I had to accept the fact that I would probably have to deal with a steady stream of reward-seekers knocking on my door despite my best efforts to conceal my location.

When I had spoken with the TV people, we had arranged to meet in a small park at the base of a hill to the east of the main plaza. I began walking at a brisk pace, eager to get to the interview on time. Hopefully, it would air quickly, reaching a broader audience than just newspaper readers and enhancing the chances of receiving some valuable information. Focused on what I would say at the up-coming interview, I suddenly felt a prickling of the hairs at the back of my neck. Some sixth sense told me that I was being followed. Taking a cue from countless movies, I stopped suddenly to stare into a shop window. With a quick glance over my shoulder, I saw a gray-suited guy about thirty feet behind me stop in his tracks and imitate my maneuver, pretending to find something in a storefront of intense interest. *Who could it be?* My money was on the police. My visit to Calderón must have aroused the inspector to have me tailed. I wondered if the gray-suited guy had been shadowing me ever since my trip to the police station, including my lunch with Enrique Rodríguez. Probably so. While I found it momentarily disturbing, I figured it was not that big a deal. It's not as though I was trying to hide anything. Let the police follow me all they wanted. Maybe they could actually be on some assistance, although at the moment I couldn't imagine how.

I resumed my walk, hearing my tail's footsteps echoing behind me. He must have known he had been made, but continued on my heels nonetheless.

I arrived at the little park at the appointed time. It was a pleasant spot, with neatly trimmed grass, colorful vegetation, and a burbling fountain in the middle. There were benches scattered around under the trees, mostly occupied with what I presumed to be nannies looking after their small charges who were playing on the grass. The sound of childish laughter filled the air, to my cynical ears still one of the greatest sounds on earth. I had a momentary flashback of playing with Heather and Willow in their backyard, squirting one another with water pistols, all three of us running, giggling, and screaming our heads off as we soaked each other.

As I took in the scene, a young woman dressed in a stylish light blue suit approached me, followed by a bearded, scruffy guy with a TV camera and a boom microphone on his shoulder. Showtime.

"Señor Jackson?" she asked, extending her hand. "I'm Elena Sánchez."

I took her hand. "Clint Jackson. Pleased to meet you."

"And this is Pablo, our cameraman."

Given that he was using his right hand to balance the camera on his shoulder, we skipped the handshake and simply nodded.

Elena looked to be in her mid-twenties. She was an attractive brunette with a dazzling smile and a pleasant voice, perfect for TV. Gesturing to a spot on the other side of the fountain, she said, "Shall we go over there, Señor Jackson? Where it is quieter?"

"Fine with me," I said, as we headed to an unoccupied bench. We settled in on the bench, adjusting our postures so that we were facing each other at a three-quarter angle while Pablo fiddled with his camera. I looked over his shoulder to see gray-suit guy taking a seat on the other side of the fountain. I could care less. Nothing secret going on here.

"Before we begin the interview, Señor Jackson, which language would you prefer? Spanish or English?"

Up to this point, Elena had been speaking English as had I. I spent a moment debating with myself. An interview in English would help make sure I didn't make any mistakes or say things that might be misinterpreted. On the other hand, speaking in Spanish would eliminate the need for subtitles on the screen and enhance the chances of reaching a larger audience.

"Let's try Spanish," I said.

"Fine, Señor Jackson. If you have any difficulties, just let me know and we can stop the filming at any time."

"Okay," I said. "Let's get started."

Elena was a good interviewer, letting me do most of the talking. I essentially gave her the same story as had been printed in the *Eco*, again being careful not to incriminate anybody. At one point, I thought she was going to press me for more information on my sources but decided to let me continue. I added a bit more information about Mel, drawing a fuller picture of my remarkable sister, hoping that would resonate with the audience. I tried to stay calm and relaxed, but as I dredged up some of my memories I began to choke up. For a moment, I felt a sense of panic build. Reality was setting in again. Here I was, in what seemed an almost surreal setting and situation, the only real hope, it appeared, for finding Mel. The weight of the responsibility began to overcome me. Up until now, I had focused on following leads, one step at a time, keeping busy and with little opportunity for reflection. Now, all of a sudden, I felt everything crashing in on me. Up until this moment, I had been certain that I could find Mel and everything would turn out okay. *But, what if I couldn't? What if she was already dead, her body buried in some distant location? What if...?*

Elena sensed my distress. "Señor Jackson. Would you like to take a break?"

I felt tears well up in my eyes and my hands begin to tremble. Maybe some time to gather myself made sense. But, why not let the public know how upset I was, how much my sister meant to me, how desperately I needed to find her? What harm could that do? I took a couple of deep breaths and, controlling my voice as best I could, said, "No. That's all right. Let's continue."

Elena looked at me with sympathy. "All right, Señor Jackson," she said, signaling for Pablo to keep on filming.

I managed to keep it together for the rest of the interview. At the end, Elena asked me, "Tell me, Señor Jackson. Do you think your sister's disappearance has any connection with the actions of the 'Atahualpa Brigade'? You are familiar with the current national crisis, I assume."

"Yes. But I cannot see that it has any relationship to my sister's disappearance, which occurred more than a week ago. And, my family has received no ransom demands."

She nodded, turned from me and faced the camera directly, recapping the gist of the interview and repeating my plea for information along with my phone number. She signaled Pablo to stop filming and then turned back to me. "I am awfully sorry about what happened to your sister, Señor Jackson." I think she meant it. I could hear a throb in her voice and her eyes were glistening. Of course, I presumed that TV news personalities in Peru were like those in the States, part journalists, part actors. But I wanted to believe she was genuine, able to identify with my anguish over the disappearance of a young woman of her own age.

229

"We'll be running the interview as soon as we get to the studio and do some editing. It should be on our local news at five o'clock, Channel Thirteen. Ordinarily, it's the kind of story that might be picked up by the national networks. But with the current crisis, I wouldn't count on it. At any rate, let's hope it produces the kind of leads you are hoping for."

"Yes. Let's hope so. And thank you for your help." When I shook her hand, she used both of hers to hold mine for a moment. I think she had the urge to give me a hug, but that would not be professional. I thanked Pablo as well and we parted company, they back to their studio, me back to the hotel. As I crossed the little plaza, gray-suit guy was still there, pretending to find something intensely interesting in his phone. I was tempted to confront him, but decided that would cause more trouble than it was worth. I simply walked on by, knowing that in a few seconds he would be on my heels. He was welcome to follow me back to the hotel, where, I presumed, he would set up a stakeout either in the plaza or the lobby. It did make me feel a little creepy, being followed like this. If surveillance followed the script of dozens of movies, the next scene might well have me attacked on the street or bundled into a police car destined for a rough interrogation, or worse. At any rate, there was no sense hyperventilating and imagining the worst. I had made progress and would continue to focus on the task at hand – doing whatever it took to locate my missing sister.

Thirty-Three

B ACK AT THE COSTA del Sol, I switched on the TV in my room. I didn't expect my interview to be on the air yet, but tuned into Channel Thirteen anyway. It was now about four o'clock, so what I got was some kind of soap opera. I switched to the national news channel, which was providing wall-to-wall coverage of the hostage crisis. The U.S. ambassador was on again, issuing warnings to the kidnappers and trying to look resolute. Maybe I was biased, but he gave off the vibe of being totally out of his depth. In the corner of the screen, the countdown clock was approaching twenty-four hours to go.

I had my phone out and was hoping for a call at any minute. But so far, nothing. Not a peep. I began to worry that the *Eco* article had been a waste of time. I told myself to be patient. It was still early.

Just then, the phone rang. I picked it up immediately. My first call! "Señor Jackson?"

It was a male voice. "Yes. This is Clint Jackson."

"I have information about your sister's disappearance. When can we meet?"

"What kind of information?" I asked.

"I'll tell you when we meet. And please bring the reward money with you."

I might be a naïve gringo, but not *that* naïve. We arranged to meet at a location on the outskirts of the city, but I had no intention of showing up. I just wanted him off the line. In my mind's eye, I saw him calculating how to rob me once he had lured me to some out-of-the way location. I let him think he had suckered me in and enjoyed the prospect of him sitting around hours waiting for me to show up.

The first call was a disappointment. But I wasn't surprised. It was more or less what I expected.

Over the next hour, I got several more calls in the same vein. Each time, I promised to show up for the meet, getting some satisfaction in picturing the callers' frustration when I failed to appear.

At five o'clock, I switched to Channel Thirteen for the local news. It began with a recap of the national crisis, and then the anchor announced a special interview concerning the disappearance of a young American woman working on an archaeological site near Cumbe Mayo. Elena appeared, introducing the taped interview, which began to roll. It was unreal to see myself on screen. They ran the whole interview, including the part where I begam to tear up. Hopefully, my public display of emotion would produce some positive results. On the other hand, it might encourage more scammers to try to play on my sentiments.

Over the next hour, the number of calls increased dramatically. Being on TV had done the trick. Unfortunately, they were all of a piece: "I have information. Meet me in an obscure location. Bring the reward money." They all got the same answer: "Sure. See you soon."

I was growing increasingly frustrated. So far, all I had done was potentially piss off a lot of locals, many of whom might not take too kindly to being scammed themselves. Well, too bad.

My watch said six-fifteen when the phone rang again. I heaved a sigh and answered, fully expecting more of the same. Instead, I was thrown for the proverbial loop. "Hey, Clint," a female voice I had known since childhood said with a tremor, "It's me, Mel."

I was momentarily speechless. "Mel, where...?"

Another voice interrupted. It was male and hostile. "Yes, *Clint*, that is indeed your sister Melanie. Now, if you want to see her alive again, you need to follow our instructions to the letter. If you don't, the consequences for you both will be severe. Do I make myself clear?"

I was momentarily stunned. It seemed as though I was in a movie or a TV show I had seen countless times. And in almost all of those, the person being contacted by kidnappers asked for "proof of life."

"How do I know you have my sister? You could have anybody call me, pretending to be her. I need proof."

He paused. I could hear him give a muted snort on the other end.

"I'm sending you a video right now, Clint. That should give you all the proof you need."

I heard a chime on my phone and opened the attachment. What I saw sent chills down my spine. I felt like I'd been punched in the gut. It was Mel all right. Her hair looked dirty and bedraggled and there were hollows under her eyes, but it was my sister, no doubt about it. What was most disturbing, however, was not her appearance. It was the fact that in the corner of the screen, I could see a hand holding a pistol pointing squarely at her head. "Please do as they say, Clint. I'm so sorry…," she said, desperation in her voice. A hand emerged from the edge of the screen, clamping down on her mouth before she could finish.

I was furious. That old anger boiled up again, fiercer than ever. I imagined all sorts of punishment I would inflict on the guys who had Mel if I had the chance. But reason prevailed. I had to keep calm and follow orders. Maybe her kidnappers were bluffing. But I couldn't take the chance. "Okay, Okay," I shouted into the phone. "I'll do what you say. Just don't hurt my sister."

The male voice responded with a chuckle. "We thought you'd see reason, Clint." Unlike everybody else I had met in Peru, this guy seemed to relish abandoning the formal Señor Jackson for the more familiar Clint. What was he trying to do? Pretend we were friends? Not likely. I detected a sardonic edge to his voice when he uttered my name, as though he enjoyed taunting me with presumed familiarity.

I decided to try some mind games of my own. "You know my name. But I don't know yours. If we are to be in a negotiation, I'd like to know the name of the person I am dealing with."

That seemed to upset him. "You are in no position to negotiate anything, *Clint*. And my name is not important. All you need to know is that I hold your sister's life in my hands."

"Okay, however you want to play it," I said.

"Now here is what you need to do. At around eight o'clock, the crowds will begin to fill the streets for the nightly protest. At that time, you will leave the hotel…"

"How did you know…?"

"No interruptions, Clint," he said harshly. "Just follow the instructions. Leave the hotel by the side entrance and try to blend into the crowd. Make sure – and this is *very* important – make sure you are not being followed." I pictured gray-suit guy on my heels. "Then pass through to the southern side of the plaza. From there, follow Jirón Amalia Puga until it intersects with the Prolongación Ayacucho. Wait on the northeast corner. Someone will meet you there and bring you to us. Do you understand?"

I repeated the instructions. "Very good, Clint. Now, *do not* contact anybody between now and when you meet with us. Be sure to bring your phone with you so we can check if you make any calls. And, if you are thinking of using the hotel phone, I strongly advise you not to."

That warning confirmed my suspicions that they had somebody on the hotel staff who had informed them of my whereabouts and was monitoring my activities. "Don't worry. I won't."

"Remember, Clint. You must follow these instructions exactly. Any deviations, and the next picture of your sister will not be a pleasant one." As though seeing her with a gun to her head was "pleasant."

"Don't worry," I promised. Then I tried to push my luck. "Can I talk with Mel. I'd like to be sure that she is all…" But he, whoever he was, disconnected without a word. If he wanted to send a message that they were deadly serious, message received.

A jumble of thoughts and emotions raced through my mind. *Mel was alive!* That was the most important thing. And against all odds, I had somehow managed to find her. But what next? Would I be able to get her out of the mess she was in? The chances were not very favorable. I had no back-up. I'd be operating strictly alone, going up against a group, whoever they were, who seemed well organized and very careful. I knew that at least one of them had a gun, and I presumed there were others who were armed as well. I had confidence that I could hold my own in a fight, even if outnumbered. But going up against guys – and maybe gals – with guns was way beyond my skill set.

I was sorely tempted to call John. First, to let him know that Mel was alive. Second, to get his advice as what to do next. Maybe he could even get Lamar Jenkins to lend a hand. But it was too risky. The guy who held Mel had made it crystal clear that there would be dire consequences if I violated the instructions. And, for all I knew, they had some way to monitor my cell phone. And, realistically, what could

John or anybody else do in the next two hours? No, it was all up to me, like it or not.

My eyes settled on the mini-bar. If ever there was time for some Dutch courage, this was it. Just a nip from one of the little bottles of Johnny Walker to steel my nerves. Once again, however, I resisted temptation. Maybe I was finally growing up. Who knows? But I knew that one little nip would lead inevitably to me cleaning out the bar, rationalizing every step of the way. I faced enough of a challenge sober. Being shit-faced would only make everything worse and lead to total disaster.

I was, however, hungry and thirsty. I debated going to the dining room for a quick meal. But decided instead to consume all snacks available along with a couple of bottles of water. Not exactly healthy, but at least some nourishment.

As I chewed and sipped, I pondered my next moves. When the phone buzzed, I was momentarily startled. I didn't know if the kidnappers' instructions included incoming calls, but decided not to take a chance. If it was another reward-seeker, I didn't need them anymore. I turned off the phone and let all calls go to voice mail.

It seemed weird to be cut off from the outside world, especially from my brother. The irony of having voluntarily isolated myself from my family for years until just a few days ago was not lost on me. Now I was desperate to connect with them but couldn't. And, if John did not hear from me sometime tonight, I knew he would be worried. As he had warned me, it was bad enough that Mel had gone missing. My disappearance would only deepen the family anguish.

If I couldn't call, at least I could leave a written message. Sitting down at the little desk in my room, I gathered the notes and time line I had been working on and began to scribble down all that had occurred since my last entry. When I had finished explaining the details of the kidnappers' instructions, I folded the sheets and placed them in an envelope. I wrote John's name and contact information on the outside, sealed the envelope, and placed it in the room safe. If I didn't make it, at least there was the possibility that any investigation would turn up my chronology. Of course, if Calderón were in charge of the investigation, chances were good that little would result.

By the time eight o'clock rolled around, I was both apprehensive and excited. The challenge ahead was daunting, but I determined to do everything in my power to get Mel out of the dangerous situation she was in. I might fail, but I would give it my best. I tried to push the long odds aside and focus on what might be possible once I was with her.

Leaving the hotel as instructed at the side door, I joined the crowd of mostly young people who were streaming toward the plaza. I made my way into the middle, dodging banners, signs, and people beating drums. The police were already lined up on the sidewalks leading into the square, their face shields down and their hands on their tear gas guns. I wondered if Calderón was somewhere around, keeping his falcon eyes alert for any recognizable trouble-makers, ordering his men to swoop in and arrest them. Maybe my imagination was running away from me, but I would not have been surprised if I was right.

Blending in was not easy. My dress – leather jacket, khaki cargo pants, running shoes, ball cap – was not all that different. But I was clearly more light-skinned than most and stood a head taller than the majority. Not much I could do about that but try to bend over some so as to hide my height.

When I reached the plaza, it was already jammed with protestors. Before I merged into the crowd, I stole a glance at the hotel entrance to see if I could spot gray-suit guy. He might have been there, but I didn't see any sign of him. Good, I thought to myself. Maybe he got called to riot duty and was off my back. I suppose I should have told the kidnappers that I was being tailed, but, if so, they might have called the whole thing off. Nothing to do for it now but to forge ahead.

Getting to the plaza had been relatively easy. I was going with the flow. Getting to the other side was a different matter. I would have to force my way through the crowd, making myself conspicuous and probably arousing some suspicion among the protestors.

I had no choice. Issuing "excuse me" and "pardon me" every two seconds, I elbowed my way through the crowd. I drew some dirty looks along the way but no one blocked my path. About halfway through, I felt a tug on my arm and someone calling my name. Startled, I bunched my fist, ready to swing.

"Clint. Clint. What are you doing here?"

It was Ken, from the team at Cumbe Mayo. We were face-to-face, the crowd jostling us on all sides with some staring at us curiously. I had to think fast. "Well, Ken. I could ask you the same question. Didn't Professor Cartwright tell you guys to stay away from these protests. And now, here you are, right in the middle of it."

He looked embarrassed. "Yeah. You're right. But you know how it is. We agree with the protests and want to show our support. Besides, as anthropologists we are used to living among our subjects, studying their culture. So, if the professor found me out, I'd tell him that I was just practicing a little 'participant observation.'" Then, with a look of concern, he asked, "You're not going to squeal on me, are you?"

He knew his excuse would not fly with the professor. "No, Ken. Don't worry."

Relieved, he repeated his question: "So, Clint. What are you doing here? Any luck in finding Mel?"

A number of protestors were watching us, listening in and showing some interest. The last thing I needed was to get into a lengthy conversation with Ken. The clock was ticking and I needed to move. "Sorry, Ken," I said, looking at my watch. "But I've got an urgent appointment. Maybe later we can catch up. Right now, I have to get going."

"But, Clint," he persisted, "What about Mel? What's going on?"

I ignored the question and began to push my way through the crowd toward the south side of the plaza. I sincerely hoped Ken would not follow me. That would be a disaster. But when I reached the other side, I glanced back and saw no sign of Ken, lost in the maze of people.

Running into Ken had been both unexpected and unwelcome. I consoled myself with the morbid thought that if there were an investigation into my disappearance, he would be able to provide a useful clue as the last person to see me before I went off the grid.

As instructed, I walked briskly along the Jirón Amalia Puga. After a few blocks, the noise from the plaza faded to a distant hum. Looking over my shoulder from time to time, I saw no indication of anyone following me along the mostly deserted street. By now, night had fallen and there was only faint illumination from the occasional overhead light. There were many shadowy places into which a pursuer could duck, but I didn't detect any sudden movements behind me. I did my best to relax while still keeping alert to the possibility that I was being tailed. If so, there was not a whole lot I could do about it. After all, I wasn't some sort of secret agent trained to handle such situations. Whether the kidnappers would take this into consideration when we made our rendezvous was another story.

I arrived at the designated corner at the intersection with Prolongación Ayacucho at precisely eight-thirty. It was empty, no cars, no people. During my walk, I had felt sweat on my forehead. Standing still, the sweat cooled and I felt a chill as the wind picked up and the temperature dropped. I zipped up my jacket against the cold and fought to control my impatience and anxiety, trying to ignore the dire thoughts that began to creep into my head as I cooled my heals. *What if the kidnappers had decided to call the whole thing off? What if they figured it was too dangerous to pick me up, unsure that I was not being followed and might lead the police to their lair? What did they want with me anyway? They already had Mel. What added advantage did I provide? What if...?*

Then a dark SUV suddenly pulled up at the corner, cutting off further speculation. *They were here. Showtime!* Through the tinted windows, I could see a driver and a passenger in the front seat. The back door opened and a man in a ski mask beckoned me inside. "Hurry, Señor Jackson."

I didn't ask any questions and didn't hesitate. I hustled into the back seat and the vehicle took off a mini-second before I had closed the door. As I fumbled with the seat belt, the guy who had opened the door slipped a hood over my head without a word. I thought about protesting, but decided to keep quiet. It was not unexpected. And it didn't really make a lot of difference. In the dark, I wouldn't have been much good at memorizing the route even if I could see it.

"Your phone," the man beside me demanded.

I reached into my pocket and handed it over.

After a few seconds, he said "The code." It wasn't a question; it was a command.

I gave him the four-digit number and I could hear him tapping it in. I held my breath as I pictured him scrolling through my messages. I had obeyed my instructions to the letter, but who knew how he might interpret what he saw on the screen. I breathed a sigh of relief when I heard him say to the others, "All clear on the phone. No messages." I then heard the faint click as he turned off the phone. I expected to hear a window roll down and the sound of my phone hitting the pavement. But apparently the man at my side determined to keep it. I heard what I guessed was him putting it into his pocket. They must have some use for it in mind, I speculated.

I was tempted to ask some questions, but decided to keep my mouth shut. If they wanted to talk, they would talk. If not, better to let sleeping dogs lie. So far, I had followed their instructions faithfully and been as cooperative as possible. I hoped that attitude would work to my advantage later on. In the meantime, I sat back and tried to draw up a game plan for when we arrived at our destination. That is, *if* we arrived at our destination. Maybe the whole idea was to get me out of the way, remove an inconvenience. If so, again, there wasn't much I could do about it. Try to stay calm and carry on, as the Brits would say. Easier said than done, I thought to myself as I listened to the sound of the motor, the tires on the pavement, the breathing of my three captors, and the pounding of my heart.

Thirty-Four

I QUICKLY LOST TRACK OF time. With my head covered, I couldn't check my watch. Never having been in this predicament before, I was unable to orient myself. I had read novels where victims in my circumstances had been able to register the stops and turns and, combined with traffic sounds, later give investigators clues to the route of their captors. Somehow, they also seemed able to estimate the length of the trip through some uncanny ability to keep a mental clock in their head.

Well, I had none of those skills. I was able to figure out that we had soon left the city and had picked up speed once we had reached the outskirts and the open road. That hardly took a genius. But from that point on, I gave up trying to use any of the tricks I had read about and just succumbed to the ride. Soon, I could feel my head grow heavy and my chin drop toward my chest. Despite the dangers of the situation, and the chilling realization that this might be my last ride *ever*, being unable to see, reluctant to try to communicate with my captors, lulled by the smooth ride, and exhausted by the events of the day, I dozed off.

I don't know how many minutes had passed, but I was jolted awake by the sound of the radio being turned on. It was tuned to a national news network that was giving blow-by-blow descriptions of developments in the "Atahualpa Brigade" saga. I could hear the two guys in front speaking in low voices, reacting to what they were hearing. I could feel the backseat shift as the guy who had my phone leaned forward to join the discussion. Again, I was tempted to ask some questions, but decided not to. What could I say that wouldn't get me into hot water? That I sympathized with what the 'Brigade' was doing? My best guess was that these guys were part of the same organization or something similar. Maybe if they thought I was on their side, that would help me negotiate the release of Mel. *Yeah.* But that was one big maybe. Better to keep quiet and let things unfold as they would.

I closed my eyes again, but kept my ears tuned to the sounds of the radio. At one point, I heard the time: nine o'clock. That meant we had been on the road for half an hour, which meant we probably were twenty-five to thirty miles from Cajamarca. Just then, we turned sharply to the left and I could feel the tires hit gravel. We began to climb, taking numerous twists and turns. Soon, I felt the air thin and my breathing become labored, not helped much by the hood over my head. We traveled this way for what I judged to be about fifteen minutes, when we made another sharp turn, this time to the right. The terrain became rougher and the pace slowed. No surprise. We were clearly headed for some out of the way mountain hideout.

After maybe twenty minutes of bumps and jostles, we came to a stop and the driver turned off the engine. It was now eerily quiet and my senses went on full alert. Either we had reached the hideout where these guys were holding Mel hostage or they had found a convenient spot to eliminate me from the equation, a place where my body wouldn't be found for a long time. If it was door number two, I did not plan to go quietly although realized the odds were stacked against me.

I heard the two guys in front get out and close their doors. Then my door opened and the guy next to me said, "Time to get out, Señor Jackson."

A hand grabbed my right arm from the outside and pulled me out of the vehicle, supporting me as I struggled in my blindness to gain my footing. Then I felt another hand take a firm grip on my left arm. "This way, Señor Jackson. Just one step at a time. Slow and easy."

I had a moment of panic. Again, the nasty choice between meeting up with my sister or ending up at the bottom of a chasm somewhere. Hooded, they could well be leading me to a sharp cliff where I would simply step off of my own accord. I slowed to a shuffle, anticipating the possibility that the next step I took could send me into oblivion. One of the guys chuckled, perhaps sensing my fear.

The next sound I heard was reassuring. It was a door opening.

"There are two steps in front of you, Señor Jackson," one of the guys said as they guided me up and through the doorway. Inside, I could feel the heat from a fire and smell a mixture of woodsmoke, tobacco, and something cooking. I reflexively reached up to remove my hood, when the voice I had heard over the phone, presumably the boss of the outfit, said, "Not yet, Clint. Not yet."

I lowered my hand and the two guys who held my arms led me across a wooden floor. I didn't resist, although I was getting tired of the rigamarole and felt the old anger welling up inside of me. My heart said, time to start swinging, get in a few good punches. My head said, don't be foolish. You are outnumbered by at least four to one. And although I had not seen any weapons, I had to presume they were all well-armed.

The next sound I heard was the unlocking of a door and then the creak of hinges as it was opened. Without a word, the guys holding me pushed me through the opening. As I stumbled through the doorway, I heard it close shut behind me and the key turn in the lock.

The next voice I heard was the sweetest sound in the world. "Clint. Clint," Mel cried out. Snatching off my hood, I felt tears well. Through the mist in my eyes, I saw my sister for the first time in years. I took her in my arms and cradled her against my chest as she began to sob uncontrollably.

Patting her on the back, I said, my voice cracking, "Mel. Thank God I've found you. Thank God." I wasn't very religious, to say the least. But what do they say about "Foxhole Christians?" I understood now. Chalk me up as a convert. And, I thought, it would take further divine intervention for us to get out of our current predicament without losing our lives.

While I waited for Mel to regain her composure, I looked around the room. There wasn't much in the way of furniture: a small table in the corner with a lamp that cast only a feeble light; a cot against the far wall with a pillow and blanket; and, two wooden chairs. There was a window above the cot, but it was shuttered closed.

Mel took some deep breaths and stepped back. "I'm so, so sorry I've gotten you into this mess, Clint. It's all my fault. All my fault. For being naïve and stupid."

She was totally crestfallen and was about to break down again.

"Take it easy, sis. We both need to stay calm if we are to get out of this alive."

She began to smile. Here I was, Clint Eastwood Jackson, "Mister Hot Temper" personified, telling my cool and rational sister to take it easy.

Mel nodded. "You're right, Clint. You're absolutely right. Let' sit, okay."

She plunked down on the cot and I pulled up one of the wooden chairs facing her. Just then, the door opened and one of the masked kidnappers entered, carrying some water bottles and a sleeping bag. Without a word, he put them down and then closed and locked the door. I grabbed two of the bottles, handing one over to Mel while I unscrewed the top of the other and began to dink. Mel followed suit.

While I drank, I took a moment to look Mel over. As I had noticed in the phone video, her hair was a tangled mess and there were hollows under her eyes. I could also smell the body odor. She seemed a little thinner than I remembered but not drastically so.

She uttered a little laugh. "Not at my best, am I?"

"You look beautiful to me, Mel." I began to choke up. "Especially when compared to how I pictured I might find you."

She reached over and grabbed my hand. "Well, you can see me now. I'm okay, Clint. I'm just so sorry that…"

I let go of her hand and held mine up. "Enough, Mel. Enough. Let's focus on what needs to be done, not dwell on the 'might have beens.' Now, how have they been treating you?" In the back of my mind, I imagined her being beaten, her bruises hidden under her sweat shirt and jeans. Or even worse.

"Not great, Clint. But not too badly, either. They give me plenty of food and water. They were a little rough when they kidnapped me, but since the first night they've been okay." Looking around the room, she continued, "I've been cooped up in here for what? Eight, nine days. I've lost track. They keep the window," pointing over her shoulder, "closed tight. The only time I see the sun is when they take me outside to go to the bathroom. No chance to take a shower or," she added, holding one of her blonde tresses, "wash my hair. But I'm kind of used to these conditions. Working on archaeological sites often leaves personal hygiene far down the list of priorities."

From all I could tell, Mel's spirits seemed good. "What about the gun pointed to your head? I doubt that's a normal part of archaeological work."

She shivered. "Yeah. That *was* uncomfortable, to say the least. But I was pretty sure it was just a threat. A way to scare you and get you to follow orders. I'm too valuable alive for them to get rid of me. At least for now."

"So, Mel. What's the scoop? Why are you here? Why am I here?"

"That's a long story, Clint. And a pretty complicated one, to which I don't have all the answers."

"We have plenty of time, Mel. I'm listening."

She smiled. "Let's start with why you are here." She paused to gather her thoughts. "Late this afternoon, they ordered me out of here and into the main room," she said, pointing to the door behind me. "They told me they had just seen you on television. You were in Cajamarca. You were looking for me and had offered a reward for any information regarding my disappearance.

"You could have knocked me over with a feather. I had absolutely no idea that you were in Peru, much less Cajamarca. I did imagine that John or Mom or Dad had contacted the embassy when I was reported missing. But that one of my family might actually come to Peru to try to find me never entered my mind."

And especially not your irresponsible, alcoholic brother, I thought to myself.

She seemed to read my thoughts. "I'm so glad you are here, Clint. Even though we are in this terrible mess, it means the world to me to have you by my side."

"I'm glad, too, Mel. No matter what happens, we are now in this together."

She nodded and smiled. "So, where was I? Yes. Well, I can't always figure these guys out. But they seemed to want you under their control rather than acting as a free agent, stirring up a fuss. That's why they called you and used me as bait to lure you here."

"And having another gringo hostage would give them more leverage," I said. "Are they part of the 'Atahualpa Brigade'?"

Mel looked surprised. "You know about them?"

"Sure. Now, everybody in Peru and beyond knows about them."

She had a puzzled look. "What do you mean?"

"You haven't heard the latest news about their actions?"

She shook her head. "I've been kept totally isolated for more than a week. What's going on?"

"The 'Brigade' has kidnapped Americans associated with mining operations in about half a dozen locations throughout the country. They are threatening to kill them one by one if their demands were not met within forty-eight hours." I looked at my watch. "That deadline expires about sixteen hours from now. It's all over the television news. The Peruvians and the U.S. embassy have mobilized forces to try to locate the hostages, but so far as I know, no luck. And it's not entirely clear how the demands can be met within such a short time span. I was half expecting to see you on the news as one of the hostages."

She put her fist under her chin in a thoughtful pose I knew all too well. Usually, it was followed by some sort of admonishment for me to clean up my act. "So that's what's been going on. Things are beginning to make sense. First, yes, these guys are part of the 'Brigade.'"

"Then why...?"

"Why haven't I been on the news?"

"Well, yeah."

"It's kind of complicated. Let me explain. You know that I've been working at a site near Cumbe Mayo on the outskirts of Cajamarca, right?"

"Sure. I went there as soon as a I arrived and spoke with Professor Cartwright and your team members. One of them told me on the sly that you had planned to meet secretly with a guy named Jaime on the night you disappeared. I even tracked Jaime down. He's hiding in the far north near San Ignacio, fearing that he's the prime suspect in your disappearance. He told me you never showed up for their meeting and that he had no idea why you had gone missing."

Her eyes widened. "You *have* been busy, Clint. I'm impressed." Then she turned serious and an edge of bitterness crept into her voice.

"Well, Jaime was lying. In fact, he led me into a trap that resulted in me being here." She sighed deeply. "Maybe this is all my fault for being a soft-hearted idiot. Jaime and I had worked together for months and I had grown fond of him, kind of a big-sister little-brother thing. I knew he was deeply involved in the anti-mining protests in Cajamarca and was one of the ringleaders. You might not guess it from his appearance, but he is a riveting orator with a lot of charisma. He swore to me that he was opposed to violent actions and believed that real effectiveness came from constant pressure through peaceful protests."

She shook her head ruefully. "And, I believed him." She paused for a moment, then continued. "At any rate, a few days before I was kidnapped, he told me that threats had been made against his family if he did not cease his protest activities. And, he needed to speak with me in private to get my advice and maybe even my help. And I fell for it. We arranged to meet secretly that night. After I was sure everyone was asleep, I snuck out and walked to his car, which was parked on the side of the road about a hundred yards from the turnout into the site. He was there all right, leaning against the driver's side door. He beckoned with a gesture for me to hurry, looking around as though he were being followed. It was all a trap. When I got closer, I saw two other guys emerge from the car, both wearing masks. I turned to run, but it was too late. They grabbed me before I could escape, threw a hood over my head, tied my hands behind my back, and bundled me into the car. One of them stuck a gun into my ribs and told me to keep quiet and stay still. I kicked myself for being such a sucker, but there wasn't much I could do. They had me."

She halted for a moment to take a sip of water, and then resumed. "We drove for more than an hour. From time to time, I could hear Jaime chuckling and saying something about *gringa sonsa,* stupid gringa. If my hands hadn't been tied, I would have reached over the seat and slapped him silly. But what really hurt was that he was right. I had been a *gringa sonsa* and now was paying the price for my foolishness."

"Don't be too hard on yourself, Mel. You were acting out of your good heart. And I can understand how you could easily have been taken in by those sad-looking puppy-dog eyes. And if it's any consolation, when I spoke with him, I believed his story as well. He's a pretty good actor." I didn't mention that I had some nagging doubts about his truthfulness, doubts which turned out to be well-founded. Nor that I had gone to extreme lengths to keep him out of the story, not wanting to lead the authorities to him. Nor that if I had him in front of me at the moment I would do more than slap his face. But, no sense wallowing in what might have been. Time to face the present.

"So, Mel. Any idea why you were selected for kidnapping? Why not one of the others? I presume there were other members of the team who would make valuable hostages. Someone else who could have been lured into a trap."

"I've been thinking about that myself, Clint. And the only thing I could come up with was a conversation I had with Jaime a few weeks ago when I told him that I had a brother who was a lawyer on the firm representing Amalgamated Mining, the outfit that is caught up in the current controversy over the granting of mining rights near Cajamarca. You know about that dispute, don't you?"

"Yeah. I've been filled in. So, as I get it, Jaime probably told his 'Brigade' comrades that there was an American student whose brother might be subject to pressure if she were to be kidnapped and held for ransom. That through her capture, the brother could in turn pressure the company to give up the attempt to establish operations in Cajamarca."

"Something like that. Yes."

I rubbed my cheeks. "So, we get back to the question. Why isn't your kidnapping on the news? Why are you the exception? Especially given the symbolic importance of the relationship between Atahualpa and Cajamarca?"

Mel laughed. "I am really impressed, Clint. You have learned a lot in a short time." Then she turned serious. "I've been pondering that ever since you mentioned the 'Brigade's' actions. The only thing I can think of is that maybe they are holding me – us – as a kind of reserve in case things don't work out elsewhere. A new threat to pressure the government. However, there is also the possibility that they are holding off while they negotiate behind the scenes with the departmental governor. That relationship seems to be very complex, well beyond my limited knowledge to explain."

I nodded. "Yeah. People I've spoken with have told me the same thing."

"Again, I'm impressed. You really have been digging. Maybe you should think about becoming some sort of investigator."

"You mean like Inspector Calderón?"

She gave the typical reaction: a look of total disgust. "Don't tell me you've had to deal with *him*? That's a waste of time."

"That seems to be the universal opinion." I then filled her in on the rest of my adventures in Peru, beginning with the frustrating visit to the embassy, the fact that the responsibility for looking into her disappearance had been placed solely on Calderón, and the hope that Lamar Jenkins could help out, a hope that was dashed with the widespread kidnappings.

"The upshot, Mel. Is that we are on our own. No cavalry to the rescue. I wasn't even able to tell John that I had heard from you and your kidnappers, although when I don't make my usual call, he'll guess that something is up. What can he do, though? Even if he were to come to Peru?"

She nodded her head in agreement. "By the way, how are John and Mom and Dad? I hadn't been in touch for a while, even before this," she said, waving her hand around the room.

I debated how to respond. The last thing she needed was more guilt. But, I reasoned, if I didn't give her the straight scoop now, she would be angry and resentful once we got out of this jam – that is, *if* we got out. I pushed that negative thought aside. *When* we got out. Besides, unlike me, I was confident she could handle the truth, no matter how unpleasant. No hiding in a bottle or curling up in self-pity for my self-reliant sister. Still… "Well, as you can guess, they are all stressed and worried, anxiously waiting some word from me as to what happened to you. John is under a lot of pressure. Ordinarily, he would be here instead of me. But he's bogged down with work and family obligations." I didn't add that there seemed to be some cracks in his marriage. "Plus, he needs to look after Al and Mae. They are both in pretty bad shape."

She paled, tears forming at the corners of her eyes. "What's wrong with them?", she asked, her voice quivering.

"Well, Al has had a stroke. A serious one. You wouldn't recognize him. He's probably lost a hundred pounds and can't speak, although he can still see and hear. But he's wheel-chair bound. Mom, too, has lost weight and is on the edge of breaking down altogether. Sorry, but that's the way it is."

She put her face into her hands and began to sob. I sat next to her on the cot and put an arm around her shoulder and pulled her to me, letting her cry herself out. When the sobs died down, I said, "The best news they could get right now is that you are safe and sound, and on your way to see them."

Mel rubbed her eyes, looking up at me as I let go of her. "And just how are we going to do that, Clint?" she said, with a tone of despair. "Let's be realistic. We are in the middle of nowhere, held hostage by four guys with guns, and, as you say, no chance of the cavalry to the rescue. What are we going to do? Develop super-powers? And it's all my fault," she wailed.

"Come on, Mel," I said, "We can't give up. There must be a way out of here. How about through that window?" I said, gesturing over my shoulder, but knowing the response as soon as the question was out of my mouth.

"You think I haven't tried that. It's bolted shut. It hasn't been opened since I've been here."

I just nodded. "Okay. We'll think of something. I'm not going down without a fight, no matter the odds."

That brought a smile. "Oh, yes. My impetuous brother. Always ready to let his fists do the talking." I flashed back to the look on her face when she saw me and Al duking it out in our last confrontation. I saw a shadow cross her eyes as she was likely reliving that awful moment herself. "But," she said soberly, "let's be real. Two fighting Jacksons, unarmed, going up against four ruthless guys with guns. We need to think of something a little more creative than that, although for the life of me I can't think of what."

At least, she was thinking of possibilities. The sense of hopelessness seemed to have passed for the moment. "Yes. But first, we need to get some rest. I'm out of my feet. It's been a long, long day. Right now, I'm struggling to stay awake, much less to think straight. Things will be clearer in the morning."

She smiled again. "What has come over you, Clint? Are you becoming the sensible one?"

I grinned at her. "Maybe, finally, I have, sis. But it's early on. Let's see if it sticks."

"Okay," she said with a wink, "A work in progress." Then she gave me a hug. "God, it's good to see you, Clint. I can hardly believe it. It's like a dream."

"Great to see you too, Mel. Now, back to practical matters. How do we get to the bathroom? I've been drinking a lot of water."

"We have to get one of the guys to escort us outside to the privy." She rose from the cot and knocked forcefully on the door. Seconds later, one of the guys, still wearing a ski mask, opened it.

He sensed what we needed. "Bathroom?"

Mel nodded. "Yes. Both of us."

"One at a time," he said. "You first."

Mel accompanied him out the door and I waited. She was back in five minutes. "Your turn," the guy said, and I followed him out into the main room where the three others glanced up at me quickly. Then they returned to watching a small TV, absorbed in the news about the kidnappings.

My escort took my arm and led me outside. "No false moves, Señor Jackson," he warned, sticking a gun into my ribs. I just nodded and grunted.

The privy was located about ten yards away. I tried to take in my surroundings without making any sudden moves. We were clearly somewhere high up in the mountains. The air was bracing, with a cool wind blowing. A quick look upward and I saw a star-filled sky. I had never paid much attention to astronomy, but I did know the constellations in the southern hemisphere were different from the northern. Aside from that, I had no idea how to orient myself. No north star to guide me. But it was a spectacular sight nonetheless.

I did my business and we walked back to the house, my escort's gun prodding me along the way. From the outside, the house looked to be someone's weekend retreat. It was relatively modern, a fancy kind of cabin. I noticed a satellite dish on the roof. From what I could see, it was also quite isolated. There were no flickers of light in the distance. A perfect hideaway.

I was led back to the room. Once I stepped inside, the door was shut and locked behind me. Mel was sitting nervously on the cot, awaiting my return. There was a look of relief on her face as I entered. She probably had been worried that despite my current conversion to practicality, I had returned to type and tried something foolish like attacking my escort. "Time to get some sleep," I said.

"Yes," she replied, removing her sweatshirt and jeans, revealing a tee shirt and shorts underneath. "I can't wait to have a shower and get into some clean clothes," she said wryly. "Hope you can stand the stench."

"Don't worry, sis. I've smelled worse myself without the excuse of being held captive." I didn't mention that some of the women I had taken to bed had also left a lot to be desired in the personal hygiene department.

She slipped under the covers, pulling a heavy blanket up to her chin. "It gets pretty cold here at night," she explained. "But your sleeping bag should provide enough warmth."

"No problem," I said, taking off my jacket and stripping to my undershirt and shorts. I unrolled the sleeping bag on the floor next to the cot, feeling like some kind of guard dog. If anybody came for Mel in the middle of the night, they would have to get through me first. I made a pillow of my jacket and before I closed my eyes wished Mel a good night's sleep. She wished the same for me and turned off the light on the table near her cot, plunging the room into darkness. Exhaustion washed over me and in seconds I fell fast asleep.

Thirty-Five

I WOKE SUDDENLY, A HAND over my mouth. Before I could respond, a voice whispered in my ear: "Don't move, Señor Jackson. I am here to help."

I recognized the voice. It was the guy who had been with me in the back seat, the one who had taken my phone. Despite his warning and assurance, I balled my fist, ready to strike. "I am working with Enrique Rodríguez. We want to get you and your sister out of here as soon as possible. Please believe me," he pleaded.

What choice did I have? I relaxed my fist and nodded my assent. Slowly, he pulled his hand from my mouth. "What do you want us to do?" I asked in a whisper.

"You need to wake your sister. Carefully. No noise. Then you both need to get dressed as quietly as you can. Once you are ready, I'll help you escape. But, please be careful. If the others hear you, it will not go well for any of us."

I nodded again, hoping he could see me in the pitch dark of the room. Carefully, I unzipped my sleeping bag and knelt next to the cot. I could hear Mel snoring peacefully. It seemed almost a shame to wake her. But our salvation seemed to be at hand. Maybe the cavalry had arrived, just in the nick of time. I whispered into her ear, "Mel. It's me. You need to wake up." I put my hand gently over her mouth. "Please don't say anything. We need to keep absolutely still. It's a matter of life or death."

She stirred and I felt her jerk against my hand. She put her hand on mine and gradually pushed it away, whispering, "What's going on,

Clint?" She then sensed the presence of the other guy in the room. "Who's that? What does he want?" There was tinge of fear in her voice.

"He's working with a guy I met in Cajamarca yesterday. We can trust him." I wasn't absolutely sure of that, but we had little choice.

"Your brother is right, Señorita Jackson," he said in a whisper. "I am an undercover agent for the municipal police force. Right now, it is four o'clock. In an hour the police will be here to surround this hideout and arrest the three other men. We want you safely out of the way before we begin the operation. There will probably be some shooting. These men are fanatics and will not give up without a fight. We don't want you caught in the crossfire. But you need to hurry. I am supposed to be on guard duty outside. If for some reason, one of them wakes and finds me missing, we'll all be in danger."

I held Mel's hand and could feel her relax. "Okay," she said. "Clint. Please pass me my clothes. They are the end of the cot."

Grabbing her clothes, I handed them over and could hear her getting dressed. I quickly did the same, being careful not to make any unnecessary noise. I had an image of somebody defusing a bomb, working as meticulously as possible not to cause an explosion. Once we were dressed, the guy whispered. "I have unlocked the window. You need to crawl out and climb down. It is not far to the ground, but watch your step. Once you are outside, you will see a dirt road. It is very important that you turn to the left and start walking as quickly and as quietly as you can. The attack force will be coming from your right and it is best to avoid them. We don't want there to be any confusion. Walk for about thirty minutes down the road." He pressed something hard and smooth into my hand. It was my phone. "You will see a gray jeep parked on the side of the road. Here are the keys." He handed them to me and I put them and the phone in my pocket. "You can drive the jeep to Cajamarca. If you have any problems, I see you have Enrique's number in your contacts. Call him and let him know your situation. He'll do his best to send help."

"I understand," I whispered.

"Good. Now I am going to open the window." By this time, my eyes had adjusted to the darkness in the room and I saw the guy brush past me, kneel carefully on the cot, and begin to push open the shutters.

I braced myself for any telltale squeaks as he made these maneuvers, but there were none. Maybe he had oiled the hinges on the shutters beforehand. At any rate, using both hands, he extended them to either side until the whole window was open. Outside, moonlight illuminated the ground below.

The guy got down from the cot, and gestured for me to get to the window and out onto the ground. I did just that, grabbing the sides of the window with both hands and sliding my butt onto the frame, my feet dangling. "It is only a few feet to the ground," the guy whispered.

As I prepared to lower myself down, I turned my head and whispered, "Thank you."

"You are welcome, Señor Jackson. And good luck to you."

I let myself go and landed safely on the ground. Mel followed in a few seconds. I grabbed her legs and helped guide her down. When she had made it, we saw the shutters close above us. I held my breath for a second, listening for any signs that we had awakened our captors. The only sound I could hear was of nocturnal insects and the gentle stirring of the wind. I grabbed Mel's hand and without a word we headed for the road, only a few yards away. When our feet hit the dirt, I had a moment of panic. *What had the guy said? Left, or Right?* Sensing my indecision, Mel pulled me to the left and we began to walk down the road, slowly and carefully at first. We didn't say a word and kept a close watch on where we were stepping. The road was rough, and the last thing we needed was a twisted ankle. I looked over my shoulder every thirty seconds, fully expecting to see flashlights and hear barking dogs and the shouts of our pursuers. But so far, nothing but silence. It was eerily quiet. I had the perverse thought that maybe we should stick around for the attack. I would enjoy seeing the guys who had caused our family, especially Mel, so much suffering, get their comeuppance. But common sense prevailed. We weren't out of the woods yet.

After about ten minutes, I felt it was safe to talk, although I still kept my voice to a whisper. "Looks like we're going to make it, sis. Free and clear."

She grabbed my arm and grinned. "Yes. Thank goodness. And I owe it all to you, Clint."

I didn't know about that, but wasn't going to argue the point. We picked up the pace, still taking care not to trip and fall. Twenty minutes later, as promised, we saw the gray jeep parked on the side of the road, covered in shadows. We approached it carefully, ready for any unpleasant surprises. I imagined Mel thinking that her whole misadventure had begun by approaching a vehicle in the dark.

There were no surprises. The jeep was empty. There were no signs of anyone hiding to ambush us. No unusual sounds. In my paranoia, I had let in the thought that the whole thing was some kind of elaborate set-up. That the guy who freed us had an ulterior motive. That we were pawns in some bigger game that we did not understand. I considered sharing these fears with Mel, but then decided not to. Let's just focus on what we needed to do to get back to Cajamarca in one piece and let the chips fall where they may.

I took the keys from my pocket and opened the driver's door. Getting in behind the wheel, I reached over and opened the passenger door. Mel hopped in. I turned the key and the jeep started up with a comforting hum. I slowly pulled onto the road. Even though we were both anxious to get away from this place as quickly as possible, we had to take it easy. It was still dark, although the sky was beginning to lighten behind us. I didn't want to hit any potholes or other obstacles that might derail our ride. I kept my eyes peeled on the road, Mel helping me to navigate, and kept the speed at around fifteen or twenty miles an hour.

The guy hadn't told us exactly what route to follow, so we had to presume that the secondary road we were on would link up with a main highway at some point with signs that would lead us to Cajamarca. I handed my phone over to Mel, who was keeping an eagle eye ahead, and asked her to see if the map app worked. She fiddled a bit, but no luck. We would just have to feel our way forward as best we could.

Finally, after an hour of navigating hairpin turns, bumping our way over the uneven surface, we hit a paved highway. A green and white marker with an arrow pointing to the right indicated that Cajamarca was eighty kilometers away. We turned onto the highway, letting out a celebratory whoop. From that point on, it was smooth sailing and we arrived in front of the Costa del Sol just as dawn was breaking.

I left the jeep in front of the hotel, not knowing exactly what to do with it. At the moment, it was a minor issue. When we entered, the lobby was deserted with only a night clerk still on duty. His eyes were glued to the TV on the wall in the far corner, the sound low. He was so engrossed by whatever was on the screen, that he jumped when we arrived at the check-in desk. For a moment, a look of startled surprise, even shock, appeared on his face. That was quickly replaced with an ear-to-ear smile and a loud shout of joy: "Señor Jackson," he said with a grin. "You have returned. And with your sister. How wonderful! When you didn't return last night, we were all worried something bad had happened. But, look. Here you are – and with your sister."

He couldn't contain himself. He came around and gave us both a hug, tears of joy in his eyes. I didn't know what to say or how to respond, but Mel just beamed at him. Suddenly realizing that maybe he had gone too far, had violated some protocol, he pulled back. "I'm sorry, Señor Jackson. Señorita Jackson. It's just that…"

"Don't worry, Oscar," Mel said, getting his name from the badge on his shirt. "We are delighted to see you. And please call me Mel."

"Very well," he said, regaining his composure. Then, pointing to the TV screen, he said, "I suppose you have not heard the news, but the government has just announced they have conducted simultaneous raids on the kidnappers around the country. I'm afraid that some have led to casualties, including the deaths of several of the victims. And I knew, Señor Jackson, that you were looking for your missing sister. And I thought that somehow…"

His eyes began to mist over again, but he took a deep breath. "You know, that…"

I gave him a reassuring smile. "No, Oscar. We were not involved in any raid." I didn't go into the details of how that might not be strictly true. We had simply avoided a raid. If not, our fate might well have been to join the list of casualties. Thank goodness for the intervention of Enrique Rodríguez.

"Now, we need to go to my room and clean up. Could I have the key please?"

"Certainly, Señor Jackson. Certainly," he repeated as he returned to his station behind the desk and pulled my key from the slot behind him. As he turned it over, I asked him to keep the news of our arrival confidential for the time being.

"Of course, Señor Jackson. Of course. Not a word, I can assure you."

"Thank you, Oscar. We appreciate your discretion."

He nodded and smiled in a conspiratorial manner. *Our little secret.* But I wondered how long he could keep it. Probably not for long.

Thirty-Six

WHEN WE GOT TO the room, we immediately called John. We had tried on the road, but couldn't get a signal. It was now six o'clock in the morning. I doubt if John had gotten much sleep, especially after I had failed to contact him as planned yesterday evening. He picked up on the first ring. "Hey, John. Great news. I found Mel. She's here with me now."

Before he could respond, I gave Mel the phone. I could only hear her side of the conversation. "Hello, John. Yes. Yes. It's me. Yes. Tired, dirty, and hungry. But, otherwise Okay." There was a pause. "Clint saved my life, John. If it hadn't been for him, who knows what would have happened to me."

After another pause, she handed the phone to me. Although I too was bushed, I was trying to think my way through our next steps. "Listen, John. We need to get out of Peru and back to St. Louis as soon as we can." I saw Mel nod in agreement. "I'm going to try to book the earliest flight I can, but it might take a while. I'll let you know when you can expect us."

"Great, Clint. This is just great news. I've been following developments in Peru and when I heard an hour ago about the raids and the deaths of some of the kidnapped victims, I feared the worst. When you called, I didn't know what to expect," he said, his voice chocking. "How did you manage it?"

"That's a long story, Bro. I'll fill you in later. Right now, we need to clean up and get some food. How are Mom and Dad?"

"Not so good. Al is going fast, I'm afraid. But I'm going to call them right away and tell them the news."

"Should Mel call them?"

"Sure. As soon as she can. But let me brace them first. I'm not sure how they will react hearing from Mel out of the blue. They are both in a very fragile state. Tell you what, I'll call them, then call you back. Then you can proceed."

I agreed and disconnected. While we waited for John's call, I went to the trusty mini-bar and got out two cold water bottles, which we opened and greedily gulped down. Then the phone rang again. "You can call Al and Mae," John said. They are overjoyed."

"Will do, John." Before disconnecting, I remembered. I didn't have their number. John gave it to me and hung up. I dialed it, then turned it over to Mel. "Hi, Mom," she said. "Yes. Yes. I'm okay, thanks to Clint." After a pause, she continued, "I'm so, so sorry I have put you all through this. You can't imagine, I…." She chocked back sobs and said, "We'll be coming home as soon as we can." She listened to what Mae had to say, and answered "I love you, too. See you soon" and ended the call.

Looking at me with tear-stained eyes, she said, "Mom told me that Al was right next to her, listening to every word. She wasn't sure how much he comprehended, but thought he understood the basic fact that I was now safe and sound, thanks to you."

I hoped Al got at least the first part. That Mel was now out of danger. As to "thanks to you," I withheld my judgment.

"Now," Mel said, "I really, really need to take a shower and wash my hair."

I grinned. "Have at it, sis. There is a robe in the closet and lots of soap and shampoo in the bathroom."

"I could really use a change of clothes, Clint."

"Sorry, but I can't help you there. I only brought enough for myself. But maybe we can improvise."

I dug into my duffel and pulled out some shorts, socks, a tee shirt, a dress shirt, and an extra sweater. "These should do the trick," I said, "even though they're going to be a bit large on you. Not much I can do about the pants. Guess you'll have to soldier through with your jeans."

She wrinkled her nose. "Well, at least most of what I wear will be clean. Maybe we can find a place nearby that sells women's clothes. Until then, this," she said, waving at my offerings, "will have to do."

"Okay," I said. "While you take your shower, I'll try to get us out of here as soon as possible."

Grabbing the robe from the closet and gathering up the clothes I had offered, she went to the bathroom and closed the door. A minute later, I could hear the water running. I hoped it was good and hot.

Picking up the house phone, I called the front desk. Oscar picked up on the first ring. When I asked him to book us on the next flight to Lima, he told me that was a service the hotel did not provide. I would have to go directly to the local office of the national airline a few blocks from the hotel, which, unfortunately, did not open until nine o'clock.

I pounded my fist on the bed in frustration. But, what could I do but wait until nine? "By the way, Señor Jackson. You might want to turn on your television to the local news channel. I think you will find it interesting."

Disconnecting, I grabbed the remote and switched on the TV, which was already tuned to the local news channel. What I saw was surreal. There was my interviewer, Elena, breathlessly reporting on site of the local kidnapping drama. In the background, I saw body bags being carried out of the cabin from which we had escaped scant hours earlier. Grim-faced police dressed in swat-team gear were moving around in the background like gray ghosts. Elena had the microphone in front of the guy who seemed to be in charge. He was explaining what had happened. The authorities had gotten word from an unnamed source that the local branch of the "Atahualpa Brigade" was holding two North Americans captive in the cabin behind him. They had deployed their forces and, after making sure the hostages were safe, attacked just before dawn. There had been an intense exchange of gunfire in which several police had been wounded, fortunately none seriously. But then he said something that brought a lump to my throat. All *four* "terrorists" had been killed. He didn't reveal that one of the four had been a police undercover agent. But I knew. I also knew that he had died saving our lives. That was going to be tough to get over.

"Tell me, captain," Elena said, "Were the two North American hostages Clint and Melanie Jackson?"

"I cannot confirm their identities at this moment," he lied. "But we presume that they somehow escaped. They were not in the cabin when we attacked."

"Is it possible that they were killed beforehand and their bodies buried?"

"Anything is possible. But it seems unlikely. The "terrorists" were not expecting us. Why would they eliminate their most valuable assets?"

Elena nodded in agreement. Just then, my phone buzzed. I muted the TV and looked at the screen. It was Roberto Martínez. I was tempted to let the call go to voice mail, but reconsidered. If it hadn't been for him, I might not have found Mel. His idea of putting her story on the front page of his paper had led ultimately to the kidnappers contacting me and the ultimate rescue of us both. I owed him, big time.

"Hello, Roberto."

"Ah. Señor Jackson. So good to hear your voice. How are you? And your sister?"

"We are fine, Roberto. In large part, thanks to you."

"Have you seen the news about the attack on the local 'Atahualpa Brigade'? And the speculation about what happened to the two captives?"

"I was just watching it on TV."

What came next was predictable. "I would like to interview you and your sister, if that is possible." He wanted a scoop, and I couldn't blame him. And it seemed a small price to pay in return for his assistance.

"Well, Roberto. My sister is in the shower right now. When she comes out, we'll see if she is okay with an interview. She is still pretty shaken up. And, we are planning to leave Cajamarca as soon as we can get on a flight out. So, let me call you back once I talk things over with her."

"Sure thing, Señor Jackson. Whatever you say. And, once again, I'm very pleased that you two are safe. It's been quite an ordeal for you."

"Thanks. Yes, it has. I'll get back to you soon. I promise."

After I disconnected, I could still hear water running in the shower. Mel was making up for lost time. The TV was still on and I saw the four bodes being loaded into a van. The thought hit me that if I owed Roberto Martínez a large debt, I owned an even bigger one to Enrique Rodríguez. If not for his intercession, both Mel and I would be corpses number five and six. He was probably swamped, but I decided to call him anyway. I was expecting to be sent to voice mail, but he answered right away.

"Ah, Clint. You are okay, I trust? And your sister?"

"We are both fine, Enrique. Thanks to you and your undercover guy. I'm really sorry he got caught in the crossfire," I said, my voice cracking.

"Yes, Clint. So am I. He was our best agent. But, I'm afraid, such risks go with the job. The important thing is that we caught the *brigadistas* and you and your sister escaped without harm."

He paused, "I presume you have seen the television news of our raid."

"Yes. That's how I knew your agent had been killed."

"Well, you should brace yourself for an onslaught of journalists once they know where you are. Our leader on the scene tried to deflect questions about your whereabouts, but it's only a matter of time until they track you down. There are probably reporters from Lima already on their way here to interview you." He paused again. "I can't tell you what to say, but I would appreciate it if you keep my involvement and the role of our agent out of the story. There are lots of complicated reasons why we don't want to have the full story distributed widely. I hope I can count on your discretion."

"I understand, Enrique. Absolutely. It's the least I can do to repay you for your assistance."

I got the feeling that he was not all that sure I could stick to my pledge, but he simply replied, "Thank you, Clint."

"By the way," I said, "Your jeep is parked in front of the Costa del Sol, the keys in the ignition."

He chuckled. "No, it's not, Clint. We've already moved it. We've known you were in the Costa del Sol for some time."

"So, the guy in the gray suit who was following me. One of yours?"

"Yes. One of ours. Hope he didn't get you too upset."

"No, No. Not really," I said. "Good to know you were keeping an eye on me."

"Well, Clint. There is a lot going on, so I need to hang up. But, if anything comes up that I can help you with, don't hesitate to call."

"Thanks, again, Enrique. And maybe next time, I'll share some pisco sours with you."

He laughed. "I look forward to it," and we ended the call.

By this time, I could hear that the shower had stopped. When the bathroom door opened, Mel stepped out of the swirl of steam behind her wrapped in the hotel robe with a towel wrapped around her head. She grabbed my clothes and retreated back. "Be done in a minute, Clint," she said through the door. My guess is that it would take longer, but to my surprise she emerged in record time, dressed in my clothes, which, I thought, looked a lot better on her than on me.

While she sat next to me on the bed, I filled her in on that latest developments. When I mentioned the four body bags, she blanched. "We owe that guy our lives," she said. I thought she was going to dissolve into self-blame, but she stiffened. When I asked her if she was willing to do the interview with Roberto Martínez, there was some hesitation. But she agreed that we owed him too. When I called him back, it was nearly seven o'clock. I realized he was anxious to meet us, but I had to shower, we had to have some breakfast, and I had to be at the airline office at nine. We set up the interview for ten, depending, of course, on my luck in getting plane reservations. If we were lucky and got a morning flight, then the interview was off. Roberto agreed to those conditions, having little choice. I did want to repay him. But getting back to St. Louis was now our top priority. He seemed to understand.

I showered, shaved, and shampooed. By this time, Mel and I were starving. When we got to the hotel restaurant, it was still relatively deserted, but we did attract some curious stares. I wondered if Oscar had stuck to his promise of discretion. Probably not. Too juicy a bit of news to keep to himself.

We went to the buffet and filled our plates with sausage, eggs, rolls, fruit, and juice. The waiter brought us coffee, Peruvian style. The coffee was in a small container in a concentrated dose. We added hot water, sugar, and cream and downed several cups. During breakfast, Mel told me she had called Professor Cartwright while I had been in the shower, informing him that she was safe and planning to head back to St. Louis as soon as possible to deal with a family emergency. But she also promised to return to the site as soon as she could. He said he was okay with that and would tell the rest of the team at once that she was okay. Her voice wavered a bit, but I could sense her getting steadier and stronger by the minute. Good old Mel. But I also realized she had been through a terrible trauma. As tough and as resilient as I knew her to be, she was going to need a lot of support and some counseling to get through to the other side.

"So, Clint," she said between bites. "What have you been doing these past few years? Mom told me you were living in San Francisco. How's that been?"

I told her about my work in construction and how I had become a big fan of the Bay Area.

"Do you plan to go back there, after this little adventure?"

"Sure. Unless something comes up. I really like it there."

She hesitated. "And what about your…?"

"My drinking?"

"Yes, that." The elephant in the room.

No sense lying to her. "Not so good. I've tried to give up a million times, but no luck. In fact, despite all my best intentions, I got pretty drunk at the Miami airport waiting for the flight to Lima. I'm surprised they let me on."

She gave a sigh, but no recriminations. She knew me well. "But I haven't touched a drop since I got here. I've been focused on finding you." *Big deal,* I thought to myself. *It's been what? All of three days.*

Mel reached her hand across the table to grasp mine. "Thank you again, Clint." Then, with a chuckle, she added, "I hope I don't have to get kidnapped again just so you go on the wagon."

It was a joke, but it hit home. Maybe I could turn the corner. Only time would tell.

Looking over my shoulder, Mel whispered. "Lots of people are staring at us. A few are pointing to the screen and then back at our table."

I glanced up to the television, tuned to the national news. From what I could tell, the coordinated raids to free the hostages from the "Atahualpa Brigades" had not gone well. Several of the hostages had been killed in the crossfire. The U.S. ambassador was issuing a statement, a grim look on his face. Then, suddenly I saw pictures of me and Mel on the screen. Reading from the scroll, we were identified as two Americans who had successfully escaped our captors in Cajamarca. We were a good news story and minor celebrities. The real hero, however, the guy who saved our lives, was not mentioned. And, it seemed, the story of our escape had gone from local to national to international, featured prominently now on CNN and presumably other news outlets.

When I relayed all this to Mel, she seemed upset. "Well, let's hope journalists don't dig too deeply into the whole story, Clint. It's not only embarrassing, but I'm afraid it will put some of my friends in danger. In fact…." She stopped, her face registering shock. "Oh, no, Clint. Look who's in the lobby."

I turned to see none other than Inspector Felipe Calderón, backed by two burly guys in gray suits, heading in our direction. This could not be good. I doubted if he was coming to congratulate us on our successful escape.

Before he reached our table, I stood up to face him. He stopped about a foot away, his manner oozing hostility and resentment. "You and your sister need to come with us, Señor Jackson. Right away. We have some questions for both of you." His two-man entourage glowered at me, trying their best at intimidation. Under normal circumstances, it might have worked. But these were not normal circumstances.

"What a coincidence," I said, my voice dripping with sarcasm. "I have some questions for *you*. Like why didn't you carry out a real investigation of my sister's disappearance rather than dismissing it with some cock and bull story about her eloping? Were you under orders to just go through the motions, or was it your own idea? How do you think that is going to play out when I do interviews on national television, letting the world know how incompetent and corrupt you are?"

I said all this in a loud voice, so that everyone in the room could hear me. Looking over Calderón's shoulder I saw that we had a transfixed audience, hanging on every word. Good.

Calderón's eyes narrowed and his face flushed. I saw his hands ball into fists and I readied myself to counterpunch. "You are very insolent, Señor Jackson." Then he played the nationalist card. "Typical of you arrogant Americans who think you are above the law in Peru. Well, you are soon going to find out that things are different in Cajamarca. You will either come with me willingly, or by force. Your choice."

My blood was boiling. I could feel the old anger swelling and I got ready to swing at him if he or his minions laid a hand on me or my sister. Mel saw what was happening, and intervened. Grabbing my arm, she said, "It's all right, Clint. It's all right." Turning to Calderón, she said, "We will be happy to answer your questions, Inspector. But please give us time to attend to some urgent matters. You must realize that we have been through quite an ordeal. We have yet to recover. Just a few hours. Then we'll come to your office on our own accord. Let's say around ten o'clock?"

I could tell that Calderón was about to object. But the optics were not good. He could sense that the crowd in the dining room, some of whom were filming the entire encounter, was not in his corner. They might even have been ready to intercede on our behalf. In fact, some of them began to shout out their support, telling him to leave us alone. I guessed that most of them were tourists, unaware of the fear that Calderón stirred among the locals. Finally, after glaring daggers at me, he relented. "Very well, Señorita Jackson. I'll expect you both in my office at ten o'clock precisely. If you are a second late, you will be in serious trouble."

"We'll be there, inspector," Mel said, "I promise."

Giving us one last withering stare, he turned on his heel and along with his entourage left the room. As soon as he was gone, the others in the dining room erupted in cheers and applause and came to give us handshakes, hugs, and congratulations. Mel and I were caught up in the emotion of the moment, grinning and laughing along with everybody else. It was a great catharsis, but we still faced the dilemma of how to get around our commitment to meet with Calderón at ten.

Once things had calmed down, I called the waiter over to pay for the breakfast. "No need, Señor Jackson. It is, how do you say it? On the house." I tried to insist, but he refused and Mel indicated that it was best to let it go and express our appreciation, which we did.

Back in our room, I thanked Mel for keeping me from punching Calderón, which would have been a disaster no matter the momentary satisfaction. "Well," she said, "We bought some time. But we have to think of a way to avoid any further contact with that jerk. He wants to pressure me to reveal Jaime's whereabouts, and there are a variety of ways for him to do that. He could, for example, place us in preventive detention, keeping us from leaving for up to forty-eight hours. And maybe other things even less pleasant. What are we going to do, Clint? Any ideas?"

I thought for a minute. There weren't many realistic options. We had to leave Cajamarca as soon as possible. From John's tone, it was clear that Al was in the last stages. I had to get Mel to him before it was too late. But we didn't even have our plane tickets. It was now eight o'clock and we had another hour to wait until the airline office opened. We might be able to rent a car and drive to Lima. But Calderón could set up roadblocks and we'd be in jail before we knew it. Maybe Enrique Rodríguez could intervene on our behalf, but I didn't know how much sway he had over Calderón and was reluctant to ask him to take yet another risk on our behalf.

After talking things over with Mel, we decided to touch base with John to see if he could help. When I called, He answered immediately and listened carefully as I explained our dilemma. "Maybe you can reach out to your friend at the embassy, Macalister, and see if he can get the ambassador to intercede. I know they were less than helpful before, but the situation has changed. I guess you know by now that we are some sort of international celebrities. Tell Macalister that it is not going to make the embassy look so good if two Americans go from being heroes who escaped terrorist kidnappers to ending up in a Cajamarca jail."

"That's a good point, Clint. I'll get on it right away. And by the way," he chuckled, "Mel's photo shows what a beauty she is. You, my brother, not so much."

I laughed. "Yeah. The stoner hippie look. But actually, I am more clean-cut these days, closer to the All-American hero the press wants me to be."

"Later, Bro. Hang in there."

"Will do, John. And thanks."

After I disconnected, I told Mel that John was going to see what he could do to get Calderón off our backs. "I sure hope he can, Clint. That guy gives me the creeps. I'm sure he wants to press me about Jaime and the last thing I want is for that kid to have more problems."

She saw me frown. So far as I was concerned, we could throw that jerk to the wolves. How much consideration had he shown my sister? Leading her into a trap and letting her be kidnapped. But I knew Mel, she of the good heart. "I know what you are thinking," she said. "But as I told you, it's complicated. I'm sure Jaime was under considerable duress, squeezed by the police on the one hand and by the 'Atahualpa Brigade' on the other. I saw a look of real regret on his face when they bundled me into the car."

I wasn't going to argue the point. She knew Jaime and the overall situation a hell of a lot better than I did. "Well," I said, "He's probably in Ecuador by now. He seemed to be leaning in that direction when I saw him in San Ignacio."

"You're probably right. But, even so, I don't want to give Calderón the slightest hint that we know where he is or that he was involved in my kidnapping."

"Okay. Agreed. Let's hope John can save us from the inspector's evil clutches. If not, if we have to talk with him, mums the word on Jaime."

She smiled and nodded. "Now," I said, "we need to get our stories straight as to what happened at the hideout a few hours ago. If we get interrogated by Calderón or are interviewed by the press, we need to tailor our story in a way that doesn't get Enrique Rodríguez into any trouble. We're going to have to be a little creative in telling our story."

Just then, my phone buzzed. I looked at the screen. It was Elena, my TV interviewer. "Yes, Elena."

"Hello, Señor Jackson. Congratulations on your escape. And the rescue of your sister. It's all over the news. And I was hoping you would let us interview you and your sister. I would greatly appreciate the opportunity, if, of course, you are willing."

"Hold on a minute, Elena. I need to consult with my sister." Turning to Mel, I said, "It's the woman who interviewed me yesterday. The interview that led my arrival at the hideout. Just as with Roberto Martínez, I think we owe her. She wants to interview us both. What do you say?"

"I guess it's okay. But I need to find some new clothes. No offense, but wearing your shirt and sweater is not the look I want to display to the world."

I was about to make a sexist remark, but bit my tongue. Whatever her outward calm, I knew that Mel was struggling to keep things together after all she had been through. If she wanted to make sure she was dressed properly, who was I to judge? "Understood, sis. We'll get on it as soon as we can."

I then told Elena that we were ready to do the interview and set the time at ten o'clock. By now, everybody in Cajamarca probably knew we were staying at the Costa del Sol. There was no sense hiding the fact and we agreed to do the interview in the lobby. Although I didn't tell Elena, I also realized that ten o'clock was the time we promised to be at police headquarters. When we didn't show, I figured Calderón would come to get us. When he found himself interrupting a TV interview that was going to go national to arrest us, maybe he would have second thoughts.

After arranging things with Elena, I called Roberto Martínez. I didn't know how he would take to being scooped by the local television outlet and suggested that he come over right away for his interview. "That's very thoughtful of you, Señor Jackson. But I know you have a lot to do. Elena and I have worked together before and we can do it again in this case. I'll see you at ten, if that's all right with you."

"Fine, Roberto. See you then." Turning to Mel, I said, "Well, that's that. I hope you are okay with all this."

"Frankly, I'm not looking forward to it. But you are right that we owe these people an interview. Now the sixty-four-thousand-dollar question: What are we going to tell them? And the wider world?"

We hashed it over for about twenty minutes. We finally decided that Mel would keep the details of her kidnapping purposely vague, saying only that she had been lured to a secret rendezvous and been taken captive by the "Atahualpa Brigade," keeping Jaime's role out of it. From then on, I would describe my arrival and my search for Mel, again trying not to be too specific as to the details but highlighting the importance of the interviews, which led to my own capture. Then came the tricky part. How to explain our escape without involving Enrique Rodríguez and the guy who facilitated it? We had to be creative, constructing a narrative that left them out and concocting a tale of somehow forcing open the window, making our way down the road, stumbling on to the jeep, hot-wiring it, and ending up back in Cajamarca. It had more holes than swiss cheese. *How had we known to go left on the road, not to the right? How likely was it to find a jeep in such a remote location? Wasn't it all too convenient?*

But if would have to do. If someone like Calderón decided to carry out a thorough investigation, I don't think the story would stand up for very long. However, all we needed was for it to stand up long enough for us to get out of the country and back to the States. Of course, another thing that worried me about the story was that it made me seem more heroic than I really was. The brother dedicated to finding his missing sister at all costs and against all odds, bringing her safely home. A nice picture, but one with lots of flaws. So far as I was concerned, the real heroes were Enrique Rodríguez and the guy who died in the firefight. Maybe someday I could tell the true story. But for now, I had to stick with the false one.

We had just finished tying the bow on our account, when John called. "Good news, Clint," he said, excitement in his voice. "I was able to get a hold of Charlie Macalister right away. He, in turn, put me in direct contact with the ambassador, who happened to be meeting with the minister of the interior who is in charge of the national police. The minister assured the ambassador that you and Mel don't have anything to worry about from the local gestapo guy, Calderón."

I had put the call on speaker, and could see Mel breathe a deep sigh of relief when she heard that news. "Now, about getting you home as soon as possible, the ambassador is greasing the wheels. We got you both on a noon flight out of Cajamarca landing in Lima at one. Then on a three o'clock to Miami with connections to St. Louis, arriving here at around midnight. A long trip, but you'll be flying first class, courtesy of Uncle Sam."

Mel interrupted. "John. I don't have a passport. It's with my stuff at the dig. And I don't know if we'll have time to retrieve it."

"Not to worry, sis. We have that covered. The ambassador anticipated you might not have your documentation, given the circumstances. He has issued a special temporary passport for you."

"Thank goodness, for that," Mel exclaimed.

I was bemused by the ambassador's sudden attentiveness to our needs given the hands-off attitude he and his underlings had displayed when I was at the embassy a few days ago. "So, Bro," I said, "We are getting the royal treatment. Better late than never, I guess."

John got my drift. "Yeah. Well, the whole kidnapping story has turned into a major disaster and major embarrassment, both for the Peruvian government and ours. The raids were carried out by local troops, but with considerable oversight and planning from us. I don't know how closely you've been able to follow the details, but the raids were successful only in killing everybody, kidnappers and hostages alike. Five U.S. citizens dead and one on life support. So, you are the sole survivors, the 'feel good' story of the entire messy affair. Heads are going to roll, and the ambassadors might well be among them. The finger-pointing and the blame game have already started."

"And we get the royal treatment as a result," I said. "I shouldn't complain, I guess. At least, we seem to have smooth sailing getting out of here and back home. It could be a lot more complicated and a lot more difficult. Thanks, Bro. For all the efforts on your end. I guess you have some juice among the powers that be."

He laughed. "Yeah. Maybe. But nothing is cost free, Clint. You will be met by the ambassador at the airport, along with plenty of press. Just grin and bear it, although if I know you, you would rather punch the ambassador in the face than shake his hand."

I laughed in return. "Guilty as charged. Don't worry. I'll play nice."

"Okay, guys. Keep in touch and let me know how things go. By now, all your airline passes and special documentation should be at the local LAN Peru office. Let me know if there are any foul-ups."

"Will do, John. And thanks again."

By this time, it was a little after nine o'clock, the time when the airline office should be open. I imagine that under normal circumstances, that opening time could be flexible. But I assumed that pressure was being applied to make sure we could pick up what we needed the moment we arrived.

When we exited the hotel, a small crowd had gathered outside. When they saw us, they began to cheer and applaud. Some approached, shaking our hands and patting us on the shoulder. We practically had to run a gauntlet to get to our destination. We smiled and thanked our well-wishers, explaining that we had important business to attend to and asking them to excuse our haste. They took it good-naturedly and began to disperse. I hoped we could avoid such encounters in the future. It was heart-warming to receive such attention, but it also made us a little uncomfortable. Our sudden fame – or was it notoriety? – was going to take some getting used to.

The airline office *was* open. I didn't even have to show my passport. The clerk recognized us immediately and turned over the documents, wishing us a safe journey home. Leaving the office, Mel asked if she could do some clothes shopping. She offered to go on her own, knowing that waiting for women to buy clothes was not on my top ten list of favorite things to do. But I wasn't going to let her out of my sight until we got safely home.

Mel had asked at the hotel where to find women's clothes and had been directed to a place a few blocks to the north. As we headed there, we could see heads swivel, fingers point, and words whispered: "There are the two gringos who escaped the terrorists." Pretty soon, I feared, we'd be asked for autographs. But we made it to the store unimpeded. Fortunately, Mel found everything she needed in her size in less than ten minutes. As we left the store, I teased her. "I bet if you had been alone, it would have taken you at least half an hour, tops."

She laughed and poked me in the ribs. Good. Signs that she might be getting back to normal.

When we got back to the hotel, it was nine-thirty. A mob had gathered in the lobby and we were greeted with flash-bulbs going off and phones stuck in our faces to record answers to their many questions. I held up my hand to ask for quiet, scanning the room for any sign of Roberto and Elena. I spotted them to my left in a section of the lobby where coca tea was served and small tables were surrounded by comfortable couches and chairs. I nodded in their direction and held up one finger that we would be over to talk with them in just a minute. By this time, Oscar and the hotel staff had come to our rescue. He and some of the waiters maneuvered between us and the mob. "Please, ladies and gentlemen" Oscar said. "Leave our guests in peace."

"Thank you, Oscar," I said. Then, addressing the horde, I said, "We have arranged interviews with two press outlets. After we are finished, if time permits, we would be happy to answer your questions."

Mel looked at me and in a low voice, said in English, "Gee, Clint. I didn't know you had diplomatic skills. I'm impressed."

The crowd was not happy. I could hear grumblings in the ranks. But they gave way and I took Mel by the arm and we walked over to meet Roberto and Elena, who was there with her trusty cameraman, Pablo. After introductions, Mel excused herself to go to our room to change and freshen up. Elena flashed a smile of understanding. While we waited for Mel to return, we sat and had some tea. After a few minutes of desultory conversation, Mel reappeared, dressed in her recent purchases and with some minimal makeup applied. While we had been waiting, we had determined that Roberto would begin the interview without the camera rolling, taking notes and recording our conversation so that he could write it up and get the story out as soon as possible. Then he would leave and Elena would take over, filming our interview, which would be broadcast as soon as possible. Ideally, she would have preferred to do it live. But given the fact she had rushed from the kidnapping site to Cajamarca, they had not had time to arrange the live feed. Nonetheless, they would rush the film over to the studio and put it on the air at once. We should be able to see it before we left.

The hotel staff had managed to move the crowd back into the central lobby and set up a phalanx between them and us. I could see various onlookers craning their necks and cupping their ears in attempts to hear what we were saying. They would just have to wait for the news to hit the *Eco* and appear on the airways.

We told our story to Roberto as we had rehearsed it. He nodded and occasionally interrupted, but for the most part just let us talk. Every once in a while, a look of surprise appeared on his face, but for the most part he seemed to accept our narrative without question. When we had finished telling our tale, he asked some personal questions of Mel to provide background and human interest to his story. Wrapping up the interview, he thanked us and we thanked him. I told him that if he hadn't taken the opportunity to feature Mel's plight on his front page, we probably would not have been alive to tell the tale. His eyes glistened. "I'm so pleased I was able to be of some assistance, Señor Jackson, and we have this happy outcome." With that, he hugged us both before he left quickly to get back to his office.

Our TV interview followed the same course and we told the same story. Occasionally, as with Roberto, a quizzical look appeared on Elena's face and I thought she would follow up with some additional probing. But she refrained and we wrapped up after about twenty minutes. "I'm rushing the film over to our studios," she told us. I repeated the words of gratitude I had uttered to Roberto, and she responded much the same way. She also said, with a slight grin, "Thanks to you as well, Señor Jackson. My interviews with you will put our ratings through the roof. It's a great story, and we appreciate the opportunity of getting the first chance to tell it on camera. It's the biggest, how do you say it? 'Scoop' that we have ever had." She didn't say it outright, but I knew she was also thinking that it was a heck of a career boost for a local reporter, with the interview likely to make not only the national news but the international outlets as well.

After we finished the interviews, we headed to my room to pack for our trip home. Much of the curious crowd stayed around. I'm not sure how many were journalists or would-be journalists or simply gawkers, but the hotel staff continued to keep them from pestering us.

When we were safely inside, Mel asked, "How do you think it went, Clint? I could feel my palms sweating when we got to the part of how we escaped. Good thing we weren't hooked up to a lie detector."

"I know what you mean. And there were times I thought Roberto and Elena had their suspicions that the story didn't really hang together. But I guess that the general sympathy there is for us – and especially for you, held captive for more than a week – they weren't going to press it. I wouldn't be surprised, however, that they or some other journalists will begin to dig deeper once the excitement dies down. Not much we can do it about it at this point," I said with a shrug.

Mel just nodded. But I knew that she was still suffering internal turmoil from her experience and was worried that her actions might put others in danger. It would take her time to recover.

It didn't take long for me to assemble my belongings. At the desk, Oscar greeted us with a broad grin. After being on night duty and then in charge during all the excitement, he should have been dead on his feet. But he showed no signs of fatigue. When I turned over the key and took out my credit card to pay the bill, he waved me off. "No, No, Señor Jackson. We are not going to charge you. It's the least we can do. After all," he said with a wink, "You have provided us with a year's worth of free publicity. Now everybody will want to stay in the hotel where the famous gringo hero had a room. We might even charge double for whoever books it."

I couldn't help but laugh. "Okay, Oscar." Then, pulling several hundred dollars from my money belt and handing them over to him, I said, "But you and the staff deserve something extra for all your efforts this morning." He was about to decline, but I shoved the bills into his hand. "Please, Oscar. I insist."

"Very well. Thank you, Señor Jackson. You are very kind," he said, pocketing the bills.

It was a little after eleven when we headed to the street for our ride to the airport. I had already contacted Daniel and, as usual, he was there waiting at the curb. There was still a crowd in front of the hotel and they greeted us with whoops, whistles, and applause. I wondered if somewhere in their ranks there wasn't a police agent or two, assigned by Calderón to continue to keep an eye on us. I couldn't imagine that he had taken the orders to stand down with good grace. He wasn't the type. I didn't think he would actually try to block us from leaving, but I didn't put it into the "absolutely impossible" category either.

I had called Daniel for a reason. If there was a follow-up investigation, which seemed almost certain, it would soon turn up the fact that Daniel had driven me to the University and then to San Ignacio in search of Jaime. I had mixed feelings about Jaime, but I didn't want him or any of the students to get into trouble. Mel and I had discussed this possibility in the hotel, and she agreed that we had to do what we could to get Daniel's help in covering my tracks. It was going to be a big ask. He could get into a lot of trouble if he was caught lying to the authorities, especially Calderón. But we had to try.

Daniel was waiting, holding the car door open for us and with an ear-to-ear smile on his face. Flash-bulbs popped again as we got into the car and Daniel closed the door. Once behind the wheel, Daniel turned and said "It's is so good to see you Señor Jackson. Señorita Jackson. We are all so happy to see you are both safe and freed from your captors. And we are all very sorry that you had to suffer such an experience. Please believe me. Not all Peruvians are terrorists."

"Thank you, Daniel. We appreciate your concern," I said. In the back of my mind, however, I thought, *well, you might not be so happy once you understand what I have to tell you.*

As we exited the plaza on the way to the airport, I explained to Daniel what he might expect from the inevitable follow-up investigation. Watching his reaction in the rear-view mirror, I saw his face wrinkle with concern. "The last thing we want," I assured him, "is to put you or any of the local students in danger because you helped us. I hope you understand."

I saw him nod. "I don't want to tell you what to do, Daniel. But if you are asked, I hope you can plead ignorance as to what I was up to when you chauffeured me. Maybe you could tell them that you were only the driver and stayed in the car while I went out on my own to the University and to San Ignacio, which, after all, is the truth."

He nodded again. "Don't worry, Señor Jackson. You can rely on my discretion."

"Thank you, Daniel. We both appreciate it," Mel said.

I couldn't help feeling guilty that Daniel might be under the gun simply because he had been my driver. And I imagined a scenario where all his good intentions to remain discrete crumbled like dust when confronted by someone like Calderón. But there was little we could do beyond warn him. The rest was out of our hands.

When we arrived at the airport, Daniel got out and held the door for us, his broad smile back in place. We all exchanged hugs and good wishes. In the process, I slipped a C-note into his hand. I didn't expect it to buy his silence, but he deserved the generous tip regardless.

I grabbed my duffel, slung my backpack over my shoulder, and we headed for the entrance. Before we got there, a blue-suited guy with what looked like aviator wings on his lapel came to greet us. "Welcome, Señor Jackson. Señorita Jackson. Please come with me. My name is Martín and I have been assigned to assist you with your boarding."

We exchanged handshakes, and followed him into the terminal. There was a sizeable crowd, waiting for the flight to Lima. They were all transfixed by the televisions on the walls, all tuned to Elena's interview with us. It was a surreal moment, as we passed by virtually unnoticed while Martín led us to a VIP lounge where we were the only passengers. "Please make yourselves comfortable, señores," pointing to two leather-bound chairs arrayed in front of another television screen, where we could see ourselves being interviewed. "I need to check with the flight crew," he said. "I'll be back soon."

With that, he closed the door, leaving us alone with ourselves in the flesh and on the screen. Mel and I looked at each other and giggled. *This was all so weird!* We watched the interview, mentally pinching ourselves that what we were watching was real. I listened carefully to hear if we had made any slips in our story, but to my relief could find none. When the interview ended, Elena came on to explain that we were heading back to the United States to reunite with our family. She then provided an up-date on the events of last night, telling the audience that an extensive investigation was already under way into all aspects of our kidnapping.

I felt a shiver. We were not yet free and clear. *What if Martín was not who he said he was? What if he had placed us in this room so we could be more easily apprehended by the authorities?* I half expected Calderón to burst through the door and place us both under arrest. I was about to share these fears with Mel, when Martín opened the door to the suite, a reassuring smile on his face. "The plane is ready for boarding, señores. Please let me escort you to the ramp. You will be the first to board. We have assigned you the first two seats at the front of the cabin. As you might guess," he said with a wry smile, "everyone boarding will recognize you. I hope you don't mind the attention."

Relieved that my fears had been overblown, I chuckled. "We are getting used to it, Martín. By the way," I added, "Don't you need to see our documents and our papers."

I began to pull them out of my backpack, when he put a restraining hand on my arm. "No need, Señor Jackson," he said with a laugh. "I know who you both are, as do most Peruvians by now. And we have special instructions from the president of the republic to make sure your flight to Lima goes as smoothly as possible. It is the least we can do after all you both have been through."

We walked out onto the tarmac, where the plane to Lima was warming its engines. He led us to the bottom of the ramp, where a flight attendant was waiting. "Margarita will show you to your seats, señores. And *buen viaje.*"

The attendant, Margarita, had the standard smile. But somehow, it seemed genuine, not pasted on. "Right this way, Señor Jackson. Señorita Jackson."

We followed her up the ramp and into the plane. She pointed to the front row and we settled in, Mel at the window, me on the aisle. While Mel took her seat and buckled in, I stored my gear in the overhead bin and then followed suit.

I grinned at her. "I could get used to this royal treatment."

She grinned back. "Yeah. Beats what we're used to. But I wouldn't want to have to repeat what it took to get us here."

I nodded. "No. Once was more than enough."

The rest of the passengers filed in, all of them giving us smiles and a few handshakes as they took their seats. When we took off, Mel looked out the window, a wistful look on her face. I knew she had mixed emotions about leaving. We saw the valley, with its beautiful colors, unfold below us on another crystal-clear day. Everything looked calm and peaceful from a distance, making it hard to believe we had been in such danger on the ground. Mel spotted Cumbe Mayo and then the site where she had spent so much time and her eyes glistened as she held tightly onto my hand.

Thirty-Seven

ONE HOUR LATER, WE descended into Lima. Once the plane came to a halt, Margarita announced to the passengers, who were already scrambling to pull their luggage from the overhead bins, that they should remain seated until two honored guests were allowed to disembark. *Uh-ho, there goes our popularity.* But the other passengers seemed to take it in good spirits and as we were led out of the plane, they burst into cheers and applause for the *gringos valientes.*

Yet another blue-suited guy with wings on his lapel greeted us at the end of the ramp and led the way into the terminal, where we were ushered into another VIP lounge. Awaiting us was the U.S. ambassador as well as a coterie of security agents, embassy personnel, and Peruvian officials. The ambassador, all smiles, approached us with his hand outstretched. "Mister Jackson. Clint. And Melanie. So very happy to see you, safe and sound. Your country is very proud of you."

I was tempted to ignore his hand, but Mel gave me a gentle nudge and I reluctantly went through the ritual. I took quiet pleasure in giving his hand a tight squeeze that produced a surprised wince on his face. He was enough of a professional to ignore it. Mel was smiling as he took her hand, whether from genuine appreciation or stifling a laugh from my little show of disapproval. *Yeah, "safe and sound" – and no thanks to you!* But I stifled my resentment. No sense stirring the pot at this point. But when I got home, I planned to raise some holy hell with the State Department for the way the embassy had brushed me off.

Good ole Charlie Macalister was the next to greet us. "Clint. Melanie. So good to see you. And congratulations on your escape. It's one bright spot in what has been a pretty terrible twenty-four hours."

I decided not to play any macho handshake games with him. I wasn't happy with how he had behaved, but figured he was only following orders.

"I can only imagine," I said, taking his hand. "And sorry about what happened to the other captives."

He replied with a somber nod. Then the ambassador said, "Mister Jackson. Miss Jackson. I would like you to meet the Minister of the Interior who is in charge of national security, Señor Adolfo Díaz Canseco."

The minister, dressed in a well-tailored charcoal gray business suit, was a fit looking guy in his fifties, with dark hair graying at the edges. He was wearing dark glasses, but took them off when we began the handshake ritual. His brown eyes were rimmed with red and he clearly had not gotten much sleep in some time. "On behalf of the Peruvian government," he intoned, "I want to offer my deepest apologies for what you have endured in our country. I want to assure that the terrorists who kidnapped you make up only a tiny percentage of the Peruvian people, who are overwhelmingly peaceful. I also assure you that everyone associated with what happened to you will be rounded up and dealt with in the harshest terms possible."

I saw Mel's face turn pale. She was undoubtedly thinking that his promise of retribution was no idle threat and might bring harm to the innocents, including the Peruvian students with whom she had been working. I was thinking along the same lines and hoped that the people who had aided me in finding Mel wouldn't be caught up in the web as well. I was tempted to tell the minister that if anyone should be punished, it was Inspector Felipe Calderón, who had failed miserably in his duties and who was undoubtedly corrupt. But I curbed the temptation and simply said, "Thank you, Minister. We have been very touched by the friendliness and concern shown to us by so many Peruvians."

"Thank you, Señor Jackson. That is most gracious of you."

"Well," the ambassador said, "I know you two," nodding to me and Mel, "are anxious to get to your plane and be on your way home to the U.S. But I hope I can prevail on you to spend a few minutes to talk with the press. There's quite a horde waiting outside," he said, pointing beyond the door. "And we promised them you would make an appearance and perhaps answer a few questions."

I looked at Mel and could see that she shared my reluctance. Enough, already. We *were* in a hurry to get home. The ambassador sensed our hesitation. "I know you are not eager for any delays. But, like it or not, you and your escape are now all over the news, both here and around the world. Given what a disaster the rescue operation was otherwise, it would be of great help to both the U.S. and Peru if you would at least spend a few minutes in front of the camera."

I was tempted to tell him to shove it. After all, he couldn't force us to face the press. And for all the talk of the greater national good for both nations, I knew that he and the minister were undoubtedly taking a lot of heat for having botched the rescue operation. Having us appear at their sides, as John said, the "feel good" story of the moment, might help deflect some of the criticism.

I asked the ambassador if I could have a moment alone with Mel before coming to any decision. He agreed. What else could he do? We talked it over and decided it wasn't worth making a fuss over. Let them have their photo op and then we would be on our way. Also, Mel pointed out, it might provide some good will that would work to our advantage if we wanted to protect the people who had helped us.

The ambassador heaved a sigh of relief when we told him we were on board with the press appearance. The only condition we had was a limit of no more than three questions. He wasn't happy, but nodded okay. "Okay. Agreed. Now, please follow me," he said, pointing to a door that led into the terminal.

When we filed out, flanked by officials and security agents, there was the expected jam of cameras, the now familiar flashes of light, and hands raised with phones outstretched in our direction. The ambassador led us to a make-shift podium, with a microphone. Taking his place behind the podium, he used both hands to gesture to the crowd to quiet down. In front of him, in a rough semi-circle, were dozens of reporters, separated from curious onlooker by makeshift barricades manned by uniformed airport personnel. Beyond the barricades, crowds craned to catch a glimpse of what was going on. Some seemed to recognize me and Mel, shouted out words of congratulations and best wishes. I grinned back at them, acknowledging our thanks with a wave of my hand.

The ambassador began his remarks by thanking the Peruvian government for their assistance in rescuing us. By his side, the Interior Minister stood stoically, making only a slight nod of appreciation for the diplomatic gesture. I struggled to remain expressionless. So far as I was concerned, the Peruvian government per se had done diddly to help rescue us. It had all been thanks to local authorities like Enrique Rodríguez. I was tempted to say something along those lines when it was our turn at the podium, but knew that under the circumstances I had to bite my tongue.

After a few more words of gratitude, the ambassador told the reporters that we had a flight to catch and only had time for three questions. He ushered me and Mel to the podium, where we were greeted by more shouts of encouragement from the crowd beyond the barrier, which was continuing to grow.

The first two questions were easy. "How are you feeling?" "Are you anxious to return home?" We both answered to the first with "Tired but happy and relieved to be free." The second was an obvious "Yes we are. Very anxious to be reunited with our family." The third was trickier. "What will you tell your fellow countrymen about Peru when you return?"

Mel and I looked at each other. She gestured for me to respond first. If there was a time for me to dump my frustrations with the roadblocks I had encountered from both governments onto the world stage this was it. Instead, I said, "We both deeply appreciate the warmth and affection of the great majority of those Peruvians we have met." Pointing to the crowd beyond the barrier, "And the words of encouragement and congratulations we have received ever since our release. Thank you."

This produced an overwhelming round of applause and more shouts from the assembled crowd. If I had been a Peruvian politician, I would have reveled in the adulation. But instead, I wanted to get through this press conference as quickly as possible and on to the gate for our flight. But Mel grabbed my arm, a look I couldn't read on her face. "I'd like to say a few words, Clint," she whispered in my ear. "It won't take long."

"Sure thing, sis," I said, as she moved behind the microphone. "I would like to echo my brother's appreciation for the warmth and support we have received from the people of Peru," she began, her voice firm and resolute. "We know that the grand majority of Peruvians want what we all want, peace and stability. And we know that the grand majority also rejects acts of violence. And we also know that we were extremely fortunate to have escaped the fate of the other hostages. Before we go, I want to offer my condolences to *all* those who died in the rescue attempts this morning. Thank you."

Mel's words brought more cheers. But the ambassador and the interior minister were not among them. The ambassador drew on his diplomatic skills to quickly replace his momentary frown with his practiced smile, as he began to escort us from the podium. But Díaz Canseco looked stone faced behind his dark glasses. Neither one of them were happy that Mel had emphasized her condolences for *all* those who had perished in the fouled-up rescue raids. It was a not too subtle hint that the members of the "Atahualpa Brigade" also deserved some sympathy.

We were steered back to the room where we had met the ambassador and his entourage. At the door, the ambassador told us that Macalister would accompany us to our plane while he attended to other matters. "Thank you for agreeing to meet with the press," he said. "It was important for them to hear from you first-hand." *Yeah. And for you to be seen with us, as though you were somehow instrumental in our escape.* He seemed to read my mind and said in a low voice, "And I'm sorry that I couldn't do more to assist you in your search for your sister. But I was constrained by larger national security considerations. I'm sure you understand."

His apology was a day late and a dollar short. I was once more tempted to mouth off, but swallowed my smart comeback and simply nodded.

"Well," he said, "I hope you have a safe trip home. I am sure you are anxious to reunite with your family."

He shook hands with me and Mel and then, accompanied by his flunkies and security detail, walked out into the terminal. Before the door closed, Minister Díaz Canseco turned and stared at us. The dark glasses hid the look in his eyes, but his whole posture emanated hostility.

Clearly, Mel's inclusion of *all* Peruvians rankled. I could imagine him thinking of Mel, *so maybe you are not the innocent victim the public thinks you are but rather a secret supporter of terrorist groups in our country.* I was almost ready to give him the finger, when he turned abruptly and followed the ambassador out the door, leaving a sense of menace lingering in the air.

We were left with Macalister and a group of half a dozen others. Two wore suits and were introduced as embassy personnel. The four others were uniformed armed guards, automatic weapons slung over their shoulders. Pointing my head in their direction, I asked Macalister, "Why all the fire power? I thought we were home free once we got into the airport. What's going on?"

"I don't want to alarm you two," he said. "But we have gotten some communications that the 'Atahualpa Brigade' has put targets on your back. You were the two who got away, while all of their comrades were gunned down. It may just be talk, but we don't want to take any chances. These men have been assigned to us by a private contractor and are completely reliable."

I raised an inquisitive eyebrow. "It's not out of the question that the 'Brigade' has infiltrated the state security services and even have sympathizers among airport personnel. It may all be bluffing, but we don't want to take any chances."

Mel looked more repentant than frightened. "Clint," she said, her voice shaking, "I am so, so sorry I got you involved in all this."

"Don't worry, sis. We can manage. And, after all, you have made me a celebrity. A little danger just makes me that more appealing to the public."

She smiled and gave me that familiar elbow dig in the ribs. "Sure, Bro. You're welcome. Anytime."

Macalister interrupted this poignant family moment. Pointing to his watch, he said, "Time to get going," and led us out a back door and into a corridor that, he told us, would lead to the other end of the terminal and the departure gate for international flights.

The corridor was completely empty and our footsteps echoed off the walls as we began to make our way down it. After a few steps, Macalister asked the security detail to move away a distance so that he could speak privately with me and Mel. Once they had accommodated him, he turned to me and with a semi-apologetic look on his face, said "I know you are pissed at the ambassador for not helping to find your sister. Looking back now, we should have lent you a hand. But you know what they say about hindsight being twenty-twenty."

He could see that I wasn't buying it, but soldiered on. "The ambassador isn't a bad guy. But he's a political appointee and really out of his depth. This crisis has put him on the spot and he's just not up to the challenge. He let the whole hostage situation get out of hand and turned too much authority over to the Peruvians, who prefer blunt force to negotiations. Part of the legacy of their long struggles against terrorist groups. The ambassador didn't understand that and while maybe nothing would have worked in the end, the result is five dead Americans. He's going to meet some of the relatives of the victims who are arriving at the international terminal in about," he looked at his watch, "fifteen minutes. It's not going to be easy or pleasant. So, maybe you can cut him some slack."

I didn't know where he was going with all this. My guess is that he feared I would somehow unload on the ambassador and the entire embassy once we got home. I figured that journalists would continue to besiege me and Mel for a while, until our story became yesterday's news – which probably would take about forty-eight hours. At the moment, I was in no mood to reassure him. He was right. I was pissed. And while I felt some sympathy for the spot the ambassador was in, I wasn't about to give him a free pass either. So, I was noncommittal. "We'll see," I said, with a shrug. "Right now, I just want to get me and my sister out of here as soon as possible."

"Understood," he said. But he couldn't let it rest. Turning to Mel, he said "And you, Melanie, certainly didn't help matters with your condolences for *all* those who had died in the rescue attempts. Your sympathy for the 'Brigade' couldn't have been clearer. And you had to broadcast it to the entire world. Don't you realize that if hadn't been for your brother, you would have been among the victims. What were you thinking?"

Macalister's tone reminded me of a parent scolding an errant child. I also saw the name "Lori Berenson" flash in front of my eyes. The look on his face seemed to say that Mel was just another naïve American girl letting her idealism get in the way of rational thought. But if he expected Mel to express regret over what she had said or offer an apology, he was sadly mistaken.

Sticking out her chin, she said "Listen, *Mister* Macalister. If you got out of the embassy more and spent less time on the cocktail circuit, and maybe mingled with the common people of Peru, especially the Indigenous people, you might have a better understanding of this nation's reality. You might appreciate how giving free rein to multinational mining companies, ignoring Indigenous rights and the environmental costs of extraction, and reaping most of the profits for themselves, would find resistance among those who have been trampled on for centuries."

He looked almost bemused by the tirade, giving Mel a condescending look. It did not deter her. She took a deep breath. "Look. I don't approve of the violent tactics of the 'Brigade' or of any other group, although I wish our government showed a little more concern for the Peruvian government's excessive use of force against peaceful protestors. Come up to Cajamarca sometime and see how forces under people like Inspector Calderón treat the innocent. Clint told me that you and the embassy had let Calderón take the lead on looking into my disappearance. How did that work out?"

She had struck a blow. Macalister looked a little embarrassed, nodding that Mel had made a valid point. "And, another thing," she continued, her voice firm and her gaze steady, "How do you know that the 'Brigade' would have followed through and actually executed their prisoners? Maybe they were open to negotiation. In my case, I didn't have the sense that my captors really wanted to do me any harm. They treated me well. By giving the Peruvian government *carte blanche* to deal with the hostage situation as they saw fit, you could have predicted the outcome. So, don't you dare chastise me for showing sympathy for those Peruvians, who no matter how misguided, were only struggling for justice."

Macalister looked at me for support. But it was a vain exercise. I just shrugged. *That's my sister, pal. She is not one to let you or anybody else intimidate her.* In the back of my mind, I also pictured how proud Al would have been of her at this moment. Mae, too, of course. But her toughness reminded me of my father, and in this case, in a good way.

"Well, Melanie," Macalister said, "That's all well and good. But the reality is that the Peruvian government is going to react to this episode with a brutal campaign to wipe out the 'Brigade' and all those associated with it. And we have been ordered by the White House to give them all the assistance they need. We cannot let the deaths of five innocent Americans go unpunished. So," he added, "It probably is a good thing you are going home. If you stayed, I'm not sure we could protect you. And, I wouldn't count on coming back to Peru anytime soon."

That got to Mel. I thought for a moment that we would have a real role reversal and I would have to restrain *her* from punching Macalister in the face. But she regained control. "We'll see about that. Maybe when I get back to the States and tell the story of how the embassy failed to lift a finger to find me, you'll sing a different tune. I have every intention of returning to Peru to continue my work here, no matter what you and others might say or do to convince me otherwise. I won't be intimidated by you or by anybody else."

It was an effective counter-punch. Macalister had to realize that the optics were all on Mel's side. She was going to get a very sympathetic audience for having survived a real ordeal. And she was spot-on to criticize the embassy for their lack of action, no matter how officials tried to spin it. Who were most of the public going to believe? Some bureaucrat in a suit or a spunky American girl, who was articulate, impassioned, and beautiful? It was no contest.

Macalister realized he had lost the fight. Looking at his watch, he said, "We had better get a move on."

We walked quickly in silence to the end of the terminal. Macalister led us up an enclosed stairway to the second level of the airport. Taking us through a series of corridors, we found ourselves at the gate for our American Airlines flight to Miami, scheduled to depart in about five minutes. We had circumvented all passport control and Macalister handed me our boarding passes and the claim ticket for my duffel which had already been checked through to St. Louis. All other passengers were boarded and the gate area was empty except for the airline staff. Before we headed into the plane, he said, "We'll stay here until you take off, just in case there are any hiccups. Have a safe flight. And please see hello to your brother for me."

"Will do," I said, and relenting a bit, thanked him for his help in avoiding the usual hassles of boarding an international flight, not to mention the armed escort that had gotten us safely to our destination. It wasn't enough for me to forgive him completely though. I still blamed him for the embassy's lack of help in finding Mel and was angry at the way he had tried to browbeat her. But I also recognized he was in a tough spot, probably doing the best he could under the circumstances. No sense dwelling on it, I decided. Let's just get home without any incidents.

An attendant showed us to our seats in the first row of business class. We barely had time to buckle up before the plane left the gate and headed for the runway. In minutes, we were aloft and headed for Miami. Mel again had the window seat, where she could see the Andes to her right as we headed north. She grabbed my hand. "Look, Clint. Aren't they beautiful?"

There was a note of longing in her voice. I could imagine her thinking that she couldn't wait to return, no matter what.

Once we had reached cruising altitude, the attendant offered us champagne. Mel looked at me quizzically. "How about it, Clint? Time to relax and celebrate?"

I wasn't much of a champagne drinker, more addicted to the hard stuff. "Not for me, Mel. But why don't you go ahead. You deserve it."

"You sure you won't mind?"

"Absolutely. And although I don't know much about champagne, that looks to be pretty high quality. Go ahead, please. Don't worry about me."

Mel accepted the glass and I took a Diet Coke. We clinked in a toast, while Mel gave me an appraising look. "Is this the new Clint?"

I knew what she meant. I smiled and shrugged. "At least for now, sis. Let's hope it lasts."

We were both starved and when our meal arrived, we ate ravenously. The food in business class was a clear cut above coach, but at this point, we would have eaten anything.

After the attendant had taken our tray, we reclined our chairs, closed the window shade, and were soon fast asleep. Before drifting into dreamland, I had a feeling that my whole experience in Peru had been sort of unreal, almost like a dream. It would take some time for me to process what I had been through and what the broader implications might be. Not for the first time, I swore that whatever else resulted, I would remain sober. But hard experience had taught me that was easier said than done. Maybe this time, however...."

Thirty-Eight

WE TOUCHED DOWN IN Miami at eight o'clock. Rubbing the sleep from our eyes as we taxied to the gate, the attendant told us we would be the first to deplane. An official would take us to our connecting flight to St. Louis, scheduled to take off at nine.

Leaving the plane, a dark-suited guy approached us and introduced himself as "Jake." "Welcome home, Mister Jackson. Ms. Jackson," he said with a smile. "Please follow me."

We did as we were told, following the by now familiar routine of taking an eerily empty corridor from one terminal to another. The only thing missing was a security detail. Presumably, we were now out of danger from terrorist sympathizers. Jake kept up a steady line of chatter, informing us of how it had been arranged for us to by-pass immigration and customs to assure that we got to the flight on time. Lots of strings were still being pulled, it seemed. "And you guys are all over the news," he told us. "But we've managed it so the press won't be hassling you here or upon your arrival in St. Louis."

"Thanks. We appreciate that."

"Yeah. But I should warn you that you are probably going to be bombarded with interview requests as soon as things settle down. If you want, we can arrange for somebody to help you with press."

I wondered who "we" were. The State Department? The White House? The CIA? This was uncharted territory for me and Mel. "Well," I said. "Let's see how things go. We should be able to handle the press on our own."

"If you change your mind," Jake said. "Here's my number. Feel free to call at any time," handing me his card. "And one more thing," he added, a serious look on his face, "You are going to be contacted by government agents who will want a full account of what happened to you in Peru."

"From which agency?"

"The National Security Council."

That surprised me. I was no expert, but I figured we would be interrogated by the CIA or maybe people from the State Department. But it seemed we were going to be questioned by a higher level. From the White House itself. I just nodded, planning to get John's take on the whole thing. He was much better versed in such matters than I was.

We hurried along the corridor, anxious to get to our flight and on our way. When we got to the end, after about fifteen minutes of walking, Jake led us through a door and into the gate area. In a repeat of what had transpired at the Jorge Chávez Airport in Lima, we found that all the other passengers had boarded. Jake led us to the check-in desk and handed us over to an attendant. "Good luck, you two," he said with a grin. "And, once again. Welcome home."

The attendant took us in tow and we headed for the gangway. Along the way, I glanced at the TV Screen tuned to CNN. There we were, in living color, standing with the ambassador. Mel noticed it too, glancing at me with a look that said *Can you believe this?*

Once again, we had prime seats in the front row. I could hear a few of our fellow passengers whispering our names as we buckled up. After we had reached cruising altitude, several passengers introduced themselves and tried to start a conversation. Neither one of us was in the mood and I explained as politely as I could that we were exhausted and needed to rest. One guy seemed determined to pester us, but I gave him my patented stony glare and he backed off.

We had to dodge some thunderstorms, but otherwise the flight was smooth and we arrived in St. Louis at around ten-thirty. Again, we were given the privilege of disembarking first. With the best wishes of the crew echoing in our ears, we trotted down the terminal to the waiting area. I momentarily flashed back to my arrival at the same terminal less than a week ago and my need to reinforce myself with liquor before I met my brother. No such desire or need now, and I pushed the memory to the back of my mind.

291

When we got to the waiting area, John, Tiffany, Heather, and Willow were all there to greet us. We rushed into each other's arms, hugging, kissing, and crying. I embraced John and he pounded me on the back. "God, Clint. It is so good to see you. And you did it. You got Mel home safe and sound. I…" he started to sob. Then collected himself. "I can't thank you enough."

While we were celebrating, a clutch of reporters and news crews approached us. They had been filming our arrival and wanted some commentary. John took charge, putting his hands up and saying, "Look. We have to get to the hospital. Our father is gravely ill and we need to be at his side. Please excuse us. Maybe another time. Right now, we need to hurry!"

There was a grudging murmur of assent and they gave way as we quickly passed through to the parking garage. It was still July in St. Louis, and when we left the air-cooled terminal, we were hit with the familiar heat and humidity. John led Mel and me to his car while Tiffany followed with the girls in her own vehicle. I took the passenger seat and Mel got in back. Once we were headed out of the garage and onto Interstate 70, John said, "Mae is with Al at the hospital. She wanted to come with us, but there's a good chance Al would have passed and she wouldn't have been there with him."

Mel said in hoarse voice. "That bad."

"I'm afraid so, sis," John said. "He's in hospice. About the only thing keeping him alive is the hope that he'll see you before he goes."

Mel began to cry. "I'm so, so sorry, John. Clint. I've caused so much pain for you all."

Once again, I tried to reassure her. Turning in my seat, I reached out and grabbed her hand. "Come on, sis. You are not at fault here. You were following your dream. We are all extremely proud of you. The only thing you are guilty of is having a good heart."

She got control and the sobbing subsided. But I knew she was going to have a rough road ahead.

After fifteen minutes, we pulled into the parking garage at St. Luke's Hospital in Chesterfield and rushed to Al's room. When we got there, Mae was standing next to the bed where Al lay, tubes stuck into various parts of his body. He looked even worse than when I had last seen him, if that was possible. Mae let go of his hand and rose to embrace Mel. "Oh, Melanie. It's so wonderful to see you. It's a miracle. A real miracle. My prayers have been answered." Both of them began to sob and John and I struggled to keep it together.

"Say hello to your father, dear." Whispering into Mel's ear, she said, "He can't talk. But he can hear and see. He'll know it's you."

Mel leaned over the bed and said softly, "Hi, Dad. It's me, Mel. I'm here." Then, glancing in my direction, "Clint saved me, Dad. He's a real hero. If hadn't been for him, I wouldn't be here."

I whispered to Mae, "How much does Al know about what's happened over the past twenty-four hours?"

She whispered back, "We've been watching the news during the brief times when he's awake. I'm not sure how much he has been able to absorb, but I thought I saw his eyes gleam when he saw you and Mel on the screen."

I just nodded. Mel leaned down and gave Al a kiss on the cheek. "I'm right here, Dad." She sat down on the chair that Mae had occupied, holding onto Al's hand. "Right by your side."

Mae gave me a little nudge. "Your turn, Clint. Say hello to your father."

I hesitated. A range of emotions ran through me. Mel let go of Al's hand. "Here's Clint, Dad. He saved me. You should be proud of him."

She got off the chair and I took a seat, grabbing Al's hand. "Hello, Dad." I struggled with what to say next. "Listen. About all this hero stuff. It's a story we had to concoct so as not to get the people who really helped us, including one guy who gave up his life, into trouble. Without their help, we wouldn't be here now. I just did what I had to do, that's all. Nothing particularly heroic about it, despite all the hype. I just want you to know the full story."

I couldn't read much from his expression, but I thought I saw for the first time in my adult life a sign of approval from my old man. Maybe, finally, I had done something that made him proud of me. Or, maybe, it was just what I wanted to believe.

John gripped my shoulder. When I looked up, his eyes were moist. "Don't sell yourself short, Clint. What you did was nothing short of amazing." Then, leaning over Al's bed, he said, "Clint did something that nobody else could have done, Dad. Nobody."

I couldn't be sure, but I thought I saw Al's head move in a slight nod of acknowledgement. Now it was my turn to let tears form.

Just then, Tiffany and the girls entered the room and took up positions around Al's bed. I pulled John aside. "Listen, Bro. We need to keep the real story of how Mel and I escaped as quiet and as confidential as possible. I'm not sure Mae heard me, but we need to keep her in the dark if we can. Same for Tiffany and the girls. I hate living a lie, but there's no choice. I can't afford to put the lives of those who really deserve the credit for the rescue at risk. Maybe sometime in the future the real story can come out. But not now. Understood?"

John gripped my arm. "Don't worry, Clint. Totally understood."

"Thanks, Bro."

"And one more thing," he said, his eyes shining, "I couldn't be prouder to be your brother than I am now."

Tears began to trickle down both our faces. We struggled to gain control or this was going to turn into a massive weep-fest. Emotions were already running high as we watched Al, a shriveled hulk of what he had once been, only able to communicate with his eyes. It seemed pretty clear that the end was near. At least, he had the comfort of having his family surrounding him as the end neared.

Just then, some of the monitors began to blink and beep. A nurse and a doctor entered the room and asked us all to leave while they checked Al's vital signs. We assembled in the corridor, engaging in desultory conversation. After about ten minutes, the doctor emerged and approached Mae. "I'm sorry, Mrs. Jackson, but your husband has slipped into a coma. I'm afraid it's only a matter of hours before his heart gives out. It is time to make a decision. There's nothing more we can do for your husband. You can wait until nature takes its course, or we can detach him from the monitors and end his life now. The choice is yours."

"Is he suffering?" Mae asked.

"That's a difficult question to answer," the doctor replied. "We don't know much about brain and neurological function when someone is in the state your husband is. But more than likely, he is not feeling any pain."

She looked at John, Mel, and me. "What do you think, children?"

None of us wanted to answer. We exchanged uncomfortable looks. Given my troubled history with my father, I was reluctant to say anything, figuring that whatever I said, it would be taken the wrong way. Finally, John came to the rescue. "Unless you object, Mom, I think we should let nature take its course. It will give us all a few more hours with Dad. And, as the doctor said, it could be that somehow he might sense our presence and that will give him some solace in his last hours." Turning to Mel and me, he said, "What do you think, guys?"

"I agree," Mel said.

I nodded. "So do I John."

Mae looked relieved. "Well, then. That's settled."

We returned to Al's bedside and took up positions around the bed. Mae and Mel took turns holding Dad's hand while the rest of us sat in chairs and tried to engage in a conversation that bordered on the normal. It wasn't easy but we managed. Heather and Willow caught me up on all that had happened in their lives during the years I had been away. Both were turning into bright, beautiful, and accomplished young women. If there were any family troubles, I didn't notice them.

After about two hours, the accumulated stress and strain of the day began to take its toll and I must have dozed off. Suddenly, the monitors went off again, jolting me awake. All the lines on the screen were flat. Al was gone. We all shed some tears while Mae uttered a little prayer that would accompany her husband of more than fifty years into the afterlife.

While I was crying along with everyone, I felt a whirl of emotions and contradictory sentiments. My relationship with Al had been a tempestuous and complicated one. You might call my feelings a mixture of love and hate, with the latter mostly prevailing. And I blamed him for most if not all the difficulties I had faced in life. Of course, you could argue that by the time I had reached thirty the "blame it on your father" excuse rang hollow. And, I had to admit, there was a lot to that argument. In my sober moments, I realized that it was time to suck it up and take full responsibility for my actions. Of course, those moments too often gave way to an alcoholic stupor, where all the old resentments bubbled to the surface.

I guess every son wants his father's approval. I rarely got that from Al. Even when he offered some "atta-boys" there was always that tinge of sarcasm in the brew. Maybe, just maybe, the fact that I had brought Mel home had registered in a positive way, a big plus on his personal scorecard of my behavior dotted with so many minuses. Maybe if he had been able to express himself, he would have shown his appreciation for my efforts. However, I could only speculate that what I saw in his eyes when I spoke with him was recognition and even pride in what I had accomplished. I would always harbor doubts that was indeed the case, given our troubled past. But it was also something to cling to. Finally, finally, I had done something right in his eyes. It might have been too late to erase all that had gone before, but it offered me some reassurance that for once I had not been a disappointment to the man who, for better or worse, had molded my life.

Thirty-Nine

THE NEXT FEW DAYS were a blur. Al's funeral drew an overflow crowd, a mixture of the St. Louis elite and the blue-collar guys who had worked for him. At the ceremony, I was reluctant to speak, knowing that everybody knew about my troubled relationship with my father. It was hardly a secret. But I managed somehow, keeping my remarks brief and even injecting a bit of humor. But it was a strain. Of all that I had gone through over the past week or so, it was one of the toughest things to deal with.

Al had wanted to be buried in his Marine Corps uniform. We did our best to accommodate, but it took some extensive tailoring by the mortuary people to get it to fit over his wasted body. We decided that a closed casket would be best, figuring that even with the best efforts of the mortuary staff, the ravages of time and his emaciated frame would not be what he would have wanted as his final image. Always strong. Always vital, Always tough. *Semper Fi.* That's what he would have wanted.

He was buried at Jefferson Barracks, that imposing veterans resting place on the banks of the Mississippi. As the Marine guard played taps and fired off a twenty-one-gun salute, I struggled to keep my emotions in check. They were still in flux and often contradictory. I mourned my father's death but at the same time held on to the sense of resentment that he had treated me unfairly throughout my life. Perhaps if we had had more time, we could have eventually ironed things out. But, in the back of my mind, I was convinced that the animosity and ill will between us were too deeply ingrained ever to be erased.

We greeted the well-wishers at the funeral ceremony, the burial, and at a reception in Al and Mae's new home in St. Albans. In addition to the condolences, the hugs, and the kisses, Mel and I received a lot of praise for our dramatic escape from the Peruvian kidnappers. I'm not sure everybody knew all the details, but our minor celebrity still resonated. Both of us accepted all the congratulations, but from time to time exchanged conspiratorial looks that said, *If only we could tell the whole story!* At the end of the day, we were all exhausted, Mel and I especially so. We still had not fully recovered from our ordeal and were dealing with the twin strains of Al's death and the need to cover up the truth of what had really happened to us.

In the days after, we managed to keep the press at bay. All the local newspapers and TV outlets wanted interviews, along with some from the national press. John did an effective job of protecting us, pleading for privacy at a time of family grief. That didn't stop some pesky reporters from hanging around, but a few of Al's construction buddies served as a kind of Praetorian Guard to dissuade them from bothering us.

Mel and I finally agreed to two interviews, one with the local newspaper, the *Post-Dispatch*, the other with the St. Louis affiliate of NBC news. We stuck to our agreed-upon stories despite some probing questions from the interviewers looking for a scoop. Emerging unscathed from those encounters, we fended off any further requests. By this time, too, our adventure had faded from the larger news cycle, swallowed up with dramatic developments elsewhere. That was fine with us.

By the third day after the funeral, things had settled down. Mel and I were staying with Mae and John, Tiffany, and the girls spent most of their days with us. Mae seemed to be doing okay. Al's death had not come as any great surprise. She had been preparing for it ever since he became ill. And the seeming miracle of having Mel and me in her presence definitely lifted her spirits. And, she was tough. Nonetheless, we worried about how she would cope once we left, all alone in a house that was too big for two much less for one. We would require some family confab to figure all that out.

While we were having lunch, the phone rang. Rosa was screening all our calls and usually she looked at the screen and made a decision as to whether she should answer or not. More often than not, she just let it ring. Most of them were nuisance calls. But this time, we could hear her pick up and answer. Carrying the receiver with her into the dining room, she said, "It's for you, Mister Jackson," she said, handing it to me, a look of amazement on her face.

I took the phone from her and when I heard the voice on the other end, I excused myself and went into the living room. After ten minutes on the phone, I returned to the lunch table, an amused look on my face. All eyes were on me. "So, who was it?", John asked. "*Sixty Minutes*, wanting to do a piece on you and Mel?" he guessed.

Tiffany giggled. "Maybe some glamorous actress who would like to meet you."

Mae chimed in. "No. No. It must be somebody really important. Maybe even the president himself."

I was enjoying the jovial atmosphere, but didn't want to keep everybody in suspense. "Well. You are not going to believe me, but that was Clint Eastwood on the phone. He wants to talk with me about doing a movie based on our exploits in Peru."

There was stunned silence for a moment. John broke it. "You're putting us on, Clint. No way. Come on, now. Who was it, really?"

"I'm not kidding, Bro. It really was Clint Eastwood, right Rosa?"

Rosa blushed. "Yes. I couldn't believe it myself when I saw the name on the screen. But, yes. I'd recognize that voice anywhere."

"Told ya," I said, with a grin. "Yeah. He saw the story on the news, noted the first and middle name, and thought it would make a great movie. He's invited me down to Carmel to talk about it. Who would have thunk it?"

"Wow," Tiffany exclaimed. "You're going to do it, right?"

Mel gave me a look that said *Not on your life!*

"Well, Tiff. I told 'Clint' that I would have to consult with my sister and would get back to him."

"Come on, Uncle Clint," Heather said. "You deserve to be famous."

"And we can come up with lots of ideas for who will play you and Mel in the movie," Willow added.

John said nothing, knowing that if we pursued this path, we would have to continue the cover-up of what really happened. Things were really getting weird. If somebody had told me a week ago that the guy I had been named after was interested in making a movie about something I had done, I would have checked that person's alcohol level. But here it was.

While the girls continued to lobby me in a good-natured way, Rosa interrupted us again. "Melanie," she said. "Someone has been calling you from a foreign number. I don't know what to do. Should I answer the next time?"

"That's okay, Rosa," Mel replied. "Just give it to me when the call comes."

As if scripted, the phone buzzed in Rosa's hand. She turned it over to Mel quickly, as though it might bite her. Mel answered and when she heard who was on the other end, walked into the living room where she would not be overheard. We couldn't make out the words, but we could hear her murmuring indistinctly. I thought I caught the word "Professor."

Twenty minutes later, Mel returned to the table, a troubled look on her face. "Who was it, Aunt Mel?" Heather asked with a grin, "One of those famous Mexican directors offering to make you a star?"

Mel tried to go along with the joke, but I could see the strain as she answered, "No. Not this time. Maybe later. We need to deal with Mister Eastwood first."

As we finished our lunch, Mel, who was sitting next to me, whispered in my ear. "It was Professor Cartwright, Clint. We need to talk in private, with John included. I don't want Mae and the others involved."

I nodded.

After lunch, John was about to leave with Tiffany and the girls when I corralled him in the hallway and asked him to stay. "Mel and I have some things to discuss with you, in private."

"Sure thing, Bro. I'll tell Tiff to take the girls and come back for me later."

I don't know what excuse John gave his wife for staying with us, but she didn't appear fazed or curious. She left with the girls, agreeing to return in a couple of hours. Apparently, the girls had some urgent shopping to do.

We waited for Mae to head upstairs with Rosa, leaving us alone while she took a badly-needed nap. When she was gone, we sat on the couches in the family room. Through the windows to the north, we could see the Missouri River shimmering in the heat and humidity of St. Louis in mid-July.

Mel kept her voice low. "That was Professor Cartwright on the phone," she informed John. "And the news from Cajamarca is a mixed bag. The national government is going full throttle to wipe out the 'Atahualpa Brigade.' The reaction has been brutal, with police and army units rounding up any and all suspects and subjecting them to 'enhanced interrogation.' After dealing with Sendero Luminoso, they have lots of practice."

"Anybody we know caught up in the net?" I asked.

"That's the good news. So far, not yet. The students who worked with us have been spared. And the governor who was trying to play both sides, has been removed and replaced with someone who may be, and I emphasize, *may be,* less corrupt. And the good news is that in the shuffle, Inspector Calderón has been fired. Professor Cartwright thinks that his mishandling of my disappearance may have had something to do with it. On the other hand, the protest movement has been indefinitely stymied. No more demonstrations in the main plaza.

"And another thing. The U.S. ambassador has been recalled to Washington and although there has been no official announcement, it looks as though he is going to get his walking papers."

"Well," I said, "Don't expect me to shed any tears."

"And guess who is replacing him, at least temporarily?"

"My old buddy, Chuck Macalister," John chimed in.

"Yes. None other," Mel said. "I'm not sure that's going to do me a lot of good if I return." She then explained to John how she had torn a piece out of Macalister's hide at the Lima airport.

John laughed. "Good for you, sis. Good for you. But don't worry about Chuck," he said reassuringly, "I can get him to be reasonable."

I turned to Mel. "After all you have been through, sis. Are you sure you want to return to Peru? I know you are devoted to your career, but are you going to be up to it? Will it be safe?"

"Yes, I do," she said with steely determination. "I've invested too much in the project to give up now. But," she added, "It all depends on Professor Cartwright. It's up to him. Right now, the situation is still very fluid. He knows how badly I want to continue, but he wants to wait at least a week or two to see how things shake out. Until then, I'll just have to cool my heels. But yes, definitely. I want to get back into the field. Hopefully, this time I'll behave with a bit more caution and less naivete."

John and I exchanged looks. I could read his mind. Neither one of us was entirely comfortable with the idea that Mel could return to Peru trouble-free. She was now probably an even more vulnerable and valuable target for any crazy group looking to kidnap a high-profile captive. I was about to make that point, but saw John give an imperceptible shake of the head. *Let's not push it now, Bro. Give her some time.*

"Okay, Mel," John said. "You know that whatever you decide, you have our total support."

I was about to add something along the lines of *and don't expect me to come to your rescue again. Luck was on our side this time. No guarantees for the future.* But I refrained. "That's right, sis. Whatever you decide is okay by me."

Mel smiled. "Thanks, guys. That means a lot." Then, turning to me, "And what do we do about this Clint Eastwood offer?"

I laughed. "Well, that's something I never, in my wildest imagination, thought I would have to consider. And as much fun as it might be to meet up with him in Carmel, there is no way we can do it. Maybe years ahead, when we are sure that everybody who helped us is free and clear, we can tell the real story. And if some film maker is still interested, we can go from there. But for now, we'll just have to forego the chance for fame and fortune."

John looked at me with what seemed admiration. *What has happened to my brother?* I imagined him thinking. *Just a little more than a week ago, he was stumbling drunk off a flight from San Francisco. Now, all of a sudden, he is acting reasonable and making the right decisions.*

Mel chimed in. "And I guess I'll have to disappoint Heather and Willow. No stardom for me either."

Just then, we were interrupted by the phone ringing. John picked it up, looked at the screen, and answered. We could only hear his side of the conversation, but from his tone and the questions he asked, it was clear that it was serious. "Okay," he said after several minutes, "We'll be there tomorrow at nine," and then hung up.

He had a sober look on his face. "That was the Feds. They want to talk to you two about what happened in Peru. As you heard, I agreed that we would meet with them tomorrow at the Eagleton Courthouse downtown and insisted that I be there as your attorney. What do you think?

The mood had darkened. "What happens if we refuse?" I asked.

John shrugged. "That's hard to say. Given your celebrity and the timing – Al's funeral and all – they may not want to push it. On the other hand, if they do, they can make life unpleasant."

"Just who are 'they'? The guy who met us in Miami warned us we'd be hearing from federal officials. He even mentioned it might be somebody from the National Security Council."

"Not that," John said. "The CIA."

I looked at Mel. She had a look of distaste. "I vote no, John," she said. "We've been through enough. Besides, the CIA has done enough damage in Peru and elsewhere. Why should we accommodate them? What about you Clint? I'll go along with whatever you think best."

I was torn. I wanted to line up with my spunky sister. But I also thought John was right. Why stir up unnecessary trouble. We'd go meet with these guys, tell our well-rehearsed story, and be on our way. "Sorry, Mel. But I think we ought to take the safe course and meet with them. Otherwise, they might keep hounding us."

Once again, the look from my two siblings seemed to say *Who has invaded the body and mind of our impetuous brother?*

In the end, we went to the meeting. The two guys who questioned us were deferential and didn't push too hard. I got the impression they were just checking boxes. Our "feel good" story still had legs. They also seemed aware that the part of the story that dealt with the embassy response to Mel's disappearance – or lack of response – would not play well if it were to be highlighted. I don't think they bought all aspects of our narrative, but in the end, they thanked us for meeting with them and offered congratulations for our successful escape. There was even a hint we might get a White House invitation. If so, it was one we would decline. We just wanted to get back to normal.

Back home after the meeting, we could all finally relax. Over lunch, we swapped some family stories, trying to avoid any mention of my fraught relationship with Al. That was something I would still have to come to terms with. But, in the meantime, for the first time in a long time, I felt I was part of the family again. A page had been turned and I was ready to move on. And whatever the future held, I knew by now that it had to include saying goodbye to my old friend, alcohol. Looking back on the adventure involving Mel's disappearance and rescue, I realized that resisting the temptation to have a drink to calm my nerves or get through the next hurdle had not been that difficult. Further tests lay ahead, but for the first time in a long time, I felt ready to meet them.

Epilogue

SEVEN MONTHS HAVE PASSED and I am back in San Francisco, living in my bare-bones apartment and working long days and sometimes nights in construction. My old boss had taken me back happily. Returning to the job, I got a lot of slaps on the back and endured some friendly kidding about my newfound "hero" status from my fellow workers.

At first, I had to continue to fend off curious journalists. The story had been told so many times by now and I had nothing new to add. Over time, the celebrity and curiosity faded and I adjusted to the routine of work. My plan was to try to save enough to start my own small company, specializing in custom-made homes. That plan, I recognized, had a lot to do with Al's example. He had caused me a lot of pain, but I began to realize – or rationalize – that it stemmed more from love than hate. For all his faults, he had set an example for me to emulate and had given me the opportunity to develop the skills that I could now put to good use. That didn't mean a total reconciliation, but it was another step in that direction.

After coming to an agreement that Mel and I were not ready to have our story the subject of a movie, I called Clint Eastwood and told him of our decision. He tried to talk me out of it, but I hung tough. Maybe if we had been talking in person, I might not have been so stubborn, especially if he treated me to that famous squint. But distance helped. He tried to sweeten the pot by offering to buy the rights to any future movie. It was a hefty sum, enough to allow me at least to find something better to live in than my crappy apartment. But I resisted the temptation and declined the offer. I could sense his disappointment over the phone, but we ended the conversation on friendly terms. "If you ever change your mind," he said, "You have my number."

"Sure thing, Mister Eastwood, I'll keep that in mind."

Looking back on that episode, I realized that there might be something else I had learned from Al: the clear moral line between right and wrong. I had chafed at his stubbornness and unwillingness to compromise, but there was much to admire in his being a straight-shooter in a business that often saw people cut corners and skirt on the edge of the law. Al was never tainted with any of that. No bribes to show favors, no pulling a fast one to avoid regulations, no cheating of his employees. Everybody got a fair deal from my father, not that he couldn't be unforgiving if anyone working for him didn't perform as expected.

I made it a point to keep in touch with Mae, John, and Mel on a regular basis. No more the loner, shut off from all contact. For her part, after a couple of weeks, Mel got the go-ahead from Professor Cartwright to return to Cajamarca. While there was still some turmoil, things had settled down considerably and he thought it was safe for her to come back. Just to make sure, John got in touch with Charles Macalister, who was still filling in for the ambassador. Macalister echoed Cartwright's assessment that the situation had stabilized and it was unlikely Mel would be in any danger, although he could not offer any guarantees. John didn't accept that and put pressure on his old classmate to make sure that Mel received some kind of protection while she was in Peru, up to providing round-the-clock bodyguards. Macalister could make no promise, but agreed to look into that possibility.

Listening in, Mel told John that she could look after herself and didn't want any special treatment. When John related the conversation to me, I thought about the guard, Gustavo, at the campsite. He hadn't been of much use when Mel had disappeared. Maybe once burned twice shy would apply to him, but it was a thin reed to rely on. Finally, John had gotten Mel to agree to have some extra security, which he would pay for. She was reluctant, but my brother could be as stubborn as my sister and he finally prevailed. For all her bravado, he reminded her, she had been kidnapped once and there was no guarantee that it might not happen again. Mel reluctantly accepted that argument and gave in as the price she had to pay to return to what she loved doing.

Back in Cajamarca, Mel was welcomed with open arms and was now happy as could be digging in the dirt of her assigned site. She wrote me some long letters, filling me in on how everybody I had met was doing. From the tone, I got the sense that it wasn't just the archaeological work that was absorbing her. She also seemed to have developed a romantic attachment to Ken, the alpha male of the team. We were no longer in the local news, our story fading into the past. She did make it a point to contact Roberto Martínez and Elena to thank them again for their help. We thought it best she not to get in touch with Enrique Rodríguez. We were still not sure what danger we might put him in if it were known how he had helped us. Jaime, it appeared, was now hiding in Ecuador. The University of Cajamarca students had been hassled but not mistreated, at least not for now. The protests had been halted but the campaign against the mining companies continued. Cartwright's students had been firmly warned again not to get involved in the local disputes, and while the sympathies remained, they adhered to the renewed warning. Mel's experience had been a sobering reminder that the stakes of any kind of involvement in national matters could be high.

About a month after I returned to San Francisco, I got a call out of the blue from Blake Anderson. He was in the city on business and invited me to dinner that night at Sam's. I quickly agreed and we met at that storied establishment on Bush at seven. Blake greeted me on the street with a grin and a firm handshake. "Clint. Great to see you. Glad you could make it."

I grinned back. "Glad I could, too."

"Quite an adventure you had in Peru," he said, taking me by the elbow and leading me past the long line on the sidewalk waiting to be seated. Sam's didn't take reservations, but seemed to have made an exception for Blake. Our formally attired waiter led us to a back booth, where we would have total privacy. More than a few major deals, both legal and illegal, had been made behind the curtains that closed behind us as we sat.

Before leaving, the waiter asked if we wanted drinks. Blake ordered a martini straight up. When I asked for a Diet Coke, Blake raised an eyebrow but remained discrete. He had seen what shape I had been on the flight to Lima and knew that I was not unfamiliar with alcohol.

We both ordered sand dabs, one of the house specialties. Sipping our respective drinks, Blake said, "Well, Clint. Looking back on things, I wish I could have offered more help. Once I found out about how Macalister and Hogan had brushed you off, I thought about lending a hand. But we were tied up in a pretty urgent situation of our own and by the time I got around to contacting you, you were on your way to Cajamarca. As it turned out, you did pretty darn well on your own," he said, lifting his glass in a toast.

"Thanks, Blake. I appreciate that. And you did help me get the lay of the land and prepare me for navigating things in Lima." I didn't add that part of that preparation had led me to contract Manuel Rodríguez as my driver. And, if not for Manuel and his brother, Enrique – well, we probably would not be enjoying a celebratory dinner.

Our sand dabs arrived and were, as usual, spectacular. I didn't eat at Sam's often, but when I did, I always enjoyed the atmosphere along with the food and drink. Of course, in the past there had usually been more focus on the drink than on the food.

"So, Blake," I said, "What's the situation in Peru for you and the DEA these days?"

He shrugged. "Same old, same old. We keep fighting the war, gaining a few victories here and there. But it's slow going. You break up one gang and two more pop up to take its place. And each government tells us they are committed to helping us fight the good fight and each turns out to be as incompetent and as corrupt as the one they replace. Sometimes I wonder why we even try. But try we must. Until we address seriously the issue of reducing demand in the U.S., the best we can hope for is to stem the flow as much as possible."

The tone of his voice and the look on his face displayed the frustration he felt. Then he gave me a look I couldn't quite decipher. He chuckled. "Not much of a recruiting pitch, is it?"

He saw the surprise on my face. "How would you like to join the Department, Clint? We could sure use somebody like you. Tough, resilient, honest. If you are interested, I could make it happen. For all the frustrations, it is a career where you can make a difference. And with reasonable pay and benefits. What do you think?"

I sat back, astonished at the turn in the conversation. Fumbling for an answer, I said, "Well, I think undercover work would be out. I'm now too well-known, especially in Peru."

"You have a point there," Blake conceded. "But there are plenty of people who do the undercover work. I was thinking more along the lines of a recognized agent, working out of the embassy. Full disclosure, however. As I'm sure you aware, no position in the DEA is risk free. You have to assume that every second you are in the field, there is a target on your back." He looked down and shook his head. "I'm not very good at this recruiting pitch, am I?"

I laughed. "You're just too honest, Blake."

He laughed back. "Yeah. Maybe so. Still, any chance you might be interested?"

I had some time to gather my thoughts. He had been honest with me. I would reciprocate. "I appreciate the offer, Blake. I really do. But right now, I am committed to getting back to normal." I told him my plans to start my own boutique construction company and he nodded in understanding. Not as glamourous as being a soldier in the "War on Drugs" perhaps, but a laudable aspiration nonetheless.

"I'm not going to give you any more of my sales pitch, Clint. But if you change your mind, here's my contact information," he said, handing over his card. "Feel free to get in touch anytime."

I took the card and put it in my pocket, experiencing some *déjà vu*, recalling doing the same thing when we had parted company in Lima.

"Thanks, Blake. I'll do that. And I do appreciate the offer."

Over coffee and dessert, Blake gave me an overview of the current situation in Peru. The crackdown on the "Atahualpa Brigade" was still ongoing, with the government enjoying the upper hand. Most of the ringleaders who had not been eliminated in the failed rescue fiasco, had been rounded up and incarcerated. Sympathizers, it seemed, had been sidelined and silenced, knowing from painful experience that similar crackdowns had produced fatal results for anyone even suspected of being associated with the more radical elements of the movement. As with *Sendero Luminoso*, it appeared that some fragments of the "Brigade" had taken to the jungle region and teamed up with drug traffickers. The DEA was working closely with the government to locate and eliminate those groups, but it was tough going. The best to be hoped for was to isolate and contain them as much as possible.

What he told me gave me hope that Mel was going to be okay. I told him that she had gone back to Cajamarca. I got the sense that this was not news to him. "She should be all right, Clint. The fact that the Brigade is essentially off the table and that the protests have diminished, not to mention her notoriety, should shield her from any potential danger. But..."

"Yeah. Nothing is guaranteed. I know."

"Yeah. But there are risks in everything that is worth doing."

I nodded in agreement.

Blake insisted on paying the bill. "Uncle Sam's treat," he said with a wink. Out on the sidewalk, we parted company. I thanked him again for his help in Lima, the dinner, and the offer. With that, we went our separate ways. As I walked back to my apartment, I once again reflected on how lucky I had been in my little adventure in the Andes. If not for Blake, then no Enrique and no happy ending. Those and others were the real good guys in the story. While I had become the star, it was the supporting cast that deserved most of the credit.

As for me and my affliction, I was still a work in progress. I had joined Alcoholics Anonymous and attended meetings on a regular basis. I also had begun to see a therapist to work on my lingering family issues, this time taking it seriously. My long hair and goatee were gone, replaced by the clean-cut look. My eyes were beginning to clear. When I wasn't working, I tried to get involved in group sports. Some of the guys I worked with had formed a softball team in the summer and a basketball team in the winter. I joined both. It was rough at first, but I began to get the hang of both and could hit and field with reasonable accomplishment and score a few baskets from time to time. Most of all, it was fun to be involved with others and enjoy the companionship away from work. I did, however, have to beg off the ritual beers after each game. The guys didn't press it. They knew my issues and respected my efforts to overcome my disease.

Another positive was Marisol. She was the sister of one of the guys on the company team and I had met her after one of the games. She was in her twenties, worked as a paralegal, and was gorgeous. We had been dating for about three months now, and so far, so good. She knew something of my past, both the good, like saving Mel, and the bad, my alcoholism. She was another reason, as if I needed one, to stay sober. I couldn't believe my luck in finding her and didn't want to lose her. Falling off the wagon would be fatal to our relationship. She didn't talk about it much, but I knew she, her brother, my workmate, and her mother had fled from an abusive, alcoholic father. The last thing she would tolerate is falling into the same trap with a guy like me.

So, as I said, a work in progress. I was feeling good about the new me. The power of positive thinking. Always lurking in the background was the specter of taking that one drink that would lead to a dozen more. But I was on the road to recovery and redemption, one step at a time. It had been a rocky road, with many unexpected twists and turns, but for now it seemed smooth ahead. The only person I could blame if I crashed and burned, I saw every morning in the mirror.

Printed in the United States
by Baker & Taylor Publisher Services